D1544278

Practicing What You Preach

Also by Vanessa Davis Griggs

"The George Landris/Johnnie Mae Taylor" Series:

The Rose of Jericho

Promises Beyond Jordan

Wings of Grace

Blessed Trinity Trilogy:

Blessed Trinity

Strongholds

If Memory Serves

Practicing What You Preach

VANESSA DAVIS GRIGGS

KENSINGTON PUBLISHING CORP.

DAFINA BOOKS are published by

Kensington Publishing Corp.
119 West 40th Street
New York, NY 10018

Copyright © 2009 by Vanessa Davis Griggs

ISBN:978-1-60751-990-4

Printed in the United States of America

Dedicated to those who know but just need to be reminded of God's love and forgiveness and that there really is nothing too hard or too big for our God.

To the memory of my grandmother Peggy Jane Wiseman, my aunt Naomi Session, my uncle Henry Davis, my cousins Valerie Randle and Joseph "Lil Joe" Lee III —forever inside of my heart!

Acknowledgments

All that I am and all I ever hope to be I owe to an awesome and great God who truly loves me. Thank You, Heavenly Father, who gives me the victory and always causes me to triumph. To my mother, Mrs. Josephine Davis, and my father, Mr. James Davis Jr., who celebrated fifty years of marriage on November 23, 2008. You both have loved me and my siblings with an everlasting love, while having enough love to share with others who are blessed to know you, as you make them feel they're just as special.

Love to my family: my husband, Jeffery, of thirty-one years; my children, Jeffery, Jeremy, and Johnathan Griggs; grandchildren Asia and Ashlynn; sisters Danette Dial and Arlinda Davis, sister-in-law Cameron Davis; brothers Terence and Emmanuel Davis. Oh, if there were only words to express how much I love you all. My life is so much richer because of all of you.

To those in our family who carry the history and memories of our past and to those who push us toward our future. My aunts: Mary Mack, Rachel Shockley, Ruth Washington, and aunt-in-law Clara Lee; uncles Joseph Lee Jr., Abraham Lee, and Daniel Lee; nieces and nephews Bart, Alexis, Ariel, Chantelle, Charisse, Christopher, Arionna, and Rechelle. The memories we make together no one can ever take away. Let's hold the good things close to our hearts to warm us on those days when it may feel a bit cold and to hold them high to light our path when we need to see our way just a little bit better.

I am so blessed to have friends who continue to encourage me on this journey: Rosetta Moore, Vanessa L. Rice, Stephanie Perry Moore, Irene Egerton Perry, Zelda Oliver-Miles, Linda H. Jones, Bonita Chaney, Ella Wells, Pam Hardy, Shirley Walker, and Malinda Millings. There are many who read my books, and I thank you so much for that. Two people I'd especially like to acknowledge: Regina Biddings and Gregg Pelt.

To my editor, Rakia A. Clark: Do you have any idea how much I truly appreciate you and your wonderful spirit? I appreciate you! I am so blessed to know you and to be able to work with you. And I mean that from the bottom of my heart. To the staff of Kensington/Dafina: thank you for all that you do when it comes to me and my books. One plants, one waters, but God gives the increase.

To those of you who have honored me by choosing to read *Practicing What You Preach*: I love you much! I've said this before and I mean it: I don't and won't ever take you for granted. Many of you may know by now how much I pray about what I do before I ever begin. I know how much God loves you and how much He wants the best for you. I just want to be obedient to what God gives me to do. God told me to write this book because He cares about those who feel bound and are hurting. It's not I but He that dwells within me. I thank God for caring so much about us the way that I know He does.

I love hearing from you. Thank you for spreading the word about my books. May you continue to walk in God's exceedingly, abundantly, above-all-you-can-ever-ask-or-think blessings. Now, let's get started! It's good to be blessed, but even better to be a blessing.

Vanessa Davis Griggs

www.VanessaDavisGriggs.com

Chapter 1

The sunlight seemed to pour through my bedroom window even more than usual. I pulled my blanket completely over my head as soon as I realized the brightness was affecting my sleep. I didn't want to get up today. I just didn't. I was tired. Not physically tired (although working a full-time job while putting together an elaborate wedding is draining), but tired on the inside. Tired of people expecting things from me, tired of people asking if I can do things for them, automatically assuming I'll do it. T-i-r-e-d, tired! I sneaked a quick peek at the clock. Twenty more minutes until the alarm was set to go off. *Quick! Go back to sleep. Before there are people to please.*

I don't usually consider myself a people pleaser. In fact, I would describe myself as strong and independent. But lately, I've been taking on more and more. I don't know, maybe all of this can be traced back to my upbringing—the people-pleasing part, that is. It's what my mother prides herself on, although she likes to call it being a peacemaker . . . a unifier . . . a real leader. My mother, Ernestine, is the one everybody goes to when somebody needs something: time, help, money (especially money), and everything in between. She's the one who takes care of the family—immediate, extended, and those who merely call themselves family. She forever places herself last on the list, which normally means there's nothing left when her turn finally rolls around. And at fifty-two that's what's slowly taking a toll on her. It's not the high blood pressure and cholesterol her doctor has her taking pills for daily. Putting everybody else's needs and wants above her own is what's dragging her down.

Well, I've decided at age twenty-eight that my mother's fate will not be mine, no matter how much people claim I'm just like her. I want a lot out of life, and I don't intend to put my goals on the back burner. I just need to figure out how to say no to things I don't want to do and stick with it after I say it.

Those two letters—*n* and *o*—when knitted together form a definitive answer. But for some reason I've not been able to make them work for me effectively. Sure, I may start with the *n* but it will invariably come out as, "Now?" or "N . . . oh, you *really* want me to?" Or worse: "No problem."

Two days ago my friend Nae-nae called and gave me a chance to test just how far I'd come with this "saying no" business.

"Peaches, I have something I *have* to do that I absolutely can't change," Nae-nae began, calling me by the nickname reserved and used only by a few family members and my closest of friends. "Can you take my mother to the grocery store for me tomorrow?"

"No," I said firmly, fighting off my normal knee-jerk reaction to add something else to it in the form of some type of acceptable excuse.

"No?" she said as though I had no right to ever say that. "What do you mean, *no*?"

"I have some things I need to do myself," I said as I began to slip back into my usual role of not wanting anyone to be upset with me because I'd dared not please them.

She laughed. "Oh! Is that all? Well, you can just take her after you finish what you have to do. It's not like she has to be at the grocery store at a certain time or anything, although you know she is slightly disabled and shouldn't be out too late at night. Come on, Peaches, you know I don't have anyone else to help me out. I've always been able to count on you. Please don't start being like everybody else and let me down now. Pleeeaaase?" she whined.

"Okay, fine. I'll take her," I said even quicker than I suspected I would. She thanked me and hurried off the phone. I had caved in yet again.

What I should have said was, "Well, if your mother doesn't have to be there at a certain time then you can take her after you finish what *you* have to do." That's what I should have said. But no, that wasn't what I said at all. I'd merely given in once more.

It's so funny how later on you can always think of stuff you *should have* said. So my new goal is to learn how to say what I mean and stick with it no matter what. I just have a hard time telling someone I can't do something when honestly I know that physically I can. Just one more lovely trait I can attribute to my fine upbringing.

My mother never believed in telling lies, not even the little white ones folks basically say it's okay to tell. You know like, "No, you don't look fat in that." Or "Cute outfit." What about, "Oh, no; I really *do* like your hair. I was only staring so hard at you because it's so . . . *different*."

Not my mama. It was "Girl, now you know you're too old to be trying to wear something like that." Or "Somebody lied to you. Go back and try again." Or what about, "That looks good, it just doesn't look good on *you*." Still, she will do anything for you.

I started planning special events as a hobby about two years ago, but lately it appears this could someday become my real bread and butter if I continue to pursue it seriously. Everybody says I'm great at putting things together. That's what I was doing yesterday after work—taking care of some pressing business for an upcoming wedding. A wedding, incidentally, that's huge and could really put my name on the go-to-for-event-planning map.

I pushed myself to do what I had to do after work, then managed to take Nae-nae's mother to the store. It took her two whole hours to shop. Two hours I really didn't have to spare. She insisted on doing it herself. Seriously, she could have given me the list she'd already written out anyway, and I would have been done in fifteen minutes. Tops. Instead, she ended up rid-ing in the mobile cart the store provided. She'd stand up, get an item, put it in the basket, sit down, then ride sometimes just to the next group of items, only to begin the slow and tedious cycle all over again.

I don't know, maybe I really am as hopeless a case as Cass said. Cass is my ex-boyfriend. His real name is Cassius, named after his father who was named after Cassius Clay the boxer before he changed his name to Muhammad Ali. If you ask me, I'd say Cass thought his name was short for Casanova. But truthfully, he was the one who got me started on this self-evaluating journey I've been on lately. Cass flat out said I was too easy and a real pushover. Well, he should know, since he treated me like a disposable pen, then pushed me over and threw me away when he felt my ink was all but used up.

And to think he had the nerve to break up with me and make out like everything was all my fault. He claimed I was too self-centered for him. *Give me a break!* So I was supposed to believe that I was too easy, a pushover, while at the same time believe I was self-centered. *All righty then.* Looking back, the best thing Cass ever did for me was to move his narcissist-self on. Now, you want to talk about somebody being stuck on himself, then that is Cass, the guy I dated last for a whole year, to a T. After Cass, I started listening to my pastor and decided to pray that God would send the right man into my life, because I sure wasn't doing all that hot on my own.

This was all too much to be thinking about this early in the morning, especially with very little time before the alarm was going to sound. But I still found a way to doze off again. I hit the snooze button three times before finally dragging myself out of the bed. Standing in front of the window, I took in the stillness of the day's beginnings, then hurried to dress, made my way to work, and got to my desk with two minutes to spare.

Marcus Peeples was walking out of Dr. Brewer's office when I arrived. He often comes into the OB/GYN's office where I work. Definitely not the most handsome guy I've ever seen (especially with the glasses he wears), Marcus is around 5'11" and sort of lanky, particularly compared to me.

Some label my body type as thick, which means curvy in all the right places. My mother said we're just big-boned people. "Absolutely nothing to be ashamed of," Mama always said. It's never bothered me. After all, Marilyn Monroe was a size fourteen, same as me.

Marcus seemed like an all right guy. He was usually trying to push (what I assumed) his pharmaceutical products on my boss, who must be too nice to tell him to buzz off. But lately, every time he has come in here with his fancy briefcase in hand, he has tried to strike up more and more conversation with me.

Two months ago, he asked if I was married or dating anyone. Having just broken up with Cass a few weeks earlier, my answer pretty much conveyed that not only was I *not* dating anyone, but that I wasn't *interested* in dating anyone anytime soon. He promptly dropped that line of questioning for a few weeks. Then it happened. Today, in fact.

When Marcus walked into Dr. Brewer's office, he stepped over to my desk and without his customary hi or how are you said, "How about you and I go out on a date."

I flashed him a quick fake, polite smile, and replied, "Thanks, but no thanks." *Who says I can't say no and mean it?*

He nodded as he smiled back at me. "Oh, I see. You must only be interested in the kind of guys who like to break your heart, then leave you to put the pieces back together," Marcus said.

For someone who reminded me at best of a reformed nerd, at worst of someone almost anyone could take down in a fight, that statement took me totally by surprise.

"No. I'm just not interested in *you*," I said, pointing my finger at him on cue with the word *you*, not caring whether my words hurt his feelings. I was on a roll today: two *no's* in a row.

Instead of scurrying away the way I expected he would do, he set his briefcase down on my desk. "And how do you know that?"

My eyes immediately went to the briefcase, then back to him. "A woman knows these things," I said, rolling my chair back away from him just a tad. He'd gotten a little too close for my comfort.

"Just as I suspected. You're one of those women who will never give a good man a chance. That way, you can have your beliefs validated about all the men who have hurt you and feel justified without those beliefs ever being challenged."

What did he do that for? I was just about to say something smart like "Is that right, Dr. Phil?" when he suddenly took off his glasses. It's amazing how glasses can change a person's looks entirely. Right before my eyes, in just that instant, Marcus Peeples was transformed from Clark Kent into Superman—I kid you not. I noticed for the first time his hair, cut low and sort of wavy, most likely with the help of a wave cap. I took note of how perfect his hairstyle fit his caramel-colored face. His goatee, which I hadn't paid attention to, was perfect for his triangular jaw. But it was those long, thick, black eyelashes framing those gorgeous, twinkling brown eyes that now had me completely fixated and, quite frankly, at a loss for words. *Dr. Phil who?*

I scooted my chair back a little bit more, smiled, then shook my head to emphasize that his assessment of me and my situation was totally wrong as I tried to right my ship. He'd gotten me a little off course.

He placed his hand on his briefcase. "One date," Marcus said. "Come on. What do you have to lose?" He flashed me a big smile. Near-perfect white teeth, and I declare one of them appeared to have twinkled.

I maintained my coolness, breathing evenly as I began to speak. "One, huh?"

He held up his index finger. "One. And you can choose the time and the place. If you find we have nothing in common or that you don't like me, then no harm, no foul. So, what do you say?"

I had to snap out of this, and quick. I had to take back control. "Okay," I said slowly, not wanting to answer too quickly. "How about tonight?"

"Tonight?" He sounded as though *that* had caught him completely off guard. I sensed I was definitely interfering with some already laid plans.

Good! Last-minute dates usually get the ones who aren't really serious every single time. "I'm sorry. Is that a problem for you?" I projected a look of true concern and sincerity. "Do you already have something planned for tonight? Because if you do . . ."

"I did, but for you, I'll change it. Tonight works for me. So where would you like to go?"

I couldn't help but grin. "How about Bible study, my church? And we need to be there by seven o'clock." I crossed my arms. Body language experts would likely say I was putting up a barrier between us. I'd classify it as expressing my confidence as I had officially regained control.

He began to chuckle. "Oh," he sang the word, "so, you're one of *those* kind of women, huh?"

"Those kind? Is church a problem for you?" I could tell despite his smile and chuckle that I'd unnerved him slightly. *Double good!*

He continued to grin. "No problem. I said you could choose the place. I want you to see that I'm a man of my word." He took out his business card and handed it to me.

"I'm sure Dr. Brewer already has your card on file," I said.

"He does, but this card is for you." He took out his Black-Berry. "Now, if I could get your home address?" He looked at me and saw what I imagine had to be a defensive expression on my face. "Miss Melissa Anderson, I need your home address so I can pick you up tonight. That's what real men do." A boyish grin broke across his face again.

I looked at his card before glancing back at him. He put his glasses on and he was instantly transformed back into the harmless Clark Kent. The information on his card was personable enough. He had his home address and both a home and a cell phone number listed. A home number given—not foolproof by any means but a positive sign—was generally a good indication that he wasn't some married man trying to find a way to sneak around on his wife. I don't play that other-woman stuff. Got burned once accidentally. I vowed never again if I could help it.

Still, I weighed whether or not I should give him my home address at this point. After all, there are plenty of crazies running around in this world. On the other hand, I did *sort of* know him, so he wasn't a *total* stranger. He'd been in here at least ten times that I know of—sometimes when patients were here, most times before office hours began. He seemed a decent enough guy.

I rattled off my home address as he keyed it into his Black-Berry.

All right now, Mr. Marcus Peeples. Let's just see how much you like Bible study at Followers of Jesus Faith Worship Center as a first date. I already sensed, based on the way he had reacted when I mentioned the word "church" that this was going to be fun.

Chapter 2

There was a man in the land of Uz, whose name was Job; and that man was perfect and upright, and one that feared God, and eschewed evil.

—Job 1:1

Any woman who will be truly honest knows at least one good man who's gotten a bad rap about something. And this is coming from a woman who has met some real jerks in her day.

Like my friend Nae-nae, I started developing pretty early in life. My grandma said it was due to all those fast-food meals we ate all the time instead of home-cooked ones like she cooked for her children back in the day.

"When you grow chicken legs and wings the size of a turkey in that short amount of time, you know there's something unnatural," Grandma would say. "If you grow food on steroids and you feed it to your body, what other results do you expect to get? Back in my day, we used to say, 'You are what you eat.' Well, the result is gonna really show up later in life if you young folk aren't careful and don't stop eating so much junk."

My mother never paid much attention to what her mother had to say, at least not on that subject. "Mama, fast food is called fast food for a reason," she'd say.

My brother Diddy-bo, who is two years older than me, and I would sit quietly and listen to Grandma and Mama as they argued about stuff like that. I believe that's why Mama worked so hard to help get Grandma married off and out of her house.

Diddy-bo and I would find ourselves confused about the two

of them, mostly our mother. When we were in church singing, "Give me that old-time religion," Mama would always sing the part about it being good enough for her mother therefore it was good enough for her. Diddy-bo brought that to Mama's attention after a church service once when Mama and Grandma were going at it big time about something they didn't agree on. Mama told Diddy-bo she was talking about Jesus when she sang about it being good enough for her mother, and not Church's Chicken versus chitterlings or collard greens cooked with hog jowls or fatback.

"Ewww!" Diddy-bo and I said in unison. "Chitterlings!"

The thought of chitterlings still causes my nose to turn upward. Grandma lived with us for about two years, and in that time she cooked chitterlings for each of the three New Year's Days she was at our house. Apparently, chitterlings were just one of many New Year traditions or superstitions Mama allowed that Grandma religiously subscribed to and practiced.

We had to have our Christmas tree completely down before New Year's Day to ensure that bad things didn't come to the house during the year. Grandma would cook either collard or turnip greens because if you eat something green on the first day of the year, it brings green (money). Black-eyed peas (what Grandma called black folks' caviar) were for good luck. No female could step foot into the house until a man had crossed the entryway first. That, according to Grandma, was to ward off bad luck from entering the house for the brand-new year. You couldn't wash clothes on New Year's Day, because if you did, "You'll wash someone out of your life," Grandma would say. "Wouldn't want to lose anybody we love this year, now would we?"

Chitterlings didn't have any notable significance other than it happened to be a staple Grandma looked forward to. Like ribs, chitterlings were said to have their roots in the days of slavery when black folks took what was normally discarded and managed to make a meal out of it.

All Diddy-bo and I knew the very first time we smelled that so-called southern "delicacy" cooking, when we were ten and eight, respectively, was that it stank to high heaven. After we learned what it was, I fully understood the source of its smell. Mama said the only thing she didn't like about chitterlings was cleaning them, and the way the odor got into her draperies and lingered in the house all day.

No kidding?!

Still, Mama happily and excitedly ate a plateful of chitterlings and always went back for seconds, sometimes thirds.

"Some people prefer to put mustard on theirs, but I like mine with hot sauce," Mama said. "Diddy-bo, get me the bottle of hot sauce and bring it here." When he did, she shook a little hot sauce on the gray matter bunched on her plate, cut it up, put a forkful in her mouth, closed her eyes as she smiled, then looked up and moaned the way I do whenever I eat a superbly made peach cobbler.

Diddy-bo is not my brother's real name, just as Nae-nae is not my best friend's real name nor Peaches mine. Diddy-bo's name is Spencer after some famous actor from my Grandma's day named Spencer Tracy. Nae-nae is actually Denita Wilson. She's named after her daddy Dennis and her mama Anita. And me? Like Denita, I was sort of named after my father Melvin (whom most folks called Mel) and my Aunt Lisa. So I'm Melissa. Mama said I always went delightfully crazy whenever I ate peaches when I was a baby and I was as pretty as a peach. I guess Peaches just stuck.

Diddy-bo likes to tell me that I grew into my pretty.

When I think back on what a real brat I was (Diddy-bo says I still am), I can't help but think about how special my brother truly is. He doesn't let anyone mess with me, that's for sure. Ask Cass. When Diddy-bo found out Cass had borrowed my two-thousand-dollar stereo system and refused to give it back after he broke up with me, Diddy-bo paid him a little visit. I don't know what Diddy-bo said or did to him, but when Diddy-bo brought my system home to me, he asked me to say an extra prayer for him.

And people wonder why I love my brother so.

Chapter 3

While they behold your chaste conversation coupled with fear.

—1 Peter 3:2

Marcus showed up fifteen minutes early for our date. He looked amazing—different than before. When he visited my boss, he mostly wore suits and ties. For our night out, he wore a lightweight pullover sweater with a geometrical design and pecan-colored slacks. He wasn't as lanky as I'd thought. And those nerdlike glasses he always sported? Gone.

"Why aren't you wearing your glasses?" I asked as we rode to the church. I thought for sure that after coming to my door to get me he would have put them on to drive.

He looked at me and smiled. "Oh, so you noticed?" He glanced away from the road to look at me.

"Well, yeah. I'm pretty observant. So you must wear contacts."

"No. I wear glasses if my eyes become strained from too much reading. And I happen to read a lot. A lot. But mostly I wear them when I want to appear more serious."

"Glasses make you look different, that's for sure."

He tilted his head toward me and grinned. "Is that a good different or a bad different?"

I shrugged, trying to make him think it really wasn't that big a deal. "Just different, that's all." I looked over at him. With the help of streetlights, I was able to see his eyes again, and they were just as gorgeous as I remembered. I've never seen eyes that sexy on a man. I turned my gaze away from him. "Me? I have to have glasses to see," I said. "Fortunately, I'm able to wear contacts, too. But I'd love not to have to wear glasses ever."

He didn't respond immediately. I wanted to look back over at him, but I fought the urge and continued to focus my attention on the road ahead.

"Well, I suppose it might stem from when I was a little boy. Everybody in my family wore glasses except me. It was something I was a little envious about," he said. And although I didn't see it, I heard the smile in his voice. "My mother used to think I was nuts because I wanted to wear glasses when I didn't have to."

"Then aren't you being a bit dishonest by wearing glasses?" I turned to him. "If you really don't need them, aren't you merely using them to misrepresent yourself?"

"No, I don't think I'm misrepresenting myself. My doctor prescribed them for those times when my eyes feel strained. Do I need them to read every second of the day? No. Do I need them to drive? No. But when I work a lot or late into the night, sometimes my eyes do get tired, so I put them on. My ophthalmologist says it doesn't hurt for me to wear them all the time. So I wear them when I want to even though I don't really have to."

We were getting close to the church's exit. "Turn left at the light, then right about a half mile up, and you'll see the church on your right," I said.

"So, Melissa Anderson, tell me. What are your dreams? What are your goals in life?"

"Now that came completely out of the blue," I replied, a little surprised, though I was impressed that he even cared enough to ask. I turned and looked at him.

"Oh, really now? Well, I believe you can tell a lot about a person based on their goals and dreams for life."

"Is that right?"

"Yes, that's right. And I'd like to know you better. So what are your dreams?"

"Okay, if you really want to know. I'd like to own my own

business someday. A pretty big goal, since I'm not that crazy about everything I'd need to do to own a business. Let's just say that I like the creative side of what I want to do a lot more than I do the business side. I'm not all that fond of having to do all the paperwork it requires, all the records you have to maintain. But one thing I've learned in life is you do what you have to do in order to do what you want to do."

The arrowed light turned green. He started moving as the line of cars in front of us began rolling. "That's interesting. I don't know if I would have ever guessed that about you," he said.

"Wouldn't have guessed what? That somebody like me might be remotely interested in owning my own business? That I could be capable of running, let alone owning, a business? What?" I hunched my shoulders a few times. "What?"

"No," he said with an unspoken question I felt directed at me as though he were asking where that little outburst had come from. I quickly realized how defensive I must have sounded at that moment.

"Honestly, the times I've seen you at work, you appear dependable and rather comfortable with handling everything," Marcus said. "In fact, Dr. Brewer constantly comments on how he doesn't know what he would do without you. He talks all the time about how you run his office practically single-handedly. He loves your work ethic and can't seem to say enough great things about your organizational and administrative skills. I suppose I just never thought about you having a desire to leave his office and do something else entirely, that's all. But you running your own business, I can absolutely see that."

I blushed. *Dr. Brewer had told him how much he appreciated me.* "Thank you," I said when I realized he was surprised that I was interested in leaving Dr. Brewer someday, and not about my being able to own my own business. "I do my best. But I do have dreams. I don't want to work for somebody else for the rest of my life."

"Do you have an idea of what kind of business you'd like to own?"

"Yes. I *love* organizing events, putting them together, watching them work. Right now I do it more as a hobby. I charge a fraction of what I *could* get while I'm learning and working out all the kinks. At this point, it's a win-win for everybody. I started out putting together small events like baby showers, birthday parties, and various get-togethers. But the past few months, I've been working on this wedding."

I started to tell him the bride-to-be's name mostly because I thought it was pretty neat. But then I decided he wouldn't care that her name was Angela Gabriel and that she likes being called Angel, like the angel Gabriel. When I first met Angela and she told me that, I thought she was joking. But her last name really is Gabriel and most folks really do call her Angel Gabriel.

"The wedding is shaping up to be a major production, although the bride-to-be has done a lot of the work herself," I said. "But I would *love* to own an event planning business, not just planning weddings but all types of events, and do it full time."

Marcus pulled into a parking space beneath a lamppost, then turned off the ignition. I could see him clearly now with the light shining down on us. He turned toward me. "Then I think you should seriously pursue it." He smiled, and that's when I saw them. *Dimples.*

I don't know why I'd never noticed his dimples before. I love dimples. And on top of everything (gorgeous eyes, dimples, and his going to church with me), he—unlike Cass—genuinely listened to me when I talked. He got out of the car, walked around to my side, and opened the door for me just as he had when he picked me up. And even though I was fully capable of getting in and out of a car by myself, I graciously took his proffered hand. He had the gift of making me feel special. He treated me like I was royalty or something. No man had ever opened a car door for me before. But then again, we independent women can have a way of shutting a true gentleman down.

I couldn't help but thank God at this point. Here I was with a man who actually listened, seemed to genuinely care, and was not bad on the eyes at all. So far, so good.

Yet, there is one rule I have found, and it has proved itself time and time again with accuracy, at least in my life, no matter how clichéd it is. If something sounds too good to be true, it probably is.

But tonight—tonight I've decided to suspend all negative thoughts and judgments and just see where this takes me.

For tonight. And tomorrow . . . well, tomorrow is yet another day.

Chapter 4

That they all may be one; as thou, Father, art in me, and I in thee, that they also may be one in us: that the world may believe that thou hast sent me.

—John 17:21

Bible study was really good. Pastor Landris has been teaching everyone in the main sanctuary as opposed to the break-out sessions we normally have. He began a study three weeks ago on "Who we are in Christ." So even though I'm really busy these days, between my job and putting together this wedding, I'm determined not to miss even one lesson. Tapes and CDs are good, but there's nothing like being there in person.

"That was a powerful illustration your pastor gave tonight," Marcus said as we rode to my house. "The way he had that large envelope with the word 'God' on the outside, then pulling out a smaller envelope with the word 'Jesus' on it."

"Wasn't that great! Oh, I loved that, too!" I matched his tone of excitement. "And when Pastor Landris pulled out that even smaller envelope from inside the envelope with 'Jesus' on it, with the word 'Me,' and he said that the 'Me' was us, I knew it was going to be on then."

"I've never seen anything like that before. Everybody was sitting on the edge of their seats, literally, *including* me, waiting to see how he was going to bring all of that together." Marcus alternated his gaze between me and the road. I was thankful he was keeping his eyes on the road more than on me, specifically since he was so excited.

"I knew tonight was going to be good! That's why I love Pastor Landris, and I hate to miss his teachings. He brings the Word in such a way that even the children get it."

"I saw those children's eyes totally fixed on him as he spoke. And the teenagers, my goodness. They were standing up, giving high fives to each other, and praising God."

"I know. I saw them. But they're always like that with Pastor Landris. He's so good at getting across his message."

"Yes, I love how Pastor Landris held up that envelope with the word 'God' on it that second time, pulled out the envelope with the word 'Jesus,' then started teaching out of John seventeen, twenty-one through twenty-three, visually showing how Jesus abides in God and how when we accept Jesus, we abide in Him by pulling out the 'Me' envelope. And if Pastor Landris had stopped right there, that would have been enough for us to chew on for the rest of the week. But then he went and pulled out that card with the word 'Holy Spirit' from inside the envelope that said 'Me' to show how the Holy Spirit was now *in* 'Me' as '*Me*' abides in Jesus as '*Jesus*' abides in '*God.*' Oh, man." Marcus slapped the steering wheel with his hand. "That was *too* awesome! I thought I was going to get up and start running around the sanctuary myself, giving out my own high fives!"

"And then Pastor Landris flipped the script to show that when Satan or an enemy comes at me, how they have to go through God, through Jesus, just to get to me." I couldn't help but grin, thinking about that. "And even then, should my enemies happen to get to me, I still have the Holy Spirit and Jesus inside me. Oh, that was so powerful!"

"You're right. That *was* powerful. He had us all on our feet when it reached that point. I'm going to tell you, I've never heard so much praise and shouting in my life. Y'all know how to have church!" Marcus continued to shift his gaze between me and the highway. "I enjoyed myself. Thank you so much for inviting me. Oh, wow! I had an awesome time."

Marcus tightened his grip on the steering wheel, then relaxed with a smile across his face. "It's only eight-fifty. How about we get something to eat?"

I nodded. "Sounds good to me," I said. I hadn't eaten anything since a banana I had during my morning break. I had skipped lunch trying to play catch-up on my errands due to the time I'd lost last night when I took Nae-nae's mother to the grocery store.

Marcus stopped at my favorite fast-food place, and I got my usual double-decker hamburger with melted Swiss cheese, sautéed onions, and mushrooms. There was no reason to give him a false impression of me by going for a salad I didn't really want. He got the same double-decker, only with bacon. We decided to get our orders to go, which worked out perfectly. It gave us a chance to talk in private at my apartment while we ate.

"So, tell me about yourself." I took a bite of my hamburger and chewed as I listened.

"Well, let's see. I'm twenty-nine. My family moved from Dallas to Birmingham when I was five, and I've been here every since."

"Do you have any sisters and brothers?"

He took a big bite of his burger. Barbecue sauce gushed out onto his fingers. He took his napkin and wiped the sauce off. I couldn't help but think *what a waste of good sauce.* I'd have just licked it off my fingers and kept going. That's when it tastes its best.

"I have two sisters and two brothers," he said after he swallowed. "I'm the knee baby, which, growing up, could be quite interesting at times." He bit into his burger again.

"Do they still live here?" I asked.

"No." He chewed, then swallowed hard. "My sisters married and moved away. My older brother is in the military so he moves around a bit. And my baby brother is incarcerated." The tone in his voice dropped when he spoke of his younger brother.

I dabbed both corners of my mouth daintily with my paper napkin. "I'm sorry to hear about your baby brother."

"Yeah, me too. We were close growing up, so it makes it doubly hard. It was drug related, of course. I tell you, I wish our people would wake up and see how this drug stuff is destroying our families, our communities, and enslaving our men, especially our young men," he said. "So what about you? Do you have any siblings?"

I smiled. "I have an older brother. I'm the baby."

"Oh, so that must mean you're absolutely spoiled," he said, grinning as he took a long draw from the straw of his super-sized drink.

"I am not," I whined, then caught myself. "I am not," I said again, making the words sound more grown-up this time around. "And before you ask, yes, my brother still lives here. He's real tall, about six-five, weighs about two hundred and fifty pounds, and he adores his little sister. So I would watch myself if I were you," I half teased.

He smiled and nodded. "Duly noted. I'll definitely keep that in mind."

"Okay, you don't wear a wedding ring, but I still like to ask just to be sure. Are you married, or separated, legally or otherwise?"

He shook his head. "Nope."

I grinned. "Gay? On the down low? Attracted to men in any way, shape, or form other than sheer admiration?"

He tilted his head downward as he looked at me. "No," he said. "Now, what would make you ask me something like that?"

"It's just one of my dating rules' questions. My mantra is: assume nothing, and if you want to know, ask."

"I'm divorced," he said, volunteering the information before I could ask. He took another bite of his burger and chewed a few times before adding, "and I have a child."

My grin instantly fell from my face. "Divorced? And you have a child?"

"Yes and yes. A little girl. Her name is Aaliyah, and she's five." He then leaned down and over, I can only assume to get a better look at my face. "Is something wrong?"

"No," I lied.

What I should have told him was the other one of my three rules when it comes to the men I date. I don't date married or separated men. I don't date men I even *suspect* may be on the down low. And I don't date men who are divorced. I once dated a guy who was younger than me, although I prefer a guy who is older. So I'm no prude or anything like that. I've even dated a guy who had two children, so children weren't a deterrence for me. My rules are in place to protect me before I get too deeply involved with a man, any man, no matter how awesome or heaven-sent he may appear to be.

The first two rules need no explanation. And it would have been too much trouble to go into full details regarding my third rule. Suffice it to say: there are too many scriptures in the Bible about being with someone who's divorced for me to deal with anyone who is divorced. I don't profess to be a Bible scholar by any means. Nor do I imply that I know all that's behind those scriptures, either.

But what I do know is that there is something about it being a cause for a charge of adultery. And honestly, I have enough problems and sins of my own to have to ask forgiveness for; I really don't need to add someone else's charge of sin to my ever-running account.

"So"—I flashed him a smile as I finished up my sandwich— "tell me about your daughter."

Listening more out of politeness now, although the way he spoke of his little girl was truly endearing and inspiring, I knew full well this would be the last time the two of us would be seeing each other. At least seeing each other on any type of personal basis.

Such a waste. God, this is so unfair! Do you hear me, God? I really liked him, too.

Chapter 5

But ye are a chosen generation, a royal priesthood, a holy nation, a peculiar people; that ye should show forth the praises of him who hath called you out of darkness into marvelous light.

—1 Peter 2:9

I must admit: Caller ID is a wonderful thing. I really had a great time with Marcus. And had I answered the phone when he called the day after our date, I most likely would have let him talk me into another one. With Caller ID, I ended up allowing his call to go to the answering machine, fully planning on calling him back when I felt strong enough to turn down any and all invitations or continuing relationship talks. Friday, he called me at work.

"Well, I suppose you're really busy, since you haven't returned my call," he began.

"Yeah, it's busy everywhere. You know how it gets sometimes. And I have this wedding that I'm working hard on." I immediately began to look for an excuse to get off the phone as quickly as possible. "It's also really jumping here today," I said.

"I enjoyed our date on Wednesday night," Marcus said, his voice deep and strong. "To be honest, it's the most fun I've had in years, other than with my daughter, of course."

"Yes, it was nice," I said. My heart started to pound faster, then skipped one beat.

"What do you say that we do it again? Go on another date. Your choice again."

I allowed the silence as I searched for the right words. "You know, I don't think so." I made sure the tone of my voice was not mean. I wasn't trying to put him down.

Now it was his turn to be silent. "Oh, so you don't care to go out with me again? Well then, I suppose things didn't go as well on our date as I had thought."

I could feel myself softening. I didn't want him to think I didn't like him or that there was anything wrong with him personally. He really is a nice guy. "Marcus, honestly I'm just so busy these days. That's all."

"I realize you're working hard on that wedding. I'm scheduled to be in a wedding. I know a lot of work goes into planning one, even though my part has so far only entailed being fitted for a tux and committing to a night for a rehearsal and that one day for the actual wedding. What I'm saying to you is that I don't mind waiting. After you finish—"

"Listen, Marcus, I think it would be best if we just let this whole thing go. It was fun, but I really do need to stay focused. All right? I have dreams, and I just realized I really need to work hard at them if I want any of them to manifest themselves. You understand."

I heard him sigh. "Sure," he said. "Of course. I understand."

"Okay, then good. Well, I need to get back to work now. Okay?"

"Melissa." Marcus said my name with such tenderness. "Will you keep my phone number? And if you change your mind, if you ever want to go to Bible study again together, or anything, anything at all, even if you just want someone to talk to, I'm a great listener. Will you please give me a call?"

He was making this so hard. "Sure. Yeah, sure," I said. "Listen, I need to catch this call. Good-bye." I took the other call. After I finished, I placed my forehead firmly in the palms of my hands. "God, why is it nothing ever seems to work for me?"

I hadn't lied when I told Marcus I was too busy to pursue a relationship or to talk to him. He's seen how busy this place gets. A few times, even he has had to come back because things were so hectic. Dr. Brewer's schedule gets all out of whack when he has to do an emergency C-section. This leaves me having to call and let patients know we're running behind and having to reschedule those who either can't wait or can't be here at a later time.

Two years ago, when Dr. Brewer worked in an OB/GYN practice with four other doctors (one of whom was a female), they were able to cover each other easily. The downside was the complaints from patients who preferred a certain doctor but were forced to see all of the doctors so they would be familiar with whoever was on call. A lot of Dr. Brewer's patients were upset when they were in labor and found they had no real say-so when it came to which doctor would deliver their baby.

The breaking point for Dr. Brewer came when one of his patients was treated badly by one of the associates. On top of that, she was a high-risk patient. He'd asked why she hadn't called him, since he happened to be available that day, especially since the doctor on call was already tied up and a backup doctor was required to come in.

"I did ask for you," she had said. "In fact, I begged for you. I was told very nicely it didn't matter what I wanted. Then that doctor came in, and he treated me like I was some charity case or something. There I was in pain and in trouble, and he talked to me like I was some kind of a bother to him. To be honest, he talked to me as if I should be glad he was doing anything at all for me. He eventually told me that I should have thought about all this before I went out and got pregnant. Although he tried to laugh it off like he was merely joking, I didn't appreciate his sense of humor one bit."

Well, that was the last straw for Dr. Brewer, and the last time he allowed one of his patients to go through anything like that. He informed me he would be moving back into his own private practice again. And when it was time for that patient's six-week checkup, our new office is where she came.

"I'd rather get a backup to fill in for me when I can't be there than to have my patients go through something like that ever again," Dr. Brewer said. I think he hated that practice as much as his patients did.

If you knew Dr. Brewer, you would have known he wouldn't stay with those others for too long. I've worked for him for ten years. He was impressed with my skills and hired me right after I graduated from high school. I can say this with conviction: he truly cares about the people who come to him. I think it broke his heart to have those patients who had sought him out—including one who had been with him from the beginning of his twenty-three-year practice—have their babies delivered by one of the other doctors. He's just that kind of physician, a relationship doctor. Dr. Brewer cares about people.

His love for people is why I think he lets Marcus come and talk with him as much as he does. Although I wholly admit that Marcus also seems to be a nice guy. Maybe nice people just need to learn how to tell people to take a hike—in a nice way, of course. I'm working on that myself. It's too bad Marcus is divorced. I was totally feeling him. In fact, I was starting to believe he may have been sent to me by God, an answer to a prayer.

Oh well, I'm sure one of these days the right man will come along for me. I just need to wait on the Lord, although it is getting hard. And I know You know this already, Lord, but I'm not getting any younger down here.

In the meantime, I have this big wedding to pull off in stellar fashion. Angela's family will begin arriving next week for the wedding. The rehearsal and rehearsal dinner are scheduled for that Friday night. With the wedding party Angela was having along with all of her and Brent's families, the rehearsal dinner was proving to be almost as large and as much work as the actual wedding and reception.

One positive thing about being this close to the wedding is that I will be too busy to dwell on what *might have been* with Marcus. After all, it was only one date. One date where we'd done nothing grand or spectacular other than go to Bible study and talk afterward while eating a burger.

Get over it, Peaches. Let's move on. Peaches, are you listening? Forget about Marcus. Face it, it just wasn't meant to be. Onward and upward! I said to myself.

The ringing phone cut through my thoughts like a hot knife through soft butter. I shook my head as I answered the phone. "Dr. Brewer's office, this is Melissa speaking."

Chapter 6

Bear ye one another's burdens, and so fulfill the law of Christ.

—Galatians 6:2

Gayle Cane, Angela's cousin from Asheville, North Carolina, arrived on Tuesday evening the week of the wedding. She had apparently decided to come early enough to help out wherever she could. She was staying at the designated hotel. Seeing it was needed, I took off the rest of the week starting Wednesday. To help out Angela, who was becoming more and more stressed as Saturday drew closer, I picked Gayle up from her hotel on my way to Angela's apartment that morning.

Gayle told me she had been a home care nurse for an elderly woman for the past three and a half years. From what I gathered, Angela and this second cousin weren't all that close, but Gayle needed to talk to Angela before everyone else arrived in town.

With so much to do and so little time to do it, I suppose that's why I was around to hear most of their conversation. In and out of the room, working in my space away from Angela and Gayle as they feverishly arranged the names of those who had RSVP'd for the reception on the seating chart, I guess they must have forgotten I was there as their conversation grew deeper and more intense. I could have told Gayle that this really wasn't a great time for talks, especially not ones rooted in family secrets.

Gayle was bringing Angela up to speed on things that had happened after Angela left Asheville four years ago.

"After Grandmother—well, your great-grandmother—died, you decided to leave and come to Birmingham to live," the tall and rather slender Gayle said. "You know I bought her house to keep down all that confusion and arguing about who should inherit the house, since Grandmother didn't have a will."

"I know, and I appreciate you for stepping in and doing that. It's amazing how people, family folks, start acting all crazy after a relative dies and has something everybody thinks they're entitled to when they're gone. I couldn't believe how everybody started fussing and fighting after Great-granny died. I'm sure she never thought they would act in such a way."

"I know. That's why I just offered to buy the house outright at fair market price and let them divide up the money. Anyway, shortly after that, I took a job working for this woman named Sarah Fleming."

"Sarah Fleming? You mean, *the* Sarah Fleming?" Angela asked. "You knew her?"

Angela stopped writing and turned her full attention to Gayle. "Not personally, but I kind of know the story surrounding her. I was there at the beginning of things, when she first came back to Asheville. I was the one who took Johnnie Mae Landris to the house to meet Montgomery Powell the Second that first time she went to see him and to try and see Sarah after she moved back to Asheville. I never got to meet Sarah Fleming. So how did you end up working as a nurse for her?"

"Grandmother and I had this long talk. Do you remember when I came to visit her for two weeks right before she died?"

Angela thought, then nodded. "Yeah."

"Well, she shared a lot of things with me, one of those being things about Sarah Fleming. Grandmother asked me to do her a favor. She said if there was ever a time I could do anything to help Sarah Fleming, to please do it, for her. So when I learned Sarah was looking for an in-home nurse, I applied for the position and got it."

Angela started smiling. "So how is she to work for? I know

their family was really rich." Angela had put down her pen, and all I could think about was how much she *wasn't* getting done. We had too much to do for this. And I wanted to make it to Bible study tonight.

Gayle smiled. "Sarah Fleming died a few months ago. But she was a remarkable woman. And I'm not just saying that to be polite, either. She was remarkable. Her mind was so sharp. She had a wonderful spirit, and she was loving and giving, not just to her family, but to people like me." Gayle pressed her hand against her chest as she spoke.

"So where are you working now?" Angela asked, her eyes fixed on Gayle.

"I'm not working anywhere right now. I didn't take off very much when I was working for Miss Fleming." Gayle nodded. "That's what I called her—old habits are hard to break. So I absolutely needed some time off to recuperate. She paid me for the time I never got to take, and on top of that, she left me money in her will, quite a bit, considering I wasn't expecting anything. She was more than generous in what she paid for my services, more than generous. So I'm sitting pretty as I decide what I want to do next."

Angela put the palms of her hands together and brought her fingers up to her bottom lip. "That has to be a great feeling. Knowing you don't have to worry about money while you take your time to decide what you want to do next."

When Angela brought her hands down, Gayle reached over and quickly squeezed one of them. "It really is. Besides giving me time to rest up, I can spend some time with family without having to worry about anything. I can visit my two adult children. They're both out of college with great jobs now. My daughter, Sherrie, lives in California; my son, Patrick, in Chicago, is interested in politics. I'm healthy and blessed. Life is good."

"I, for one, am glad you're here with me." Angela picked up the printout again as she began to glance between the paper and Gayle. "You know our family a lot better than I do these days. Your helping me make sure that everybody ends up sitting in the right place at the reception is really a blessing to me. I definitely don't want to start a family feud at my reception just because I grouped folks at the wrong table. I want this to be a joyous time for everyone. No family drama."

Gayle looked as though she wanted to say something but she wasn't quite sure how to bring it up. Angela must have picked up on it as well. She put the paper down on the coffee table. "Gayle, what's wrong? Is there something else on your mind?"

"I was just thinking about Grandmother and something else she asked me to do. I thought that what I'm about to say was going to be a lot easier than it's turning out to be."

"What is it? Tell me," Angela said.

Gayle scooted forward. "It's about your grandmother."

"My grandmother? Great-granny talked to you about *my* grandmother?" Angela had a puzzled look on her face. I felt wrong for being there, so I stood up and tried to find a reason to leave and give them some privacy. Angela looked over at me and shook her head as though she knew I was trying to exit. For whatever reason, she was asking me not to go. Maybe she *did* understand how much work we had to do and how far behind this was making us. I sat back down and continued with what I was doing. "What did Great-granny say to you about my grand-mother?" she asked Gayle.

Gayle took a deep breath and released it. It was as though she knew what she was about to say would be extremely difficult both to say and to hear.

"Grandmother asked me to see if I could find your grand-mother, her daughter, if I ever got the chance. She told me her name. It's Arletha."

"She said her name?" Angela asked. "No one in our family ever said her name. Not as long as I've been on this earth. It was as though she never existed. No one spoke of her; no one had ever even told me her name. So my grandmother's name is Arletha?"

"Yes, Arletha Williams would have been her birth name."

"Did Great-granny tell you where she is? Was she in contact with her? After my mother died and Great-granny took guardianship of me, I asked her, when I was older, about my family. She wouldn't talk about my grandmother. She said she didn't know whether she was alive or dead, but either way, her daughter had chosen not to be part of our family, so there was no reason to ever discuss her. As far as I know, my grandmother never came back to Asheville, and you already know that Great-granny was a homebody who rarely veered far from Asheville's city limits."

Gayle took Angela's now trembling hand. I had already perked up when I heard the name Arletha. Arletha is not a common name. Interestingly, I happened to know a woman named Arletha. She lived in the community where I grew up, several houses down the street from our house. Her name was Arletha Brown.

"Do you know if she's alive, and if so, do you know where she might be? Did Great-granny tell you that much?" Angela began to wipe away a few tears that were now rolling down her face. I could tell this was an emotional discussion for her. I couldn't imagine not ever having known my grandmother, especially if she was still alive.

"Grandmother didn't know. She just asked if I ever got a chance, for me to see if I could find out anything. One of the problems I ran into is legal records. All of grandmother's children were born at home. You know her mother was a midwife, too. And even though Grandmother's children's births were recorded, back in those days, birth certificates and records weren't kept as meticulously as they are these days. Grandmother once told me that a midwife was required to send in the birth records logged in some kind of a small book, but there were times when it might not have been sent in. Those people's births were not properly recorded. I haven't been able to find anything on an Arletha Williams, or an Arletha Black for that matter."

"Why would you look for Arletha Black? Great-granny was a Black but she married a Williams."

"It's possible, not that I'm saying it's the case, but it's possible Grandmother might have had Arletha before she married," Gayle said. "If she did, it would have been recorded as Arletha Black. I've been searching for Williams, but I'm a realist, too."

I thought it was interesting that the Arletha I knew had a last name that was a color, Brown, and this Arletha could have been a color, Black.

Gayle continued explaining. "I did what I could, given my other obligations at the time, but I've run into nothing but dead ends."

"So you don't know any more than any of us. Except Great-granny did at least tell you her name, which is more than she ever told me. And you've known all of this since Great-granny died and you never said a word to anybody? The least you could have done was say something to me about it," Angela said. "I don't have anybody like the rest of you do. If there's a chance my grandmother is alive and still out there, I would like to have known that before now."

"Angel, it's not like you kept in touch with any of us after you moved down here. Besides, Grandmother asked me not to say anything to you unless and until I was able to locate Arletha."

Angela leaned forward and pursed her lips. "So you've located her?" She held her breath.

"No," Gayle said. "And I had all but quit looking. Then I was talking with a woman, a relative of Sarah's actually, after the will was read. She counseled me on how bad secrets, especially a secret like this, can be for everyone involved. She felt I shouldn't keep this to myself or from you. She felt you at least had a right to know what I knew."

Gayle stood up and took a few steps away from Angela. "When I was telling this woman about it, I just happened to mention Arletha's name. She then told me she'd met a woman in Birmingham, Alabama, named Arletha. Since Arletha is not a common name, it was something to follow up on. She had her phone number, and she gave me that number."

Angela stood up and walked over to Gayle. "Here in Birmingham? *That* Arletha lives here? So have you called yet?"

Gayle nodded as she sat back down on the couch. "I have."

"And what did she say?"

"She asked if this was some kind of a sick joke, then she hung up on me. When I tried calling her again to explain myself better, she told me to stop calling and harassing her. She said if I called her house again, she would report me to the proper authorities and let them take care of me."

"It's her," Angela said as she began to pace back and forth in front of the sofa like a caged lion. "I just know the Arletha you called is my mother's mother." She turned and faced Gayle. "Well, we've got to go see her. We have to find out for certain, once and for all. We owe that much to Great-granny." Angela began to pace again as she continued, "We need to go see her today. That's what we need to do. There has got to be a way to find out where she lives."

As soon as Angela said that, I looked at all the work we had left to do and the little time we had left to do it, and I realized how unwelcome a distraction this was.

"I checked to see if there was an address listed in the phone book for her, and there's not. Besides, Angel, you're getting married in a few days," Gayle said. I slowly began to exhale and thanked God for Gayle's voice of reason during this volatile time.

"That's one of the reasons why I was debating whether or not to mention this now," Gayle said. "The timing is all wrong."

"Give me her phone number." Angela held out her hand. "I want to call her myself."

Gayle got her purse, took out a piece of paper, and handed it to Angela. "Chances are this woman isn't your grandmother, Angel. Now don't go and let this interfere with the life you're about to embark upon with Brent. I knew I shouldn't have said anything to you just yet." Gayle shook her head. "I knew this would be a mistake."

"Yes, you should have." Angela headed for the phone. "And I'm calling her right now." She picked up the phone and held it. A smile came over her face. "If it turns out this woman really is my grandmother, then what better time for me to find out than right before my wedding. In my spirit, I don't believe this is happening by some sheer coincidence." Angela looked at the paper as she pressed the numbers. "I mean, look at the timing of all of this. It's almost like it's some sort of setup."

After a minute, with the phone at her ear, Angela looked up at the ceiling. She clicked the end button and slowly placed the phone back into its base.

"What happened?" Gayle asked.

"The number is no longer in service." Angela went over to the couch and gingerly eased down onto it. I could see she had just had the wind knocked out of her. I knew all too well what that felt like.

Gayle sat down beside Angela. "I'm so sorry. I *knew* I shouldn't have brought it up now. I should have followed my first mind and just kept this information to myself." She leaned over and hugged Angela. "Okay, here's what I want you to do. I want you to forget I ever said anything. Okay? You know your grandmother's name. It was Arletha. We don't know where she is or even if she's still alive. You're getting married on Saturday. So let's just get back to the happy place we were before I opened my big fat mouth. Let's finish seating family and friends and concentrate on the glorious day you're about to embark upon. Angel, please don't let the devil steal your joy. Not now."

Angela shook her head repeatedly. "I can't." She looked at Gayle. "And I'm not sorry you said anything." Angela looked down at the paper again. "If this Arletha Brown happens to be my grandmother, I want to know. I know other family members and close friends are going to be attending my wedding. But can you imagine how much it would mean, not having my mother alive to be here for this, not having Great-granny here, but finding my grandmother, if she's still alive, and to have her sitting out there in the audience?"

"We don't know that she is still alive, and we definitely don't know that this Arletha Brown is your grandmother. Chances are more likely that she is not. All of this is sheer speculation. It's a distraction. And even if you wanted to, we have no way of locating Arletha Brown to find out one way or the other," Gayle said.

I sat there debating what, if anything, I should do at this point. If I kept my mouth closed, maybe they would drop this, at least until after the wedding. But if Angela's thoughts were on finding this woman, we might not get anything done, and everything she and I had worked so hard to accomplish these past months would be ruined.

"Well, I'll just see what I can do. I have to at least try and find her. I'll get on the computer. I'll start calling around to see if anyone has heard of her," Angela said. "I'm sorry, but I'm not going to give up so easily when I could be so close. I'm not."

"I think I may know where she is," I said. Both Angela and Gayle turned and looked at me. "Arletha Brown. I believe I know where she lives. At least, I used to."

Gayle and Angela exchanged looks, then Angela stood as she looked at me. "Melissa, can you take us to her house? Please. Can you take us now?"

I nodded. "Sure. But I don't want you getting your hopes up. I don't know if she still lives there. She may be in a nursing home. She might have died. And like Gayle said, it's very likely this Arletha is not the woman you're looking for. I just know we have a lot of work here to do on this wedding, and you really don't need to be distracted right now. So if this helps you to get back on track, I'll take you, but only on one condition."

"What's that?" Angela asked.

"If she no longer lives there or if she says she's not who you're looking for, that you'll drop this. You'll put this out of your mind, at least until after the wedding," I said.

Angela shook her head, then nodded, then shook it again before she nodded again and said, "Of course. Of course. If you take us and it turns out she's not the person we're looking for, we'll come back here, finish what we need to do for my wedding, and I'll work on searching for her after I get back from my honeymoon."

Angela looked toward heaven. "Thank You, God. Thank You, God. Thank You." She looked over at Gayle. "Now, don't tell me this isn't God. Don't tell me it's not God."

Chapter 7

These be they who separate themselves, sensual, having not the Spirit.

—Jude 1:19

Sasha called Marcus. This wasn't his weekend to have Aaliyah, but Sasha said it was an emergency and she really needed him to get her.

"And if you don't mind, instead of bringing her back on Sunday, could you possibly keep her until Thursday for me?" Sasha asked. This was becoming a habit.

"Okay, so what's the emergency this time?" Marcus asked.

"Look, Marcus, either you can get your daughter this weekend and keep her or you can't. I told you it's an emergency. Now if you just don't want her—"

"Sasha, don't do that," Marcus said. "You know I have never said I didn't want my child. Never. And I'm not going to allow you to even *try* and go there with me."

Sasha's voice changed to a softer, more patronizing tone. "Oh yeah, that *is* right. You *were* the one who was pushing hard for me to have a child when you knew good and well I wasn't ready. I married you when I was twenty; had her when I was twenty-two. I'm only twenty-seven now. Maybe if you had listened to me more, things would have turned out differently between us."

"So what are you trying to say, Sasha?"

"I'm just pointing out the fact that at twenty-two, I wasn't ready to have a child and that you were the one who kept pressuring me until I finally gave in. You knew I was dealing with a lot of stressful things, being married for only a year. Maybe, just maybe, if you and I had waited to have a child, things might have turned out differently for us. Not that I don't love our daughter, because you know I do."

Marcus sighed. No matter what else he may have thought about his ex-wife, he did know that she loved Aaliyah. "Sasha, all I asked you was: What's the emergency?"

"And the answer is: It's none of your business. In case you've forgotten, you and I are no longer married. Remember that little thing called a divorce that became official two years ago? You know, that legal piece of paper you fought me on tooth and nail, causing us both to have to spend more money than we would have, had you just signed the thing. Well, here's a quick refresher course on what that document means. It means *you*, Marcus Antoine Peeples, no longer have a right to know what *I*, Sasha Antoinette Bradford Peeples, am doing."

"I know what it means, Sasha. All I asked is: What's your emergency this time? Last month . . ." Marcus stopped and began to count to ten.

He and Sasha did this very same thing every single time something like this came up. She would ask him to do something, claiming something either came up, happened, or some other reason she desperately needed his help. He would find out later the only emergency was some party she wanted to go to, a shopping trip to another city with one or several of her girlfriends or some other type of girls' night or girls' weekend out, or her just feeling like she needed a break.

A few times her emergency had turned out to be a weekend trip with some guy she had "fallen in love with" who, at the time, was definitely "the one." The same guy who would later send her into a state of depression. She would then need Marcus to keep Aaliyah because she was too depressed to take care of her. He knew about some of these guys because during a few of her bouts of depression, she also needed someone to talk to. She ended up talking to Marcus, the only person who seemed to care enough to reach out and check on her when she withdrew, to try and help her get better.

"Sasha—" Marcus began speaking again after he reached his count of ten.

"Marcus, either you can keep Aaliyah or you can't. If you can't, then don't worry about it. I'll get—"

"I'll keep her, Sasha. Okay." He knew Sasha was headed toward dumping Aaliyah on anyone she could get to take her no matter how incompetent that person was. "I'll keep her, but I'm in a wedding on Saturday so I need you to bring two of her dressy dresses with her."

"Sure, no problem. I mean, you buy her so many clothes and dresses it's not like she doesn't have a closetful. Most of her clothes still have tags on them. I believe that child has more clothes than me, and you know how I am about clothes. So, can I bring her over right now? I'm sort of short on time."

"Sure, Sasha. You can bring her over now."

"Thanks, Marc," Sasha said, calling him by the name she used when she was feeling in friendlier spirits.

Marcus hung up the phone and went to his study, that special place in his home where he usually went to pray, study, or just be alone with God. He sat down in the chair and looked up. "God, please help me. You know I'm trying hard down here. I just don't understand. I'm doing what You said to do in Your Word. I'm doing what You say right now, acknowledging You in all my ways. I know You never promised this road would be easy, but I really don't understand sometimes. Lord, if I'm wrong or doing something wrong, please help me to see that. Please order my steps in Your Word. Teach me. Lead me. Guide me, O thou great Jehovah. I desire to walk in Your will. And God, please touch Sasha's heart so she will be the woman You have called her to be. Not the woman I think she should be, but what You have called her to be. Help me to be more patient and forgiving. This I pray, in Jesus' name. Amen."

Marcus thought back to the beginning. How happy he and Sasha had been once upon a time. He reflected on all that had happened, and how much things had changed.

Chapter 8

Then said I, Wisdom is better than strength: nevertheless the poor man's wisdom is despised, and his words are not heard.

—Ecclesiastes 9:16

1993

Marcus was seventeen and beginning his junior year in high school. He was never one to be mistaken for the athletic type. Unbeknownst to most people at his school, Marcus was really great at shooting a basketball. It was defending the ball from an opponent that caused him the most trouble.

"Here's what I don't understand," Brother Man said, his comment directed at Marcus after he and five other friends finished playing a spirited game of basketball at the park. It was a community park that served as the official dividing line between the rich section of the neighborhood and the middle class. The four of them from the middle-class section were walking back to their side of the divide to go home.

Brother Man's real name was Darrell, but everybody (with the exception of a few of his teachers) called him Brother Man. "Here's what I don't understand. How come you can shoot the ball and hit the goal almost every time, but you don't seem to be able to dribble the ball and chew gum at the same time, forget about dribbling the ball and walking. Why exactly is that?"

"I keep trying to tell y'all that shooting the ball is mathematical," Marcus said. He understood math better than anyone in school, which was why he could hit the basket almost every time he shot the ball. "It's the same thing with shooting pool. Both are a lot of geometry and mathematical principles with touches and flashes of science mixed in."

"Ah, man, you keep trying to sell us that brain stuff," Brother Man said. "I know my moms is telling you to try and push that junk on us just so we'll do better in school. I'm telling you, I don't need to know math or English or science, and I especially don't need to know no world history. Not where I'm headed. 'Cause in case you haven't heard, the Brother Man has got mad skills." Brother Man pretended to shoot a basketball, then acted like it had hit nothing but net, with the appropriate hand follow-through and the required hamming it up afterward. "Brother Man is headed for the NBA and slated to become the next Michael Jordan, y'all mark my word. I'm telling y'all, watch and see what I say."

"Well, you still need to know math and English," Marcus said. "You still need to know how to read and to count. How else are you going to know when you're being cheated out of your money or signing away your best interest?"

Brother Man started laughing along with Slim Jim and Pretty Ricky, the two other guys with them from the neighborhood. "That's what you hire accountants and lawyers for," Brother Man said. "Geez, and here I thought you were supposed to be the smart one out of all of us."

"Well, let me give you your word for the day: embezzlement," Marcus said as he proceeded to walk away from them, headed toward his house.

"Embezzlement? So what does embezzlement mean?" Brother Man asked.

Marcus stopped and turned, flashing Brother Man his signature smile, the one he used when he knew he had the upper hand. He then said, "Look it up in the dictionary."

"He can't," Slim Jim said as he began to laugh uncontrollably. "That would require him knowing how to spell."

Brother Man threw a sharp look Slim Jim's way. "I know how to spell. I just don't know what some of these stupid words mean off the top of my head."

Marcus grinned as he walked backward while talking to and facing his friends. "That's good! When you get home, look that word up," he said, directing his comment to Brother Man. "Embezzlement, a form of the word embezzle."

"Fine. If you won't tell me, I'll go home, look in the *m*'s and find what the word means myself."

Marcus shook his head. "You might want to check in the *e*'s."

Brother Man frowned. "*E*'s? Where does an *e* come from?"

"The *e* is silent. The same way you're going to be if you don't do better in school and get serious about your education," Marcus said. "Because all this noise you're making is going to go straight out the window when you find out you're not going to be able to get into a college unless you pass the high school exit exam, graduate from high school, and get a certain score on an ACT or SAT test."

"I keep telling you, I'm going to be so good I won't need to waste my time in college." Brother Man started pretending that he was dribbling a basketball again. "The scouts are going to be flocking to snag me. Coach Nick told me some people are already taking note of me. I'm going straight from high school to the NBA. Forget college. None of these colleges pay you to play. And I ain't about to let some college make all that money off of me and my skills, everybody including the coach getting rich, while I don't end up with a dime in my pocket. Paying my room, board, books, and classes, but I won't have enough to take a girl out because I don't have a car or the money to buy gas or to buy me or even her a Happy Meal. Nope, not going out like that. Then if I get injured while playing in college, what am I left with? No money and no chance at the NBA."

"What you'll end up with is an education that no one can take away from you. They'll give you a scholarship to further your education, and that education belongs to you," Marcus said. "And you're going to need that college degree even if you do plan on going to the NBA. That way, if things don't work out with your NBA dreams or if they do and you end up getting injured and can't play, you'll have your degree to fall back on."

Brother Man shook his head, then shot his imaginary basketball at Marcus. "Not going to happen. Look at me." He held his hands out as he drew attention to his body by beating his chest a few times. "I'm in great shape. I'm not lanky or a geek like you."

Marcus smiled. "You still need your education. I'm not going to say you won't make it to the NBA. But it sure would be bad to make all that money and have some geek like me come along and embezzle it because you can't read or you can't count. That's all I'm saying. Trust me: there are plenty of folks out there waiting, praying, and looking for people just like you to take to the cleaners." Marcus pretended to throw the imaginary ball back at Brother Man. "And you can take *that* to the bank." Marcus walked up to his house, unlocked the front door, and walked inside.

Fifteen minutes later, his doorbell rang. Marcus couldn't hide his surprise when, thinking it was one of the guys he'd just left, he opened the door.

"Sasha?" Whenever Sasha was around, which wasn't often since they didn't run in the same circles, it was as if his brain took a temporary leave of absence. "Sasha."

Sasha was two years younger than Marcus but only one grade behind him. She lived in virtually the same neighborhood as he, Brother Man, Slim Jim, and Pretty Ricky, except that her house was in the wealthier section across the divide. Growing up, she didn't have much to do with or say to Marcus, but everybody knew she was crazy about Pretty Ricky and had been spotted on their street a few times throughout the summer. But Pretty Ricky didn't seem to give Sasha the time of day.

"Don't get me wrong, now. Sasha's fine," Pretty Ricky had said. "But I'm not interested in no jailbait."

Sasha was a cheerleader and had been since the seventh grade, second runner-up in the school beauty pageant in eighth grade, and voted Most Beautiful, Class Favorite, and Homecoming Queen in the ninth grade.

Then there was Marcus, who still rode the school bus.

Sasha's mother took her to school and paid someone to pick her up every day after school. Or Sasha would ride home with some of her friends who had their own cars and drove to school. Marcus knew this because the bus he rode was the one she would have ridden had she ridden the bus, which she never did.

Sasha smiled. She had the most beautiful smile. "Hi, Marcus," she said.

"I'm sorry. Hi. I was just shocked to see you standing here. Are you looking for my mother? Because she's not home yet." Marcus concluded she had to be looking for his mother, maybe to sell her something. The cheerleaders did a lot of fund-raisers.

"No, actually, I was looking for you."

"For me?"

"Yes." She took her hand and, like a choreographed move, pushed her hair that rested on her chest to the back. She crinkled her nose as she smiled. "I'm sort of in need of your help."

"*My* help?" Marcus's voice squeaked.

She smiled even more. "Yes, *your* help. It's algebra. I just don't get it. That's why I didn't take it in my freshman year. My mother hired a tutor to help me, but I still don't get it. I hear you're a whiz with this kind of stuff. Mercedes tells me you helped her. She was the one who suggested I get with you."

"Mercedes suggested you get with me?" Marcus realized he wasn't being cool at all. Here was the hottest girl in school, almost (after Mercedes to everybody else, but not to Marcus), and Mercedes had told Sasha—a girl he had dreamed would one day come to his front door, ring the doorbell, and ask for him—that she should get in touch with him. Marcus was starting to think the power of prayer his mother and the pastor at church always preached about really *did* work.

"I'm sorry," Marcus said. "I keep repeating what you're saying. I did help Mercedes, but I didn't know she thought all that much of me. She rarely speaks to me when I pass her in the hall at school. I really didn't think she even remembered me, let alone have anything nice to say about me."

"Oh, Mercedes speaks *very* highly of you. Anyway, I was wondering if you could possibly help me with this algebra stuff. I *have* to pass this class, Marcus. If I don't make a passing grade this semester, I'm off the cheerleading squad. Please."

Marcus found it interesting how people in his age group didn't seem to care about making good grades for good grades' sakes. Many of them were motivated more by sports-related requirements, other social engagements, or money paid by their parents for A's, B's, or C's. In a few cases, some parents were so desperate they even paid if their child just came home with a D. Only a handful of his peers seemed self-motivated, wanting to make good grades for the pride of what you can achieve if you put your mind and heart to it. He just didn't get it.

His mother often told him how no one ever had to pay her to make good grades. How she was harder on herself than anyone else, even when she got a B. "We knew education was our ticket out of poverty and into us contributing to a productive society. If we were ever going to attain our dreams, we had to do our best," his mother had said. "That's why I'm so proud of you, Marcus. You get it. You get what this is all about. Short-term pain for long-term gain. That's what life sometimes teaches us."

Marcus looked at Sasha, who now had placed one hand on her hip as she waited for his answer. "I can help you if you want," he said. "When do you want to start?"

"Tomorrow. And my mother said for me to tell you she's going to pay you."

Marcus adjusted his body to appear a little taller, a little more debonair than he really was. "You can come anytime after six. And you don't have to pay me." He bowed as though he were bowing before a queen as he said, "It'll be my pleasure to assist you."

"Right. Well, that's what you say now." She giggled. "You don't have a clue how much trouble I can be," she said. "Well, I'll see you tomorrow at six." She turned to leave.

Later, when Marcus looked back over his life, he realized what prophetic words Sasha had spoken that day. And had Marcus only listened to her, he might have saved himself a whole lot of trouble later.

A whole lot.

Chapter 9

Folly is set in great dignity, and the rich sit in low place.

—Ecclesiastes 10:6

Sasha and Marcus began her algebra lessons the following day after she came home from cheerleading practice. It was the beginning of September and the leaves were starting to change. There was just something different about autumn air. At least, Marcus thought so. When he opened the door for Sasha, he felt that the air was cleaner, crisper than even he had ever noticed it to be.

"My mother's not home yet," Marcus said, trying to decide what he should do. He and his mother, Sharon Peeples, had a great relationship and talked about everything. She had told him and his younger brother not to have anyone in their home when she wasn't there.

Sharon was a single mother. She had raised Marcus and his four siblings practically single-handed. His father had been to see them maybe three times since he and his mother divorced. She'd moved from Dallas to Birmingham when Marcus was five in order to keep her job, which ended up being outsourced overseas four years later anyway. Marcus and his younger brother, T. J., were the only ones still living at home now. Born on November fourth, T. J. was exactly one year and two days younger than his older brother Marcus.

T. J. usually sneaked off to hang out with his buddies after school. He knew what time his mother got home, and he always made it in the house by the time she arrived. She had no idea he was disobeying her by being with "those thugs," as she had called them when she had forbidden him to hang out with his so-called friends anymore.

Sasha stood outside his door wearing a short cheerleading-practice outfit and high heels. "I'm sorry, Marcus. I know you told me to come over after six. But we finished practice early today. I was just so excited to get started, I couldn't wait. Besides, I sort of have a little emergency that popped up at the last minute. I figure if we could get started earlier, we could finish up early enough for me to handle it. But I *have* to get this algebra or else I'm sunk!"

Marcus looked at his watch, a gift his father had sent him two Christmases ago. It was five thirty-three. His mother normally got home around six—six-fifteen if traffic was backed up. *Sasha being there almost thirty minutes early shouldn't be too bad.* And he wasn't doing anything wrong. Besides, she was a girl. He was sure when his mother said she didn't want anybody in her house whenever she wasn't home, she was merely wanting to keep out the boys who would tear up the house.

Still, Marcus didn't like disobeying his mother even on small technicalities. He saw how hard things were for her. He tried his best not to be the cause of any added stress or problems in her life.

That's one of the reasons Marcus stopped tattling on T. J. It was really stressing his mother out. Marcus tried doing what he could with his brother. He went so far as to tell their older brother, Ronnie, who talked to T. J., to no avail. His mother gave so much of herself. Marcus knew there were times when his mother went without just so her children could have. She had sacrificed her life for them, given them more than she would ever let them know. But Marcus knew.

He had seen her many nights mending an outfit just so she wouldn't have to buy herself anything new to wear. He saw the day his mother dropped her head when T. J. came in excited, asking—begging—for her to buy him a pair of Michael Jordan tennis shoes because all of his friends owned a pair and he was the only one who still hadn't gotten any. How she cried later that night after T. J. told her she was just being mean, how he was the laughingstock of his class because of how he dressed.

Marcus knew his mother couldn't afford a two-hundred-dollar pair of shoes. She was taking her lunch to work every day just so she could give them money to buy *their* lunch. He knew all of this, not because she had burdened them with this information but because he had paid attention. He saw her when she prayed to God to provide the money to pay the light bill because their electricity was scheduled to be cut off.

Marcus saw her emptying her purse as she searched for whatever change she could find, then begin to count it, sometimes smiling and looking toward Heaven when she finished, with a nod of yes. Sometimes looking upward, still smiling, with a shake of no. He would see her later bring that money to one of his sisters or brothers for something they needed or wanted for school. No one else in his family seemed to notice how much money they received in change. No one except Marcus.

And that's what motivated Marcus from a young age to do well in school. His mother was sacrificing too much for him to allow her sacrifice to be in vain. Marcus suspected his older brother knew how difficult things were. That's one of the reasons Ronnie chose to enlist in the navy as soon as he graduated from high school instead of going off to college. The navy had promised him a chance to receive money for a higher education. Ronnie saw that as his pathway to rise up. After reenlisting that first time around, Ronnie decided to make a career with the navy.

Marcus's older sisters, Tia and Brianna, went off to college after they graduated from high school. They both took out student loans, but college was difficult because they still needed money for so many things besides tuition. Books certainly weren't cheap, even the used ones. Ronnie sent money home to help out when he could, but once he was married and had two children, he had his own responsibilities.

Tia met a guy in college who was a senior when she was a freshman. They fell in love and decided to get married after her first year with every intention for her to continue her education. She got pregnant in her first year of marriage and hadn't gone back to finish college yet.

Brianna went wild the first few months of college, despite her mother's warnings. She got pregnant, then married the guy after the baby was born. She also dropped out of college and never went back.

Marcus was determined not only to go to college and graduate with honors but to win scholarships that would pay for everything, including his books. Marcus was on a mission. He talked to the school counselor when he first arrived at high school to find out what was available to him and what he needed to do in order to get it. He wasn't going to wait until his junior or senior year to get it together. He knew that everything he did from the ninth grade on up would have an effect on his well-thought-out plans. He was going to make something of himself, then give his mother something so she could stop working so hard and take a much-needed and well-deserved rest, if she chose to.

When he first told her of his plans while he was in middle school, she smiled. "You know what, Marcus? I believe you'll do just that." She hugged him. "I believe in you."

Marcus was amazed at the power and impact of those four words: "I believe in you." That's what his mother had given him. A vision of what was possible if one would only believe and work hard for it. And whatever you do in life, to always put God first.

"Marcus, if you don't remember anything else I tell you, just know that with God all things are possible," she had said. "God has a calling on your life. There's something different about you. Yes, my dear Marcus, like all of us, God has a purpose and a plan for your life. There's something truly special about you. And I'm not just saying that because you're my child." She nodded and smiled. "You're destined for great things. I just know it."

That was the other thing Sharon Peeples had given her children: the knowledge of who God was in their lives and the power that is available to those who have the wisdom and the desire to connect and hook up with Jesus. There is grace, favor, and guidance to those who allow Jesus to be the Lord of their life and not just their Savior. Marcus knew what prayer could do. He had seen the effects of prayer, time after time, again and again, in his mother's life.

"Earth to Marcus, earth to Marcus," Sasha said, before she finally yelled, "Marcus Peeples! Are you planning on making me stand out here all night or what?!"

Marcus looked up from his tennis shoes. He hadn't realized his mind had wandered so far from the present as he had wrestled with what he should do about Sasha showing up at his house early. Sasha did say her mother was going to pay him for tutoring her. That was money he could either give to his mother or use to buy something he needed so she wouldn't have to worry about it. High school kids, especially juniors and seniors, had lots of expenses, so every little bit of cash he could make would help.

Besides, he was seventeen, turning eighteen in a few months. His mother had married when she was eighteen, so he should be allowed to have someone in the house and be trusted to be responsible. It wasn't that much time before she would be home. Sasha appeared harmless enough. Definitely not one of the thugs his mother was concerned would steal something out of their house. And they wouldn't be doing anything except studying.

"Come on in," Marcus said after his brief deliberation. "Did you bring your algebra book?"

"Yep, it's in my bag," she said, turning so he could see her oversized backpack.

"We can go in the den and work in there," Marcus said. "Unless you would prefer the dining room table?"

"Where's your computer?" Sasha asked. "Don't you need a computer to teach me?"

"Nah. Not yet, anyway."

"But you do *have* a computer, right?" Sasha asked. "Just in case we find we need one, you do have one, right?"

"Yes, I *do* have one. It's in my room. But for now, we don't need one. I'm going to show you how to do things the good old-fashioned way." He led her to the den and motioned for her to have a seat on the couch. He gathered the magazines spread out on the coffee table and placed them in a stack. Thus began their journey of variables and equations and expressions.

"I still don't get if *a* equals *b* and *b* equals *c* how *a* can equal *c*," Sasha said. "It just doesn't make sense to me. I don't understand variables and expressions and equations. I don't get why we need to use alphabets instead of just inserting the numbers and be through with it. Algebra is just crazy! Why would anyone go to so much trouble to make something easy so complicated?" She fell back against the couch and folded her arms. "And tell me, when will I *ever*, in the real world anyway, *ever* have a need, *or* for that matter, a *reason* to have to add using alphabets? When?"

Marcus loved watching her being so passionate about how she felt, even if she was complaining about and bashing something he absolutely loved.

"Okay, think of algebra as a way to say something without having to keep repeating certain information." Marcus racked his brain to try and think of some way to bring this to life and turn it into something that Sasha might be interested in and therefore get.

He looked down at her shoes. Despite the fact that she had come from cheerleading practice, she had arrived wearing high heels with red painted on the bottom.

"Take a pair of shoes, for instance," Marcus said. "Okay, let's say that *a* represents one pair of shoes and *b* represents a second pair, and *c* represents a third pair of shoes. Let's say you were trying to tell Mercedes or one of your other friends something about each pair. And you tell them that *a* equals *b*, and *b* equals *c*, then what would you be left to conclude about shoes *a* and *c*?"

Sasha smiled. "Okay, you're telling me that shoe *a* and shoe *b* are the same, and shoe *b* and *c* are the same, so that would mean that shoe *a* and shoe *c* are the same."

"Or as the equation would phrase it—"

"—*a* equals *c*!" Sasha beamed as she relaxed. "I get that!"

"So if you were to substitute a number for shoes, then what?"

"Then I would know that whatever number *a* represents and if it equals *b*, and if whatever the number *b* is it equals *c*, then logically *a* must equal *c* since *a* equals *b*!" She clapped. "Oh, that was fun! You really *are* good." Sasha touched his hand, allowing her hand to linger on his.

And that was when he felt something that equaled electricity flowing from her hand to his body, and he fully realized just how much of a role science played and the impact it had in real life.

"Mama's pulling up in the driveway!" T. J. said as he burst in the door and headed toward the kitchen. He stopped, backed up, and walked into the den. "You're Sasha, aren't you? Wow, you look even better up close." He held out his hand. "My name is T. J. So tell me, which part of heaven did you fall from?"

Just then, Sharon walked in the house. She stopped when she saw her two sons and one young lady in her den. "Boys," she said, "what's going on here?" She directed her gaze at T. J., since he was the one holding Sasha's hand.

T. J. immediately held up both of his hands in a show of surrender. "Ask Marcus. You told us not to have company in our house when you're not here. I know better, so it wasn't me. I wouldn't *dare* disobey you, Mama."

Sharon looked at Marcus, feeling bad that his brother had embarrassed him.

Marcus stood up. "Mama, this is Sasha Bradford. She goes to my school. I'm helping her with algebra."

Sasha stood, walked over to Marcus's mother, and firmly shook her hand. "How do you do, Ms. Peeples? Your son agreed to tutor me in algebra. I must apologize. He told me to come after six. I got here a few minutes early and he's such a gentleman, he didn't want to make me wait outside until you arrived. I had an emergency come up so I sort of put him on the spot showing up like I did. He has been absolutely wonderful so far. Marcus has actually gotten me to understand some of this stuff. And to think, we just got started. Your son is really smart."

Sharon grinned as she nodded and wrinkled her nose. "He is, isn't he? Especially when it comes to anything mathematical. I'm glad he knows how to do this stuff because if I had to help him, we would both be in trouble." Sharon leaned over and whispered, "Between me and you, math was not my strongest suit either."

"Oh, I know. My mother has hired tutor after tutor for me, but I've still struggled. But I must say, no one has ever managed to make it come alive the way Marcus just did. I'm actually looking forward to learning more."

"Do you live around here?" Sharon asked. "I didn't see a car when I drove up."

"I live in the subdivision next to this one. A friend dropped me off after school, after cheerleading practice. Oh, I'm a cheerleader, which is why I'm dressed this way. But it's not all that far to walk over here. My mother is sending someone to pick me up."

"Oh, yes, I know," Sharon said. "Back when I was walking more to stay in shape, I would walk over there and back."

"She lives in the *rich* folks' neighborhood," T. J. said with a smirk. "You have to make some serious Benjamins to own one of those addresses, unlike over here on this side where we can't seem to ever be able to afford something as simple as a pair of Michael Jordan shoes."

"T. J.," Sharon said with a scold in her voice. "That's not nice. I've taught you better. We're thankful for what God has blessed us to have. And I'm happy for those who manage to have even more."

"It might not be nice, but it's true. And I ain't hating on them. One day I plan to have a house like the ones in her subdivision, if not bigger. In fact, you gonna see my house featured on that show called *Lifestyles of the Rich and Famous*. Watch and see."

"Well, I'm not going to interrupt you two from your schoolwork," Sharon said to Marcus and Sasha as she started out of the room. "I had a really rough day at work today. I'm going to go upstairs and change out of these oppressive clothes and find me something comfortable." She smiled. "T. J., have you done your homework yet?"

"Yes, ma'am," T. J. said. "I finished all of it about fives minutes before you came in the house. I'm going to go get on the computer now."

After Sharon and T. J. left, Marcus and Sasha went back to the books. "Marcus, I hope I didn't get you in any trouble being here. So, you didn't tell your mother about me or that you were going to be doing this?"

"I didn't tell her yet because, honestly, I wasn't sure you were serious. I thought I'd wait and see if you showed up, then I'd tell her." Marcus tried to get comfortable. For some reason, Sasha sitting so close to him was making him more and more tense. He could only hope she hadn't noticed just how much.

After an hour of tutoring, a car honked outside. Sasha got up to leave. "Mama said you need to let us know how much you charge. She sent this today." Sasha pulled out twenty dollars and gave it to him. "She said if I liked you and if I think the two of us will work out, we can schedule as many lessons as I need."

"I wouldn't charge you twenty dollars for a one-hour session, though."

"Oh, it's okay. My daddy is pretty loaded. He's an investor. He works for some big investment company or something like that. Daddy's paying for this so I feel good knowing that his money is going to good use. And Marcus, you are *so* worth it! In fact, if you like, I'll tell Mama you're charging twenty-five, or better yet, thirty dollars a lesson. And if they think it's too much to pay, I'll have one of my little tantrums, tell them how awesome a tutor you are. Make them understand what all I'll possibly lose if I don't get a passing grade. Trust me. I have my routine down pat."

Marcus smiled as he looked at her shoes and then back up at her. "Twenty dollars is more than enough." He looked into her big beautiful brown eyes, then hurriedly looked away as he opened the door for her. "Thank you, though."

She touched his hand again. "No, seriously, I thank you. For the first time, I'm actually looking forward to class tomorrow, if you can believe that. Imagine how I'll be when you and I are finished."

"If you keep up this enthusiasm, you just may decide to become a teacher and teach algebra one day. Wouldn't that be something?"

"Now let's not get carried away, Marcus. I plan on becoming a top model or an actress. Maybe a model, then an actress. I've even had a few ad shoots. But teaching is not something I would ever be interested in doing. Besides, I'm not all that great with children. Trust me, a model or an actress is what I was born to be."

Marcus suddenly heard his mother's words replaying in his mind as she spoke.

"I saw Maya Angelou on *Oprah* one day," his mother had said. "Maya said something that is so true and has stuck with me. She said, 'When someone tells you who they are the first time, believe them.' I can tell you Maya Angelou hit the nail on the head with those words of wisdom. Definitely something all of us should take heed of."

Chapter 10

Cast in thy lot among us; let us all have one purse.
—Proverbs 1:14

"Melissa, we'll go in my car," Angela said to me as she grabbed her purse and we headed out the door to go find Arletha's place. "I appreciate this so much. You just don't know how much."

"At least we can follow this one lead, and if it turns out it's not the Arletha we seek, we can table this until later," Gayle said. She stopped Angela by grabbing her by her shoulders. "But you have to promise me that if this is *not* the Arletha we're looking for, you'll put this out of your thoughts, at least until after your honeymoon."

"I know I shouldn't have let this mess me all up the way it has. I just never thought this would mean so much to me. Apparently it does." Angela walked over to the door of her apartment and held it open as we filed out. "I also know I don't want this to drive me crazy and ruin my and Brent's special day. We have been so looking forward to this wedding. You just don't know how hard it's been having to wait. Now this comes up. On the surface it looks like it might be a gift from God, but who knows for sure? To learn that my grandmother could possibly still be alive and could be right here, in a place I can get in my car and drive to today, I can't put it into words."

"I know it's messing with your mind," Gayle said as we walked toward Angela's car. "But you're going to make me feel bad if I put even the slightest damper on your wedding for telling you this news today of all days."

We were close to Angela's navy blue Cadillac Seville.

"Melissa, why don't you sit in front so you can show Angela how to get there?" Gayle said. After Angela unlocked the doors, Gayle got in back behind Melissa.

I got in front and closed the door. My old neighborhood was only about thirty minutes from Angela's place. With the exception of the oak tree in the front yard being much bigger, everything else looked pretty much the same. Angela pulled into the driveway. She sat there, frozen, not moving one way or the other.

Gayle leaned forward and stuck her head through the opening between the front seats. "Are you going to be all right? Do you want me to go in and check for you while you wait out here?"

Angela continued to hold the steering wheel firmly without saying a word. After a minute, she released it and grabbed her purse. Shaking her head a few times, she seemed to snap out of it.

"We can go in together," Angela said. "If this is where Arletha Brown lives, I'll just explain everything to her. If it turns out we have the wrong Arletha, I'll let it go. For now anyway. And when I return from my honeymoon, and Brent and I have had a few weeks to adjust to being husband and wife, I'll see what I can do to locate the *right* Arletha." She nodded a few times as though someone had asked her a question that required a yes answer. "We'll just have to play this by ear."

"Should I stay in the car?" I asked.

Angela turned to me. "How well did you know Arletha Brown when you lived here?"

"Not all that well. She didn't have children and most of us children avoided her house as much as possible. Honestly, she didn't seem to enjoy being around other people all that much, adults or children," I said. "But whatever you want from me at this point, I'm ready and willing to do."

I was sincere about that, but I was also thinking about those place cards for the reception that still needed our attention back at her apartment. The sooner we took care of this, the sooner we could get back to taking care of them and all the other business that was screaming for our attention. There are just some things a wedding planner can't do without the assistance of the bride. That's if you want a bride happy with the end results. If my going in with her would help move things along that much faster, then whatever I needed to do, I was willing to do.

"Then let's go," Angela said to both me and Gayle as she opened her door.

We walked up to the front porch. There wasn't a doorbell. Angela took charge even though Gayle was the oldest of us three. She opened the green-trimmed screen door and knocked on the main door. After a minute, she knocked again. Either no one was home or the person inside had peeked out, saw us standing there, and decided not to answer it.

Angela knocked again, harder, in rapid succession. The door suddenly opened. A chain kept the door from opening any wider than a crack large enough to see through. "Yes?" the elderly woman said as she eyed us through the crack.

"Hi. Yes. We're looking for Arletha Brown," Angela said.

"Who is *we*?" the elderly woman asked.

"My name is Angela Gabriel. This is Gayle Cane and Melissa Anderson." Angela touched us as she spoke our names.

"Sorry, but I don't talk to Jehovah's Witnesses. So y'all can take your literature and whatever else you're trying to peddle and, in Jesus' name, get off of my porch."

"Ma'am," Angela said, speaking quickly before the woman could close the door in our faces. "We're not Jehovah's Witnesses."

"Then who are you?"

Angela's hands began to shake a little as she held them up. I took what she was doing as her way of letting this woman know we didn't come to do her harm. "Ma'am, might you be Arletha Brown?"

"Ms. Arletha"—I moved up around Angela so the woman could see me better—"I'm Melissa Anderson. I used to live up the street from here. I'm Ernestine Anderson's child, Ms. Cora Belle's grandchild."

I threw in my grandmother's name because I remembered my grandmother had befriended or at least tried to befriend Arletha a few times, back when she lived with us. My grandmother had been looking for more people her age. They would speak on occasion when my grandmother saw her outside. They would chitchat if she caught her before Arletha spotted her and scurried back inside her house. Nothing much ever came of it. My grandmother said Arletha was a little more fanatic than she cared for when it came to religion. Eventually, my grandmother quit even bothering and just waved if she saw her.

"You're Cora's grandchild?" the woman asked as she took the chain off the door and opened it. She looked me up and down, then said, "That you are. I see a little bit of Cora in you. Same bone structure, same nose." She looked from me to Angela and Gayle as she seemed to size them up. "So, what can I do for y'all?"

"Ms. Brown, would you mind if we came in for a minute?" Angela said.

"That depends," Arletha said. "Are you selling something? 'Cause if you are, I can tell you right now that I ain't the least bit interested, so don't bother wasting your time or mine."

"No, ma'am," Angela said. "I can assure you we didn't come here to sell you a thing. I promise, if you'll give us just a few minutes of your time, I'll explain everything."

Arletha motioned for us all to come in. I had never been inside her house before. It was spotless, everything in its place, with a real antiquelike feel to it. The couch and chairs in the living room still had plastic on them, the hard kind that when cracked could do some damage to a leg if you sat or moved the wrong way. The kind of plastic I thought everyone had gotten the memo about stating that it was no longer chic or cool to have on your living room furniture. I sat down. I was thankful— no detectable cracks.

"The clock's ticking," Arletha said. "You might want to start your pitch right about now."

Gayle sat, not having said a word. She looked over at Angela, who sat down, pressed her lips together several times, then quietly and slowly exhaled.

"My name is Angela Gabriel."

"That much I got when you were outside my door," Arletha said.

"Ms. Brown, my mother's name was Rebecca. After my mother died, I was raised by my great-grandmother, Pearl Black Williams." Angela took in another deep breath. "I have reason to believe you may be my grandmother," she said, releasing that breath along with those words.

All eyes were now fixed on Arletha.

And that's when I suddenly realized, that's when it struck me . . . I had forgotten how to breathe. As much as I was trying to, I couldn't remember how to breathe. Something we all do day in and day out without ever thinking about it. But as we sat there, eyes glued on Arletha, all I could hear my brain saying, at first calmly, was, "Breathe. Breathe." Then in a more panicked tone, I heard my brain begin to scream, "Hurry up, girl. You need to breathe!"—then scream louder—"Breathe!"

Chapter 11

Arletha sat there, not moving a muscle. She looked at Angela, then Gayle, and finally, she stared at me. "What did she say your name was again?" she asked, directing her question to Gayle.

"I'm Gayle Cane."

"You were the one who called my house a few times a few months back, aren't you?"

"Yes, I am."

"And I told you to stop harassing me, did I not?"

"Yes, but—"

"Yes, but nothing!" Arletha said with obvious anger lacing her voice. She stood up, then turned her attention to Angela. "Young lady, your minute is up," she said, as she indicated we had officially worn out our welcome.

Angela spoke in a hurried manner. "Ms. Brown, I don't want anything from you. I'm merely searching for my grandmother, that's all. Surely you can appreciate that. Her name was Arletha, just like yours. I hate to confess this, but I just learned this today. When my cousin, Gayle, here"—she looked over at Gayle and nodded—"came in for my wedding and told me. You see, even though I live here now, I'm originally from Asheville, North Carolina. My mother, Rebecca, died when I was only five.

So I don't remember a lot about her. Just the bits and pieces I have been able to hold on to."

Arletha shrugged. "I'm sorry to hear that. But none of this has anything to do with me."

"My great-grandmother who raised me, her name was Pearl, she died four years ago. I'm getting married on Saturday to this wonderful man. His name is Brent . . . Brent Underwood." Angela spoke passionately. "I didn't think it would mean so much to me since I had never known much about my grandmother, but when I learned today, for the very first time, my grandmother's name—"

"You'd never known your grandmother's name before today?" Arletha asked.

"No. My great-grandmother never talked about her daughter, at least not around me. And the other family members didn't either. I don't know what that was all about, I don't know what happened, but that's how things were. No one talked about it. Ever."

Arletha shrugged her shoulders a few times. "Sounds messed up, if you ask me. In fact, it sounds like your family pretty much disowned her. I'm sorry for what you have probably lost in all of this, and I'm also sorry that I can't help you."

"So are you saying you never lived in Asheville, North Carolina? That there is no way you could even remotely be my grandmother?" Angela asked. She looked directly into Arletha's eyes as she stood close to her.

"I'm saying that I wish I could help you, seeing as you seem to be a nice young lady, a very pretty young lady at that. But my advice to you is to have a wonderful wedding and to forget about this nonsense of finding some grandmother that may or may not still be alive and may or may not want to be found," Arletha said. "That's just my opinion. I've been on this earth a long time, and I can tell you that this world brings you enough trouble without you going out looking for it unnecessarily."

"But it's not trouble I'm searching for right now. I'm looking for family. And if that's you, then I want you to know that I love you. I truly do. No, I didn't grow up knowing my grandmother, but if you are my grandmother, I love you."

Angela began to cry as she spoke. "I don't have a mother to sit on my side of the aisle for my wedding. And yes, when I heard my grandmother might still be alive, of course I was going to stop whatever I was doing and go look for her. And when I learned there was a possibility the woman I seek might be you, of course I was going to come over and do all I could to see you, to talk with you. I promise I don't want anything from you. But there's something I can't explain and don't quite understand myself about knowing that your own blood is out there somewhere that causes a person to want to find them." Angela broke down. I reached in my purse and handed her my packet of tissues.

"I never fully appreciated why, when it came to adopted children who are raised in loving families, they still feel a need to locate that missing parent," Angela continued. "But for some reason that I can't explain, you have this burning need, a desire to connect. You want to look into the eyes of where you came from. In some ways, you feel it will possibly help you find yourself. It's hard to put what I feel into words."

Gayle hugged Angela. "Ms. Brown. I'm Angel's second cousin. My grandmother, Pearl, Angel's great-grandmother, asked me to do this for her right before she died. She asked me to try and find her daughter Arletha. At the very end of her life, she wanted Angel to know her grandmother, if by God's grace she happened to still be alive."

Gayle's voice became softer. "If there's even the smallest chance you are Angel's grandmother, please do the right thing. Please do whatever you can. And if you're not sure, for whatever reason, please—"

"What do you think? That I have amnesia? I'm in stages of dementia, Alzheimer's or something where I don't remember whether I had a child or not? You think I don't know who I am? Who my own mother was? Where I came from?" Arletha asked.

"No. I'm just saying we can do a DNA test and put this to rest for all concerned," Gayle said. "It's a pretty simple procedure to administer. They swab the inside of your cheek with a Q-tip, send it to a lab equipped to handle DNA tests, and it will tell us once and for all whether you are any kin to Angel . . . and to me."

"And what are you supposed to be, some kind of DNA specialist?" Arletha asked as she stared at Gayle, who had moved even closer to Angela.

"No. I'm a nurse."

"Well, as I've already stated, I do feel for you, young lady," Arletha said, directing her attention back to Angela. She led us out of the room. "I'm sure you're going to have a lovely wedding. My advice to you—and you can take it for what it's worth or not—is to forget about what you don't have and learn to concentrate on and appreciate what you *do*. I'm sure your husband-to-be doesn't want or need all this drama." Arletha opened the front door and held it as she waited for us to leave.

Angela took out her business card, turned it over, and wrote her home address on the back. "Here is my card with all of my contact information on it, including my cell number." Angela handed the card to her. "If you need anything, anything at all, or if something comes up, will you please get in touch with me?"

Arletha shrugged as she took the card. "I'll take your card, but I don't know anything more I can do for you. I can't make it any plainer than that."

Angela looked at Arletha one last time. She stepped outside, then smiled. "Thank you for your time. We didn't mean to bother you."

"Yeah. Sure," Arletha said as though she didn't really believe that. Suddenly, her countenance began to soften a tad. "And whether you believe this or not, I *am* sorry things didn't work out for you. I'm not totally unsympathetic to your plight. And for the record, if I really *were* your grandmother, I'd be proud to have you as a granddaughter."

"I'm sorry, too." Angela put on her shades. "But I'll keep

praying, and we'll see what God does next. I know that His ways are not our ways, nor His thoughts our thoughts. And like Great-granny always told me: there's nothing too hard for our God."

"You're preaching to the choir now. Especially when you start talking about God," Arletha said. "You just need to let God be God and start actually practicing what you preach. And if it's God's will, you'll locate your grandmother, one way or another."

Angela thanked Arletha for her time, apologized again for showing up the way we had, and said good-bye. A little bit despondent, we got back in the car.

"Well, you gave it your best shot," Gayle said, patting Angela on her shoulder.

"Yeah. You followed up, and it turns out she's not the one you were looking for," I said.

Angela took off her shades. "Oh, y'all both think so?" She started backing out of the driveway. "That Arletha we just met, Arletha Brown, that's my grandmother." Putting the car in drive, Angela turned her head back and looked at Gayle. "Didn't you see all of those little moles on her face and neck? Those are Black moles," Angela said, facing forward, while alternating between looking at the road ahead and back at Gayle.

"Black moles? Okay, so her moles were black," Gayle said.

"No, they were *Black* moles as in Pearl Black. Her oval-shaped face was Great-granny's face if I ever saw it. I've seen pictures of Great-granny when she was in her sixties. I see the resemblance. That's how Great-granny looked before she got older."

"Angel, okay now. Be reasonable. I *knew* I shouldn't have said anything to you about this. That's what I get for listening to somebody else," Gayle said.

"I *am* being reasonable. And for the last time, you were right to tell me, and you were right on time to tell me now," Angela said. "But don't worry. I'm not planning on letting any of this interfere with my wedding. Brent deserves more than that from me. I say that I trust God. I say that God will make a way out of no way. I say that my God will supply all of my needs according to His riches in glory. Well, Arletha Brown was absolutely correct earlier when she said I need to start practicing what I preach."

Angela stopped at a red light and looked over at me. She grinned. "Melissa, when we get back, I need to put one more invitation to my wedding in the mail, pronto."

"Dare I even guess to whom?" I asked.

She smiled. "You're guessing correctly. I'm sending one to Ms. Arletha Brown."

"She's not going to come," Gayle said with a tone of force along with a touch of weariness in her voice.

"Oh, she's going to come. I just have a feeling that if I invite her, Ms. Arletha Brown will come."

Chapter 12

A gracious woman retaineth honor: and strong men retain riches.

—Proverbs 11:16

I was *too* happy that after Angela put an invitation in the mail to Arletha, she got back on track for the wedding. I was also glad Gayle was around. Angela convinced Gayle to check out of her hotel and stay with her. All of us went to Bible study Wednesday night. Neither Angela nor I was planning on missing the final installment of Pastor Landris's teaching on "Who we are in Christ." Gayle loved it so much she bought the other lessons in that series.

Gayle has a great sense of humor and wonderful comedic timing. She could say something that wasn't supposed to be funny, and we would end up laughing just because of how she said it. She had us laughing so much Thursday night that I suggested she look into stand-up comedy. Angela and I both threatened her and told her not to say another word for fear that we would never finish from laughing so hard.

"Like my grandmother would say, you are a hoot a minute," I said.

"A hoot?" Gayle said as she laughed at the word. "What in the world is a *hoot*?"

"It means you're really funny. You crack me up," I said.

Angela had ordered the programs for her wedding. She had

wanted to handle that part, so I had no input whatsoever. Gayle helped us so much on Thursday.

The bulk of the family members arrived Friday morning, with the rest Friday afternoon. The rehearsal dinner included both of the families as well as the wedding party and their families. I asked Nae-nae to help me out for both the rehearsal dinner and the reception. She needed some extra cash and I was in a position to throw some her way.

Even though Nae-nae has borrowed money from me that she has yet to pay back, and she owes me for all of the little "favors" I've done for her, I still wanted to be a blessing to her by offering her the opportunity. She would be paid pretty well for the two nights. I was still left to wonder, though, how people can borrow money from someone, remember that you said they could get it, but can't seem to remember they haven't paid you back.

Nevertheless, Nae-nae is my friend. And she has a good heart. If anyone knows her situation, I do. She has children, I don't. Enough said.

One good thing going for me with this wedding was how much Angela had already done. She only hired me after she'd gotten it going and decided she could use some help. My friend Tiffany Connors was the one who told her about me. How I had done an outstanding job planning another wedding (it was small, but it turned out so well), and that she should seriously give me a call. Angela did, and here I am.

Knowing Tiffany the way I do, I'm sure she knew this would be the big boost I needed to get my name out there in a big way. I love that Tiffany.

I mainly worked on the staging and decorating aspects of the wedding. Angela hired a caterer for the rehearsal dinner being held at the church's fellowship hall and for the reception to be held at Ross Bridge, an upscale golf course, for the well-to-do community. I took care of all the other necessary details. Angela handled the wedding party details and anything that needed to be printed.

Angela was going to hire a director, but I told her I was great at multitasking. "Consider me your one-stop shopping," I said. "We can bundle my duties."

She knew exactly what she wanted to happen at the wedding. I was to shadow the rehearsal along with her so I could execute everything during the wedding just the way she wanted it.

So when everyone arrived for the rehearsal, I had received my stage direction script from Angela on how the entire wedding, from start to finish, would proceed—from the number of groomsmen lighting candles, to how many groomsmen would stand with the groom, to how many bridesmaids and junior bridesmaids there would be. And of course, the customary ring bearer and flower girl duties. There were only initials or the first name of who was to do what and when—Angela's shorthand to herself. That's probably why I was shocked when I looked up and saw Marcus standing before me.

"So are you not going to speak?" Marcus asked. "I said hello."

I shook my head to show him just how busy I was. "Oh, I'm sorry. Hi." I began to fumble with the paper I held in my hand so he could see what I'd been busy doing when he walked up. "It's really jumping around here," I said. "I didn't see you at first. I'm so focused, trying to make sure I know what's going on and staying on top of things."

Marcus glanced around the room. There were a lot of people at the rehearsal. "Yes, I see," he said. "This is going to be really nice. So, this is the wedding you were working on?"

I looked around the room again, not because I hadn't already, but to make sure when I spoke my voice didn't crack. "Yes. The one and only." I looked down at the paper again to see how I had managed not to know Marcus would be part of this wedding. That's when I saw MP beside Best Man. "So, you're the best man, huh?"

He leaned over and looked on my paper. Tapping the top of the paper, he said, "Yep. That's me right there."

I happened to finally look down and saw Marcus holding the hand of a little girl. Her jet-black wavy hair was pulled up into a ponytail. She was so pretty. And when I looked into her face, there was no mistaking who her father was. She was the spitting image of Marcus.

"Well, hello there," I said, bending over slightly as I spoke. "Aren't you the prettiest thing? What's your name?"

She looked up at her daddy. He nodded. She smiled and looked back at me. "Aaliyah Peeples."

I stood up straight. "Aaliyah? What a beautiful name for such a beautiful little girl. So Aaliyah, how old are you?"

"Five," she said as she held up her hand showing me all five of her fingers spread wide.

"Wow, five. Well, you sure are pretty."

"Say thank you," Marcus said as he looked down at her with such love and admiration even I could feel it.

"Thank you," Aaliyah said. She began to twist the way most little girls do.

"Marcus, hey man! I'm so glad you made it," Brent Underwood said as he walked up to Marcus and gave him some dap first, then a manly hug where they merely bumped shoulders. "I was starting to get a little worried about you. Thinking maybe you'd gotten cold feet on me or something."

"Me? Get cold feet? You're the one who's getting married tomorrow. I'll just be standing there with you to give you moral support," Marcus said. "Not that you'll need it. You're marrying a jewel and a truly virtuous woman, from everything I've seen of her."

"Well, I know how seriously you take marriage. I'm just sorry things turned out like they did for you," Brent said as he looked down at Aaliyah. He touched Aaliyah's chin. "Well, hi there, little princess. You're hanging out with Daddy tonight, huh?"

Aaliyah hugged Brent. "Yes! But what are *you* doing here?"

"I'm here because I'm getting married tomorrow to a beautiful angel, and we have to practice to make certain it's a beautiful day. We want to be sure we do it right. You know how you practice your ballet dancing?"

Aaliyah nodded. "I practiced yesterday, but I didn't get to practice today."

"Just like you practice your ballet to make sure it's great, we're going to practice what to do for the wedding tomorrow so we can be great like you," Brent said.

"So are you really marrying an angel, Uncle Brent? A *real* angel? With wings?"

Brent smiled. He wasn't really her uncle, just what Marcus had her call him. "Well, not a *real* angel the way you're probably thinking. She's more like an angel in disguise. She doesn't have wings, but she reminds me of an angel."

"Oh," Aaliyah said, disappointed.

Angela came rushing up. "Marcus, I'm glad you made it." She kissed him on his cheek when he leaned down to hug her. "There's always something, always something," Angela said, turning to Brent. "Why can't things ever go off without a hitch?"

"What's wrong?" Brent asked.

"It's the flower girl. She can't make it. She fell off the swing today at day care. Her mother took her to the doctor and they said she sprang her arm," Angela said.

"That's good it was just a sprang," I said, remembering the time I broke my arm when I was younger, and I fell out of that tree. *Pretty is as pretty does, Grandma said. Climbing a tree to throw stuff at your brother was not pretty. I told you: God don't like ugly. You'd better be glad all you did this time was break your arm.*

"Yes, I'm thankful that was all it turned out to be. But now I don't have a flower girl for tomorrow. I'm trying to think what we can do."

"Aaliyah can do it," Marcus said. He squatted down to her height. "Sweetheart, how would you like to be in Uncle Brent's wedding?"

"You mean the wedding Uncle Brent says he's having with the angel?" Aaliyah said. Everybody laughed. Angela looked at Brent and smiled.

"Yes, that one," Marcus said.

Brent chimed in. "I would really love it if you'd be our flower girl."

"Are you the angel?" Aaliyah asked Angela.

Angela tried to keep from laughing but she wasn't doing a great job of it. "My name is Angela, but they call me Angel for short."

"No," Aaliyah said, shaking her head. "Uncle Brent says he's marrying an angel, only she doesn't have wings like the angels I've seen on a shelf at my grandma's house."

"Yes," Brent said. "This is the angel I was talking about. So what do you say about being our flower girl? Do you think you can throw flower petals in the aisle before my angel comes down it tomorrow? Will you do that for us?"

"Of course I can do that. I've done that before so I'm pretty good at it." Aaliyah placed her little hand on her hip and tilted her head to one side as she grinned. "I guess you can say I've practiced already, so it's no problem, Uncle Brent. I'll be *happy*," she threw her head back, "to do that for you and your angel, even if she doesn't have wings."

Everybody laughed again. I stood in awe of how smart this little five-year-old happened to be. Marcus seemed to practically beam around her. He rubbed her hair as she stood close. There was no doubt, he loved his little girl.

Angela took Aaliyah by the hand to give her the basket she would practice with. Brent and Marcus stayed close to where I was. They spoke as though no one was there.

"I thought you said this wasn't your weekend to keep Aaliyah?" Brent said.

"It's not. But you know Sasha. She called yet again with an emergency. Besides, I don't have a problem keeping my daughter, you know that. As it turns out, looks like it was a good thing, a blessing, really, that she was here. She's going to be the flower girl."

"Oh, there's no question about how much you enjoy having her," Brent said. "And I know you would like nothing better than to have that little girl with you all the time. I was just wondering what happened with Sasha, since it seems lately this is becoming the norm. So, what did she say was the emergency this time?"

"She didn't. Just that it was an emergency, and she needed me to keep Aaliyah."

"You're going to have to stop reinforcing Sasha's bad behavior, Marcus," Brent said. "She does this to you because she knows she can. And you just keep letting her get away with it."

"I hear you, Brent. But if I didn't get Aaliyah, Sasha would just dump her off on anybody she could get to take her. I don't want my child being passed off to anybody and everybody. She's at an impressionable age. And some of Sasha's associations are at the bottom of the barrel. Cousins sleeping with everybody while exposing those children to their reckless behavior. Having all kinds of men hanging around their place—perverts and whatnots. And I'm going to be frank with you, Brent. If anyone touches my child in an inappropriate way or something happens to her, preacher or not, I'm not sure what I might do. Lord, forgive me, but I really don't know. And I don't ever want to find out."

Brent leaned in. "Marcus, don't go there. Don't get yourself worked up about this. Sasha does this to you every time. That girl still knows how to push your buttons."

"I know. I know," Marcus said as he nodded. "I know the Bible tells us to forgive, and Lord knows, when it comes to Sasha I've bent over backward to do it. But my little girl is counting on us adults to love and protect her. I'm her father, and yes, I am a minister, too. But lately with Sasha and all that she's taken me through and truthfully still takes me through every chance she gets, it can be hard to actually practice what you preach. 'Turn the other cheek. Go the extra mile.' Talk about praying without ceasing."

Marcus clapped his hands, shook his head, then began to roll his shoulders as though he were trying to shake something loose. "Listen, I'm sorry I went there," Marcus said. "I just needed to vent, I guess. I'm sorry, Lord. I'm sorry, Brent. Please forgive me."

"It's all right. You know I got nothing but love for you," Brent said. "You and I have been friends since college. I know the real deal. If you needed to get that off of you, that's fine. Now, let's have a word of prayer, Mister Preacher Man. Just me and you."

Marcus smiled and nodded. They bowed their heads and Marcus prayed. I closed my eyes, too. When he finished, I found myself wiping tears from my eyes. I had no idea Marcus was a minister. And I sure didn't know he could pray like that.

Chapter 13

And whatsoever ye do in word or deed, do all in the name of the Lord Jesus, giving thanks to God and the Father by him.

—Colossians 3:17

The wedding went off beautifully without too much drama. Anyone who has ever been part of a wedding knows there will always be a few snafus, even if the guests never know it. Pastor Landris officiated at the ceremony. There were so many people crying tears of joy. It was something to see.

Of course, Nae-nae didn't show up to help me like she promised, so that left me more than a little stressed at first. But true to form, Pastor Landris's wife, Johnnie Mae Taylor Landris, and about three other members of the church stepped up in true servants' fashion and offered their services. They helped out with whatever they were asked to do and wherever they were needed. I learned a valuable lesson from this: hire wisely or you'll pay for it later.

I must admit that I'm always in awe of how someone like Johnnie Mae Taylor, the name she continues to use on her books as an author, can be so down-to-earth. I know some folks who wouldn't dare serve others because they think they're above them. If I were the wife of a famous pastor and world renowned for my own books (I hear one of hers has been optioned for a movie), you wouldn't find me asking anyone if I could help them. I don't care if I saw them pulling their hair out; I would be sitting around waiting for people to take care of me. But not Johnnie Mae.

She has the cutest little girl named Princess Rose and a little baby boy named Isaiah. It was touch-and-go there for a while with little Isaiah. There was concern back in the summer over whether he and his mother were going to make it. But it just goes to show what the Bible says: "The prayers of the righteous availeth much." And there was definitely some fervent praying going from June through August before mother and child came home from the hospital.

Then the pastor's mother passed away, and that was hard. I wasn't sure how Pastor Landris could take so much happening, one thing after another. He and his family were definitely under spiritual attack. But Pastor Landris has often said that his trust in the Lord is not based on what's happening around him.

"If the world falls down around me, I'm still going to trust God and His Word," Pastor Landris has said many times. "I don't serve God for what He's going to do. If He doesn't ever do another thing for me for the rest of my life, I'm going to be right here praising Him. You see, I don't praise God only for what He does. I praise God for who He is." These past months especially, his words had definitely been put to the test.

After the ceremony, Angela and Brent, along with the rest of the wedding party, were taking pictures for the wedding album. I was on my way out of the sanctuary to get over to the reception hall at Ross Bridge before the wedding party got there. The caterers were taking care of the food setup, so that was good. The reception hall was beautifully decorated. All I needed to do was to make sure that nothing had been overlooked. As I was on my way out, I stopped in my tracks.

Sitting in a seat at the back of the sanctuary was none other than Arletha Brown. Dressed in a lovely chiffon baby-blue gown, I almost didn't recognize her. Her hair was freshly curled. And for one who I'd heard, from people she went to church with, never wore makeup, she had on wine-colored lipstick.

"Ms. Arletha?" I asked with a smile. "I *thought* that was you. It's good to see you again."

She looked over at me and did not seem impressed that I had recognized her.

"I'm sorry. Do I know you?" she asked.

"I'm Melissa Anderson." By the look on her face, my name did not ring a bell.

"I came to your house on Wednesday. I'm Cora's grand-daughter," I added, deciding to skip the family line and go straight to the one she'd originally had a favorable reaction to.

"Oh yes. Now I remember you."

I was wrestling with how to ask her what was she doing here. I knew enough about Arletha Brown to know that she had a sharp tongue and wouldn't hesitate to use it if asked what she considered to be a dumb question. I knew we had sent her an invitation to the wedding. But honestly, I didn't think she would actually come.

"It's *so* good to see you," I said again, still debating.

"I *was* invited," she said as though she were reading my mind. "I didn't have anything else to do today, so I thought I would come see what all the hoopla was about. Besides, I've had this dress hanging up in my closet for years now. This was as good an excuse as any to wear it."

I was relieved she had been the one to break the ice. "Well, we're glad you made it. I thought everything turned out beau-tifully." I waited to see if she had anything to say. She merely sat there with her lips buttoned tightly. "Have you had a chance to say hello to the bride yet?" I asked.

"Now, why would I do that?" Arletha said almost frowning, or maybe that was just the way she always looks. She certainly was a bitter woman.

"I was just thinking how much she would love to know that you came."

"From the number of people here, I doubt very seriously she would care if one more person was in attendance or not. It's like I said, I got an invitation. I wasn't doing anything today. So I came. I almost didn't recognize the pastor, though. I see he finally got rid of those dread whatever they call them. Maybe there's hope for him yet."

I didn't know what that comment was all about. There was nothing wrong with Pastor Landris when he wore dreadlocks, and there was nothing wrong when he decided to cut them off. I was starting to feel sorry for her. I could see now, this woman was really hurting. I thought back to Marcus's prayer the evening before. He prayed for people to be more understanding of one another, to be more compassionate, more like the Lord, loving without conditions. I would have preferred that Arletha not be so nasty and negative about everything. But I knew I needed to love her where she was right now. I had to be the bigger person. I had to be Christlike, which is what a real Christian is.

"Ms. Arletha, if you don't mind my saying this, I know Angela would be so excited knowing that you came. If you don't mind, I'd love to take you up there and let her know you're here."

"Why?" Arletha said. "Why is my being here such a big deal to you or to her? I'm not who she thinks I am, and your insisting that I let her know I'm here is just plain being messy, if you want to know what I really think about it." She stood up and grabbed her rather large black pocketbook.

I wanted to ask her if what Angela thought wasn't true, then why had she stayed long after the wedding was over. But I knew antagonizing someone like Arletha wouldn't garner much toward the desired goal. "Ms. Arletha, I just know what a great heart Angela has, and I know how much she appreciates everyone who took the time to come share this day with them. I understand it may not be that big a deal to you, but it would mean the world to her. Just knowing that you came would mean you weren't offended by our visit the other day."

Arletha turned back toward me. "I'll speak to her at the receiving line at the reception. They are planning on having a receiving line, aren't they?"

"Yes, they are."

"Good. That's the only reason I was sitting back here, just in case you were wondering," Arletha said. "I was planning on going to the reception. I didn't want to get there too early and have to sit and wait, having folks trying to talk to me and carry on a conversation when it's obvious I don't want to be bothered. Sort of like now, when I was sitting here minding my own business before you came up."

She took a few steps, then turned around once more. "You helped put together this wedding?" she asked.

"Yes, ma'am. Although Angela did a lot of it, I did have my part."

She nodded once and sharp. "Well, you did a nice job. You tell your grandmother, Cora, I said hello. She is still living isn't she?"

"Yes. When she remarried she moved to Jacksonville, Florida, with her husband."

"I remember she told me she was getting married. She's a good woman, your grandmother. I've not met many like her."

"I'll tell her you said hello."

Arletha left. I looked at Angela and Brent. The photographer was taking a picture of Brent, his mother, father, and grandmother, and I couldn't help but think how much it would have meant to Angela had her grandmother been there to take a photo with her.

But if you were to ask me my real thoughts when it comes to Arletha Brown possibly being kin to Angela, I would have to come down on the side of no way. And as much as I hate to say it, Arletha was right not to go down there and speak to Angela. It just would have made Angela start thinking of what she didn't have at this moment. And today had been too good a day to end it like that.

Chapter 14

Wherefore receive ye one another, as Christ also received us to the glory of God.

—Romans 15:7

The reception was packed to capacity. The individually candle-lit tables were decorated with red and gold: red tablecloths, gold canelike chairs, and gold chargers holding white china surrounded by crystal. Dozens of red roses standing tall in golden vases alternated with white ones on adjoining tables.

Everybody was having such a great time. The first dance of Mr. and Mrs. Brent Underwood was electrifying and romantic and spiritual—it was poetry in motion. People say I'm a sap for love. I suppose it's true. Everything was so beautiful and so genuine. I couldn't believe I had actually been a part of this great day.

And true to form, when the music opened up for everybody, the dance floor filled up quickly as the live band Brent had hired began to play the theme song for the electric slide. Young, old, black, white, those who could dance, those who couldn't, all out there having a good time, laughing as they dipped and did all the other moves associated with the slide. Two people had already asked for my business card to plan their wedding.

Later, when things began to taper off, Aaliyah came over and sat beside me.

"Hi," she said, dressed in her white satin dress I was told her father went out and bought especially for the wedding after the other girl was unable to participate.

"Hi, yourself." I smiled. "Are you having fun?"

"Lots," she said. "But I always have fun when I'm with my daddy. He gives me a lot of attention. My mother says too much. She says he's spoiling me."

"Well, I don't think there's such a thing as spoiling a child, myself. I think your daddy is great the way he is with you. That's what I think. You're a very lucky little girl," I said.

"My daddy says there's no such thing as luck. He says we're blessed!" She threw her arms in the air as though she were throwing something up when she said the word blessed.

"You know, your daddy is not only right, but he's a really smart man." I touched her hair that had been styled with Shirley Temple curls.

"Well, thank you," a voice behind me said, startling me just a tad.

"Daddy!" Aaliyah said as she jumped up and hugged him. "Dance with us."

"What?" Marcus said.

"*She* wants to dance"—Aaliyah pointed at me—"and so do I."

"Oh, *she* does, does she?" Marcus asked, smiling.

I was about to protest (I didn't want him thinking I had put her up to that) when he continued speaking to his daughter. "And who is *she?*"

"*She* is *her*," Aaliyah said, pointing at me again.

"I never said I wanted to dance." I looked directly at Marcus. "I never said that."

"But she does want to," Aaliyah said. "And I want to, too. We can all dance together, the three of us. You know, Daddy. Like the way we used to with me, you, and Mommy." She started jumping up and down. "Please, Daddy. Please." She gave him her puppydog look. I knew he was a goner then.

"Well, Aaliyah, first off her name is Miss Melissa," Marcus said, holding his daughter's hand.

"I know, I know," Aaliyah said as she bounced a little. "She was the one who told me when to walk out today and to throw out the flowers, not too fast, not too slow, just right."

"And you did an awesome job today," Marcus said to her. "In fact, you both did." He was now looking at me with a slight grin. He held out his other hand to me. "Well, you heard my daughter. She wants us to dance together."

"Oh, you two go on. I'm fine right here. It's been a long day, a good one but long."

Marcus grabbed my hand and pulled me up before I could protest anymore. "That's precisely why you need to enjoy yourself. It's bad to work at something and not enjoy the fruits of the labor. Besides, you wouldn't want to disappoint a sweet little girl, now would you?" He looked down at Aaliyah, who smiled at her daddy's words.

So we danced. The three of us together. And I must admit: that evening, with the two of them, was the most fun I'd had in a long, long time. I laughed, I danced, I felt like I belonged. I didn't feel as though anyone wanted anything from me except to be in my company.

And Marcus is quite the dancer, especially when inspired by his daughter.

Angela and Brent were getting ready to leave the reception. Brent hadn't told Angela where he was taking her on their honeymoon. But from everything I was picking up, I knew it was somewhere exotic. I hadn't thought any more about Arletha until I spotted her standing off to the side, watching intently as Angela and Brent waved good-bye to everyone. I was about to go over and speak to her when Gayle walked up.

"Don't bother," Gayle said.

"What?"

"Don't bother trying to go say anything to Arletha. I saw her earlier at the reception. Whenever I tried to approach her to speak, she walked away from me."

"I talked to her at the wedding," I said, as I watched Arletha leave.

"She was at the wedding?" Gayle asked.

"Yes. She said she was coming to the reception. I tried to get her to let Angela know she was there while they were taking pictures. She insists she's not who we think she is and she only came to the wedding, and I suppose this reception, because she had nothing better to do." I took a sip of the punch I held in my hand. "She told me she would speak to Angela during the receiving line. Do you know whether she did or not?" I asked.

"She didn't. In fact, Angel has no idea she was even here. In a way, I'm sort of glad. I feel bad that I brought this up in the first place. If I had known—"

"But you didn't know. And personally, I think you did the right thing by telling her what you did. It could have turned out wonderfully. Had Arletha been her grandmother, it would have been the best gift she could have gotten during this time. As it turns out, she wasn't."

"I'm just grateful that Arletha stayed in the background, keeping Angel from knowing she'd come," Gayle said as she looked around the room. "It wouldn't have served any purpose, and Angel deserves this day of happiness without all of the 'what ifs' it would have generated. I'm just trying to figure out why Arletha decided to come to a wedding for someone she just met on Wednesday. That's the part that's puzzling me. It doesn't make sense. You say you're no relation, but you come to a wedding and a reception." Gayle shrugged. "I don't know."

"If you knew Arletha Brown, it would make sense. She probably really was bored. We sent her an invitation. She thought we were bold to send one after she told us she wasn't the person we were looking for, so she throws it all back in our faces. It was like a dare, a challenge to her. From what I remember, she hated people challenging her. That seems to motivate her even more to fight."

"I guess," Gayle said. "So, what's up with you and the best man?"

"Nothing's up," I said. I could feel my face beginning to warm up.

"I saw you two dancing over there."

"It was the three of us. His daughter is a little doll, and she wanted to dance."

Gayle grinned. "Yeah. Okay. I get it now. But from the outside looking in, it looked like it was just the two of you. In fact, when I noticed, and I by no means was gawking or anything, it looked like there was no one else in the room except the two of you."

"I don't know him like that. I know him from his visits to the place where I work, but I don't really know him. And we did have one sort of date a few weeks ago, but I—"

"Don't know him," Gayle said, finishing my sentence. "Yes, I heard you already."

"I didn't even know he was a minister. I just learned that last night," I said.

"And that makes a difference how?" she teased me.

"It doesn't make a difference. But he's divorced and that does make a difference."

"Him being divorced makes a difference? I don't get it," Gayle said. I could tell she was serious about that.

I really didn't want to get into my thoughts and rationales regarding dating a man who is divorced with Gayle tonight.

"It's just a quirk with me. You know, some people won't date outside their race. Some people won't date people who are a certain shade of color. Some won't date certain heights or certain weights. I mean, I have a friend who loves heavy men. She won't give a skinny man the time of day. Some women won't date men who are younger than them."

"That's me. I don't date younger men."

"See," I said. "Well, me, I don't date men who are divorced."

"Divorced or divorced with children?" Gayle asked.

"I have nothing against a man with a child. In fact, were I to meet a widower or a never-married-before man who had a child or children and I liked him, I wouldn't have any problems with dating him."

"Okay, so it's just divorced men?"

I sighed. "Yes, just divorced men, period." I was looking for an out now. "I need to take care of some things before the reception is officially over. It's been a long day," I said.

"Well, you did a fantastic job, both you and Angel. This has been quite a memorable day. My family can't believe how great this all turned out. Little old Angel from Asheville doing it up big time."

I saw Marcus pick up a now exhausted Aaliyah. She laid her head on his shoulder.

"Yes," I said in response to Gayle's statement. "It certainly has been that—a great day."

Marcus spotted me looking in his direction. He winked and nodded, then carried his daughter toward the exit.

Chapter 15

For we are his workmanship, created in Christ Jesus unto good works, which God hath before ordained that we should walk in them.

—Ephesians 2:10

After I got home from church, I lay down on my bed and took a long nap. I was completely exhausted. Marcus called me Sunday evening, thirty minutes after I woke up.

"How was church today?" Marcus asked.

"Anointed as always. Pastor Landris really brought the Word home today," I said as I continued to lie on the bed.

"I was wondering if you'd even make it to church today. I have to give you your props: that was some kind of a wedding and a reception you put together. You're good."

I smiled. "Well, I thank you. But I have to be fair and say that Angela did a lot of the work herself. She called me in for reinforcement."

"Oh, I'm sure you're being much too modest. Angela told me herself that she never would have pulled all of that off so wonderfully had it not been for you," Marcus said. It was amazing how much deeper his voice sounded over the phone than in person.

"Well, don't get me wrong, I did a lot of work for sure. And there were plenty of things she didn't think about that I suggested and handled." I sat up on the bed. "I just don't want to mislead you and make you think I did everything all by myself."

"Can you just say thank you and leave it at that?"

"Excuse me?" I wasn't totally following him.

"When someone pays you a compliment, can you just say thank you instead of trying to take away from what great thing they've said to you?"

I thought about what he had just said and I blushed a little bit. "I thought I did say thank you."

"You said thank you, and then you used the word most folks use that generally means forget everything I just said and pay attention to this part only," he said.

"And what word is that?" I stood up and began to walk around my bedroom.

"But."

"But?" I repeated.

"Yes. You said, 'Well, thank you, but' and that one word practically erased the thank you." I could hear a smile in his voice. "Learn to take a compliment. When someone says you did a great job, just say thank you and close your mouth after that. No one needs to know what you messed up on while doing the great job. Just practice that. You know, become more conscious of how often you're using that nasty little qualifier after someone says something nice to you. Stop sabotaging yourself. Trust me—there are enough people out there to tear you and what you do down without you jumping on the bandwagon to help."

As I thought about what he had just said, I started smiling. He was right. I did have a habit of saying something negative after anyone said something nice to me. No one had ever pointed that out to me before. I suppose I thought I was using humility by pointing out my flaws and shortcomings when in essence I was sabotaging my self-esteem.

"Let's practice," Marcus said. "You did an outstanding job with that wedding and reception yesterday. It was a beautiful day from start to finish."

"Thank you," I said, then realized just how awkward it felt not adding something to that. I really was fighting the urge to say something more. "So, how is your daughter doing?" I asked, opting to hurry and change the subject away from me.

"Believe it or not, she's knocked out right now. When she was younger, I always made her take a nap around two or three in the afternoon if she hadn't taken one by then. After she turned five, it became harder to get her to cooperate. She fights me about taking a nap now, saying that she wants to play with me, or she'll try and distract me by hugging and kissing me, telling me how much she loves me."

Marcus laughed a short laugh. "And when I insist she lie down, she just closes her eyes and pretends to go to sleep, then five minutes later, she gets up and acts like she's just waking up. She's a great little actress, I must say."

I thought about when I was little. I remember being five and doing the same thing. "I think when children get to that age, they just don't want to miss out on too much. And I'm sure that, having you for her father, she *really* doesn't want to miss any time with you." I couldn't believe I had just spoken that part out loud. I clasped my hand over my mouth to keep anything else from slipping out.

"Well, thank you, but I'm sure it's not just me she doesn't want to miss out on," Marcus said.

I now grinned. "Oooh," I said like a little child, "you just said a bad word."

"What?" he said, and I could imagine the wheels turning as he replayed what he had just said. "Oh," he snickered. "My bad. I used the dreaded 'but' after my thank you."

"I suppose that just proves how hard it is to practice what you preach," I said. "And speaking of preach, why didn't you tell me you were a preacher?" I flopped down on the couch in my den.

"You didn't give me a chance to tell you much of anything, remember? We went out that one time, and after that, for some reason, you cut me off completely. So does it matter that I'm a preacher?"

I took one of the pillows from behind my back that was bothering me and moved it. "No, it doesn't matter that you're a preacher. I just had no idea."

"Is that why you thought it would be great to go to Bible study for a first date with me? You thought that would turn me away?" Marcus asked.

"I wasn't trying to turn you away," I said.

"Yes, you were. You have a fear of getting too close to men. I don't know what happened, but somebody burned you and now you have a wall up to keep most men out."

"So you've seen me at work about ten times when you visit with Dr. Brewer once a month for whatever reason you come by. Go to Bible study with me one time. Talk once or twice to me on the phone. See me at a wedding. And now you think you know everything there is to know about me and you feel you can effectively analyze me?"

"Don't forget we did eat a burger together," Marcus said.

"What?"

"Oh, and we danced together, too," Marcus said. "Don't leave that off."

"What?" I said with annoyance.

"Last night, we danced together. You were recapping our life together and you left off the dance."

"We didn't really dance together," I said, throwing my feet up on the couch. I could feel the heat coming into my face, but it wasn't anger. It was a warm feeling accompanied by a few butter-flies in my stomach. "Not really," I added.

"Yes, we did."

"It was me, you, and Aaliyah. That hardly counts as you and I dancing together." I said it with pretend aggravation in my voice, though I was far from being aggravated.

"So, you didn't enjoy going out with me that one time?"

That came out of the blue. "Yes, I enjoyed it."

"Then why did you seem to turn cold on me?" Marcus asked. "I called you and you were different. What did I do that turned you off from talking to me?"

"You didn't do anything."

"Then how about we go out again? Your choice of place and time." Marcus waited as I struggled to find the right response.

"Melissa, are you still there?" he said.

"Yes, I'm still here. Look Marcus, you're a great person—"

"Uh-oh, here's comes the dreaded word," Marcus said. "But . . ."

"But"—I hated that he was right about that word—"I just don't think we're compatible."

"Wow," Marcus said. "Talk about misreading the same situation. I thought we hit it off wonderfully. In fact, last night I was even more convinced there was something there." He paused for a second. "May I ask you something and you give me an honest answer?"

"Sure," I said, hoping it was something I *could* answer honestly.

"Is it because I have a child? Is that the problem you have with me? Don't feel bad if that's what's bothering you. I promise I'll not judge you on that. I know there are all these horror stories out about the drama that can come with men who have a child or children with other women—"

"So you have other children with other women?" I asked, not having thought about that question before.

"No, I wasn't talking about myself. I was speaking in general. You're not trying to change the subject, are you?"

"No. You brought up other children, and I hadn't even thought about that. I knew you had the one daughter because you told me that the first time we went out," I said.

"And I've tried to be up front with you about everything," Marcus said. "But I don't understand why a date that seemed to have gone so well in my mind ended up going nowhere. I know you said you were working on a big wedding. Now that it's over, I'd like to take you out again, or if you'd prefer, we can just hang out together at your place or mine and just talk."

I wanted to say yes, Lord knows I wanted to say yes. I really enjoyed being with him and around him. I forced the necessary words out of my mouth. "No, I don't think so."

"Tell me why?"

"It's nothing about you. It's me," I said.

"That's a cop-out. So, it's because of Aaliyah. You just don't want to have anything more to do with me because I have a child. Admit it."

"Marcus, it's not about your having a child. In fact, seeing how you are with her proves just how great a person you really are."

"Yeah, okay," Marcus said with a touch of sarcasm. "It's not me, and it's not my daughter. Okay."

"Marcus, please don't take what I'm saying and try to twist it around."

"I asked you to be honest with me," Marcus said, his tone still even and pleasant. "If you just don't want to say it, then it's fine. That's your right."

"It's not you or your daughter," I practically yelled.

"Then what is it?" he asked.

"It's because you're divorced!"

I waited for him to say he got it. But he didn't say anything.

"I'm sorry," Marcus finally said, "I must be missing something here. It's because I'm divorced? Not that I'm separated and saying that I plan on getting a divorce, because *that* I could understand. But you're saying it's because I'm already divorced?"

I sighed hard. "I don't date divorced men."

"Okay. Well, if that's a rule you have—"

"It's not my rule. It's because of what the Bible says. In several places, the New Testament speaks about divorce, but the one I know I've seen is in the fifth chapter of Matthew." I looked over at where I had put my Bible when I came home from church. "Hold on a second, let me get my Bible and I'll tell you exactly." I laid the phone down on the couch and went over and got my Bible.

I went back and sat on the couch, turned to Matthew 5, and flipped through a few pages, skimming quickly to find the verses I was searching for. When I found them, I picked the phone back up. "Okay, I'm back," I said.

"I already know what scripture you're referring to," Marcus said.

"I'm sure you do since you're a preacher and you should know a lot of what's in the Bible. I just want to read it again myself. It's in Matthew five, verses thirty-one and thirty-two. 'It hath been said, Whosoever shall put away his wife, let him give her a writing of divorcement. But I say unto you, That whosoever shall put away his wife, saving for the cause of fornication, causeth her to commit adultery: and whosoever shall marry her that is divorced committeth adultery.' Almost the same thing is in other scriptures found in Mark and Luke, I think. And I've also heard there's something in the second chapter of Malachi about God hating divorce, although I admit I've never thought enough to find that one for myself."

I closed the Bible. "Now, I don't know the circumstances behind your divorce, and it's quite possible the acceptable offense was so in your case." I waited to hear what he had to say now.

"You know what? I'd like to come over one day, and you and I discuss divorce and the truth behind those scriptures you just read, as well as the others in the Bible," Marcus said.

"What's to discuss? It's plain what God has to say on the matter. And what I just read to you, those words are in red, which means those are the words that Jesus said. There's no argument or discussion when it comes to what Jesus has to say regarding a matter."

"Melissa, if I can show you what those scriptures you just read are really saying and address it to your satisfaction, will you consider dating me then?"

"Marcus, you're a nice guy and all—"

"If I can show you, will you give me the opportunity to get to know you better? Now, if you're just really not interested in me at all, then that's another matter. But if your only objection to me right now is that I'm divorced, and you feel that having a relationship with me that might possibly lead to marriage will cause you to be in sin, then let's have a discussion, face-to-face, and see where we end up."

I thought about what he was saying. I knew that some people, including preachers, had ways of taking scripture and making it fit into what they wanted it to. The scriptures I had read were pretty clear, so I didn't see any way he could possibly twist them. Still, if there was something I had missed or didn't know when it came to what the Bible had to say about divorce or, more to the point, remarrying after divorce, then I owed it to myself to become educated. It would be a shame to let a good man get away and find out I was wrong about my reasoning for doing it. The least I could do was hear him out.

"Okay, Marcus. When is a good day for you?"

"I'll have Aaliyah until Thursday. How is Friday night for you?" he said.

"Friday is fine for me."

"Then I guess we have a date," Marcus said. "Seven o'clock?"

I started to argue that it wasn't really a "date" date. But even I knew that was being too trivial.

"Seven is fine." I hung up the phone after saying good-bye, then placed my hand over my heart. For some crazy reason, I was missing talking to him already.

"Okay, God. I really need your help down here. Please don't let me be bamboozled. If this is not good for me, please don't allow me to be led astray."

Chapter 16

A man hath joy by the answer of his mouth: and a
word spoken in due season, how good is it!
—Proverbs 15:23

Sasha called Marcus on Thursday evening. He had just finished preparing supper for him and Aaliyah. They were
about to sit down to eat.

"Hi, Marcus. How's my baby doing?" Sasha asked.

Marcus had to hold himself back from what he really wanted
to say. Sasha hadn't called to check on Aaliyah or say hello
since she'd dropped her off last week. "She's fine," he said,
tamping down any hint of frustration he had with her question.
"We were just about to eat."

"Oh," Sasha said in an upbeat voice. "So what all did you
cook?"

"Baked chicken, fresh spinach, and macaroni and cheese."

"Macaroni and cheese. Aaliyah's favorite."

"Yep," Marcus said, his patience quickly wearing thin. He
knew Sasha. When she was chitchatting like this, it meant she
was either up to something or she wanted something. "What
time are you planning on coming to get her? That way I'll have
all of her things ready when you arrive."

"That's why I called. I was wondering if you could keep her
until Saturday. They're having a surprise birthday party for
Memphis's sister and he wants me to go with him." Memphis
was Sasha's latest boyfriend. They had been together for a

whole six months, which was three months longer than with any of the other guys she had dated since she and Marcus had parted ways. "I promise I'll be there early Saturday morning, no later than noon. Please."

"Sasha, I have plans tomorrow night," Marcus said.

"Well, take Aaliyah with you. You know how she likes to hang around you. And you know, technically, this really was your weekend to get her."

Marcus shook his head as he listened to Sasha.

"Come on, Marcus," Sasha said. "Don't make me have to beg you. You know you want to spend more time with your daughter. I promise, this will be the last time I ask you to do something like this. I promise."

"You mean the last time this week," Marcus said. "Because we both know this won't be the last time ever."

"Okay, Marcus, whatever. So what do you say? Will you keep her until Saturday?"

"I told you I've already made plans for tomorrow night."

"Whatever it is, knowing you, it's church related. Marcus, just take Aaliyah with you like you usually do. She likes going to church with you."

Marcus looked over at his daughter. She looked up at him and smiled as she played with some of the fruit in the bowl on the table.

"Oh, wait a minute," Sasha said with a slight giggle. "Are you trying to tell me you have a date? Is that your plan for tomorrow night? Marcus finally has a date."

Marcus wasn't sure how he wanted to answer that. Melissa didn't consider it a date, but he was looking forward to spending some time with her. He also knew that if Sasha decided she wanted to go out, she had no problem taking Aaliyah and dumping her with anyone who would agree to keep her. That was one of the things that frustrated him the most about Sasha. She never thought any further than her next desired thing.

He walked over to Aaliyah and took the orange she was rolling on the table like a ball out of her hand and put it back in the fruit bowl. She looked up at him, tilting her head as she wriggled her nose at him. He leaned down and kissed her on the nose, then tapped it lightly.

He walked away from Aaliyah. "Fine, Sasha. You can get her on Saturday."

"Thank you, thank you, thank you, Marcus," Sasha said. "You really are great! I owe you big time for this. Memphis says he has a surprise for me tomorrow. I can't ask my mother to keep Aaliyah. She's always too busy. She's so wrapped up in her new boyfriend, she doesn't have time for anybody else, let alone to do anything to help me out like she promised she would. I wish my daddy was still here. Things would be different."

Marcus had heard all of this before. He really didn't care to hear it again.

Sasha's father had died of a heart attack shortly after Sasha's divorce to Marcus became final. Their family had always lived the high life, and mother and daughter were never denied when it came to their desires. Even after Sasha was married and Marcus couldn't give her what she wanted, her father delivered every time. So much so that it frustrated Marcus because he was being treated as less than a man, as someone who couldn't take care of his bride.

So when her father died, no one was more shocked than Sasha. She and her mother grieved heavily after his death. And both of them thought they'd be set for life with all the money he'd accumulated and invested over the years. And both were certain he had at least a million-dollar insurance policy that they would share.

Then came the big surprise. He was broke and heavily in debt. And that insurance policy? It had lapsed the year before. That was why Sasha and her mother both found themselves having to get out and get a job.

"I'm getting off the phone now," Marcus said.

"Yeah, sure. I'm sorry, you did say you and Aaliyah were about to eat. Well, give my baby a kiss for me," Sasha said.

"Would you like to say hello?"

"Oh, yes. Put her on for a second."

Sasha talked to Aaliyah for a minute. Aaliyah handed the

phone back to Marcus. "She says she wants to talk back to you," Aaliyah said.

"Yes," Marcus said to Sasha.

"I just wanted to thank you again. For keeping Aaliyah like this and for taking such great care of her. You're really the best," Sasha said. "I mean it."

"Yeah," Marcus said, "the best." He clicked off the phone after she said good-bye and placed it back in its holder. "Are you ready to eat?" Marcus asked Aaliyah as he got Aaliyah's Dora the Explorer plate out of the cabinet.

"Yes!"

He fixed both of their plates and set them down on the table. "I know I told you Mommy was coming to get you today, but how about you stay here with Daddy for a few more days."

"Yeah," she said as she clapped.

Marcus smiled at her as he pondered what he would do now about Melissa and their date for tomorrow night.

"Let's bow our heads and say grace," he said as he clasped his hands together and looked into the eyes of his daughter as she happily followed his lead.

Together they began to say the grace he had taught her just as his mother had taught him.

"God is great and God is good . . ."

Chapter 17

Then the Lord put forth his hand, and touched my mouth. And the Lord said unto me, Behold, I have put my words in thy mouth.

—Jeremiah 1:9

I couldn't quite explain why, but I was really looking forward to seeing Marcus on Friday night. I didn't consider it an actual date, but I have to admit, I enjoyed being in his presence. It had been four days since we'd talked on Sunday. I was kind of hoping he would stop by Dr. Brewer's office the way he usually does. He comes in once a month. By my calculations, it was close to the time he should show up.

I didn't understand that situation either. Dr. Brewer never had him on his calendar, yet he seemed to show up like clockwork. Whenever he came, Dr. Brewer always saw him, without an appointment, but he never said anything to me about him. It seems I was learning more and more about Marcus Peeples everyday.

Marcus called me around nine o'clock Thursday night.

"Are you busy?" he asked right after we both said our hellos.

"No, just watching a little television." I couldn't help but notice how queasy my stomach suddenly felt as soon as I heard his voice. I put my hand on my abdomen to calm myself. "I'm looking forward to my personal Bible study tomorrow," I said. After I heard the words come out of my mouth, I wish I hadn't said it *quite* like that.

"That's sort of why I'm calling," he said. I could hear in his voice that something was wrong. "I have a slight problem."

I tried to sound cool. The last thing I needed was for him to think I was actually *excited* about tomorrow's get-together. "What's going on?"

"I suppose I shouldn't say a problem. But we may need to reschedule for another day. Maybe Saturday afternoon or night if you're not already busy. My ex was supposed to get Aaliyah today, but now she needs me to keep her until Saturday."

"Oh," I said, relieved that's all it was. "That's fine. Whatever you want to do. We were just going to talk about Bible stuff anyway, so that's fine." As soon as those words left my mouth, I lightly tapped my forehead a few times with the heel of my hand.

He cleared his throat a little. "Well, I was looking forward to talking about that Bible stuff with you."

"I didn't mean anything by that. I was only saying it wasn't like we had a date or anything." I'd said the 'D' word in a sentence. "I know things come up. Of course, had you wanted to, you could have brought Aaliyah with you. Not that she would be interested in our discussion, but I do have several children's DVDs she could watch while we talk."

Okay, I could see now that I was really showing just how much I was looking forward to this nondate. I had to fix it so he wouldn't get the wrong idea and think I was interested in anything more than studying the Bible. "Saturday is fine."

"Thank you," Marcus said.

"Thanks for what?"

"For wanting Aaliyah to come over. That means a lot to me. It really does. You just don't know how much," he said with a **warm**th to his voice.

"I think your daughter is wonderful. And honestly, I love having her around. It wouldn't have bothered me if you brought her over. But I understand if you'll feel more comfortable doing this another day." I paused a few seconds. "Besides, I'm sure you'd rather spend this time with your daughter. You and I can meet anytime. Time with family and friends is precious. We should grab every opportunity with them that we can."

He chuckled. "You're something else."

"Is that right?"

"Yeah. That's right."

I suddenly realized we were in a slight flirting mode and that was definitely not where either of us needed to go. *He's divorced, he's divorced,* I told myself. *Get a grip! He's divorced.* "So you want to change it to sometime on Saturday?" I asked to get us back on track.

"Yeah. Any particular time you'd prefer?"

"Since it's Saturday, the afternoon works for me," I said. "What about two o'clock?"

"Great," he said.

So on Saturday, he came to my apartment with his Bible, along with lots and lots of typed papers. "Wow, you're serious," I said. I looked at everything he was taking out of his briefcase as we sat next to each other on the couch.

"Yes, I'm serious. When it comes to the Word of God, I don't play with that. If I'm going to tell somebody something, I want to have all of my ducks in a row—"

I started laughing. "I'm sorry. But hearing that phrase coming out of your mouth just took me a little bit by surprise."

"Oh, so you think I'm too stuck-up to say something like that?" He had a serious look on his face.

"No," I said as I quickly cut off my laugh. "No, I'm sorry. It's just, if you don't mind me saying, you are a little nerdlike. Especially with those glasses on." I pointed to them. "I thought you said you didn't need them to see. But every time I see you, you have them on."

"Would you prefer I take them off?"

I sat there beside him remembering how I felt the first time I saw him without his glasses. "No, I think you should keep them on."

"And what do you mean, I'm a little nerdlike?" He cocked his head to the side.

I glanced at the stack of papers he had placed on the coffee table. "Okay, every time I see you, you have your briefcase with your serious look and those glasses. You just remind me of this

guy I went to school with who was always studying, forever raising his hand whenever the teacher asked the class a question.
And trust me: he was a serious bookworm. In fact, he used to
tutor the other kids who couldn't get what the teachers were
teaching. Especially algebra, of all things. Who tutors folks in
algebra?"

"I used to tutor folks when I was in school. Algebra, in fact."

I smiled. I could tell he enjoyed this back-and-forth.

I took a deep breath and made a show of letting it out.
"While I've got my foot in my mouth, there's something I've
been meaning to ask you."

"Shoot."

"Why did you get divorced?"

He stroked his chin. "I don't mind answering any questions
you might have about me. I met my ex-wife when I was in high
school. She was a cheerleader and one of the most popular
girls in our school. I was, as you like to put it, nerd-lite in
school."

"Now, see. You're wrong for that. You shouldn't be taking my
words and using them against me," I said playfully. "Nerd-lite? I
like that." I giggled.

He sat back on the couch. "I'm not using your words against
you. It's not like it's the first time I've ever been called a nerd.
Anyway, my ex-wife and I didn't date until we were both in college."

"Did you attend the same college?" I asked.

"No. She went off to Howard University while I stayed here
in Birmingham and attended UAB. With my SAT scores I could
have gone to any school I wanted. In fact, I was accepted at
MIT. Boy, was I excited when I received *that* letter in the mail."

"Then why didn't you leave and go to a college out of state?
Was it too expensive?"

"Actually, I had been offered over one hundred and sixty
thousand dollars in scholarships." He took in a deep breath
and released it slowly as he twisted his mouth several times.

"Since I can remember," he continued, "I've watched my

mother struggle as she raised us, practically single-handed, working hard to put food on the table and keep a roof over our heads. I told you about my younger brother whom I love dearly. T. J. was forever finding ways to get into trouble. He hated that we didn't have the money to buy the name brands of the world and other things the other children at our school had, let alone the little things he felt everybody was entitled to. Things like not having to worry about the lights being cut off. He hooked up with the wrong crowd, started selling drugs, among other things. Somebody was killed. They claimed my brother was in on the deal. He was close to seventeen at the time. It was the summer I graduated. They decided to try him as an adult."

I could see how much telling me this was affecting him. I wanted to reach out and touch his hand but I fought the urge.

Marcus looked down at his hands before looking back at me. "Fourteen months later, he was found guilty of second-degree murder—guilt by association. It took the jury eight hours to decide what to do with possibly the rest of my brother's life. He's in prison now. T. J. was not a bad kid. He just needed direction, a father figure with a strong hand steering him in the right place. I suppose my hands weren't strong enough to do that.

"His conviction broke my mother's heart. I didn't want to leave her, not while all of that was going on. So I decided to stay in town and attend UAB. After he was sentenced to twenty-five years with the possibility of parole, it didn't feel right leaving her here still struggling to pay the bills in addition to paying the lawyer she'd hired. So I continued to stay, attending college while holding a part-time job on the side."

I realized that my asking him about college had taken him off the path to telling me about his ex-wife. But I also sensed that he needed to tell me about his brother and his mother. The more I talked to Marcus, the more I was seeing his true heart. And he did appear to have a big heart.

Marcus smiled at me. "I'm sorry. You ask me why my ex-wife and I divorced and I wander off into my other family troubles."

"I asked you about college as well. And honestly, I appreciate you for being so open and honest about your brother and your mother. It makes me feel good to know you're that comfortable with me that you feel you can tell me something like that."

"It still makes me mad when I think of our young black men becoming old black men in prison. There's got to be a better way for us to approach this problem," Marcus said. "There's got to be." I heard the quiet anger in his voice.

"Yeah, it's definitely causing a hardship on us women out here. I have a friend whose boyfriend is in jail right now. On the one hand, you wish our guys would stop putting themselves in the position for them to even be caught up in that situation. My friend's boyfriend robbed a store. They know this stuff is wrong. And they know they're likely to get caught. So why even try it?" I asked rhetorically.

"The young especially feel invincible," Marcus said. "They believe they will be the one person who outsmarts the system. I tried telling my brother that, as did my older brother, Ronnie, in the navy. It's hard enough, even with all the strides we as a people have made these days, to be black and not find oneself in trouble with the law. Ask any black man whether he truly feels okay driving while black, especially at night in certain places. He'll tell you the embedded fear you have when it's dark and a police light flashes behind you."

"Driving while black," I said.

"Absolutely. I was pulled over once, simply because I was in a white neighborhood and I happened to be black. They pulled me over for a bogus reason, asked for my ID, then told me I looked like someone they were looking for. Mind you, it was nine o'clock at night, dark, and no way for them to see my face until they pulled me over. But I *looked* like someone they were looking for. I had my daughter in the car with me. Afterward, she wanted to know if I had been bad and if that was why the police had stopped me. Broke my heart for my little girl to see that, particularly when I'd done nothing wrong."

"Wow," was all I could say. "I've only been stopped by the police once in my life, and even then, they let me off with a warning."

"It's different for black men, that's for sure." He shook his head slowly, then clapped his hands once. "Okay, but you asked about Sasha."

"Sasha?" I acted like I hadn't heard her name before, although in truth, I had overheard him when he and Brent were talking about her the night of the rehearsal.

"Sasha's my ex-wife's. So, why did she and I divorce?"

"You don't have to tell me," I said. So far I had caused him to be sad about his brother, his mother, and the plight of the black man.

"Yes, I have to tell you. If I want to move forward with any kind of a relationship with you, I need to put everything on the table." He turned more squarely toward me as he stared, then broke into a full smile. "Melissa, I really want to get to know you better. There's something special about you. And your laugh is infectious. The first time I saw you sitting there at that desk, I saw how special you were. I think if we can get past some of the things that concern you regarding my past, you and I just might have something going here."

"Marcus, I don't want to mislead you. I do like you. In fact, the more I'm around you, the more I find to like about you. But I grew up believing it was wrong to divorce. As I grew older and began to read the Bible for myself, I found that maybe it wasn't divorce that was the problem so much as remarrying after a divorce. Being with a divorced person, according to how I interpret the Bible, is to commit adultery with them. Adultery to me is a very serious offense in the eyes of God. And from what I've read, God *hates* divorce." I took a deep breath.

"Now, I know there's the exception due to fornication that Jesus spoke about in that passage of Matthew I read to you over the phone the other night," I said. "And that may well be what happened with you. I don't know. If it is, then maybe it would be acceptable for the two of us to get together."

Marcus began to smile. "So, you're saying you would be interested in dating and even possibly marrying me?"

I looked at him and tried not to smile. He had an uncanny way of taking my words and going to a whole 'nother place with them. "We're adults. I don't know where things would lead if we took it a step further, but being adults means we need to think some things through before we just dive into it."

"Count the cost," Marcus said.

"Count the cost?"

"Yeah." Marcus readjusted his body, getting even more comfortable as we sat on the couch together. "The Bible says before a man decides to build, he should count the cost. That's a metaphor to use in life. Too many people do things without first thinking about it and counting what it will cost in the end. That includes dating a person. I believe, and it just may be only me"—he placed his hand on his chest—"but I believe if you're *thinking* about dating a person, you need to think it all the way through. That includes the possibility of marriage. Count the cost up front. Minimize surprises later."

"Women do that more than men. I mean, we are bad about seeing a guy and then letting our minds leap ahead to the wedding day, the kids, and the home to follow," I said.

"Men need to do more of that, especially when it comes to dating. But we're wired differently. People believe men are only moved by sight. Women are definitely moved by feelings. But men are also moved by feelings." I noticed that Marcus tightened up a little as he spoke. "We care a lot more than women will ever know."

"Would you like to tell me about your ex-wife? Would you like to tell me what happened with you and Sasha?" I touched his hand. He looked at me with the most sincere look in his eyes. He then nodded.

I sat back and made myself comfortable.

Chapter 18

For the stone shall cry out of the wall, and the beam out of the timber shall answer it.

—Habakkuk 2:11

Before Marcus began, I got him a can of soda. He took a sip, put the can on the coaster on the coffee table, then turned back toward me. "I don't want this to sound like I'm placing my failed marriage on Sasha's shoulders, because I'm not. I just wanted to say that up front. We were both young and inexperienced. I think we had fantasies about what married life would be like. My mother tried to tell me real life was different."

He picked up the can again and took a few swallows before he continued. "In fact, when I told my mother we were going to get married, she thought we should wait a while. Sasha's mother told her the same thing. When I talked with Sasha's father privately, he tried his best to talk me out of getting married, at least until I'd had time to save up enough money. He told me that having money problems was the leading cause of most marital problems, so the more money I had, the better my chances would be at making our marriage work, especially when it came to his daughter, who had learned 'at the feet of her mother.' His words, not mine."

"So he thought marriage was about money?" I asked.

"No. He was saying that love alone would not sustain the marriage."

"I don't think I agree with that. I think if you love someone, it doesn't matter if you have to do without sometimes. Love shouldn't be conditional. It shouldn't be based on your income or what you possess," I said.

"I agree," Marcus said. "But love doesn't pay the bills. Love doesn't put a roof over your head. Love doesn't put food on the table and clothes on your back."

"I don't know if I agree with that. Love is what paid the bills in our house. Love put food on our table. My mother was a widow, but she loved us richly."

"I think you've misunderstood what I'm saying. I know love will do all of that. I saw my mother do just that, and she did it with love. I'm talking about in a marriage. You have two people who may have had some lust going on. But the level of love that's needed to be able to stand the test of hard times may not have risen to where it's needed yet to withstand the reality of life." Marcus took another sip of his drink. He held on to the can this time as though occupying his hand made him feel better.

"Case in point," Marcus continued. "I loved Sasha. I absolutely did. But I had not long graduated from college when we decided to get married. I was looking for a job and told her we could get married after I found one. Her father got me an interview at the investment company where he worked. I didn't really want to work there, but because I loved Sasha and she wanted to get married in a hurry, I took the job. I knew we couldn't afford a house, so I found an apartment. After the wedding, Sasha seemed fine with us living there. Two months later, she was going ballistic to get a house. I told her we couldn't afford a house just yet. We needed to save up, which I figured would take until our one-year lease on the apartment was up. I had plenty of love, but I guess that wasn't enough for her."

He shook his head as he smiled. "Next thing I know, her mother is over to our apartment handing me the keys to a house she and Sasha had picked out and she'd put money down on. It turns out she and Sasha had gone and found the house 'they' liked. I tried to tell both of them it was too much house for me and my salary alone. That the way they had done that wasn't right."

"Sasha didn't work?"

"No. She was supposed to be finishing college. She had transferred to Miles College after six months of being at Howard." He set the empty can down on the table. "Her parents were paying for her college even though I told them as her husband she was my responsibility now. Sasha wasn't serious about finishing college. Part of Sasha's problem came from her mother still trying to run her life. If you hadn't known better, you would have thought her mother was purposely trying to sabotage her. It was like she didn't want Sasha to be happy, almost like she was jealous of her own daughter. After I figured out what was going on, I tried to tell Sasha her mother had a spirit of Jezebel."

"Spirit of Jezebel? I thought Jezebel was like a floozy or something," I said.

"That's what most people think when they think of Jezebel. The truth is a Jezebel can be male as well as female. Jezebels are religious, which generally fool people into feeling comfortable enough to let their guard down. Jezebels are intimidating. Jezebels tend to use authority that's illegitimate."

This was fascinating. To think that Marcus came over to teach me about divorce and what the Bible had to say about that, and I was now learning things about Jezebel that were different from what I'd ever heard before. "Illegitimate?" I asked, wanting to know exactly what he meant. "Can you explain that for me?"

"Okay, let's take Sasha's mother as an example. She had a husband. However, she never allowed him to be the husband. It was her way or no way, although in public she let people believe she was the good wife who dutifully followed and supported her husband. In reality, she gave that man a run for his money. Then, when her daughter got married, there she was in our marriage trying to run things. She was acting like she was the husband in our marriage and Sasha and I were under her authority.

"A Jezebel spirit usually gets what it wants, mostly through manipulation. Someone with a spirit of Jezebel will get other people to do their dirty work for them. They are extremely jealous, always know better than you, know what's best for you and you'd better do it or else. And should you give in to someone with the spirit of Jezebel, he or she will take from you and you'll find yourself living in lack and without. Jezebel's name means 'Where is the Prince?' referring to Baal, a false god. In Hebrew, the word Jezebel means 'without cohabitation.'

"Jezebel will not live with or cohabit with someone he or she cannot control *and* dominate. It's all about control or getting you to do what he or she wants. And when that comes into play—I'm talking about manipulation and control—whether folks realize this or not, *that* is a form of witchcraft. Jezebel stays in the background, but don't be fooled. It's Jezebel who's calling the shots."

"This is really something. I've never heard Jezebel put in quite this context before," I said.

"You can read all about Jezebel starting in First Kings around the sixteenth chapter, verse thirty-one, through chapter twenty-one. Then go to Second Kings and read the entire ninth chapter. Pay attention to how Jezebel influenced all those around her, especially her husband, Ahab. How she even had the prophet Elijah fleeing for his life purely through intimidation." Marcus shook his head as though he were trying to shake loose something inside him.

He continued, "Jezebel was having prophets killed, and the words Elijah was speaking were coming against what she was doing, so she wanted to silence him, just like the Jezebel spirits today want to silence those who would speak God's truth. But people have to recognize it's a spirit. The same spirit Herodias had in the New Testament when she came after John the Baptist. Manipulating and using her daughter to have John the Baptist beheaded. That spirit is referenced with Jezebel's name in the book of Revelation two-twenty. Queen Jezebel just became the poster child for this controlling, evil spirit."

I sat there thinking about how I could actually listen to this man forever. The passion he had for teaching the Word of God, even when it was one-on-one like right now with me, was something to behold. He had a gift, that's for sure. I thought about the Jezebels in my life that I hadn't recognized as Jezebels because I would have been looking for a woman poised to take somebody else's man. I now see that Jezebel was more than that, and people were being taken down and taken out without ever knowing what hit them. *Hey! Cass was a Jezebel!*

"I know you're a minister. Are you the pastor of a church?" I asked.

"I'm not a pastor, but I preach at my church. There are quite a few pastors there, and Reverend Walker—that's my pastor—gives us an opportunity to preach once every three months or so during our Wednesday night services," Marcus said, smiling.

"Do you teach a Bible class?" I asked.

"When my pastor asks me to teach. But it's usually on a subject he requests be taught."

"So you have all of this talent and all of this knowledge and you don't get to use it that often?" I stood up. "I'm sorry. I'm sorry. I'm just all up in your Kool-Aid."

He frowned and looked puzzled. "Excuse me," he said, laughing.

I flopped back down on the couch. "Oh, don't act like you don't know what I'm talking about. You know you used to drink Kool-Aid."

"I know what you're talking about. I was the Kool-Aid king. Straight up. I could make some Kool-Aid now. I just hadn't heard that in a while, that's all." He snickered.

I turned more toward him. He really was a great guy. "All right. Let's see. How would someone like Sasha say it, because it doesn't sound like she knows anything about Kool-Aid." As soon as I said that, I thought of how petty I just sounded. "I'm sorry. I shouldn't have said that. I had no right."

"It's okay," Marcus said. He reached over and took my hand and held it. "I know where you're coming from."

"Let's start again, minus the Kool-Aid reference. Here I was again getting all in your business."

He continued to hold my hand. "And honestly, I like that about you. I like that you care about what I do. Sasha hated it when I became a minister about two and a half years into our marriage, six months after Aaliyah was born. Don't get me wrong, she liked the attention it brought from people who admire what your husband does—a 'Man of God.' But having to be at church so much or going back to a church when I was asked to preach"—he shook his head—"that was not her cup of tea."

I pulled my hand out of his. "Well, I love listening to you teach things about the Bible. You have a way of making it come alive. That's why I love Pastor Landris. I don't mean love in that way," I said, becoming a little flustered as I spoke. "I love his teaching and preaching and his spirit in general. He and his wife are both pretty special people."

"Yeah, I loved when I visited with you that time." He licked his lips. I didn't know whether he was trying to make me nervous or whether he was just nervous himself. "Now, you want to talk about something funny?" he said. "You taking *me* to church as a first date. Now *that* was funny."

I smirked and rocked my head from side to side. "Yeah, yeah, yeah."

"And it was the best date I'd ever been on. I said right then and there, this woman is the woman for me."

I stopped smiling. "But you're divorced."

"Yes, I know. And you have a problem with dating men who are divorced. And I was supposed to be showing you what the Bible really says about that, but instead, I'm talking about my brother, my mother, my ex-wife, my mother-in-law, and my pastor. Meanwhile, I'm no closer to getting you to go out on another date with me than when I first walked in here," Marcus said. He looked at me as though he were waiting for words to scroll across my forehead.

I scratched my head. He was a lot closer than he knew. "Why did you and Sasha divorce?" I asked again. All he had to say was that she cheated on him; that would be the escape clause acceptable to me. More important, in the case of divorce, it seemed acceptable to God.

"She wanted out of the marriage," was what Marcus said to answer my question.

My whole body just slumped. *No deal.*

Chapter 19

Who is as the wise man? and who knoweth the interpretation of a thing? a man's wisdom maketh his face to shine, and the boldness of his face shall be changed.

—Ecclesiastes 8:1

Marcus looked at his watch. "What say you and I go get something to eat? My treat."

I checked the time. Two hours had passed since he first walked in the door. At this point, I had two choices. I could go out with him and prolong the inevitable, or I could decline and end this now. If I prolonged things it was only going to make it harder to walk away from someone I was clearly falling hard for. My grandmother would tell me it was time I bought a clue and figured out there was a pattern in my life I was apparently missing.

I did it with Cass. I find a guy I'm attracted to, see there's a major problem should I choose to proceed, then lunge headfirst, knowing my heart is going to get smashed in the end. I knew Cass was a narcissist. He would always be first in his world, and that world would always revolve around him. Lawrence, the guy I dated before Cass, was dating a woman when I met him. He said they were over and he was looking to move on with his life. He and I got hot and heavy into a relationship and the next thing I know, the two of them are getting married in three weeks. And he had the nerve to send *me* an invitation. Then there was Dwight, who was a straight-up dog.

Yes, a straight-up dog. He was dating three of us at the same time. And he would have gotten away with it had he not taken us to the same places on some of our dates. Valentine's Day he said he had to work overtime. My friend Nae-nae wanted to go out, since her boyfriend had conveniently broken up with her right before Valentine's Day. We both knew that was the oldest trick in the book. Break up with your girlfriend a little before some major holiday so you don't have to buy her anything, then conveniently make up after it's over.

So Nae-nae decided she wasn't going to sit around while everybody else had a date for that night. She had asked me about going with her and I had originally declined. At that time, Dwight and I had Valentine's Day plans. Then he called at the last minute apologizing and upset. His boss had told him he needed him to work essentially half a shift of overtime because some guy didn't show up and they were shorthanded. Dwight promised he would make it up to me on the weekend. He sounded really disappointed.

"I'm in no way trying to get out of celebrating Valentine's Day," he had said. "Every day you're my valentine. We're not limited to man-made days." It sounded good.

I thought it was cute and endearing when he said that. I called Nae-nae and told her I'd go with her. Nae-nae, Denise (Nae-nae's other friend), and I were sitting at the table having just ordered our food when Nae-nae started drumming her fingers on the table to get my attention.

"Isn't that your new beau?" Nae-nae asked. "Over there." She used her head to point in the direction she wanted me to look.

I followed where she was leading me and sure enough, it was Dwight sitting over there all goo-goo-eyed, caressing some other girl's hand.

"Girl-l-l," Nae-nae said, "I would not sit here and take that. You need to go over there and let him know he just got busted. Overtime my foot. Oh, he's working overtime all right. Overtime to two-time you."

Even though it really wasn't my style, I was about to get up and go over to confront him just to let him know he hadn't gotten away with cheating on me. Lo and behold, somebody else even more ghetto than Nae-nae ever could be (when she chooses to) goes over and curses him out. Now, I don't condone fighting, but that girl slapped him upside his head like nobody's business. Then that girl Dwight was with had the nerve to want to get up and fight her. Now, that's where I'm totally different. Had that been me sitting there with Dwight when she slapped him for cheating on her, I think I would have shaken her hand as I congratulated her while telling her he was all hers.

Now here I sit with Marcus Peeples, who seems to be a really great guy. He's smart and funny, from all I've seen of him, loving and caring. But he's divorced. He could have given me a clean go-ahead by saying she had said she was a virgin but when they married he'd found out that wasn't true, or he could have said she cheated on him, thus committing adultery, during their marriage—end of my dilemma. But instead, all he had said was she wanted out of the marriage.

Well, according to the Bible, that's not an acceptable reason to get a divorce. And if this was only about him that would be fine. But that scripture I read said that whoever marries that person who is divorced, that person is committing adultery. Now that would affect me and my standing with the Lord. And I don't care to be saddled with committing adultery when all I would have done was marry a guy who happened to be divorced.

I suddenly found myself silently praying as I sat there. Praying because I really liked Marcus and it didn't seem fair. Why should I have to pay for something he and his wife did? They married, it didn't work out, they divorced, he meets me, we hit it off, he and I date, let's say we get married, then I get saddled with committing adultery? No.

"What's wrong?" Marcus asked. "Melissa, what's wrong?"

I don't know what happened, but there I was crying and Marcus was holding me.

I pulled away from him. Having him hold me wasn't helping. I mean it was, but it wasn't. "I can't be with you. I just can't. And the more we're together, the more I find myself falling for you.

Marcus, I love God with all my heart. I try to do right. I'm not saying that I succeed all the time, but I'm trying my best. I don't want to be charged with committing adultery just because we get together and decide to get married. I know God forgives us for our sins when we confess them. But I know if you and I go forward, I'm attracted to you. It's hard enough not to fornicate. Now, if I do the right thing—don't fornicate but say marry you—I'm still in sin." I looked at him and started to laugh.

"I'm just being honest with you here," I said. "Cass, my last boyfriend, started out pretending like he was saved and celibate. We weren't together two weeks before he started pressuring me for sex. Acting like he was so in love with me, he just couldn't help wanting to be with me. Saying we were going to get married someday anyway so in God's sight we were already like husband and wife. Saying we didn't need a piece of paper to join us together as man and wife in God's sight."

Marcus sat back as I spoke. I continued. It was like a purging for me to keep talking.

"I tried to live right, but I fell more than a few times with Cass. Then Pastor Landris taught on Strongholds earlier this year. And I sat there hearing not Pastor Landris's voice, but the voice of God speaking to my heart. I knew I had to die to my flesh, and I had to die daily. Fornication was wrong. No matter how I tried to justify what I was doing, it was wrong. Yes, God knows our heart. Yes, I knew I could ask for forgiveness. But God deserved better from me than I was giving. I didn't go up to the altar that day when Pastor Landris called for those who wanted to be released from their strongholds. I prayed right there in my seat. And you know what?"

"God heard you right where you were," Marcus said.

"Yes. He heard me. I asked Him for strength to walk in His Word. And I set my mind and my thoughts on Jesus, the author and the finisher of my faith. When Cass wanted to make love and I was tempted, I thought about Jesus being right there with us. I pictured Jesus with us. The thought of Jesus having to be there while I was about to do something I knew was against what He desired for my life—that's powerful."

I grabbed Marcus by the hand as I spoke. It was mostly a reflex. "I pictured Jesus' wrist, the holes left from Him being nailed to the cross. And I reminded myself how He'd done all of that for me. Little old me. What He was asking of me was for my good. To sin is to hurt myself. God being an awesome Father is just like any parent who cares for his children. Parents tell their children things, not to take away all of their fun but to keep them safe. They tell them not to do things they believe will hurt them in the end. I realized that day, sitting there in church, that strongholds come to keep us from achieving God's best and all the good things God desires for us to have."

I took a breath as I realized I was still holding his hand. I laid his hand down gently, almost embarrassed. Here I was going on and on about fornication and sin, and I was holding this man's hand.

I continued. "I was up front with Cass about how I felt. I loved him, but I loved God more. He said he understood and that he agreed with me. Then two days later, there he was trying to get me in bed. But I stood firm. It only took him a week to start talking about how self-centered I was. How I let everybody run over me. He was just looking for ways to tear me down. That's when God showed me how he was protecting me because I was seeing what I would have ended up with had I stayed on the path with Cass. Cass broke up with me a month later so he could be with 'a real woman,' as he put it."

"Melissa, I appreciate you and your honesty just now. I respect you and I want you to know I would never do anything to be a stumbling block to you or to hurt you. This divorce thing is a problem for you. I see just how much. I told you I would come over and show you some things about the scriptures regarding divorce."

"Why couldn't you have just said your wife cheated on you? Then I wouldn't be so conflicted. I don't know if we move forward whether anything will come out of it or not. But I know me, and I know that when I fall for someone, I fall hard. After a person's heart gets involved, it can be a lot more difficult to listen to your head."

"I know. So tell me. What do I need to do to fix this? Because I'm really attracted to you, and I would like to see where God is leading us in this." He leaned forward. "I just thought you might have been hungry, that's why I suggested we get something to eat. I'm not trying to run a scam on you. There's a lot in this book"—he picked up his Bible, then put it back down— "I want to show you in regards to your concern. It will just take a little time to do it. I got a little sidetracked with other things earlier. But I do want to show it to you and let you judge for yourself."

"I have some chicken salad in the refrigerator. Why don't I make us some sandwiches? Then you can show me what you wanted to show me on divorce." I looked at him; he nodded.

I had a decision to make. Door number one was to cut my losses and get out now. Door number two was to hear him out.

I got up, made us sandwiches with potato chips on the side, and came back for round two of our Bible session.

I chose door number two. Yes, I had fallen for Marcus. And now I could only pray that what he had to say about divorce would be enough for me to be justified in not having chosen door number one.

Chapter 20

Being then made free from sin, ye became the servants of righteousness.

—Romans 6:18

"Okay, if there's anything you have a question on as I go through this, feel free to ask," Marcus said after we finished eating.

"Absolutely. I'm not just looking for what I want to hear. This is nothing to play with. We're talking about something that could come between me and my relationship with God. I've had enough hard times in life. I don't need to purposely bring things upon myself and become guilty by association," I said.

Marcus opened his Bible and began. "First off, I need you to know you must keep and apply scriptures in their context and setting, as well as recognize the history that goes along with them."

"Pastor Landris tells us that all the time," I said, suddenly realizing how often I was comparing him to Pastor Landris. "Well, not that *exactly,* but he talks about context."

"This scripture you read in Matthew five, it used to bother me as well. I didn't believe in divorce even though my parents had divorced. I had every intention when I married to be married until death us did part. I saw how divorce affected our family. It's always best, especially when children are involved, to have both parents working as one. But sometimes, that's not possible. My mother never remarried, and not that she and I ever discussed it, but I believe it was because she felt as you do about divorce and remarriage."

He picked up a piece of paper as he spoke. "When Sasha and I started having problems, I really buckled down to do all I could to make things work. But every time we had an argument, she would say she wanted a divorce. Here I was, this young minister, on fire for the Lord, and I was having problems in my marriage that God didn't seem able to fix. Sasha knew people were watching us, and I do believe there were times when she purposely did things to make me look bad. Don't get me wrong, Sasha's not a bad person, but when she wanted to hurt me, she knew what to do to accomplish that."

"I know people like that. They're hurting and they want you to hurt so they try to hurt you," I said.

"Precisely. That's how Sasha can be. Part of why she acts that way is because she was used to getting her way. I tried to tell her it doesn't work like that in a marriage. Marriage should be give and take."

"Not just marriage, relationships in general," I said, adding my two dollars and ninety-eight cents. "Although some people act like that means you give and I take."

Marcus laughed. "That was pretty good. I may use that," he said. "I'm not trying to put anyone down in telling you these things. I just need you to have some background on what caused me to go deeper into learning more about divorce and the Bible. It wasn't because I needed something to get me off the hook. God spoke to me and said there were too many of His people in bondage over this divorce thing. He wanted me to help them to see what was really going on. In fact, when God started me on this quest to go deeper, I told him I didn't want to do this. I was not the right person for this job."

My eyes widened. "You talk to God like that?"

He chuckled. "Oh, you should hear some of the conversations God and I have. He'll tell me to do something, I'll tell Him I'm not qualified and that He really should find someone else preferably *more* qualified. But He doesn't seem to listen because He keeps on talking to me about doing it."

It was my turn to chuckle. "I never thought of it that way. I talk to God but I never thought about it in the way you just described it. It's almost like you're arguing with God."

"Not arguing exactly. I like to phrase it as having a healthy debate. A debate, I might add, I always lose. But then, I am going up against God the creator. He knows what I'm going to say before I even say it."

"Okay, I'm going to be quiet and let you finish."

Marcus proceeded to give me a history lesson as well as a lesson on words. "You believe that divorce is only okay in God's sight when it comes to sexual immorality," he said. "Many people believe that. That's one of the reasons why some women—and yes, there are men as well, although we as a society don't like to discuss them—who are being physically and emotionally abused and feel stuck in their marriage. There are a lot of women being grossly mistreated, but because they believe divorce is wrong, they stay in the marriage and take it. There are others who have divorced, and God has a special someone out there for them to partner with. But they believe remarrying will cause them to biblically be branded as adulterers."

I started to say something again but realized if I kept this up he would never get where he was trying to go.

"Here's a little history. In the old days, men had more rights than women. When a man married a woman, the woman's father gave them a dowry. If the marriage didn't work out, the dowry was to be returned with the woman. A man could keep the dowry if he thought he was marrying a virgin but it turned out she wasn't. But he couldn't lie and say that—marring her name—if that wasn't the case. Before Moses instituted the act of a certificate of divorcement, all a man had to do was say, 'I divorce you, I divorce you, I divorce you,' three times, and you were divorced. The problem with that was, when the woman wanted to remarry she had nothing to prove she was divorced.

"So Moses instructed the people that to legally divorce your wife she had to be given, in her hand, a certificate of divorcement or a bill of divorcement, and send her out."

Marcus turned to Deuteronomy 24:1 and let me read that scripture for myself.

"Now, this is important, as it is relevant to the scripture in Matthew five thirty-one where you read that Jesus was being asked about divorce. In Deuteronomy twenty-four one, where it says, 'When a man hath taken a wife, and married her, and it come to pass that she find no favor in his eyes, because he hath found some uncleanness in her,' that uncleanness cannot be referred to as adultery."

"Really?"

"Really. And here's why. Adultery was punishable by death. You can find that in Deuteronomy twenty-two, verse twenty-two." He turned to that scripture. " 'If a man be found lying with a woman married to a husband, then they shall both of them die, both the man that lay with the woman, and the woman.' Also, in the New Testament, in the book of John, chapter eight, do you remember when those scribes and Pharisees brought unto Jesus a woman caught in the act, caught in the very act, and they brought her to Jesus?"

"Yeah, I remember that. They caught her in the act, which means she wasn't by herself, but they only brought *her* to Jesus," I said as I looked at him intently.

"Precisely." Marcus turned to the book of John, chapter eight, and pointed to the fourth verse as he read it to me. " 'Now Moses in the law commanded us, that such should be stoned: but what sayest thou?' Okay, the Pharisees were *always* trying to trap Jesus. The Law of Moses said that one caught in adultery should be stoned to death. They caught this woman *and* the man she was with. But instead of carrying out that law, they brought her to Jesus trying to set Jesus up. When Jesus said to them, 'He that is without sin among you, let him first cast a stone at her,' they all left. That's because the Law of Moses addressed a lot of other sins and the punishments for those sins as well.

"People talk about Jesus writing with His finger on the ground. Some wonder what He may have written. I can't answer that. But what we *do* know is, everyone who stood accusing this woman must have thought about their own sins and the consequences that should be applied for them to have left without having cast even one stone."

"Wow, that's something, how you were able to tie all of this together." I was truly impressed.

"That's why I wanted to get something to eat before I began. There's a lot to this, and it can get pretty deep. It may take a little time to peel away all of the underlying layers. But I want you to get at least enough of this to help you understand the history and context."

"I'm definitely being schooled here," I said. "So in Matthew, Mark, and Luke, where it speaks on divorce—"

"The Pharisees were trying to trick Jesus, to test Him on His knowledge of the scriptures. They were trying to trap Him. That's why they misstated the referenced scroll, what we call the Old Testament scriptures, or more accurately, left off part of what the entire scripture said." He turned to Mark 10:1–12 and read it, then to Luke 16:18.

"But see," I said as I looked at Luke 16:18 and read it back to him, " 'Whosoever putteth away his wife, and marrieth another committeth adultery: and whosoever marrieth her that is put away from her husband committeth adultery.' Then in the book of Mark, chapter ten, verse nine"—I turned back to it—"it clearly states, 'What therefore God hath joined together, let not man put asunder.' And in verses eleven and twelve it speaks again, 'And he saith unto them, Whosoever shall put away his wife, and marry another, committeth adultery against her. And if a woman shall put away her husband, and be married to another, she committeth adultery.' That's where I keep getting hung up. You put away your wife and marry another, you commit adultery."

"There is so much to this, but I'm going to try to go straight to the point to help you get this as quickly and as easily as possible. Let's address the words 'put away' that you saw in these scriptures." He found a typed page with notes on them. I leaned over to see what he was reading.

"I love the King James version of the Bible, but I also like to go back to the original word or words in their original lan-

guage. The word you'll find in the Old Testament is the Hebrew word *shalach*," Marcus said, pronouncing it *shaw-lakh*. "I
have a *Strong's Concordance*, and the appropriate Hebrew number for *shalach* is 7971. They do that because most of us can't
read Hebrew characters."

"Okay," I said. I did understand that most folks can't read
Hebrew, me included.

"Now the renderings of the word for *shalach*—"

"Renderings?"

"Sorry, definitions," Marcus said. "It's that nerdlike thing
again, you know."

I laughed and felt bad that I'd called him that, but good that
he could make me laugh about having said it. "Renderings, definitions, got it! Just call me a nerd-in-training."

He shook his head as he smiled. "*Shalach*: to send away, for,
or out, cast (away, out), forsake, leave, let depart, push away,
put (away, forth, in, out). Nowhere in these renderings does it
say it means divorce. Now here's what I've learned about this
Old Testament word. It is used eight hundred and seventy-eight
times in the Old Testament, thirteen times relating to intimate
relations or marriage. Again, but not divorce. The word *shalach*
in relationships means a separation. The Greek word compara-
ble to *shalach* found in the New Testament is *apoluo*." He pro-
nounced it *ap-ol-oo-o*. "*Apoluo* can be found ninety-four times in
the New Testament, eighteen of which relate to relationships
or marriage."

Marcus turned to the book of Jeremiah. "I want to show you
where the word *shalach* would be in the Bible, and I want you to
see something." He pushed the Bible toward me. "Read Jeremiah three eight."

I did. " 'And I saw, when for all the causes whereby backslid-
ing Israel committed adultery I had put her away, and given her
a bill of divorce—' "

"Stop right there," Marcus said. "See where God is speaking,
and He says He had 'put her away' *and* 'given her a bill of divorce.' If put away meant divorce, then why follow up with saying 'and gave her a bill of divorce'? I know, one could argue it's

saying divorce, then gave her a certificate, but it's really saying there was a period of separation and if that didn't work, if they didn't reconcile, a divorce was given. Is any of what I'm saying making any sense?" he asked.

"Yeah, some." I didn't want him to think I was slow, but when it came to things of God, I wasn't looking for someone to bamboozle me with sleight of hand and fast or double talk. Not that Marcus was doing that. He was actually making this quite plain.

"Okay, let's look at it this way. You get married, and according to the law back then, contrary to what you see sort of happened with even some of our most respected Bible figures—think Kings David and Solomon—you were only supposed to have one wife at a time. We know this to be the case in America right now. If you marry one woman and you marry another woman without having gotten a divorce, it's called bigamy. And those who marry several women are called polygamists. In America, that's a crime."

"I got that. I'm with you on that."

"Good. In biblical days, they were to marry one person and only one at a time. If a man sent his wife away, which was something men could easily do at will for almost no reason, and he had not done the legal thing applicable at the time, which was divorce her, he was still considered to be married to her," Marcus said. He readjusted his body.

"Just like it is today here in America."

"Right. And if you were *legally* married and you had sex with someone else while you were still married, then that was called committing adultery."

I smiled. "Again, as it is today."

He nodded. "But back then, if you committed adultery, there was no getting a divorce because of it. You know, like, 'I want a divorce on the grounds of adultery.' There was: you get stoned to death for having committed adultery. And dead people don't get divorced, and dead people don't remarry. But if you were *separated* from your spouse and either spouse *married* another during this time of separation, put away, without a legal divorce, it was not a legal marriage and adultery was being committed. The Bible says that because of the hardness of the people's hearts, which meant the men were taking advantage of the women and God didn't like that, steps were taken."

"Okay, I think this is starting to make sense," I said.

"When the Pharisees asked Jesus this, they were trying to trap Him. Think about it. If you understand the law, you can see where the Pharisees were trying to show that Jesus *didn't* know the Old Testament like a rabbi—a teacher—would. Jesus knew that to put away his wife meant they were separated while they either worked things out or were deciding what they would do next. And while they were separated, they were not allowed to marry another."

Marcus closed the Bible and placed it on the table. "When you're divorced, you are legally no longer married. But to put away is *not* the same as divorce. There are lawful requirements that must be taken for divorce. Now, if while they are separated and either is trying to sexually be with another, then that constitutes adultery. And the penalty for adultery back in that day was to be stoned to death. Death *was* and still *is* a legal release from marriage. If your spouse dies, you are no longer married. No divorce papers are necessary. If you divorce them, technically, that's considered a death, as it becomes the loss of the marital union. Until death do us part—death by dying, death by divorce."

The more Marcus talked about the Bible and those things associated with it, the more I wanted to hear. But I knew he was probably tired. This was a lot of information. He must have read my thoughts.

"I suppose I should give you a break, huh?" he said.

I flashed him a warm smile. "This really is quite interesting."

He looked at his watch. "I suppose I should go now. I hope I didn't confuse you more than I helped," he said.

"No. It was enlightening when you consider there was more going on in those scriptures about divorce than I ever knew. And to see how Jesus knew when people were trying to trap Him, and the way He handled them. I knew the Pharisees and Sadducees were after Jesus, but I didn't know to what extent they really had gone to get Him, even before He was led to the cross."

"History and context," Marcus said. "History and context along with guidance from the Holy Spirit. I am forever in awe of God. I told Him when He was first trying to show me this that I was the wrong person for Him to be coming to. If you only knew how strongly I felt about this divorce thing before God sat me down and showed me all of this, you would know that I would be the very person arguing that what I just said to you right now on divorce is just wrong."

"Like me," I said. "All I knew was what I saw Jesus saying in red. And there wasn't anything anyone could say to me to make me see things any differently. But you have presented a compelling case, Mr. Peeples."

"I'm not trying to give people a license to get a divorce. But there are so many people who felt as I did about divorce. If they've gotten a divorce, they're hurting because they feel they will be in sin if they ever want to partner with anyone else in life until that previous spouse dies and frees them. Waiting on someone to die just so you can be free? How sad is that? I don't believe that's how God wants us to live."

Marcus opened the Bible once more. "But even in Mark ten, verses six through eight, it tells us, 'But from the beginning of the creation God made them male and female. For this cause shall a man leave his father and mother, and cleave to his wife; and they twain shall be one flesh: so then they are no more twain, but one flesh.' God *never* intended for us to be alone. In fact, in Genesis, God said everything He created was good, with the exception of man being alone."

Marcus closed the Bible again. "Some of us picked the wrong people to begin with. We should have prayed more about God's desire for our lives. Some of us chose what seemed to be the right person, but they may have changed after the fact. Regardless, God is a God of forgiveness, He's a God of healing, and yes, He's a God of restoration. That's why there was the putting away, the separation time allowed. God can restore. And many know this personally." Marcus gathered up his materials and put them back in his briefcase.

I walked him to the door. He had come over as promised and shown me things I never knew when it came to what the Bible has to say about divorce. Yes, there were other questions I still had when it came to this subject. But there was yet one more question I was burning to ask him.

"Are you still looking for restoration of your marriage?" I asked as calmly and unpretentiously as I could.

He smiled. "I am no longer in a marriage. Legally, my marriage is dead. I no longer have a wife. She is my ex-wife. Look, I know how you feel when it comes to me. I won't hound you anymore. The ball is in your court now. All I ask is that you pray about this, and that you allow the Holy Spirit to be your guide. Pray and let God guide your heart."

He leaned down, gave me a quick peck on my cheek, smiled, and left.

Chapter 21

Be ye angry, and sin not: let not the sun go down upon your wrath.

—Ephesians 4:26

It was now Tuesday, and Marcus hadn't heard from Melissa. He figured she had a lot swirling around inside her head since their talk on Saturday. If she was anything like him, she likely wanted to talk to someone else to see what their thoughts were on what he'd had to say. Particularly if she hadn't bought into it entirely—not that he was selling anything. Marcus knew this was all in God's hands now. He of all people knew the scripture that spoke on how one plants, one waters, but God gives the increase.

Sasha stopped by his house that night.

"Marcus, how are you?" she said as she waltzed inside. Although it was late October, she was wearing a satin nightie-looking top. Classy, but like a halter top.

"Hello," Marcus said. "And where are you coming from?" he asked.

She went to the kitchen area and sat on the bar stool at the counter. "Please don't start with me. Not tonight."

"I wasn't starting anything with you. I was just asking—" He stopped, realizing it was useless to have this type of a discussion with Sasha. "Where's Aaliyah?"

Sasha took a deep breath and released a loud, long, and purposeful sigh. "Could you please just concentrate on me for just one minute before we move on to your daughter? I've had a rough day, Marcus. I need a friend right now, not an adversary."

"I'm not your adversary, Sasha. I've never been, and you know that." Marcus sat on a bar stool, skipping the one next to her, opting to keep one seat between them.

"So what happened with you that caused your day to be so rough?" Marcus asked.

She turned away. "Oh, you don't really care."

Marcus buttoned his lips, silently counting to three. He spoke with slightly more of a lift in his voice. "I really want to know."

She turned back to him. "Really? Or are you just trying to humor me? You know I can tell when you're not being honest, Marcus. You're not good at twisting the truth."

"Yes, I *really* want to hear it."

She smiled then leaned over, grabbed a banana from where it hung, and started peeling it. "I really don't care much for bananas." She bit it. "I know you say they're good for us, but—"

"Sasha, are you going to tell me what happened?"

"Oh, it's that *stupid* job. I hate it. Actually, it's not the job I hate as much as it is those *stupid* people who work there." She took another bite of the banana and shrugged.

"Well, Sasha, we all have things in our lives we have to endure, whether we like them or not. You're strong; you'll be all right." Marcus reached over, pulled off a banana, and started to peel it.

"But I shouldn't have to put up with constant stupidity. Why do companies hire these types of people anyway? And why can't you say something helpful?"

"I don't know what else to say. I don't know what you want from me."

"Fancy that. When we were married, you always seemed to have the answers. You always had an opinion or some advice for me," Sasha said.

Marcus replied, "And when we were married, you didn't have to work if you didn't want to, let alone work at a place you didn't like. Then you decided you had to have a divorce, because *you* weren't happy being married to me."

Sasha got up, stepped on the pedal of the steel trash can,

and threw the banana peel away. The top made a thud when it came back down. "We shouldn't have gotten married when we did. And we shouldn't have compounded things by having a baby so soon after we got married."

"And we should have worked harder on staying together, but it wasn't what you wanted," Marcus said.

"Well, you worked hard enough at it for the both of us. And like your mother told you, you knew I was a spoiled brat when you came after me, so you knew it was going to be work keeping me after you got me," Sasha said. She walked over to the den and flopped down like a ragdoll on the couch.

Marcus followed her into the den. "My mother never said that."

"Oh, that's right. Your mother, unlike mine, was more polite about the things she had to say about me. Let's see, how did she put it?" Sasha put her feet up on the couch and crossed her legs at the ankles as she lay back a little. "'Marcus, now you know that girl is high maintenance,'" Sasha said, mocking Marcus's mother. "'You need to find someone more in your league. Somebody with a good heart.' That was it. And you know what, Marcus? It looks like Mommy knew best. She was *so* right about us. So I have moved on, and now everybody should be happy."

Marcus caught himself. He didn't know why he let Sasha get to him every time. "My mother liked you fine, Sasha. My mother did nothing except show you kindness and try to help us."

"Yeah, until I took you through all I took you through. Mommy dearest wasn't too pleased about that. And part of the way your mother feels about me is your fault."

"My fault?"

"Yes, your fault. If you had just signed the divorce papers and given me everything I wanted, we could have had a quick, civil, and quiet divorce." She crossed her arms.

"You were trying to cut me out of Aaliyah's life. You wanted me to pay you alimony, give you money to pay for a car you bought *after* you left me, pay child support, *and* sign over my rights to my daughter," Marcus said.

"Yeah, well, I guess I miscalculated your love for your daughter and overplayed my hand," Sasha said, leaning her head back and staring up at the ceiling.

"How could you ever think I would consent to not being in my daughter's life?"

Sasha pressed the palms of her hands into the sides of her head. "I knew that was a mistake, but I was so mad at you. I knew that was the one thing that would hurt you the most. Again, I overplayed my hand, and I was wrong." She put her hands down, sat up, and looked at Marcus as he sat in the chair across from her.

"And Aaliyah is where right now?"

"You mean *right* now?"

Marcus pressed his lips together tightly, then relaxed them. "Yes, now."

Sasha leaned forward. "Over at my cousin's house. I asked her to pick her up from after-school day care for me."

"Which cousin?" Marcus asked, letting his head tilt slightly.

"My cousin Thelma."

"I know you're not talking about scatterbrained Thelmalina. I just know you aren't." Marcus's jaw visibly tightened.

Sasha waved off Marcus's comments about her cousin. "I wish you would quit insulting her like that. And you call yourself a preacher."

"Have you checked to be sure Thelma didn't forget to go pick Aaliyah up? Goodness, Sasha. You know how she is."

"Chill out, Marcus. I'm sure Thelma went and got her." Sasha got up and headed back to the kitchen.

"We're talking about your cousin who is so busy sleeping with fathers and sons she forgot to pick up her *own* child from day care. Not once, not twice, but three times—that we know of anyway. Who knows what else the ever-so-brilliant Thelmalina has done that no one knows about." Marcus said. "Thelma is an airhead, and you know it."

"Wow, what a great example of a Christian you are. Talking about folks. Not forgiving at all." Sasha took her cell phone out of her Gucci purse and pressed a button.

"What are you doing now?" Marcus asked.

"Shhh!" she said to Marcus who was standing next to her in

the kitchen. "Hi, Thelma. It's Sasha. I was just checking to see how Aaliyah's doing. What? You didn't remember to go get her? You're leaving now?"

Marcus was about to say something when Sasha put her hand on his chest to quiet him. "Girl, don't be playing with me like that," Sasha said. "Oh, I knew you were just kidding." Sasha widened her eyes at Marcus, who wasn't laughing. "I'll be by to pick her up in about an hour. All right, Thelma, thirty minutes." She paused. "What? Where am I?" she said, repeating the question.

Marcus shook his head to show his disgust as well as to let Sasha know he didn't want her speaking his name to her cousin.

"On my way to your place," Sasha said. "I'll see you in a little bit." She clicked the phone off.

Sasha bit down on her bottom lip. "Marcus, I just wanted to stop by and thank you again for keeping Aaliyah for me like you did. You really are a great father. I just wanted to tell you that in person."

"No problem, Sasha. She's both of ours. But I will say that I *really* don't like her being around Thelma. I really don't. Thelma smokes and who knows what else, and I don't want our daughter in that environment."

Sasha picked up her purse and put her cell phone back in it. "Well, I appreciate your thoughts on the matter, but Aaliyah is my child just as much as she's yours. And Thelma is my cousin. Even though I know she's not the greatest example around children, at least she'll help me out when my own mother won't."

"Oh, you mean the same mother who was encouraging you to leave me when she knew the real deal going on with you?" Marcus said. "The mother who told you that you didn't need me because you had her and your father to back you up? That they would step in and take care of anything that I was doing in your life. You mean that mother?"

Sasha looked at him stunned at first. Marcus was normally sensitive to her feelings when it came to this, especially not bringing up her father. "Marcus, let's not go there, okay. You know how much I miss my father." She let her head drop and began to visibly shed a few tears.

Chapter 22

Neither give place to the devil.
—Ephesians 4:27

Marcus felt a little bad about having mentioned her father. He was only trying to point out that it was her mother who had come into their relationship and egged Sasha on. Sasha knew how her mother was. Yes, her mother loved her. But for some reason that even Sasha couldn't explain, her mother didn't seem to want her own daughter to be happy—ever.

Marcus suspected it was because of the adoration Sasha's father showered on his daughter. Sasha knew how her mother was. Still, she allowed her mother to meddle in their marriage. And Sasha was elated when her mother seemed to give her stamp of approval for Sasha to act like she wasn't married even before she officially wasn't.

"You don't need him," Stella Bradford had said as she sat at her daughter's kitchen table, drinking a glass of her favorite red wine. "You were doing fine before he came into your life. You'll do fine without him. I know money-wise Marcus does right by you and Aaliyah. And yes, he's a great father when it comes to that child, although I think he's a bit too fussy and protective. He's strict but he spoils her, just like your father with you." She took a sip and threw back her head before continuing.

"Yes, Marcus helps you out by getting her ready in the morning time and taking her to day care so you don't have to. Then he picks her up in the afternoon, again so you don't have to. That's all great. But if you need us, me and your father are here for you. We'll help you."

"Mom, you're making a mountain out of a molehill," Sasha said as she sat down across from her mother, having paced the floor for the past few minutes while her mother talked.

Sasha had been upset with Marcus when she'd found a letter sent to him by one of his college classmates, a girl named LaTrice. When she'd asked Marcus about it, he'd gotten a little upset because she had searched through his things to find it. It wasn't that the letter was that big a deal. His classmate had sent the letter to his mother's house, since that's where he was living back when she knew him.

In the letter, LaTrice told him how horrible her life was, being married to a man who was constantly fighting with her and had resorted to physically beating her. This was happening at least once a week now and she just couldn't take it anymore. She needed to talk to somebody.

She wrote that she wanted to divorce her husband but she was a religious person who believed divorce was wrong. She didn't have anyone else to turn to about this. LaTrice said Marcus had always given her sound advice in the past. In fact, it was Marcus who had warned her against pursuing a relationship with this guy in the first place. In the letter, she acknowledged he had been right and that she wished she had listened to him.

She couldn't tell her family what was going on because she was ashamed and didn't want to make things worse. She quoted the scripture: "For this cause shall a man leave his father and mother, and cleave to his wife. And they twain shall be one flesh." She took the leaving of father and mother to apply to both her and her husband, and that meant neither party should go running back home every time a problem popped up.

Her pastor had also advised her that she didn't need to let others know what was going on in their house. One reason was that people often tell others the horrible things that are happening, sometimes with exaggeration because they really don't want people to judge *them* badly, and then they end up working things out. But everybody who knew what they were being told is still upset and holding a grudge when the couple has moved past it. Then that becomes yet another problem in their relationship.

Her pastor was also the one who had insisted she needed to stay in the marriage and work things out. He felt too many Christians were turning to divorce and violating the Word of God as demonstrated in Matthew, Mark, Luke, and John. It was a lengthy letter, but she just needed someone to talk to about this. LaTrice had put her phone number in the letter for him to call her if it was at all possible.

Marcus did call her, not thinking there was anything wrong with doing so.

"I can't divorce him, Marcus," LaTrice had said. "I don't want God mad at me. I made a vow, a covenant with this man. And part of what we said during that covenant ceremony was 'until death do us part.' I've searched the scriptures. I've talked extensively with my pastor. Nowhere is there anything that says it's okay to get a divorce if your spouse is beating on you. It says 'saving for the cause of fornication,' which I take to mean there has to be some sexual immorality to qualify for a divorce. It's possible he could be cheating on me, but that's not what I'm dealing with."

Marcus could hear her crying between her words.

"My pastor tells me I need to find a way to work things out. That this is what marriage is about. Finding ways to make things work, not running away when something doesn't feel good," LaTrice said. "I've tried so hard, but it's just getting worse."

"What? He thinks it's okay for a man to beat his wife and that she should stay there and just take it while she's working things out?" Marcus shook his head. "No. It's like he's trying to say it's your fault and your responsibility to make him do right even though the person who is wrong is not being called on it. La-Trice, that's not of God."

"But as my pastor pointed out, I did make a vow—for better

or worse. I suppose this counts as for worse. He and I entered into a covenant, an agreement before God. I don't want to break that covenant."

It was right then and there that Marcus saw something he had never realized before. People recognized marriage as a covenant but didn't understand what that entailed.

"A covenant," he began, "is an agreement between two or more people. God made several covenants Himself. But in all covenants, there is something one party agrees he or she will do as long as you do what you say you will do. When one person violates the terms of that agreement, it nullifies the agreement. A covenant was not meant to bind one person to it while the other person is allowed to do whatever they want without keeping their end of the agreement. Even God said if you do this, I'll do this. But when man didn't keep his end of the agreement, God was not bound to just do it anyway. He could, but He was no longer obligated to do it."

"I hear you, Marcus, but we did promise to stay together until death do us part."

"And I hate to say this, but if things continue with your husband as they are, if he doesn't seek help or stop his destructive behavior, it very well may lead to your death."

"I know, Marcus. That's why I don't know what to do. I want to honor my vow. I don't want God turning away from me because I'm in sin just because I divorced."

"You and your husband both made vows to each other. Your marriage is contingent on each of you keeping your part of that agreement. Correct?"

"Yes," she said rather timidly.

"He promised to love, honor, and cherish you, right?" Marcus said.

"Yes," she said, stronger than before.

"How is beating you a form of loving you? How is degrading you verbally and physically honoring you? How is hurting you cherishing you? How is what your husband doing right now loving you the way Christ loves his bride, the church?"

She sighed loud enough for Marcus to hear her. But it was

more a sigh of release. "I see what you're saying, Marcus. We made a vow in the context of a covenant, a contract of sorts, an agreement between the two of us. When one of us breaks the terms of that agreement, it affects the whole contract."

"Exactly. If you sign a contract to buy a house and you take out a loan, you make an agreement with the mortgage company. As long as you abide by the terms of that agreement, making your mortgage payments on time, you get to stay in that house. But if you miss a few payments, you are then in violation of the contract. The mortgage company is no longer bound to its agreement to let you stay in the house."

"Great analogy," she said. "A problem we're having with our mortgage now."

Marcus looked at his watch. He needed to start dinner, since this was his night to cook. Sasha would be home shortly. "Listen, LaTrice. I'm not saying you should get a divorce. I really think people walk away too easily from marriages when times get tough or they get bored. I think we really do need to fight for our marriages."

"But I guess we should be smarter and more prayerful about it before we even get into them," LaTrice said.

"Yeah, well, most of us learn that piece of advice a little too late," Marcus said.

"I was actually thinking about getting a divorce and just never remarrying. I mean, it looked to me that when it came to God and divorce in the scriptures, you were all right as long as you didn't marry again. At least not while the first person you married was still alive."

"I don't think God intends for you to do that, either," Marcus said. "We are subject to the sins of the heart in today's time. It's like when the Bible says in Matthew five, twenty-seven and twenty-eight, 'Ye have heard that it was said by them of old time, Thou shalt not commit adultery. But I say unto you, that whosoever looketh on a woman to lust after her hath committed adultery with her already in his heart.' Sins of the heart. In my observation of that scripture, I would say that if you feel something in your heart, it's just like you've actually committed it."

That was when Marcus knew he needed to learn more about God's Word on divorce and remarrying. He went on to tell La-Trice, "If a person is married and feeling like their only way out under God's terms is if that person dies, then it's almost like in your heart you're killing them. If you're divorced and wanting not to be alone, just as God said when He made Adam, that it was not good for man to be alone, then why have to sit around essentially waiting on that person to die to feel free to marry another? It's what could be labeled spiritual murder."

"You know, I never thought about it the way you've just put it. Thank you, Marcus. You have certainly given me some things to think on and pray about. I don't know what I'm going to do, but I do know God loves me. That I do know."

"When the Bible speaks on divorce, it's mostly addressing the person who is causing the hurt and harm. It's like God is telling them He hates divorce and they need to get their act together. It wasn't to keep people being hurt in the hurt. God is love, and He wants us to treat one another with love. I absolutely believe that," Marcus said. "But if that person remains the same, God is not trying to punish the person who is innocent by making them pay the price while the guilty one has the benefit of getting off scot-free. I just don't believe that, I don't."

"I hear you, Marcus. Again, I thank you. And will you please thank your wife for me for allowing you to minister to my life."

"Well, I'm not really a minister."

"Oh, yes, you are," LaTrice said. "Everybody except you seems to know that already. You've been called, you just haven't answered your calling yet. And if you want to get technical, a minister is merely a servant of God. I know for sure you're that. At least, that's what you were when we were in college."

Marcus laughed. "Okay, LaTrice. Well, I'm going to go start dinner. My wife will be home shortly, and I want to have it close to being ready when she gets here."

"And he cooks, too," LaTrice said, speaking of Marcus as though she were talking to someone else. "Is there anything you can't do?" LaTrice said with a laugh. "I sure hope your wife knows and appreciates what she has in you. Thanks again, Marcus. And I'll try not to bother you again with my problems. I realize how some women can be when it comes to their men. I know I'd be concerned if another woman was talking to my husband like this."

"Oh, Sasha's pretty cool," Marcus said, although he had noticed his wife had become a lot more possessive than he'd realized she was in all the time he'd known her.

Marcus did tell Sasha he'd spoken with an old classmate from college when she got home. He even told her LaTrice's name. And Sasha seemed fine with it at the time.

After that, Marcus noticed that whenever he'd log on to the Internet, Sasha would stand over or near him. He didn't realize it at the time, but she was trying to obtain his password.

He found out that Sasha had e-mailed a friend she'd become angry with a virus disguised as a love postcard just so she could capture the keystrokes her friend used from her computer and be able to access her account. He later learned that she'd sent out damaging e-mails from her ex-friend's account. Sasha used the very same spyware on his computer to capture his keystrokes.

It hadn't mattered, since he wasn't doing anything wrong, but it was the principle that had bothered him.

It was only after she searched through his things and found the letter LaTrice had written to him that Sasha blew up. She accused Marcus of not telling her everything. He'd had no idea Sasha was like that.

"I told you I talked to her a few weeks ago," Marcus had said when she waved the letter in his face. "Remember?"

"Yeah, but you didn't tell me she'd written you a letter," Sasha said.

"There's nothing in the letter. She said she was having problems, she explained some of her problems, and she said she needed someone to talk to," Marcus said.

"So, why come to you? What was so special about the two of you that when she needed someone the most, you were the one she sought out?"

"LaTrice and I were never like that. We were just friends. That's all, friends."

"Just friends, huh? Then why did she send this letter to your mother's house?" She waved the letter in his face again.

"Because that's the only address she knew where to reach me. She didn't know I was married."

Sasha began tapping her foot. "Did you and she ever date?"

"No, we didn't. I keep telling you, we were just friends. I don't see why you're so upset. She wrote me a letter. We spoke over the phone. She was having a really hard time. I told you about it as soon as you came home that day. And now you're acting like she and I are having an affair or something, which is not the case."

Sasha stopped tapping and shook her head. "Do you really expect me to believe that? Well, what if I was still talking to one of my old boyfriends? How would you feel about that? What if me and one of my guy friends were chatting up on the phone? Would you be all right about that?"

"But you do talk to one of your old guy friends. One or two if I'm not mistaken," Marcus said. "I don't jump all over *you* about that."

"I see. So this was about you getting back at me for talking to Franklin?" Sasha said.

"No, it had nothing to do with you and Franklin. I told you, LaTrice needed to talk about something she felt I could help her sort out," Marcus said.

"And you were the first person she thought of?" Sasha practically wrestled the rest of his sentence away from him. "Good old Marcus. Everybody's best friend."

"Sasha, you've been spying on my computer, so you know I'm not doing anything wrong—"

"What?" Sasha tried to fake surprise. "What are you talking about, spying?"

"You put a spy virus on my computer."

"I don't know what you're talking about." Sasha went over to the refrigerator and opened it. She took out the cut-up chicken. "How do you want this chicken? Baked or fried?"

Marcus started chuckling, but not because it was funny. "Oh, so now you want to change the subject. You put a virus on my computer. I know it's there, and I know it was you who did it. Just like you sent that virus to your friend Raven."

Sasha took the chicken and opened the package at the sink. She turned on the faucet and began to wash it. "You're crazy," Sasha said. "You know that? Both you and Raven are crazy."

"You admitted to sending Raven that virus. And she had hard proof when the Internet carrier identified the breach and traced it back to you. Stop tripping."

"Well, if you knew there was a virus on your computer, why didn't you just clean it?" Sasha continued to wash the chicken without looking his way.

"For what? So you could put it back on again later?"

Sasha turned and stared at Marcus. "So is that what happened? You knew it was on there so you tamped things down between the two of you? Is that why I couldn't catch you?"

Marcus shook his head. "Sasha, I'm not doing anything wrong; that's why you can't catch me. If I'm not doing anything to get caught in, then there's nothing to catch."

Three-month-old Aaliyah was starting to wake up from her nap. Marcus could see her stirring and began to walk toward the den to get her out of the portable crib.

"You and Franklin, on the other hand, I'm not so sure about," he said on his way to the den. "Maybe that's why you're protesting so hard. Guilty people tend to project onto other people to try and take the heat off themselves. If I were you, I'd be careful of all these accusations you're hurling around at me."

Marcus picked Aaliyah up and hugged her. "You're soaking wet," he said to Aaliyah. He laid her down on the couch. "Let Daddy change you."

Sasha turned on the stove. "Fine!" she mumbled to herself. "Fried it will be." She knew when it came to chicken, Marcus preferred it baked.

Chapter 23

Look not every man on his own things, but every man also on the things of others.

—Philippians 2:4

I picked up the phone a few times after church on Sunday to call Marcus. The first time, I put the phone down because I wasn't sure what time he got in from church, and I didn't want to call him just as he walked in the door. The next time, I noticed how nervous I was about it. *Melissa, you can do this. You can do this.* I was hoping he would call me, but he had said the ball was in my court. I've just always thought it was better when the man pursued the woman, although in truth, Marcus *had* been the one to pursue me. I had been the holdout. I was the one who had kept him at bay. Now it was on me.

I'd had a wonderful time talking and listening to him that Saturday afternoon. I would never have guessed he was so knowledgeable about the Bible and God's Word. He had definitely opened my eyes about a lot of things: my misconception of what a Jezebel was, my thoughts regarding the scriptures on divorce and remarriage. A lot of what he said made sense, especially when you knew the history and the context of what was going on at the time.

The part that resonated the most with me was about the laws in the Old and, even during certain times, the New Testament regarding adultery. The most significant fact was that if a man or a woman were married, and they were with another person in a sexual way—that was adultery. And under Jewish law, if a person committed adultery, the punishment was death, not divorce. So the scripture that said "saving for the cause of fornication," which would include a woman saying she was a virgin before marriage when she wasn't, or having sex with another while being married, could *not* have meant it was the only reason God would allow a person to divorce. Because according to the law, the punishment for sexual immorality was death and not grounds for a divorce. And with death, there's no reason to get a divorce. But if a person is married and *separated*, they were still legally married and were not legally available to marry another. An illegal marriage constituted committing adultery.

Marcus kept saying "ex-wife." When I thought about it, that meant she really was no longer legally his wife. By law, he was no longer married. God's perfect will is that we marry the one he has joined us with and we work together and make it last. But there are times when God wasn't in the joining of the two in the first place, although He recognizes that the two who marry now have become one. When that one files legal papers to dissolve the marriage and it's granted, they are no longer one but now two again.

I got it, and it was because of Marcus's teaching that it made sense to me. If I were to date Marcus, I would be dating a legally unmarried man, therefore neither he nor I could be charged with committing adultery because neither of us was legally married to another. I hadn't wanted to make this work to my advantage just because I wanted it to work. I mean, I didn't want to be saying this was okay and later find out that I was in sin. So I prayed about what Marcus had said. I went back and read the various scriptures, even the places where God said He hated divorce, but I studied them in the context of what was happening at the time that caused God to say that. Context and history.

I saw that there were times when men were just getting rid of their wives because they burned the toast (okay, so that was a slight exaggeration but on point). Some just decided they wanted some other woman and were dumping their wives for no good reason. Men were cautioned against lying about their new brides not being virgins because that put a bad light on them, and God was not going along with that.

Some men wanted another woman, so they would divorce the first wife, marry another woman, then decide they wanted the first wife back. God wasn't having that, either. The law said if you had a problem with the first wife and divorce her, you couldn't go back later to get her after you'd married another and decided you didn't want her now. There was even a time when men were marrying women who were worshipping idols, and God was absolutely not happy about that. Who we marry can have an influence on us.

I studied all of this with a different eye and a different heart, praying for the Holy Spirit to lead me and enlighten me after Marcus had taught me a thing or two.

When I had finally gotten up my nerve to call Marcus, my friend Nae-nae called. She needed me to keep her kids because she had to go out of town to a funeral and she couldn't afford to take them with her. I decided it was best to wait until after she came back in a few days and then I would call him.

Then Tiffany Connors called on Wednesday as soon as I came home from work. She was in labor, and Darius, her no-good husband, was nowhere to be found. I went over to her house and took her to the hospital. Good thing I went when I did. She delivered the baby two hours after she arrived. Tiffany has no family here, so I volunteered to keep the children until Darius got home. He didn't look too happy when he saw me sitting in his den.

"Hey girl, what's up?" Darius said. "Where's Tiff?"

"She's at the hospital," I said, trying hard not to smack him upside his head.

"The hospital," he said, with a look of concern.

"Yeah, the hospital. Congratulations, you just had a little boy."

"A boy?" Darius said. "Oh, man! It's a boy. Oh, wow, wait till my boys hear this. I have a son? Wow, that's what the sonogram said, but I didn't trust it. A little boy. I finally have a son!"

"Yeah, and your wife is fine," I said, answering a question he hadn't yet asked in all of his excitement.

"I was just about to ask, Melissa. Dang, girl. Give me a break here. I just found out I have a son!" He did a victory dance.

"Yeah, and where were you tonight? And why wasn't your cell phone on?"

He shrugged. "I was out trying to hustle up some extra cash. You know how it is when you have two children and one on the way. You have to get it whenever and wherever you can," he said.

"Get it? Get what?" I asked.

"You know what? You know . . . I'm about tired of you and your attitude toward me. I haven't done anything to you but try and be nice. When folks try to talk about your plus-size self, I'm the first one to say I think you look good, especially for your height. Me? I personally like thick chicks just as well as the petite ones."

I rolled my eyes. "And where exactly does my size and what others have to say fit into this conversation?"

"I'm just saying, you need to cut me some slack. Lose the attitude. It might make you look a little slimmer. That's all I'm saying. I come home—"

I looked at my watch. "Fifteen minutes past twelve midnight."

"There you go, all up in my business again. Tiffany knows what I'm doing. She knows I'm taking care of business for our family. She doesn't give me lip. Maybe that's why you can't keep a man. You need to learn how to stay in your place," Darius said.

I chuckled. "My place, huh? Yeah, well, looks like I'm in *your* place right now." I looked around the room. "And why is that? Oh, yeah, that's right. Because your wife was in labor and she was looking for you. Calling you on your cell phone, calling your friends, but unable to find you. So, she had to call *me*. And I take her to the hospital. Mind you, I'm still trying to reach you on your cell during this whole time while I'm sitting there with *your* children while *your* wife is in labor *alone*. So what was up with your cell phone again? Why did it keep going straight to voice mail?"

"I don't know. Maybe I was out of range during the time Tiffany and you tried to call. But I'm here now, so you can run along on home now."

I stood up and gathered my things.

"How much did the baby weigh?" he asked. "My son, how much did he weigh?"

I smiled. "Ask your wife when you see her," I said as I walked toward the door. "I might as well leave *something* for you as a surprise."

Darius called out to me. "Melissa, thank you. I'm glad Tiffany has someone like you in her life. And I really mean that, from my heart." He looked sincere.

"Yeah," I said. "And before you ask, I've already told Tiffany I would get the kids from day care tomorrow and keep them until you get home. But I'm going to tell you, Darius. I'm not Tiffany. If you think you're going to 'take care of business' while I sit here taking care of your kids, you have another *think* coming. You come straight home from work, you come get your children, then you and them go and see Tiffany and the baby."

"Oh, yeah," Darius said. "Without a doubt."

The next day, Darius came straight home and got the children. He knew I was serious. Too bad that after Tiffany came home from the hospital, he was back to his old ways again. I know this because I went over there to visit the day after she came home.

"Where's Darius?" I asked.

"Oh, he said he had some business to take care of. He should be back shortly." I hung around until ten o'clock, giving the children their baths and putting them to bed before cleaning up the kitchen.

"Melissa, thank you," Tiffany said. "I don't know what I would do if it weren't for you."

"I know one thing, you need to put your husband in check," I said.

"Please don't start on that again," Tiffany said. "I don't feel like it tonight."

"I know. But we both know you deserve better."

Tiffany rubbed the baby's hair. "He's beautiful, isn't he?" she asked.

I smiled and touched his tiny little fingers. "Yes, he really is."

Chapter 24

Let nothing be done through strife or vainglory; but in lowliness of mind let each esteem other better than themselves.

—Philippians 2:3

It had now been three weeks since Marcus had come to my house that Saturday. The longer I had put off calling him, the harder it became. What to say now?

Oh, I was going to call you that first day after you came over but I got cold feet. Then I was about to call you when my phone rang. It was my friend Nae-nae, and she needed me to keep her children while she went out of town to a funeral. She came back on Tuesday night, but by the time she'd gotten her children and gone home, it was around ten at night. I don't like calling people I don't know that well after ten. So I thought I would call you Wednesday after I got home from work and before we both left to attend Bible study.

Then Tiffany—that's the friend I spoke to when we went to Bible study that night, the woman with the two little girls who was pregnant—anyway, she called me as soon as I walked in the house. In fact, she'd called several times before that but I hadn't gotten home yet. She was in labor, and of course her husband was nowhere to be found. She has those two adorable little girls with no family in town to help her. She's sort of like me—hates to bother others, so she rarely asks for help even when she needs it.

So I went over and took her to the hospital. She had the baby, a little boy. I had to take the girls home because there was still no husband to be found and visiting hours were over. Her husband didn't drag himself home until sometime after midnight.

Tiffany came home from the hospital on Saturday. I called her Sunday evening and learned she was there by herself with those children. Darius supposedly went to get something from the store. Apparently he got lost along the way because he had been gone for an hour by the time I got there. He came back three hours later. It took him four hours to pick up a bottle of medicine and a few other items Tiffany needed.

Then I was going to call you on Monday, but that meant it had been over a week and I would need to try and explain why it had taken me so long. The cycle seemed to begin all over again with different situations popping up here and there, always someone needing something.

I could have called and told him all of that, but I didn't. He frequently came to the doctor's office where I worked. I decided I would talk to him then. Funny, I hadn't asked him in all the time we'd spoken what he did that required him to visit with Dr. Brewer so often. I hate getting too deep into other folks' business. I figure if they want you to know, they'll tell you. I knew he had a job. That's all that mattered. Because the Bible says if a man doesn't work, he shouldn't eat. Quite a few people I know must not have gotten that e-mail. They have all kinds of men hanging around who won't strike a lick at a stick, and they eat very well.

I had one boyfriend who tried that with me. He must have looked at me and thought I was truly desperate for a man. He had to have thought that because he sure tried that not working thing, I guess thinking he was going to sponge off me. "Can I hold fifty dollars until the end of the week?" *How are you going to pay me back if you don't have a job?* No way. I'm not falling for that trick. Fifty here, twenty there. The next thing you know, they owe you hundreds, maybe thousands of dollars with no intention of ever paying you back. Nickel and diming you so often, you don't even realize how much the final tally is.

But I was certain Marcus did *something* for a living. A week passed and he didn't come. Now it had been two weeks since we talked, and I was beginning to think I just needed to call him before I really messed up and made him think I still wasn't interested. I would hate to lose out on getting to know him better just because I miscalculated. But then, I do believe whatever God has for me is for me.

However, I also know that we have to do our part. Marcus had gone above and beyond. He had let me know he was interested in me. He had learned of my concerns regarding his divorce and my wrestling with the scriptures regarding that. He had given me the space not to feel pressured. And I was seemingly messing it up even though I knew now that I really wanted to see where this could lead. I couldn't believe he hadn't come to Dr. Brewer's office yet. Then I looked up from my desk the following week on Thursday, and there he stood.

He was dressed down a little more than usual, wearing just a stylish shirt instead of his usual suit and tie. And he wasn't wearing his glasses. My heart began to pound faster as I tried to act normal. Yes, I *really* liked this guy.

"Hi," Marcus said, very businesslike.

"Hi," I said back, hoping that my voice hadn't betrayed my pounding heart even with that one-syllable word.

"Dr. Brewer is expecting me." He then went and sat down.

I sat there in shock. That was it? He didn't ask how I was. He didn't chitchat. Just announced himself politely, stated his purpose for being there, then went and sat down. I put my hand over my heart and breathed in deeply. Maybe he thought I had played too hard to get. Maybe he believed there was no point in pursuing me further. Maybe he had decided I wasn't what he wanted after all.

That's the way my life seemed to work anyway. I would meet a guy who seemed interested. He would talk to me for a few days, then it was like he'd concluded I wasn't that interesting after all. But Marcus seemed different. He had called me out over two months ago. How I was making other guys pay for some of my bad past relationships. He had been right.

I let Dr. Brewer know he was here. Dr. Brewer came out immediately, which was what he always did, and personally invited Marcus back to his office. I still didn't understand why Dr. Brewer seemed to bend over backward to be nice to Marcus. But maybe whatever Marcus was selling was something he felt he needed or was at least interested in hearing about. Suddenly, I realized just how much I wanted to know what Marcus did for a living. But he hadn't said anything to me today other than to speak. I had to figure out how to get a conversation going with him again.

When Marcus came out of Dr. Brewer's office, Dr. Brewer was laughing and patting Marcus on the back. I could see how much Dr. Brewer genuinely respected Marcus. Marcus walked by my desk. I thought for sure he would stop by and chat for a second the way he normally did when he left Dr. Brewer. But this time, he just waved and walked through the door that led back out to the waiting room. I was shocked. I got up and trotted after him.

"Marcus, hold up a second," I said. There was no one in the waiting room, as Marcus generally arrived before regular office hours began.

Marcus stopped.

I didn't know what I would say to him but I knew I had to say something. "I have been meaning to call you," I said.

"Oh, really," he said. It was hard to read what he might be thinking.

I forged ahead. "It's been so hectic around my place. A couple of my friends needed someone to help them out with their children, so of course I did what I could."

"Yeah, you're great with children. Children know when you're sincere and when you're faking it. Aaliyah really likes you," he said.

"Here's the thing. I wanted to let you know how much your Bible teaching helped me that day you came over. You know, the one on divorce. Anyway, I was thinking maybe you and I could talk some more sometime. That's if you're still interested."

He smiled. "Yeah. I'd like that a lot." He seemed a bit unlike his usual self.

"Are you okay? Is everything all right?" I asked.

"Oh, yeah. Just life. You know how that is. Always something going on." He didn't elaborate further.

I was hoping he would take over the reins and guide this effort toward a date between us, but he didn't. I suppose that's what I got for having taken so long. Maybe he had lost his passion to get to know me better. Maybe I should have taken the hint and saved myself the trouble. Preemptive strike—protect my heart from being hurt.

"Why don't I call you later," he said, glancing at his watch.

"Oh, I'm sorry. I didn't mean to hold you up. Sure, you can call me later. You still have my number?"

He smiled. "Yeah. I'll call you tonight." He left in a rush.

I suddenly knew how he must have felt when he was trying to talk to me and I didn't seem to be all there. It was not a good feeling.

Chapter 25

*Then hear thou from the heavens their prayer and
their supplication, and maintain their cause.*

—2 Chronicles 6:35

Angela called me. She and Brent had returned from their
two-week-long honeymoon to the Bahamas and they spent
a week at home as newlyweds. She wanted to thank me again
for all the work I'd done toward making their wedding day one
they would never forget.

"Did you happen to see Arletha Brown there?" Angela asked
after we had rehashed many of the most memorable moments
of the wedding and reception.

I didn't know quite how I should answer that question. I
knew what her cousin Gayle had said when it came to Arletha
Brown. She didn't believe she was the Arletha they were looking for. I certainly didn't want to do or say anything to encourage Angela, but I wasn't going to lie either.

"Yes, I did."

"Why didn't someone say something to me? She was there
and you and Gayle both saw her and neither of you said a word
to me?"

"Angel," I said, "there was no reason to put a damper on
such a lovely and spiritual occasion. It was your wedding—"

"Which is precisely why one of you should have said something," Angela said. "We were taking pictures, and yes, I had
family members there, but Arletha was there, too. Maybe, just

maybe, she would have come clean. You know, as her gift to me during that time. And while Brent's grandmother stood with us having her photo taken, I could have had my grandmother up there with us."

"Angela, personally I don't believe Arletha is your grandmother."

"I know that's what she said, but I just have a feeling she wasn't leveling with us. Why else would she come to a wedding on such short notice, a wedding for someone she'd just met, unless there was some connection there?" Angela paused for a few seconds. "You really think I'm wrong about this, don't you?"

"Yes, I do."

"Yeah, well, Gayle does, too. She says I want this so badly, I'm spinning things way out of proportion. I'm a little out of control. She says I need to stop this."

"I know it would mean a lot to you to find your grandmother, but I agree with Gayle," I said.

"So why do you think Arletha Brown came to my wedding?"

"When I spoke with her—"

"You talked to her?" Angela asked, shock practically oozing through the phone.

I placed my hand up to my head and patted my forehead a few times wondering why I hadn't thought before I blurted that out. "I saw her sitting back watching while y'all were taking your wedding photos."

"Again, you didn't say a word, knowing that I had invited her and was hoping she would show up," Angela said. "You didn't just see her like Gayle did. You talked to her."

"Angela, if I had told you, what would you have done?"

"I would have come over and spoken to her. Thanked her for coming."

"And then what?" I said.

"And then, I would have hoped she would give me some indication she was actually my grandmother, and I could have hugged her, and we could have taken these fabulous photos together."

"That's exactly why I didn't push the issue. She said she wasn't who you thought she was."

Angela let out a loud sigh. "Then why did she come to my wedding?"

"Because," I almost whispered before turning up the volume in my voice, "she said she didn't have anything else to do. She told me that's why she had come. Not because she was your grandmother. Not because she cared about you. Not to surprise you. She's an old woman nobody seems to like being around, so she was probably shocked and delighted to get an invitation to anything. In fact, she said she had a dress she thought she would never get to wear and your wedding was as good an occasion as any."

"She didn't say that," Angela said. "You're just trying to get me to see the point. Just like Gayle tried to get me to see it."

"So is that how you knew she was there? Gayle told you?"

"She told me after she got back home. After I went on and on about how I couldn't believe Arletha didn't show up. She told me she had come, and she'd seen her at the reception. I can't believe you both knew she was there and never said one word to me."

"Gayle's gone back?"

"Yes, she went back right after my wedding, although I think she likes it here. I have a feeling she might be thinking of relocating to Birmingham, especially since we're in need of good nurses. From what I hear, she's top-notch." Angela giggled a little. "I see what you're doing. You're trying to change the subject."

"Who, me?"

"Yes, you. But I see what both you and Gayle are trying to get through my head. If you had told me Arletha was there, I would have focused my attention on her and it would have possibly marred the mood of my wedding. Especially if what you're saying is true," Angela said. "That she's really not my grandmother. She has said that and my saying anything different won't make it any different. If I had known she was there while we were taking pictures, I probably would have insisted she take a photo with us, kin or not. Okay, okay. You were right not to tell me."

"I know," I said, trying not to sound too smug about it. "One thing I know is planning. And interrupting such a beautiful day with a possible grandmama drama was not my idea of how I pictured your wedding coming off in the end. Listen, I love my share of drama in books, television, and the movies as well as the next girl. But when it comes to things I'm involved in, I'd prefer to skip the drama if possible."

"So what do you suggest I do?" Angela asked.

I thought about Arletha and all the things I remembered from my childhood surrounding her. "Leave her alone," I said. "She's who she is, and from my point of view, she doesn't seem at all interested in what you're selling."

"I'm not selling anything. I just thought she might be my grandmother."

"And now you know that she's not. So let it go. I'm telling you, you need to leave well enough alone."

"I have just one more thing to say about Arletha. She must really want somebody in her life. From a Christian standpoint, I feel the woman must be lonely and could use some love," Angela said.

"I won't argue with you there. But what made you say that?" I asked.

"Okay. She came to my wedding. If she's not my grandmother—and according to what you and Gayle have been saying, she's not that nice a person—in spite of my blind spot to see that, then why show up at my wedding? There's something there."

My Call Waiting signal beeped. I looked at the Caller ID. It was Marcus. "Hey, I need to take this call," I said. I hated doing it the way I did, but seeing Marcus's number pop up scrambled my brain and put me in a mode of urgency.

"Sure," Angela said.

"We'll talk again soon," I said in a rush. "Bye."

I clicked the flash button and hoped it hadn't taken me too long to switch over. "Hello," I said. "Hello."

"Melissa, it's Marcus."

I felt my heart begin to melt just a little bit more, and I knew right then and there I was truly in trouble. I really, really liked this guy. Really.

Now for the true question: Where would he and I go from here?

Chapter 26

Behold, O God our shield, and look upon the face of thine anointed.

—Psalm 84:9

Marcus and I had a wonderful talk on the phone. He asked if he could come over. Of course that was okay with me. When he came, I asked him exactly (no guessing, no assuming anymore) what he did for a living.

He chuckled. "For the most part, I'm an investor currently working for a large financial investment firm. I'm also working at a few of my own things I believe in, so I'm investing in them personally. I guess you can say I do all right."

"Oh," I said, trying to figure out how Dr. Brewer fit into this picture. "I thought you might have been in sales or something. You know, coming to see Dr. Brewer every month."

"You could classify what I do as sales since I have to sell people on the idea of investing in a particular thing, company, organization, or group," he said as he smiled while tilting his head slightly to one side and gazing into my eyes.

I hated it when he looked at me like that. Allow me to clarify. I liked it but I hated it because it made me feel like I should be doing something. I wanted to get him to tell me what connection he had with Dr. Brewer, but I knew that would be ethically wrong. Dr. Brewer was my employer. Marcus was a friend, possibly headed toward being my boyfriend. Wow, I kind of liked the sound of that although when you get to be our ages, boyfriend sounds childish. Boyfriend . . . manfriend, that's better. Yeah, my manfriend.

"You're dying to know, aren't you?" Marcus said, jarring me back to the here and now.

"Know what?" I was trying to figure out if I had been so deep in thought that I'd missed part of an important dialogue.

He wrinkled his nose a few times. "You're dying to know why I come to Dr. Brewer's office."

I buttoned my lips tighter just in case they had thoughts of their own to possibly betray me. My lips have been known to do that: say something they know shouldn't have been said. Not this time. I smiled hard, held my tongue back behind my teeth, and merely shrugged.

"Oh, so you don't want to know?"

"Yes, I want to know, but I know it's not right, especially since technically it's none of my business," I said in a mad rush of words. "Does that make sense?"

"It makes perfect sense. You don't want to ask about things you have no business knowing. I respect a woman who respects others' privacy. What I can do is tell you that your employer is a great man and what he's doing is well worth investing in."

I thought about what he said and it was beginning to click. "You're an investor?"

"Yes."

"And you invest in companies and things you believe are worth investing in?"

"Yes." He smiled, then winked at me. "And I'm generally pretty good at picking what has been underestimated and grossly under-valued. That includes people as well as businesses."

I blushed.

"And because I know you probably want to know and likely are too polite to ask, I really do make a pretty good living doing it. So what would you say to me and you seeing a little more of each other?"

"I'm game," I said.

At the end of the week we went out on a date—a movie and a sit-down dinner. The following Wednesday, he came to Bible study with me at Followers of Jesus Faith Worship Center. I could tell he loved Pastor Landris's teaching. The following Sunday, he and Aaliyah came to church with me. Aaliyah went to what we call children's church.

"I want to come back here again," Aaliyah said. "Can we, Daddy? Can we come back again? We have our own church, Daddy, with our own songs. It was so much fun!"

"Yes, honey. We can come back again," Marcus said, beaming at his daughter.

"You promise, Daddy?" Aaliyah said. She squinted at him.

"I promise," said Marcus.

"Lord, I love to praise your name," Aaliyah began to sing as we walked to Marcus's black Lexus.

We went out to eat after church, and I fell totally in love with both father and daughter all over again. We laughed so much we had other people looking at us and eventually laughing just because we were so tickled.

For the month of December, Marcus and I spent even more time together. We talked a lot on the phone. We were developing strong feelings for each other. So strong, we both found ourselves wrestling with how to keep our vows not to cross the line sexually.

I called Angela Gabriel, now Underwood.

"Mrs. Underwood," I began, trying to disguise my voice, "how are you today?"

"I'm fine, Melissa," Angela said.

"Rats, I hate Caller ID sometimes. You can't call people without them knowing who's on the line."

Angela laughed. "The thing about all of these new technologies that's good but can be bad is how they make us not think the way we used to. We don't remember phone numbers anymore. They're programmed into our phone and we just press a button to call. Either that or we have to look the number up," Angela said.

"Girl, you know, you're right. The SIM card in my cell phone went out last year, and I couldn't even remember my own mother's and brother's cell phone numbers. It was *too* funny."

"Thanks for reminding me of that. I need to write down the numbers I have programmed into my cell phone as well as the ones that have come in on my Caller ID. I don't erase some incoming numbers I want to call again. I just press a button and it makes the call for me," Angela said. "So what's going on with you?"

Angela and I had spoken from time to time. We had not been friends before the wedding, but afterward, we seemed to have developed a nice little friendship. Part of the reason, I believe, was because of Arletha Brown. I was one person she could bounce her thoughts and feelings off about her. She had told Brent everything after she learned Arletha had attended their wedding and reception. Brent had offered to hire someone to investigate Arletha Brown if Angela wanted him to. That's what happens when you marry a guy whose family is rolling in dough.

Brent sure did love Angela. I could see that the first time I saw them together. With some couples, you get the sense they're merely comfortable with the relationship, but real passion is not there. Not so with Brent and Angela. You could tell they were madly in love. I had never asked, but I believed they had kept themselves chaste until their marriage. You can never tell what people are doing behind closed doors, but I just felt they were committed to doing things God's way.

Angela had wondered whether she should pursue learning more about Arletha Brown, just to put to bed—one way or the other—whether Arletha was who Angela thought she was. She had asked what I thought about it since I was aware of what was going on. I stuck to my original thoughts that she should just leave it alone. I couldn't see an old woman who seemed to be without anyone in her life at this stage *not* embracing a family member if this were the case. Especially a family member like Angela.

"I think you should pray about that," I had said. "I believe nobody can keep God's will from happening. If this woman really is your grandmother and it's God's desire that you know it, I trust things will work out in the end."

Angela didn't seem convinced that she should sit back and do nothing. "God still desires for us to do our part," Angela said. "But I will continue to pray on it. I don't feel right having Brent pay someone to investigate her, though. That just seems wrong," Angela said. "No matter how strongly I feel about knowing."

I agreed. It's one thing to search for your grandmother independently. It's quite another thing to have someone investigated. Whatever Arletha Brown may have wanted hidden was her business. No one had a right to invade her privacy. I told Angela as much.

"What's going on with me?" I repeated Angela's question since my mind had wandered off thinking about her and Brent and Arletha Brown. "I already told you that Marcus and I are dating now."

"Yes," Angela said without trying to hide her excitement. "I think that's a great example of how God works out a thing. Who would have guessed that our wedding planner and the best man at our wedding would be dating some two months later?"

"And he is so nice, Angela. I am serious. We've been talking seriously for about a month now. I know you and Brent dated for a while before you walked down the aisle."

Angela started giggling. "And you want to know what you need to do to keep things holy?"

"Yes!" I said, my voice exploding the word. "You've probably guessed that I'm not a virgin. After I broke up with Cass, I rededicated my life to Christ and vowed to keep myself until I married. That is much easier said than done."

I thought of what I might be leading her to believe and quickly moved to clarify. "Not that Marcus has been trying to go there. He hasn't. He's a minister, and he's truly committed to keeping himself as well."

"Oh, you don't have to explain things to me. Brent and I have both been there. We may be spiritual, but we're all walking around in a suit of flesh. That flesh can raise its head and want to take over. That's why the Bible tells us not to walk in the flesh but to walk in the spirit."

I sighed hard. "So, how do we do that? How did you and Brent do that?"

"Brent and I made a choice. We both knew what we desired. That meant when one of us might have been weak, the other one had to be strong enough to pull back and leave if necessary. You talk about praying without ceasing—there were certain times when Brent and I were together that he and I were both praying at the same time. You have to take your mind off what your flesh is saying and put your mind on what God is saying. There's truly a blessing for you if you'll not be weary in well-doing and if you faint not."

"So far, it hasn't gotten too bad. My mind has wandered a few times, and that's when I find myself with thoughts I know I don't need to have when it comes to him."

"Strongholds," Angela said. "That's why you have to cast down those thoughts when they try to exalt themselves against what you know God has said on the subject."

"With you and Brent, it looks like it was a lot easier," I said.

"Can I let you in on a little secret?" Angela said. "Back in June, when we had about four months to go, Brent and I were struggling like nobody's business. It got so bad, we went to Pastor Landris and asked him to secretly marry us."

"You two were married before the ceremony you just had in October?" I shook my head and smiled.

"No, we didn't get married, but we were about to. We didn't go through with it for various reasons. One being all that Pastor Landris was dealing with at the time we were about to do it. I just want you to know that I know where you're coming from. But I also want you to know you can do this. You just need to recognize this is still spiritual warfare. Satan would like nothing more than to see you fail in this area. That way he can beat you over the head with it. Don't give Satan room to sneak in. Recognize Satan's tactics, then move, with prayer and God's Word, to cut off his access."

"Thank you," I said. "Thank you for not trying to be all religious with me. So many folks want to act like they are perfect and have never had these types of struggles. Then when we, who are trying to walk the walk, need someone to talk to about our struggles, we feel unworthy to get counsel and try to fight this battle alone. Your telling me how hard it was for you and Brent, even though to us on the outside who didn't see your struggles it looked easy, really helps me right now."

"I'll tell you who helped me a lot. Johnnie Mae Landris. She is such a down-to-earth person, both she and Pastor Landris. They are examples of how I believe God wants us to be with each other. They're not trying to beat people down. They are more into helping to lift people up," Angela said. "That's how I want to be in my walk with God. Someone who is not a stumbling block to others but a stepping-stone that leads to a higher and greater relationship with the Lord. Do I miss it sometimes in my own life? Yes. Can I go to God and ask for forgiveness? Absolutely. Will He forgive me for my sins and cleanse me from all unrighteousness when I go to Him and confess, then ask for forgiveness? Without a doubt."

I nodded to myself. "That's good. That's a Word for me. Thank you again."

When I hung up with Angela, I knelt down and prayed. I wanted to be better. I wanted to live right. I needed the Holy Spirit to guide me now more than ever. Marcus was different from any man I'd ever dated. Things were moving fast with us. And because he was a preacher, I suspected we might not have a long dating period. Especially since he told me the other night it really was better to marry than to burn.

"It's important that we practice what we preach," Marcus had said. "And that doesn't only apply to preachers. It goes for Christians in general. We can talk a good talk. It's time out for merely quoting all the right things. As followers of Christ, we need to practice what we preach."

He then went into his little mini-sermon he liked to play just for me.

"If you need peace in your life, then stop sowing discord. Start walking in peace, and start practicing what you preach. If you need joy, then walk in joy and start practicing what you preach. Are you in need of a financial blessing? Then stop speaking lack all the time and start practicing what you preach. You say you're the head and not the tail? Then start practicing what you preach. You're blessed going in and blessed coming out, then start practicing what you preach. Oh, so you're more than a conqueror? Then start *practicing* what you preach. You tell us God's grace is sufficient, then you need to start—"

"Practicing what you preach!" I said as I began to laugh. "The joy of the Lord is my strength. I can do all things through Christ who strengthens me. I am above only and not beneath. My God shall supply all of my needs according to His riches in glory. I *am* a child of the King. I *will* delight myself in the Lord and He *will* give me the desires of my heart. No weapon formed against me shall prosper. No matter what's going on in my life, no matter who may come against me, no matter what people say about me, from this day forward, I *will* practice what I preach!"

Marcus laughed. "Hey, we're talking about practice. We're talking about practice, practice, we're talking about practice," he said as he'd done before, mimicking something Allen Iverson of the Philadelphia 76ers had said once during an interview when he was being criticized for not having shown up for practice. "We're talking about practice. But you know . . . practice does make perfect. And God has called us to perfect our faith."

"Amen," I said.

Marcus had such a profound way of making me laugh while making me feel so good inside.

Chapter 27

*The burden of the valley of vision. What aileth thee
now, that thou art wholly gone up to the housetops?*
—Isaiah 22:1

"Angel, hi," Johnnie Mae said when she answered the
phone. "Isn't that something? I was just thinking about
you. So how is everything, Mrs. Married Lady?"

"Oh, it's still great! Better than I ever imagined it could be,"
Angela said. "Brent is absolutely the best husband around."

"Well, now I don't know about all that. You know I think I
have the best husband around. But we'll not go there today. I'll
let you have yours."

Angela smiled. It was the beginning of December. She
worked at the church as Johnnie Mae's executive assistant.
Both of them had decided to take some time off from working.
Johnnie Mae was taking off to spend more time with her children—soon-to-be seven-year-old Princess Rose, and almost-six-
month-old Isaiah.

Angela had taken time for her wedding, honeymoon, and
then to be a wife to her new husband. Angela planned to go
back to work the first of January.

Johnnie Mae wasn't sure when she would kick things back
into full gear. Having pushed herself for years when it came to
working outside the home, she was enjoying the work associated with being exclusively a wife and mother.

Angela had just finished praying about what she should do

concerning her grandmother when she thought to call Johnnie Mae. Angela wondered if it was even possible her grandmother was still alive. Whether she was alive or not, she wanted to know what had happened to her. And Angela now had a name: Arletha Williams.

It was funny. Before this new information fell in her lap, she really hadn't given her grandmother a second thought. She missed having her mother around early on, but her beloved great-grandmother, Pearl, had more than made her feel loved. Throughout her childhood, she had really lacked nothing of importance. It was only since Gayle had told her Arletha might be her grandmother that she had begun to let it take up residence in her mind and her waking thoughts.

Brent had noticed something was bothering her. That's why he offered to hire an investigator. The more Angela thought about it, the more she saw how ridiculous she was allowing this to become.

So, Angela told Johnnie Mae all that had transpired. How her cousin Gayle had told her what her great-grandmother had said to her. How Gayle had met a woman who just happened to mention a woman she'd briefly rented a room from in Birmingham with that exact first name.

"I mean, what are the chances that my grandmother's name would be Arletha and my cousin, Gayle, would meet a woman in Asheville, North Carolina, who had known a woman in Birmingham named Arletha?" Angela said.

Johnnie Mae was quiet for a few seconds. "Arletha, Arletha. Why does that name sound familiar?" She repeated the name again. "Arletha."

"Maybe she's been to the church before, other than for my wedding, of course," Angela said. "The woman here in Alabama is Arletha Brown."

"And you say she came to your wedding?" Johnnie Mae asked.

"Yes. It's sort of a long story, but long story short, Gayle called this Arletha here before she came down for my wedding. The woman denied she knew anything regarding what Gayle was talking about. After I heard about it, I wanted to talk to her myself. When I tried, we learned the number had been disconnected. That should have been the end of it." Angela took a swallow of her bottled water.

"It turns out my wedding planner knew an Arletha in her old neighborhood. We went to her house. She still lived there. I told her who I was and what I suspected, that she might be my grandmother. She denied it was even possible. I didn't believe her. She put us out. I sent her an invitation to my wedding. She showed up but didn't speak to me or let me know that she was there. In fact, she came to the reception but not through the receiving line. I went on my honeymoon not knowing this woman had ever shown up—"

"Which was probably a good thing," Johnnie Mae said.

"Which was probably a good thing," Angela agreed. "Brent and I had a wonderful time. We were doing fine. I was looking through the guest book from the wedding when I spotted where Arletha Brown had signed. I called Gayle to see if she knew she had been there. She confessed to seeing her but hadn't said anything to me because she thought I needed to leave it alone. The woman had said she wasn't who we thought she was, so Gayle said we needed to respect that and drop it."

"The woman your cousin said told her about Arletha, is it possible her name is Memory?"

Angela thought for a second. "I'm not sure. I didn't ask Gayle who told her. I just know that Gayle worked for Sarah Fleming in Asheville, North Carolina, and I only found that out a few days before my wedding. You do know Sarah died while you were in the hospital—"

Johnnie Mae stopped her. "Wait a minute. Wait a minute. Your cousin was working for Sarah Fleming? She was working for the woman I originally came to Asheville to find when I ended up meeting you. It truly is a small world. Arletha? Arletha? I believe Memory was the one who mentioned Arletha's name. Memory is Lena Patterson's mother, Sarah's daughter. You remember Lena Patterson and Theresa Jordan? Only it's

Lena Jordan now since she married her high school sweetheart Bishop Richard Jordan, and Theresa Greene who married Maurice Greene."

"I remember," Angela said. "I just didn't ask Gayle for the name of the woman who told her about Arletha. I'll call and ask her. She did tell me she was an in-home nurse to Sarah Fleming. It seems Sarah also left Gayle enough money to be able to take off a few months without having to worry about finances. Could it be that Sarah's daughter, Memory, was the one who told Gayle about Arletha?"

"It sounds like it to me. I know Memory was living here with a woman who put her out."

Angela began to shake a little. All of this was really starting to get to her. "Johnnie Mae, would you mind if I came over? I need to see you in person."

"No, I don't mind. Come on over. I would love to see you. It's been awhile."

Angela called Brent on his cell phone and told him she was going to visit Johnnie Mae for a little while. He was on his way home from the church where both he and Angela were employed.

"Baby, are you all right?" Brent asked. "You sound a little funny."

Angela smiled, thankful that Brent paid such close attention to her that he knew when something was a little off. "I'm fine," she said. "I'll tell you all about it when I get back home."

Angela arrived at Johnnie Mae's house. She hugged Princess Rose, who had come down from her room to greet her and then just as quickly had gone back up to her room. Angela held Isaiah and finished feeding him his favorite baby food, Hawaiian Delight, while Johnnie Mae went up to her room to find something.

Isaiah was such a happy child. Except for his smaller than normal size, attributed to his being born prematurely, you never would have been able to look at him and tell that he'd had such a rough start upon his entrance into this world. Angela was giving him a bottle when he fell asleep.

Johnnie Mae came back into the den. "He's asleep?" she said

as she smiled lovingly at him. She set a cigar box sealed with gray tape on the coffee table that was also an aquarium containing exotic fish inside of it. She carefully took Isaiah out of Angela's arms and placed him in a swinglike bassinet located in the den.

Angela looked at the cigar box. She remembered it well. Right before she died, her great-grandmother had asked her to give it to Johnnie Mae, which she'd done.

Johnnie Mae had opened it, but the things inside didn't seem to mean anything to anyone. Now here sat Angela with the box once again.

"Let's try and figure out what your great-grandmother may have been trying to tell us," Johnnie Mae said when she came over and sat next to Angela.

Angela opened the box and began pulling things out. She stopped at a birth certificate. It contained the name Rebecca. There was no mother or father's name listed.

"Rebecca was my mother's name," Angela said. She had seen the midwife's log of a female's birth. "That's her date of birth. I saw it in one of Great-granny's Bibles." There were other mementos in the box, along with three sepia photos and two old black-and-whites. "What's this?" Angela asked.

At the very bottom of the box was a notebook. Angela had to empty the box and turn it upside down to shake the notebook out.

"I didn't know that was in there," Johnnie Mae said as Angela held up the notebook. "It's a good thing you saw it."

Angela handed it to Johnnie Mae. "Great-granny left this box to you. Maybe it's something she wanted only you to see," Angela said.

Johnnie Mae took the notebook and opened it. Her instinct told her to look for a note addressed specifically to her. Sure enough, Pearl had written a note to Johnnie Mae dated just before she died. The note was safely tucked in the middle of the notebook.

It simply said, "Ms. Johnnie Mae, I know I have no right to ask this of you. But could you please help my Angel should she ever need it? And should she ever find herself needing help when it comes to her possibly trying to find or know more about her grandmother, my daughter, this is all I have left to offer in the way of help. I was wrong to have kept her from knowing about her grandmother. It's too late for me to fix it now. I know you helped one person once with something similar. Maybe you can help again. When you finish with this, please pass it along to my Angel."

Johnnie Mae scanned through the notebook as Angela sat patiently, not saying a word. She paused when reaching certain pages. Near the back of the notebook, Johnnie Mae found a single page torn out of a midwife's book. She unfolded it, read it, then folded it back. When she'd finished skimming and after reading many of Pearl's beautiful handwritten words, she closed the notebook and handed it to Angela.

"This belongs to you," Johnnie Mae said.

Angela took the notebook. "Thank you." She swallowed hard then spoke again. "If I may ask, what did you take out of the notebook?"

Johnnie Mae looked at it again then handed the paper to Angela.

Angela unfolded it and looked at it.

"It's your mother, Rebecca's, *actual* birth record. And this one happens to have a mother's name listed on it. Arletha." Arletha had been sixteen and unmarried. Her mother, Pearl Black Williams, had delivered the baby.

But even more telling in all of this was the listing of Arletha's last name. It was Black, Pearl's maiden name. That meant Pearl had Arletha before she married as well.

Chapter 28

The horse is prepared against the day of battle: but safety is of the Lord.

—Proverbs 21:31

Brent was waiting for Angela at the door. He kissed her as soon as she walked in. "I missed you," he said as he hugged her tight.

She gave him a weak smile. She didn't want him to let go of her just yet.

"What's wrong?" Brent asked.

"Nothing. I just came from seeing Johnnie Mae." Angela pulled herself away from his embrace, set the box and her purse down on the table in the foyer, and began taking off her coat. Brent helped her with her coat, then took it and hung it up for her.

He led her to the couch in the living room. "Okay," he said. "What's going on?"

Angela let out a sigh. "It's this whole grandmother thing. I was talking to Johnnie Mae and we started talking about Arletha. I told her about me having gone over to see her."

"Now, I told you I will be happy to hire someone to either check out this Arletha Brown or try and find out what happened with your grandmother. Whatever you want."

Angela smiled and looked lovingly into her husband's eyes. "I know. At this point, I'm not sure I should even keep pursuing this. When I went to Johnnie Mae's house, she gave me a box my great-grandmother had given to her. Inside it was my mother's birth record, a few photos, and a notebook my great-grandmother wrote in."

"Have you read what she wrote yet?" Brent asked.

"Not yet. That's what I'm praying about right now. I don't know if I should read it or just leave all of this alone. I mean, Great-granny went my entire life without ever saying a word about my grandmother, her daughter. And now, here I am starting this wonderful life journey with you, and what am I doing? I'm chasing a ghost."

"That's a bit harsh, wouldn't you say?" Brent asked.

"No, I don't think so. Look, honestly, I don't know whether Arletha is alive or dead. If this Arletha Brown really is my grandmother, she's made it abundantly clear she wants nothing to do with me. At least, not in that capacity. Let's say we find out she really is my grandmother. What am I supposed to do then? Make her love me? Make her want to have something to do with me?" Angela shook her head. "No. I'm not going to put us through this. Before I heard about this, I was fine. I'm not going to allow something like this to ruin our lives just because *I* don't know when to walk away. I'm not."

"Your wanting to find your grandmother, or at least to find out what happened, is not going to ruin our lives," Brent said. "So what are you going to do about that notebook your great-grandmother left?"

Angela shook her head again, then shrugged. "I'll read through it. If you knew my great-grandmother, you'd know how wise and funny she could be. I know whatever is in there will be interesting. But unless there's something that points me to a definitive answer when it comes to Arletha, I'm not going to put us through this. That's it." Angela laid her head on his shoulder.

"Well, you know I'm here for you," Brent said, snuggling up with his wife.

"I know."

After a few minutes of holding her, he looked at her. "We need to buy a Christmas tree."

"Yeah," she smiled. "Our first Christmas as husband and wife."

"Are you excited?"

Angela pushed him. "You know I am."

"So do we get a live tree or an artificial one?"

"Live," Angela said. "We can put it in here. It's going to be a great Christmas this year. Let's have a Christmas party and invite our friends."

He looked at her and smiled as he played with her hair. "Sure, let's have a party. It's going to be a great Christmas. So what do you want for Christmas this year?"

"Oh, so you're playing Santa Claus now?"

He grabbed her and pulled her onto his lap like Santa Claus. "Ho, ho, ho. What do you want for Christmas, little girl?"

Angela bit down on her bottom lip, then leaned in and kissed him softly. "All I want for Christmas is you," she said.

"Oooh," Brent said. "I see you're being a naughty little girl."

"No. I think I'm being very, very good, myself."

He made a slight jolly sound. "You know, you're absolutely right." He stood up, holding her tightly in his arms.

"What are you doing?" Angela screamed.

"Taking my wife to dinner," he said, then headed with her up the stairs to their bedroom.

"Excuse me, but the kitchen's that way," Angela said.

"Yeah, but I fixed dinner and we're having it in our room."

"Well, all righty then, Mr. Underwood. You're the man."

"Oh, I love the sound of that, Mrs. Underwood."

Chapter 29

He hath made every thing beautiful in his time: also he hath set the world in their heart, so that no man can find out the work that God maketh from the beginning to the end.

—Ecclesiastes 3:11

Marcus waited in his car for Sasha to get home. He was supposed to pick up Aaliyah on the first and third Fridays of the month, at six o'clock. It was now seven fifteen. He had called Sasha on her cell phone and she'd said she was almost there. He knew she wasn't being truthful. He couldn't say where she was, but she wasn't on her way.

At seven thirty, she drove up and pulled into her garage. Marcus got out of his car and walked into the opened garage. Aaliyah unbuckled her seat belt as soon as she saw her daddy coming her way.

"Daddy!" Aaliyah said as she held her arms up for him to pick her up.

"Hi, Pumpkin. How's Daddy's little girl?"

"I'm fine," Aaliyah said.

Marcus got Aaliyah's backpack out of the car, then closed the door.

Sasha was closing her door and walking toward the trunk of the car.

"Do you need any help?" Marcus asked Sasha.

"No, I got it. But thanks," Sasha said. She grabbed a Saks Fifth Avenue shopping bag out of the trunk and made her way to unlock the door to the house.

They went inside. Sasha clicked on the light. The kitchen was a slight mess.

"I don't even want to hear it," Sasha said to Marcus before he could say a word.

"Hear what?" Marcus asked, setting Aaliyah down gently on the floor.

"I don't want to hear about me being late and you having to wait. I don't want to hear about the kitchen not being clean. And I *don't* want to hear a word about that bag I took out of my car and what I may have bought. I'm not married to you, and I *don't* have to answer to you anymore."

"Whoa, calm down. I can say something about having to wait all this time. As for your kitchen, it's your kitchen," Marcus said. "I just came to pick up my daughter."

Sasha sat down at the kitchen table and put her hand up to her face as though she were crying. "I just can't take this anymore!" Sasha said.

"I have to use the bathroom," Aaliyah said as she patted her daddy on the leg to get his attention. "Daddy, walk me to the bathroom, please. It's dark back there."

Marcus looked at Sasha to be sure she was okay. "Come on," he said to Aaliyah as they walked to the bathroom closest to the kitchen of the home they all once shared.

When he came back, Sasha was still sitting at the kitchen table. Marcus wasn't sure what he should do at this point. He hadn't planned on sitting out in the driveway for over an hour. And now Sasha was acting like he had just dropped by to chat instead of coming to get Aaliyah for their weekend visit.

"Where's Aaliyah's weekend bag?" he asked.

Sasha made a visible show of sighing, then looked up at him. "I'm obviously hurting right now and all you can ask about is some *stupid* bag?"

"Are you in physical pain?"

She stood up. "No, Marcus. I'm not in *physical* pain. There are other pains besides physical, you know. I'm tired of my stupid job. I wish I could quit that place. In fact, they got on my nerves so bad today I left work early."

Marcus frowned, especially when he thought about how he had sat outside waiting for her. "You left work early?"

She brushed past him on her way to the refrigerator. "Aaliyah, do you want some juice?"

"Yes!" Aaliyah said. "Apple juice, please."

Sasha opened the refrigerator door and looked inside. "We don't have any more apple juice."

"All right," Aaliyah said a little disappointed. "Orange juice then."

Sasha reached in and took out a plastic bottle. "We don't have any orange juice either. You can have some cola." Sasha went to the cabinet and took down one of Aaliyah's cups that came with its own lid and had a place for a straw.

"I have juice at my house," Marcus said. He didn't really like giving Aaliyah a lot of sugary caffeine drinks like that, especially near bedtime. Sasha knew that.

Sasha poured the cola in the cup, located a straw in the drawer and stuck it in the cup, then handed it to Aaliyah. "Well, she's thirsty now," Sasha said. She then took down a glass, poured some cola for herself, and began drinking it.

Marcus could see Sasha was deliberately trying to aggravate him. "Where's Aaliyah's weekend bag?" he asked again.

"I haven't packed it yet," Sasha said. "I just told you I had a bad day. On top of that, I had to pay the day care people some extra money I didn't have all because I was late picking Aaliyah up—"

"You were late picking her up? But you just said you left work early."

"Don't *start* with me, Marcus. I'm not in the mood tonight. I'm close to the edge. First, it was the people at work. Then I go shopping to try and make myself feel better, and I couldn't get the dress I wanted at Saks because my credit cards are maxed out."

Marcus looked at the bag sitting on the table she'd brought in.

She followed his eyes, went over, picked up the bag, and opened it up. "This," she said, taking a brown colored top out, "is not what I really wanted. It was the only thing on the sale rack I could afford. I didn't even like it all that much."

"Then why would you buy something you don't like?" Marcus asked.

"Because I was in Saks. I wasn't going to leave without something. Didn't you just hear me? It was the only thing I could afford." She shoved the top into his chest. "If you gave me more money than what the court ordered you to pay for child support, maybe I wouldn't be struggling the way that I am." She walked out of the room and headed toward the stairs to go to Aaliyah's room.

Marcus followed her. "Hold up," he said, catching up with her. "You were the one who wanted a divorce. Fought for it, in fact. A divorce was the last thing I ever wanted. But you wanted to hang out with your girlfriends every weekend. You wanted to be free to, let's see, how did you put it exactly? Oh, yeah, you wanted to be free to explore other options. You wanted to see what you were missing. Then you and your mother teamed up to get me out of the picture. I fought for our marriage, Sasha, and you know that. I believe your mother's and your exact words were that you didn't need me. You could do fine by yourself. Look, I pay my child support, happily, and on time. I provide a place for our child to come to when she visits with me. I buy her clothes and other things even though I pay child support. So don't try to put your bad decisions off on me."

Sasha walked up to Marcus. "I thought it was going to be different. I know you helped me around the house when we were married. I know you brought your money home and that you were a wonderful provider. Yes, I admit, I shouldn't have listened to my mother. And honestly, had my father not died when he did, maybe things wouldn't be so bad for me and my mother right now." She poked her index finger into Marcus's chest. "But now I'm having a hard time. You know my money is tight. You know it's stressful raising a child by yourself."

"You were not *before* you left me, and you are not *now*, raising Aaliyah by yourself. I do more than my part, and you know that."

"Yeah, but you're not here in the mornings to help me get her ready. You don't have to go completely out of your way to pick her up from school or after-school day care. And then when I do find a guy I like, he turns out to be a jerk," Sasha said, rambling all over the place. "And the next one is an even bigger jerk. I have all of these *stupid* bills to pay. When I was married to you and I worked, I could use my money however I wanted to." She poked Marcus again. The force of that poke caused him to take a step back.

"My daddy took care of me and my mother like we were queens. When I married you, you did your best financially, but I still had my daddy in the background to make sure I never wanted for anything," Sasha said. "Now, my daddy's gone." She poked him again. "And the money we all thought he had turned out to be bills stacked to the high heavens. And the million-dollar insurance policy he had for years? Well, it turns out he had allowed it to lapse a year earlier. So when he died, there was nothing but debt and creditors. My mother didn't even have the money to bury him. She had to ask folks to pitch in just so he could have a halfway decent burial."

"I know," Marcus said. "I gave your mother money to help out with his burial, even though she'd treated me with such disrespect and animosity. Even though she had been pushing so hard for you to leave me, then divorce me. Even though she knew the truth behind what was going on between us."

"And what truth was that, Marcus?" She poked him in the chest again. "What truth, Marcus?" She poked him again and caused him to stumble once more.

"Stop, Sasha," Marcus said in an even and calm voice. "Just go get Aaliyah's things so I can go."

"Stop what?" she said as she shoved his left shoulder. "What am I doing, Marcus?" she asked.

"You know what you're doing," Marcus said. "I didn't come here wanting any trouble with you. I just came to get my daughter."

"You mean our daughter?" She shoved his shoulder again. "What's the matter, Marcus?"

"Sasha, please don't start this. Okay, you had a bad day. I get it. You're frustrated. I get that. But you need to calm down and think about what you really want, then move in that direction." Marcus stepped away so she couldn't touch him anymore.

"I'm not frustrated. I'm tired! Tired of no-good men who promise me things but don't deliver. 'Yes, Sasha, I love you.' 'Yes, I'll do anything for you.' 'Of course I want to be with you. I want to take care of you.' Blah, blah, blah, wah, wah, wah. 'Stop it, Sasha.' 'You're just mean, Sasha.' 'That's why nobody *likes* you, Sasha.' Well, I'm tired. I'm tired of all of you!" Her voice exploded.

"And that goes for my boyfriend Memphis. Oh wait. Let me say that again: my ex-boyfriend Memphis. That goes for my mother. My cousin Thelma with her phony, two-faced, slutty self. Always after somebody else's man. And that was fine when she was going outside of the family to do it, but this sleeping with a guy you know your family member has been with is just plain nasty. Then you're going to tell me you did me a favor? A favor? That at least you exposed him for the no-good dog that he is."

She came over to Marcus, who instinctively backed away. He knew how Sasha was when she went into her fits of rage. She would hit and throw things. And if you tried to hold her while she was having these fits, she would accuse you of physically abusing her, although she was the one doing the abusing.

Sasha got that from her mother. And when Sasha decided she needed to tarnish Marcus's image in the eyes of those who looked so favorably and lovingly upon him, she accused *him* of abusing *her*. She had even called the police on him, twice, just to make it look as though she was telling the truth.

When the police arrived, they saw the house in disarray. But it was from Sasha's outrage. She claimed he had hit her. He hadn't. It was he who had been verbally abused by her, then physically attacked. All he had done was try to cover his face from her blows. She had swung at him so hard that when he moved out of the way, she fell to the floor, hitting her arm on the table. She claimed he had pushed her. Thanks to her fall, she now had a very nice bruise to prove abuse.

Sasha knew the truth. Sasha's mother knew the truth. Marcus's mother knew the truth as well, which was why she had become so angry with Sasha at the end. But more important, God knew the truth. And that was something Sasha knew that hung over her head. God knew. Marcus wouldn't ever tell anyone that his wife was abusing him; the way she would tell him how inadequate he was as a person; how, compared to other men out there, he was not worth the time of day; that she had only married him because she felt sorry for him; that he was a loser. No, he couldn't tell people it was she who beat up on him as he did the gentlemanly thing and refrained from hitting a girl back.

That was why lately Sasha felt she was never going to get ahead in life. She knew she had sown seeds of lies and deceit. And even though at times it might not have looked like it, she was going to reap a harvest from her sown seeds. One day, all of this would come back on her.

All Marcus could do was to forgive her and to pray for her. He had fasted on behalf of her while they were married and during the time she was in the process of getting the divorce. He prayed that God would break the generational curse Sasha was under. After they were no longer married, he then began to pray mightily for his daughter. That generational curse had to be broken. And if he couldn't help Sasha break here, then it would have to end with their daughter.

Now Sasha was upset, and all Marcus wanted to do was to get his daughter and be on his way. But Sasha was wound up from all of her frustrations. Based on what she was spewing as she came at him, her mother had also done something to hurt or disappoint her. No surprise there.

Marcus knew how much Stella Bradford had already hurt her daughter. He had even tried talking to his mother-in-law when he and Sasha were married about how much her actions hurt. Stella cared mostly about Stella, although from what Marcus could see, Stella did, in her own way, love her daughter. But for some reason, she didn't want her daughter to be happy. Sasha didn't seem to get that. Or maybe she just wanted her mother to love her so badly that she would do anything to feel that love.

And if that meant getting rid of Marcus because Stella believed the best way to hurt Marcus was to take away the thing he loved the most—his family—then that's what Sasha would do. And she did. Sasha's fabrications of abuse had given her mother the one thing Sasha knew would make her mother go along with her leaving Marcus. Now that Sasha was without Marcus, Stella was doing what she had always done when it came to her daughter: leaving her to fend for herself.

The only difference was that whereas in the past Sasha had her father to make everything all right, now he was gone. There was no money to make things better. Now Sasha was upset with Marcus because she knew he was doing well financially. She felt he should step up and fill the gap her father had left in her life. And had she known her father would die within six months of her divorcing Marcus, and had she known he didn't have a bundle of money sitting there waiting for them upon his death, she *never* would have let a good man like Marcus go. Never. Mother or no mother. Never.

Now she was stuck with smooth-talking wannabees who were looking for a woman to take care of them, or at the very least take care of themselves so they wouldn't have to. Sasha knew there were still some good men out there. But finding the good ones was not as easy as she had first thought.

Sasha was hurting, and hurting people take out their hurt on others. Marcus understood this. But all he wanted on this night was to get his daughter and have peace in doing it.

Trying to make things better, trying to calm Sasha down, Marcus said, "I tell you what. Why don't you just go sit down, and I'll go up and get Aaliyah's things?"

Sasha looked at him, pursed her lips, and then popped them open. "All of her things are dirty. I haven't had time to do a wash. I'm telling you, I'm tired, Marcus. This is not how my life is supposed to be right now. I need something good to happen for me. Do you hear what I'm saying?"

Marcus cautiously walked toward her. "I'll tell you what. I'll take her dirty clothes home with me and wash them."

"Oh, yeah. Right. Then what does that make me look like?"

"It doesn't make you look like anything. You wash her clothes all the time."

"Except when we were married and you would wash all of our clothes." Sasha seemed to start winding down. She went over and flopped down on the couch.

Marcus looked and saw Aaliyah standing there watching. He felt so bad for her. He could still remember how he felt when he would hear his mother and father arguing. He smiled at Aaliyah and beckoned for her to come to him. He gave her a big hug. "Aaliyah and I are going to go upstairs and get all of her dirty clothes, put them in a bag, carry them to my house, and I'll wash them all. She and I are going to have lots of fun this weekend. Aren't we, sweetheart?"

She smiled, then nodded.

"Where are your garbage bags?" Marcus asked Sasha.

Sasha got up. "I'll get one. That's the least I can do since I'm such a *trifling* mother."

Marcus touched her on the shoulder. "You're not trifling," he said.

She smiled, went to the kitchen, and came back with a big black garbage bag. "Thank you," she said. "Thank you for everything. And don't worry about me. I'm going to be all right."

"Of course, you are. We've all had bad days. At some point in our lives, we all have a bad day."

Chapter 30

*Whoso boasteth himself of a false gift is like clouds
and wind without rain.*

—Proverbs 25:14

I was looking forward to Christmas this year. Marcus and I had really gotten close in a short amount of time. In fact, we were spending as much time together as possible whenever we could. I tried not to feel *too* left out when he got Aaliyah on his assigned weekends. I knew how important it was for him to spend time with her without feeling like he needed to show balance when we were together. Aaliyah was his child. And honestly, at this stage of the game, I wouldn't want to be with any man who did any less than Marcus was doing for his child.

We would talk on the phone after she went to bed. Occasionally, the three of us would all do something together. But it was important for him to give Aaliyah father-daughter time, and I totally respected and admired him for that.

My brother, Diddy-bo, came to see me. He and his ex-wife are always at each other. She fights him about picking up his son, Desmond, when it's his turn to get him. There were a few times early on when he didn't make his child support payment. She would keep him from seeing Desmond until he got caught up. It wasn't his fault he had lost his job and didn't have the money. But that didn't matter to her. She treated Desmond as though he were some type of collateral at a pawn shop.

"When you have my money, then you can see your son," Bernadette told him. "No money, no son."

Diddy-bo was so frustrated. "I don't know how I ended up marrying that woman in the first place," he said when he was at the end of his rope. "She could be the poster child for why one shouldn't have sex before marriage. If I hadn't gotten her pregnant, I would have had time to learn what kind of person she really was. I assure you, I never would have married her."

But Diddy-bo really loved his son. He tried explaining to Bernadette that he just didn't have the money right then. He was trying to find a job, and he would pay her every cent he owed when he did. He told her it was just as important that he be in his child's life as it was for him to give her money. "Where's the hope in all of this?"

"I'm sorry, but this boy likes to eat," Bernadette said. "He can't live off hope. Instead of worrying about spending time with him, you need to be worrying about finding my money and paying me. I tell you what. When you get the cash, you can see your son. Until then, you'd better *hope* I don't file something with the court and have them come pick you up and put you in jail for failure to pay your child support bill."

I couldn't believe it when Diddy-bo told me all of this. It made me so mad I wanted to call Bernadette up and tell her a thing or two.

"Do you know how many women wish the fathers of their children even *wanted* to be in their life? Do you know how what you're doing, in the name of the almighty dollar, is affecting your child?" But Diddy-bo told me I had better not call Bernadette and say anything to her. He would work it out.

I suppose he must have worked something out because a month later, he had Desmond. And he still hadn't been able to find a job. I understand it from both sides. Nae-nae has three children and not one of her children's three daddies wants to have anything to do with them.

"I don't care about the money so much," Nae-nae has said to me on more than one occasion. "My children are hurting because they think their daddies don't care about them. I even told them I would bring the children to them, but they don't care. All they're interested in is chasing another skirt and in the process end up making more babies they don't plan to take care of or show any love."

I don't know why Nae-nae seems to keep picking the wrong men. She and I have discussed that. I suppose I can't talk since my track record is not all that great either. At least, it wasn't until now.

Nae-nae met Marcus the other night when he came over. She had asked me to keep her children while she went out on a date with some guy she had met during the week. She was supposed to have picked them up that Friday night after the date was over. I didn't see Nae-nae until Saturday evening. She at least had the decency to call this time. That's one of the biggest problems I have with her. She will ask you to do something and just take for granted you have nothing else to do but wait on her. Then you end up having to track her down, especially if you've agreed to keep her children. She does it almost every time without fail.

So Saturday evening, when she finally came to pick up her children, she got to meet Marcus. He and I were going to a Christmas party Angela and Brent were having at their house. I couldn't wait to see their house. I'd heard so much about it.

Angela was still at her apartment when she was planning the wedding. Brent had built this house over a year ago, although Angela did tell me she had a hand in planning it. This was even before they started dating. I love a good romance story. And it certainly sounded like that's what Angela and Brent's relationship was. How romantic is it to lay out the plans for a house with a man you're not even dating at the time, end up marrying him, and then live in that same house later?

I had told Nae-nae when I agreed to children-sit that I had a date with Marcus on Saturday night. At the time, I hadn't thought she would take that to mean she could stay out on her date until my date began. I was so upset with her when she got there.

"Well, don't you look pretty in that black sparkly dress? Oooh, just look at you," Nae-nae said as she strolled through my front door. "Girl, stop looking at me like that. Now you know you can never stay mad at me."

"And you know you need to stop all your sinning," I said, keeping my voice down even though the kids were in the back watching television.

"Who said I was sinning?"

"Oh, so you want me to believe you went out on a date last night, you're just now coming back some twenty-four hours later, and all the two of you did was sit and watch the moon and the stars? Then later you watched the sun come up, and the sun go down again because you enjoyed seeing it so much the first time around and that's why you couldn't find your way home? That's the reason you're just now getting here wearing what you had on yesterday? Is that what you want me to think?"

Nae-nae gave me one of her let's-not-go-there looks. "Now I know you're not trying to judge me. You know what the Bible says about judging folks. The way you and Marcus seem to be hanging out with each other, I know you don't expect *me* to believe you and he are just holding hands and watching the stars and the moon yourself." She grunted. "You're talking to your girl here—Nae-nae. This is Nae-nae you're talking to. I know you. Of all the people who know you, *I* know you. And although you've kept mum about what you're actually doing with this Marcus fellow, I know you, Melissa."

"I told you, Nae-nae. I'm not doing that anymore. I rededicated my life to Christ, and I'm trying to live according to his Word. And that means no fornication."

"Uh-huh," Nae-nae said as she gathered up the bags with her children's things in them so she could take them to the car. "I see your mouth moving, but like I said, you're talking to me. This your girl you're talking to. You remember: your running partner? The one you tell all your deepest, darkest secrets to? That is, you used to tell before you starting hanging out with this Marcus fellow."

"I'm a Christian, and I'm not playing with this now. I'm sold out for Jesus, and I'm serious about my walk with the Lord."

"Do you know how many Christians run their mouths about being saved, sanctified, filled with the Holy Ghost, and are living in sin just as big as they want to? Do you know how many of them are sneaking around doing what they do? Trying to keep everybody else from knowing what they're really doing behind closed doors while seeming to forget that what *we* down here think really doesn't count? But the Lord up above sees them, and He's the one who matters. Then they have the nerve to say that all you have to do is ask the Lord to forgive you, and He's just and will forgive you."

"Well, if you confess your sins and ask for forgiveness, He *will* forgive you," I said.

"You're missing my point. If a Christian knows it's wrong before they do it, then why do it and then turn around and ask forgiveness for it? You knew it was wrong *before* you did it, *while* you were doing it, then after you finish, you want God to wipe it clean?"

"I thought you were a Christian."

"According to the criteria, I am. But I know I'm messing up so I try to keep a low profile so people won't confuse me with what a Christian is *supposed* to be," Nae-nae said. "In other words, the way some of these so-called Christians have messed me up when I watch them act one way at church and entirely different once they leave the church building, I've decided I don't want to be that kind of stumbling block to other folks. I'd rather work on being better, then after I get myself together, I can be a real testament to the Lord."

"I have problems with that philosophy personally," I said.

"What philosophy?"

"That you have to get yourself together first. That's why we have the Holy Spirit inside us, to direct us and guide us along the way. God knows we're going to mess up. And no, He doesn't want us out there messing up deliberately. But not professing you're a Christian just because you know you're messing up seems a little like a cop-out to me. It's almost like you're denying Christ."

"Well," Nae-nae said, "I don't want to be out there telling folks, 'Look at me, I'm a Christian. Don't pay attention to what I'm doing. Just hear me when I tell you I'm a Christian. I know I'm not living right. But God knows we're only human. You shouldn't be following me anyway. I mess up, I ask for forgiveness, that's the way we Christians do this. Come on in, the water's fine,'" Nae-nae said, mocking some folks we all know.

"Nope, not me," she said. "Now, I did go to the altar and ask Jesus to come into my heart. But there are a lot of jagged edges, a lot of impurities in my life. I am trying, though, Peaches. I also know that the way I'm living is not a testament to the Lord. I for one just don't want to be a hypocrite. If other folks do and it doesn't bother them, then more power to them. That's between them and their God."

"I hear what you're saying, and I know where you're coming from, but God will do the refining. We can't make ourselves better. When we become saved, we aren't instantly transformed. It's a process with much prayer involved." My doorbell rang and I looked at my watch. "That's Marcus," I said. "He's here."

"Well, let me get these children and get out of your way." She stood there without moving.

I headed toward the door, then stopped and looked at her. "I thought you were going to get the children."

"Not before I meet this man who has seemingly changed your life," Nae-nae said as she smoothed down the sides of her hair. "I mean, he's got you smiling, acting all giddy and everything. Got you keeping things from me, your girl. I want to see this man, and I don't want my children all over me when I do." She made a circular motion with her hand. "Hurry up."

I shook my head and laughed at her. I smoothed my dress down once more to make sure I was straight, then I put on my best smile and opened the door.

"Wow!" Marcus said. "Wow."

I blushed, then heard the clearing of a throat behind me. "Come in," I said. I heard the throat clear once more. As soon as Marcus was inside, I turned toward Nae-nae. "Marcus, this is my friend, Nae-nae. Nae-nae, this is Marcus."

"Pleased to meet you," Marcus said, extending his hand to Nae-nae.

"Oh, the pleasure is all mine," Nae-nae said.

"Well, Nae-nae was just about to leave. She came by to get her little darlings, isn't that right?"

Nae-nae smiled, then nodded. "Oh, absolutely. I was just about to go get them and be on my way." Nae-nae shook his hand once more. "Now you be good to my friend. She's one in a million," Nae-nae said, her statement catching me a little off guard.

She got her children and headed out the door. "You two have a great time," she said. I was closing the door behind them when Nae-nae turned and mouthed the words, "Call me." She made a hand gesture to let me know she thought Marcus was scorching.

I hadn't thought about him being hot, but then it occurred to me that he wasn't wearing his glasses when he came in. Without his glasses, he really did look different. I don't know why his not wearing his glasses mattered so much to me. There was definitely something going on with my thought process.

Marcus really was a nice looking-guy. Other women saw that as I began to take notice when we were at the Christmas party. I suppose I saw him in a different light. Maybe it was because of how we'd met. Then after that, I really got to know who he was on the inside. I suppose I wasn't as objective when it came to Marcus. Maybe he wasn't as nerdy as I'd originally believed.

As Nae-nae indicated, he was hot. And for whatever reason, in a very short time, he had fallen in love with me. And yes, I had fallen in love with him, too. We had a wonderful time at the Christmas party, a wonderful time for Christmas, and a wonderful New Year. And to think, I almost missed all of this.

Marcus was truly a blessing from God. For once, I was actually looking forward to next days and to holidays. And the next special day approaching was Valentine's Day.

"Don't make any plans for Valentine's Day night, okay?" he said in mid-January. "I have something special planned for us."

I smiled. "Okay." My stomach felt a little giddy after he said that.

A strange thing about your stomach: joy, giddiness, and excitement can feel the same as fear and anxiety. I knew something special was coming for Valentine's Day. I just wasn't positive what the feeling in the pit of my stomach was trying to tell me.

Chapter 31

*My son, attend unto my wisdom, and bow thine ear
to my understanding.*

—Proverbs 5:1

Marcus had bought an engagement ring for Melissa. He had thought about just asking her and letting her pick out the ring she wanted, but he didn't feel that was special enough for someone like her. He wanted to have a ring when he asked her to marry him. He would let her know that if she didn't like it, she could exchange it for one she did like.

He had really gotten to know Melissa well. She was smart and funny, qualities she often attributed to him. They were opposites when it came to some things. He loved working with numbers and hated being creative; with her it was the other way around. When it came to interpersonal attributes, he was more analytical, she was more of a driver. They were polar opposites on the interpersonal chart. And yes, there were times when they had to find a middle ground so as not to drive each other nuts.

Analytical people tend to speak slowly while analyzing the data even before they allow a word to come out of their mouths. That causes them to take longer to tell a story or give information. And when they do give the information, it's normally a play-by-play of every detail they have imported into their system. Driver personalities are the complete opposite.

They want the information fast and to the point. Whatever they do or say is right on it. They like to hurry up, get it done, and get it out of the way. "Next!"

So there were times when Marcus might be saying something and Melissa would patiently try to wait, almost pulling him, internally, to get the story out. And if Melissa told Marcus something, he would want more details and made her go back and tell him everything so he could analyze even the minutest detail.

When Marcus first recognized they were having a communication problem, he analyzed and determined what was really getting on their nerves. They talked about how different they were from each other and how that was not a bad thing. Then they talked it out to see how their differences could complement each other.

After they figured it out, whenever it was taking Marcus too long to either tell a story or explain something, or if she knew beforehand that she didn't have time to hear the longer, more detailed analogy, Melissa would just say, "Give me the short version, please?"

If Melissa wanted to plow through something off the cuff, or if she looked like she was about to dive headfirst without having properly analyzed something, Marcus would say, "Let's map this out a little better. Tell me some of the parts I'm missing."

It worked. Melissa's event planning business now had a business and a marketing plan. In fact, she was now estimating that in two to three years she might be able to quit her job and really be able to do this full time. Marcus, on the other hand, grew into a better networker than he'd ever been before. Instead of boring people with an overload of data, statistics, charts, and figures, he now mixed in a lot of the fun side of himself.

It had even helped Marcus with his relationship with Sasha. She didn't seem to be as hostile toward him as she'd been in the past.

Sasha had asked Marcus about possibly investing in something she had heard about and thought was a good deal.

"This would be a good way for me to make some extra money

quickly. I could possibly quit my job and be a happier person," Sasha said. It was the weekend of Dr. Martin Luther King Jr.'s birthday holiday, and Marcus had come to get Aaliyah.

"You need to be careful when it comes to those get-rich-quick schemes. You know what they say about things sounding too good to be true," Marcus said.

Normally a response in that vein would have set Sasha off immediately. She hated that Marcus thought he knew everything. Yes, it had been his smarts that had attracted her to him in the first place. She wished sometimes he would just turn it off, only this time, she didn't get upset with him.

"I know. That's why I wanted you to look at it and tell me what you thought about it. Who knows, if you think it's good, it may be something you're interested in getting into." She handed him a package for his review. "I got this at a meeting I went to. The person there is already making tons of money. It only cost me one hundred and forty nine dollars to get started."

Marcus shook his head. "I don't do multilevel marketing, at least not this kind."

"You haven't even looked at it," Sasha said. "I saw copies of checks these people are receiving, and honestly, they blew me away. The product is something I believe people need and will buy. And you don't have to sell the products to make big bucks."

"I know. The scheme is to get people to sign up and then for them to get others to sign up. It's great if you're in on the ground floor since you'll get something from all the people who come in below you." He flipped through the brochure on top. "Don't get me wrong, there are some people who do quite well with these things. I just know it's not something I would be interested in or ever do."

"So you don't think it's something I should have done?" Sasha asked.

Marcus was a little shocked. Sasha had never been this easy to hear him and take his recommendations without her arguing about it and accusing him of trying to hold her down or keep her back because he didn't want her to succeed.

"Actually, if you want to try it since you've already paid your money, then there's no reason not to," Marcus said, closing the brochure and putting it down. "But if you had asked me before you signed up, I would have said what I just said, and I would have advised you to do something else with your money."

"Well, my mom was the one who invited me to the little party where they talked about this." Sasha gathered up the information. "She signed up and was trying to get more people under her. You of all people know I'm no salesperson, that's for sure. But then that lady started talking about how much money you can make. How easily you can do it just by adding ten people under you who will add ten people under them, and it just keeps growing until before you know it, the checks are pouring in."

"You need to be careful, Sasha. You know how you can be sometimes. You have to think things through and not just dive into something just because it sounds good at first."

Sasha smiled. "Thanks. You're right. And I will heed your advice and make sure I think about things even more before I leap."

Marcus was puzzled but pleasantly surprised at how calm Sasha was about what he had said. "You're welcome. Glad I could help."

"I want Aaliyah to take piano lessons," Sasha said.

"Oh, that would be great," Marcus said. "She loved playing that toy piano I bought her when she was two, and then that little keyboard after that."

"Yeah. I thought so, too. Only thing is: if she takes lessons and doesn't have her own piano, I mean a real piano, here to practice on, it's almost like her lessons would be in vain."

"I agree."

Sasha turned more toward him. "I saw this great piano the other day. Actually, a lady at work owns it, and she needs to sell it in a hurry. She's asking only thirty-two thousand for it, which is a real steal."

"Excuse me?" Marcus said. "We're talking about a piano, not a luxury car, right?"

"Marcus, see, that's what used to make me so mad at you. This is not funny, so I wish you wouldn't joke about it. We're talking about your daughter's future here. Who knows where this piano may lead in her career later? If she decides to be really active in beauty pageants, having a talent like playing a piano can come in handy."

Marcus put his hand up as though he were stopping traffic. "Hold up. Hold up. Now, I'm all for Aaliyah taking piano lessons, but thirty-two thousand dollars for a piano and a used one at that"—he began shaking his head—"I'm not going for that."

"But it's a grand piano, Marcus. A grand piano."

"I'm sure it is grand for that price."

Sasha sighed. "No, Marcus. Not grand as an adjective, grand as in the type." She got up, went to the kitchen, then came back with a flyer and sat back down next to him. "Ebony Steinway M, which if new would sell for around fifty thousand. Thirty-two thousand is a steal."

Marcus started chuckling. "Yeah, I agree with you about that. That's a steal all right."

"See, that's why you make me so mad." She pouted and let the flyer float to the table. "My father bought me a Steinway M when I was young. And he was more than happy to do it. There was nothing too good for his little girl. Whatever he could do to give me the best, my daddy did it. I would think you'd want to do the same for your little girl."

"I do want Aaliyah to have nice things, but I'm not going to put myself in the poorhouse in order to do that," Marcus said. "Aaliyah is only five. She's not scheduled to play in Carnegie Hall, at least not yet. If you really want her to have a piano, I will be more than happy to check around music stores and buy her one. But I'm not planning on spending any more than eight thousand dollars for a piano."

"Just don't get a cheap one," Sasha said. "Look for name brands like Steinway, Yamaha, even a Kawai is all right. Just don't buy a cheap piano. I don't want people coming in my house and seeing an off-brand name on our piano. My mother would never let me live that down. Besides, I want Aaliyah learning to appreciate the finer things of life when at all possible."

"All right. I'll be sure to ask for a name-brand piano." Marcus picked up the flyer. "I'll take this with me to help guide me." He folded the flyer and slipped it into his shirt pocket.

"You know, you *could* just give that money to me and let me handle it. I mean, I already know what to look for. That would keep you from having to get all bogged down trying to find one."

"It's not a problem. When I find one, I'll buy it and have it delivered here."

Sasha reached into his shirt pocket and slowly pulled the flyer out. "Seriously, you could give me the money and I could go online, check with eBay and see what they have. I hear there are some great deals on that Web site. If it costs less than what you give me for it, I'll return the rest to you. This way it won't interfere with you and your new girlfriend."

That statement made Marcus sit up even straighter. "My new girlfriend?"

"Yes," Sasha said as she patted his chest where the flyer had been. "Aaliyah told me you have a lady friend, and it sounds like you've seen her more than a few times. Dancing at a wedding, her coming over to your place, you going over to hers. Miss Melissa," Sasha said, making a hissing sound with the "s" in the words Miss and Melissa.

Marcus shrugged and wrinkled his nose.

Sasha started playing with her hair, taking a strand and twisting it around her index finger, then pulling her finger out of it. "So . . . do you like her?"

He tilted his head a little. "Yeah, I do."

"A lot?"

He nodded as he pursed his lips tight, then relaxed them. "You could say that."

"Do you love her?"

He shook his head. "I don't think that's any of your business."

She moved in a little closer. "Well, Memphis and I are talking a little bit again. He claims Thelma set him up. And because I know my cousin all too well, I know there's probably some truth to that. They both claim they had been drinking." She hunched her shoulders. "I don't know. What do you think?"

Marcus was starting to feel really uneasy with Sasha leaning in so close to him all of a sudden. He stood up. "I don't know this Memphis character, but personally, Sasha, I think you can have and deserve better."

Sasha stood up in front of Marcus. "I did have better. I was just too foolish to know it." She held the folded flyer in her hand and carefully and slowly slid it back into his shirt pocket before patting it. "You know what I mean?" Sasha said.

"I will see what I can find in the way of a piano for Aaliyah." Marcus then started toward the stairway. "I'll let you know when I've gotten it so we can coordinate a good time for it to be delivered. Can you get Aaliyah for me now?"

Sasha came over next to him. "Sure thing," she said. "But if you want me to handle getting the piano for you, you just let me know. I can be quite resourceful. Of course, you already know that."

"And you need to be careful on the Internet and especially on eBay. I hope you know you can't always believe everything you see there. I hope you know that."

"Oh, I know that," she said, smiling right before she sashayed up the stairs. "Aaliyah," she said, "Daddy's here for you." She turned around, smiled at Marcus, then turned the corner. "Aaliyah!"

Chapter 32

Lo, children are a heritage of the Lord: and the fruit of the womb is his reward.

—Psalm 127:3

I spoke with Angela again, checking to see how married life was treating her after three months. She told me they were expecting a baby. I was *too* happy for her. She asked me not to tell Marcus yet because she had just told Brent and she wanted Brent to be the one to tell him.

"Oh, Angela, that's great! Congratulations to both of you," I said. "Of course, I won't say anything to Marcus. Wow, that is so exciting!"

"So tell me. What's happening with you and Marcus?" Angela asked. "Are wedding bells about to ring in the near future for the two of you?"

I wanted to tell her that I thought we might be moving in that direction, but I decided not to. "Nothing so far. We're just spending a lot of time together, getting to know more about each other. And his daughter is a little doll."

"Oh, she is. Every time I look at our wedding pictures, she makes me smile. I mean, she just stepped right in there and was the best little flower girl," Angela said.

"So, when is the baby due?"

"July ninth. Looks like I got pregnant right after I got married."

"That is so romantic." I thought for a second what it must

feel like to be married to the man you love and know you're carrying his child. I wanted to ask her if she'd found out anything more when it came to her grandmother, but I didn't want to dampen her jubilation.

She hadn't said anything else about it since telling me she'd read the notes her great-grandmother had written and had left with, of all people, Johnnie Mae Landris. For the most part, her great-grandmother had written about things surrounding her life, which Angela said was quite an interesting read. Even put in her well-guarded secret recipe for German chocolate cake. She'd also written about her children, all of them but especially the one rarely spoken of: Arletha Jane.

Angela hadn't told me everything, but she did say that her great-grandmother, Pearl, had written that Arletha had been a rambunctious child almost from the day she arrived on this earth. Like many teens, she was somewhat rebellious in her teenage years. But in her case, Arletha Jane had taken things a little further than most her age.

At thirteen, she was sneaking out of the house at night, smoking, drinking, and who knew what else. When Arletha was fifteen, her mother learned she was not just having sex but having sex for money and things. Pearl had done all she could to try and turn her daughter around. But Arletha was more than a handful. Pearl had been embarrassed and ashamed by her daughter's actions. The church folks were whispering at first, then loud talking about them, first behind their backs, then later to their faces. Her other children were starting to act out because of Arletha's defiance.

Pearl's husband tried to help rein her in. But Arletha had fought back, accusing her mother of being a hypocrite. Apparently, Pearl had had Arletha out of wedlock, which meant she'd had sex before *she* married. So how could she say anything to Arletha about what she was doing in her life? Pearl wrote of her regrets that her daughter had been able to use that argument against her. Pearl had also written of her regrets about the way she had handled things with her oldest child. She should have listened to her daughter more, talked with her more and found out the source of her rebellion. But instead, she had gotten frustrated and lost patience.

When Arletha got pregnant, she managed to keep her pregnancy a secret, even from her midwife of a mother. An easy feat when you refuse to have much to do with your family and the baby grows sideways instead of out. Even more so if the mother is not nourishing herself properly. According to Angela, Pearl delivered the baby, a beautiful little girl named Rebecca. The same little girl she would have to bring up as her own.

Having been a midwife for decades, Pearl wrote of untold truths from the common to the unusual—truths withheld from many. She'd written about delivering a baby that would be called Memory. How they had kept the truth behind that birth a secret for more than sixty years. How two babies (a girl and a boy), born to separate mothers (Sarah Fleming and Mamie Patterson), had been recorded by her as a twin birth for Mamie Patterson. How, in actuality, the baby girl had been Sarah Fleming's—a secret that most assuredly had kept that child alive since Sarah's half brother had ordered Pearl to let the baby die. It was as though Pearl had written this as a place of her last confessions.

She'd written of old friends like a guy named Ransom, and a few of the new ones. Angela had smiled at how excited she'd been to have met "a real live author," as she had put it. It was indeed a thrill for her, someone of such "humble beginnings." She was an old woman who hadn't had enough money for a proper education, and there at her door and sitting in her home had been a famous author named Johnnie Mae Taylor. She'd eaten a slice of Pearl's famous homemade German chocolate cake and had loved it.

And before Pearl had died, she'd learned that her old friend, Sarah Fleming, after all of these years, was still alive. Sadly, Pearl died before Pearl got to see Sarah again.

Angela had read to me a passage her great-grandmother had written that had touched her heart.

From some of my greatest pains have come some of my greatest joys. Had it not been for the little girl that Arletha Jane gave birth to, Rebecca, and Rebecca having had our sweet little Angel, I would have been even more alone in my life. The joy all of my children, grandchildren, and great-grandchildren have brought me—I honestly never would have known real love without them.

The sum of my life, the greatest gift from God above, has truly been the gift of love and the heritage of children. I thank you, God. For in truth, I did not choose You, but it was You who chose me.

Chapter 33

For their calamity shall rise suddenly; and who knoweth the ruin of them both?

—Proverbs 24:22

Sasha had gone online and found a piano. She told Marcus she'd found one without telling him where. The cost was five thousand dollars; she told him it was eight. He'd then asked her for the information so he could check it out. She told him she had already bought it, charged it to her brand-new American Express card. The piano was on its way.

Sasha had stopped by Marcus's house without prior warning. "I need you to give me the money so I can pay my bill. You said you were going to buy the piano," Sasha said, talking rather fast. "I asked what you were willing to spend, and you said no more than eight thousand. Well, it was hard, but I did find one for eight. I bought it before someone else did. So don't even think about giving me any grief or drama since you were going to buy the piano anyway."

"How do you know I wasn't going to charge it to *my* credit card?" Marcus asked.

"If that's what you were going to do, then just write a check to me from your credit account. I don't care where you get the money. I just need you to give it to me so I can pay *my* bill. Unlike yours, my American Express is the kind that requires that the balance be paid in full every month. I just got this account and I don't want to mess it up."

"Then why would you charge it to *that* card?" Marcus asked with a touch of frustration in his voice as he quickly glanced at his watch.

"Because," Sasha said, taking note he had just sneaked a peek at his watch, "you normally pay for everything you buy with cash. I figured you would buy this piano and pay cash for it." She put her hand on her hip. "So, am I wrong?"

"That's beside the point." Marcus shook his head. "You used to always do this when we were married."

"Do what?"

"Spend my money, then expect it to be all right."

She shrugged. "I thought it was supposed to be our money. And that was the problem. You thought you should be the one to make all the financial decisions just because you're so great with math."

"Sasha, now that's not fair. I always got your input, and you know that."

Sasha nodded. "True. But you were still the one who would say whether or not we could afford a thing. Saying we should wait, or save up so we wouldn't have to charge it." She threw her hands in the air. "You drove me crazy when it came to what we could and couldn't do. Now, I don't have to ask. I just buy *what* I want *when* I want. And frankly, I love the freedom."

"Is that right?" Marcus said. He hunched his shoulders and smirked. "So tell me, Sasha. How is that working for you?"

"It's working fine for me. Just fine. How are things working for *you*?"

"Okay," Marcus said with a grin.

"Now, can you please write me a check for the piano?" She held out her hand.

"When does the piano arrive?"

"What?" Sasha said.

"The piano, when will it get here?"

"*After* my bill is due," Sasha said. "The piano is being shipped by freight. They say it will take four to six weeks to arrive. Now quit playing and go write me a check so I can handle my business. Goodness, Marcus! Must you always make everything so difficult?"

Marcus had told her he would pay no more than eight thousand for a piano. He hadn't expected her to run out and buy one two days later before he had a chance to check around himself. Still, she had bought one and there was nothing he could do about that. Besides, it wasn't that big a deal. Sasha had asked him to buy Aaliyah a piano, he had agreed to do it, Sasha had found one, and now it was on its way. He went and got a check and wrote it out to her. "I need the receipt so we can insure it," he said.

"I'm already on that. You really are the best daddy out there," Sasha said as she looked at the check to make sure it was addressed to her and written for the entire eight thousand before placing it in her wallet. "You just wait until you see and hear your baby playing her first song on it. You're going to be so proud of her."

"I'm already proud of her," Marcus said. He glanced at his watch again.

"Are you late to be somewhere or expecting someone?" Sasha asked when she noticed that was the second time he had checked his watch. "I realize I just dropped in. I didn't ask if you were on your way out or busy."

Marcus smiled. He wasn't about to tell Sasha anything at this point. He started walking toward his front door.

Sasha threw her Louis Vuitton purse across her shoulder and smiled. "Okay, so I guess that's your polite way of saying it's time for me to leave." She caught up with him. When she reached the door, she turned to him. "Thank you, Marc. You have no *idea* what this means to us. I can't wait to see the look on Aaliyah's face when that piano arrives." She rose up on the tips of her toes and gave Marcus a quick peck on his cheek. "Thank you."

Marcus had been caught slightly off guard by that kiss. He didn't know what to think. He couldn't help but wonder what was really going on with Sasha. He did know he was getting an uneasy feeling in his stomach lately when Sasha was around. He wasn't sure exactly what that feeling was trying to tell him.

Sasha left. He hurried out to his car with only twenty minutes to pick Melissa up for their date and get to the movie theater. He and Melissa hated missing the start of a movie. And she was looking forward to seeing Tyler Perry's new one. He would have to hustle to make up the time.

Chapter 34

*But Jesus called them unto him, and said, Suffer lit-
tle children to come unto me, and forbid them not:
for of such is the kingdom of God.*

—Luke 18:16

It had been a week since Marcus had given Sasha that money.
She had deposited the money into her account, having gone
to Marcus's bank to cash it. Her bank was planning on placing
a one-week hold on it even though it was a local check. She
hated that checks written for more than five thousand dollars
were automatically held for a minimum of five working days.
Sasha felt it was a racket for them to have her money without
her having access to it. They could use it, possibly making
money off it while she, the owner, had to wait to be able to.

A friend who worked for a bank told her a lot of the tricks
they use to get over on customers. One: charging a monthly
fee, unless you maintain a minimum balance of $500, just so
you can have the pleasure of keeping your money in a checking account. The bank charging *you* if you happen to deposit
a check from someone whose check bounces. Charging customers for not being smart enough to know that the check
someone else had written them wasn't good. Sasha couldn't
believe how ridiculous that was. It wasn't enough that they
charge you for writing a check that bounces. And it was nothing for them to charge thirty-five dollars the first time the
check bounced, then put it through again a few days later

and it bounces again, generating another thirty-five-dollar charge.

Sasha had been so mad the time she had written a check that caused some other checks to bounce. What really got her was how they charged her for five bouncing checks when on the day the check bounced, she had enough money to cover those five. If they had bounced the one big check, it would have been the only one to have bounced. Instead, that night, they just *happened* to process the one big check first, thus depleting her balance, then they processed the other five and charged her thirty-five dollars for each of them.

When she went to the bank to complain, the manager explained that their system processes them as they come through. It just so *happened* that the large check was put through first and the other five checks were processed after it, through no design of theirs, on that same night.

"It's just the way the computer processed them. We don't have any control over that," the woman at the bank had said.

Sasha was getting tired of computers and machine errors. She often heard her mother talk about life BC (Before Computers).

"Back in the old days, when *people* actually ran the show," Stella Bradford had said, "a person would have seen those checks come through, and a person would have looked out for the customer. Any decent person would have processed the five checks using the money you had in the account. And they would have stamped the one big one as insufficient. It's happening with everything these days. Personally, I hate machines, and I hate all this technological stuff. I don't *want* to press one for yes or two for no. I don't *want* to have to keep pressing zero trying to get a live person to assist me."

Sasha had bought a few things since depositing the money in her account. She hadn't purchased the piano yet, but she was going to. In fact, she was in the process of going online to buy that piano she'd found for five thousand dollars when she noticed an e-mail in her inbox like ones she normally ignored. Only this one was different. It read:

I am Barrister Lim Chong
A legal practitioner with Limchong Chambers
Law Firm in Kuala Lumpur, Malaysia.
Attention: Sasha Peeples

I saw your contact and profile I then decided you could co-operate with me in this proposition. I have a client who was deceased in November, 2001, as result of Tsunami Disaster in Indonesia.

I am contacting you because you have the same surname with my deceased client and I felt that you could help me in the distribution of funding that were left in my deceased client's bank account. This funding is closing to be declared UN-serviceable by the bank as there were no indicated next of kin or next of beneficiary of the funding in the bank account.

The total amount of cash in the bank account of my deceased client is US $8.7 Million (Eight Million, Seven Hundred Thousand USA dollars) only. The bank had issued to me a notification letter to contact the next of kin of my deceased client for either to re-activate the bank account or to make claim of beneficiary of the funding in the bank account to avoid the indefinite closure of the bank account.

My proposition to you is to seek your consent, and to present your kind self as the next-of-kin and beneficiary of my deceased client. Hence you have the same last name with him. This means that the proceeds of his bank account would be paid to you as his next of kin or the legitimate beneficiary.

So that when the proceeds in this bank account are paid to you, we would share the proceeds on a mutually agreed term upon percentage 50% for me and 40% to your kind self and remaining 10% for sundry expense in cure during the procession.

All the legal documents to back up your claim as my client's next-of-kin would be provided by me. The most important thing I would need is your honest cooperation in this proposition. This would be done under a legitimate arrangement that would protect you from any breach of the law.

If this business proposition offends your moral and ethic values, do accept my sincere apology. Please contact me immediately.

Best regards,
Barrister Lim Chong (ESQ)
Phone: +60172495317

Sasha normally didn't pay attention to these types of e-mails. But this one seemed legitimate. First, it addressed her by name, and Peeples wasn't a common name. This e-mail had a phone number to call. She showed it to her mother to see what she thought about it.

"Praise the Lord," Stella Bradford said. "This is an answer from the Lord. It's a gift from heaven."

"But what if it's just a scam? I don't know if you know this, but there are lots of scam e-mails floating around in cyberspace," Sasha argued.

"I saw something on television about those, but they are mostly from Nigeria," Stella said. "This one isn't from Nigeria. They have your name on it and there's a phone number at the bottom. I tell you what: let's just call this number and see. You get on the other extension. We can determine real quick whether or not this e-mail is on the up-and-up."

Stella called the number and a woman answered who sounded quite pleasant and sincere. She said the number was indeed Barrister Chong's. The woman put Barrister Chong on the phone. He was more than happy to stop what he was doing to take the call. Barrister Chong explained to Stella and Sasha rather clearly in broken English what was needed to make this happen. They were talking millions of dollars here. There needed to be trust on both sides since they could be out of money if Sasha turned out to be a scammer and not who they thought she was.

After talking to him, Stella was ecstatic. "Daughter, you're about to be rich," she said. "I know this is God. Can't be nobody *but* God. Do you have any idea what all we can do with this much money?"

"We," Sasha said, laughing.

"Yes, *we.* Now don't be trying to act funny with me. You know had your father left me any money, I was going to share it with you. I just know you plan to share whatever you get with me." Stella clapped her hands. "Glory to God! All of our troubles are over. Our prayers have been answered. God is so good!" She turned back to Sasha. "But you need to hurry up and move on this. The good barrister said he's going to send you a check for millions. All you have to do is pay part of the processing fee. His office is paying the rest. How much did he say that would be again? Twelve thousand?"

"Yeah, he said twelve thousand."

"So, do you have twelve thousand?" Stella asked.

"No, you know I don't have that kind of money," Sasha said.

"Then can you borrow it from your ex? You and I both know that Marcus has plenty of money. That boy knows he knows how to invest. I believe he may be better at it that even your daddy was. Marcus took that thing to another level. He's not just working for a company; he's investing his own money in businesses they turn down that he believes in. Like that doctor you said he was investing his own money in, that OB/GYN. Now that's a sound investment because women are going to always need one of those." Stella chuckled. She grabbed her daughter's hand and squeezed it. "I bet you Marcus has the money. Ask him to loan it to you. After we finish this, in a week or two and you've gotten those millions, you can easily give Marcus back that chump change. The barrister says you're getting forty percent of eight point seven million dollars."

Sasha took her hand out of her mother's. "I can't ask Marcus to loan me twelve thousand dollars. Marcus might have money, but I'm pretty sure he doesn't have money like that," Sasha said.

"How do you know what he has? Since your divorce, does he tell you much of anything?" Stella asked.

"No, but I know he doesn't have that kind of money. At least, not the way you apparently think he does. Just like Daddy didn't have it the way you thought he did when he was alive."

Stella pursed her lips as she shook her head. "Don't go

bringing your father into this, God rest his soul. Your daddy just had secrets I didn't realize he had. I can assure you, had I known he was in that much debt and was going to let his life insurance lapse, we would have paid that insurance premium. I could have forgone a pair of Christian Louboutin shoes for one month to ensure *that* bill was paid. He just didn't tell me stuff, and I didn't ask. That was my mistake." Stella clapped her hands. "But now God has heard our prayers. It looks like your having been married to a Peeples is about to pay off after all, big time. God is *so* good! So good. We don't need to question this blessing from God. We just need to figure out how to act on it, and quickly, like Barrister Chong just said."

"Well, I'm not as sure about this as you are. Marcus tells me all the time I need to be careful. That if something sounds too good to be true, I need to check it out before I just dive into it." Sasha was now wringing her hands.

"Well, I'm sure about this. And you know I wouldn't steer you wrong," Stella said.

"Except when you encouraged and pushed me to leave Marcus, and then to divorce him. You told me I would be rolling in dough without having to put up with him. You said I could find another man easily, and he would be even better than Marcus." Sasha shook her head. "You were wrong about all of that."

Stella shrugged. "I'm only human." She began to pat the ball of her chignon.

"But this was my life you were playing with, Mother. And now it looks like Marcus has moved on. And me? I'm stuck with a bunch of losers. Marcus is being blessed, and I feel like everything I touch these days is being cursed."

Stella waved her hand at Sasha to dismiss what she was saying. "Child, please. You are and always *were* such a drama queen. Men come and go. Trust me, they really do come a dime a dozen. You'll find one to take the place of Marcus one day. Meanwhile, he faithfully takes care of that child of his. Thanks to me, you ended up getting the house. You were able to hang out with that guy you were sort of sneaking around with and talking to on the side while you were married. I don't care how much you deny that to Marcus, I know the real deal. Too bad things didn't work out between the two of you in the end and he cut out on you." Stella crossed her legs. "You've got to get over it and keep moving. You say Marcus has moved on? Then do what you were doing right after you left him and move on. Now can we get back to more important things, namely this money?"

"I'm not asking Marcus for any money."

"Then do you have it or do you have another guy in your back pocket with cash you can ask?"

"No, Mother," Sasha said exasperated. "I don't have any money, and I don't know anyone who has that kind of money, either. In fact, I'm having a hard time trying to pay my bills. My gas bill was so high I missed paying my light bill last month. The power company already sent me a disconnect notice. I have to pay it by next week. Fortunately, I get paid next week so I'll have it. But it's not so easy being single out here. I'm sure you know this since Daddy died. It's no cakewalk trying to pay all of these stupid bills."

"And why exactly can't you ask Marcus to loan you the money if he has it?" Stella uncrossed her legs and turned toward Sasha. "Tell him you need it for something for Aaliyah. You know that man will go through fire for his daughter. He'll find money for her if he has to, just like your daddy always seemed to find the money for you."

Sasha released a hard sigh. "I can't. I just asked him for money for something for her. He's buying her a piano. He's already given me the money for it, in fact."

Stella stood and paced for a second. "Did he give you *all* the money for it?" Stella asked.

"Yes. In fact, I had just logged on to see about buying the piano when I opened this e-mail and happened to read it. I've received similar types of e-mails before, but for some reason this one caught my eye."

"It was God, I'm telling you. That's how God works." She sat down next to Sasha. "All counterfeit things are based on the real thing. I believe this e-mail is the real deal." Stella nodded as she leaned back in her seat. "You say Marcus gave you money for a piano but you haven't spent the money yet?"

Sasha nodded at her mother's first question, then shook her head in response to the second. "He gave me eight thousand dollars." She didn't tell her mother the piano would only cost five.

Stella began to smile as she crossed her arms. "It's too bad I had to practically give your piano away when I sold it after your daddy died or I could have sold it to you for that price."

"Or you could have given it to me like I asked you to since it *was* my piano. Daddy bought that piano for me for my tenth birthday."

Stella didn't address Sasha's last comment. "Well, well, if this isn't a Holy Ghost setup," she said thinking about the money Sasha just said Marcus had given her. "Let's see now. I have two thousand dollars in my account. It's for my bills this month, but we're about to get millions so I believe I can spare this for now. One thing I learned from your father: When it comes to investing, you have to give something to get something in return."

"I don't know about this, Mother." Sasha continued to shake her head. "I don't feel good about this, none of this."

"All right. Let this pass you by then. That's the problem with you, Sasha. You never listen and you always seem to make the wrong choice. Here God is practically dropping all of this money in our laps, and what are you doing? Balking about it."

Stella leaned in to Sasha. "Do you really believe it was sheer coincidence that you would have eight thousand dollars and I would have two thousand at the same time you get this e-mail? You need twelve thousand to move things along. You get paid next week. You can use your paycheck to come up with the rest next week. That way, all of us would have contributed—me, you, and Marcus indirectly. Look, it's not like you have to send these people a check. Barrister Chong is going to send you a check to deposit in your bank account. When you deposit it, you give them permission to take the twelve thousand from your account."

Sasha pursed her lips. "After taxes and all that other junk, I don't have that much left. I only bring home about a thousand dollars after everything."

Stella shrugged. "Okay, that's a thousand more. We just need to come up with one more thousand. I believe that between the two of us, we can come up with one thousand more. Surely you must have *some* money in the bank right now."

Sasha pressed her hand against her throat. "I have one hundred dollars to my name right now. That's it."

"Okay. Then I'll just have to get someone to loan me nine hundred dollars for the week and a half to two weeks we'll need until that check for millions clears." She stood up and looked at Sasha. "Do you hear that, Sasha? We're talking millions here. Millions."

"I just don't know, Mother. Something just doesn't feel right about any of this."

Stella reached down, grabbed her daughter by the shoulders, and looked her squarely in the eyes. "Banks have ways of verifying checks. When you put that check from the barrister in the bank, they can tell if it's legit. Let's say the worse-case scenario is these people are not legitimate and the bank has transferred the twelve thousand from your account. The bank can easily transfer that money back. This is the electronic age. They have ways of tracking money. You need to think about this. I'm willing to put up my money, and you know how dire things are for me these days. In fact, if I had the whole twelve thousand, I would do this without you having to contribute anything."

Stella released her grip on Sasha and began to pat her shoulders. "It's been so hard since we lost your father. I've been really struggling here."

Sasha stood up and put her arm around her mother's shoulders. "I know, Mother. It's been hard on everybody."

"Well, then you need to look at this for what it could be. If this is from God, then we could be missing the cloud. We need to move with the cloud," Stella said, referring to the time God led Moses and the children of Israel toward the Promised Land with a cloud.

"But if this isn't from God, then what does that mean? Marcus has always told me that when I didn't know what to do, I needed to stop and pray about it. I haven't prayed about this. I hear what you're saying, but I haven't prayed about this."

"What's to pray about? You've been praying for God to move in your life, right?"

"Yes. Just as you say that you have," Sasha said.

"Now God is moving. And what are you doing? You're talking about praying some more. You've prayed, I've prayed, now God has given us an answer to our prayers. But this is on you now. You were the one who got the e-mail. You have the last name Peeples. Just don't come crying to me about it when you find out you took too long to move and the cloud has moved on without you."

Sasha didn't know what to do. Her mother was probably right. After all, she did love her and she did have her best interests at heart.

"Okay, Mother. Write a check to me so I can deposit it, or get me the cash. If you write a check, they may put a hold on it, so I'll need a check today and deposit it tomorrow. So either write me a check now or get me the cash this week, and we'll do this."

Stella began to smile as she hugged her daughter. "Oh, I love you so much! I know you don't think that sometimes, but I truly do," she said to Sasha.

Stella looked up and waved her hand. "Thank you, Jesus. Thank you, Lord. We're about to finally step into our blessing!" She did a short dance of praise.

Chapter 35

Wealth gotten by vanity shall be diminished: but he that gathered by labor shall increase.

—Proverbs 13:11

Sasha couldn't believe what she was seeing. Sure, she had expected as much after she'd done all that Barrister Chong had instructed. She understood that with millions on the line, there would be a hold on the money. Even more so with this being an overseas transaction. Then came the returned check. Sasha looked at her statement. She was starting to hate computers. This had to be another computer error. Her bank statement showed a negative balance, and she knew there was no way that could be right.

No such account. Funds unavailable. The money Marcus had given her, gone.

She had gone down to the bank and spoke to the highest-level officer she could. She was told that there were lots of these types of scams. That people should know this was a scam. She had countered with the argument that if they knew this was going on in the year 2006, why weren't they doing more to protect their customers? How much did they get out of these transactions? And maybe that was why they weren't doing more to protect people like her from being scammed.

The manager had taken offense at that accusation. They were just becoming aware of it on a larger scale, just as their customers were. It was hurting their business as well because most people who get caught up in this stuff ended up having to close their accounts and they didn't have sufficient funds to open another account as they straightened out the mess, as well as their credit ratings. "This hurts everybody," he had said.

Sasha told him that the bank needed to warn customers more about these scams. If people chose to go forward after being informed, then that was a different matter. But Sasha maintained that not enough was being done to protect the vulnerable.

"There are elderly people out there, and you know that they are being taken in by what's all over the Internet. They don't know. Look at me. I'm a young woman, and I got caught up in a scam," Sasha said.

The manager admitted that what she said was true. There were plenty of bogus e-mails targeting people with online bank accounts, online credit accounts, and other types of accounts like PayPal and eBay.

"People from all over are sending out e-mails requesting that people click on bogus links. They think they're protecting their interests, their credit and bank accounts that they're being told falsely may have been compromised. The e-mails appear legitimate, with official logos and the like. When you click the link they provide in these e-mails, it takes you to a fake Web site where they ask for your login, password, and other sensitive information like your social security number. It's called phishing." He leaned in.

"People should never give out information like that over the Internet—or the phone, for that matter—when you've not initiated the contact," he said. "I advise people not to click on a link included in an e-mail from a bank or business. I don't care how official it looks. Not when it comes to your money or your identity. If you think the e-mail could be legitimate, type in the Web site's URL yourself and log in to your account that way. If there's a problem, it will be there. Most times, there never is. It's all just a scam."

Sasha told him it was fine he was saying all of this now after she had been bilked. She challenged him, asking what the bank was doing to inform the public of these scams before people get roped in, after he reemphasized there was nothing more they could do.

"What are you doing to protect your patrons?" she asked. "You don't care because it isn't your money. Nobody cares about people anymore. Everything is for the love of money." She snatched up her purse and stormed out.

Sasha had to file a police report. There was so much involved now. She went home and cried after she left the police station, where they had told her recovering her money under these circumstances was next to impossible. She told her mother that everything was lost. Her mother was livid that she had been drawn into this deceit. She was upset that the money she had put up was supposed to cover her bills.

"How am I going to pay my bills now?" Stella asked. "Dog!"

Sasha cried even more. She was hurting as well, but no one seemed to care about her.

Marcus would be expecting to see Aaliyah's piano soon. How would she tell him what she'd done?

Aaliyah came into her bedroom and saw her lying on the bed crying. "What's wrong, Mommy? What's the matter?"

Sasha sat up and hugged her daughter. "Nothing, baby."

"Then why are you crying?"

Sasha held Aaliyah. "Mommy made a mistake, and she's not sure how to fix it."

"God can fix it," Aaliyah said. "God can do anything. Daddy says so. Daddy says there's nothing too hard for our God. And Daddy always tells me the truth."

Sasha rubbed Aaliyah's hair. "Is that right? There's *nothing* too hard for God?"

Aaliyah shook her head as she smiled. "Nothing! Daddy says so. So don't cry, Mommy, all right? Just tell God about it. He will fix it."

"I wish I could believe that, Aaliyah. But I'm not sure God can fix this."

"You need to talk to Daddy. Daddy hates when you cry. I'm sure Daddy can make you feel better."

"You think?" Sasha said, managing a laugh.

Aaliyah shrugged. "Daddy always makes *me* feel better." Aaliyah hugged her.

"Daddy will be here to pick you up soon. I need to get your things ready."

"Are you going to be all right here by yourself while I'm gone?" Aaliyah asked. "'Cause if you aren't, I can stay here with you instead. I'm sure Daddy will understand."

Sasha put on an extra effort for Aaliyah. "I'm going to be fine. You go on with your daddy. And don't tell him I was crying, all right?"

"All right. But God can still fix it." Aaliyah stood up. "You want to pray?"

"What?"

Aaliyah knelt down by the bed and put her hands together. "Let's pray for God to fix it."

Sasha knelt down. She looked over at her daughter, who had already closed her eyes. Sasha couldn't do anything after that except smile and shake her head. She couldn't help but think of the words of Isaiah 11:6—"And a little child shall lead them."

Chapter 36

Blessed is the man that trusteth in the Lord, and whose hope the Lord is.

—Jeremiah 17:7

When Marcus went to pick up Aaliyah, he noticed that Sasha looked like she had been crying.

"You all right?" he asked.

She forced a smile. "Yeah. Sure. I'm fine. You two have fun this weekend," she said.

But Marcus couldn't stop thinking about Sasha. Most of the time when he picked up Aaliyah, he would have to wait while Sasha got her things together, even though she knew it was his weekend to get her. This wasn't even his weekend. Sasha had called at the last minute and asked if he could get Aaliyah. She offered no excuses, didn't claim any emergencies. She just asked if he could possibly get her this weekend.

In the past, Sasha would find something to talk with him about or fuss about when he arrived, usually about folks on her job. She was always finding some angle to discuss having to do with money. Not this time. He thought she may not have been feeling well. It was wintertime. Flu and colds were hitting folks hard. Her eyes *were* puffy, and she'd held a wad of tissue in her hand. He didn't know, and she wasn't saying much to give him a clue.

After he and Aaliyah reached his house and he'd gotten her settled in, they talked about what fun thing they wanted to do tonight. Aaliyah enjoyed playing board games and older hands-on games like Connect Four and Candy Land. Marcus fixed French fries, chicken nuggets, pork and beans, and corn on the cob.

"Is Mommy not feeling well?" Marcus asked, turning Aaliyah's plate around so she could reach her chicken nuggets better.

"She's fine. But she was crying before you came."

"Mommy was crying?"

Aaliyah bit into a chicken nugget. "Yes, but I'm not supposed to tell you."

"Oh, you're not."

"Nope." She shook her head. "Mommy said not to tell you."

"Now, why would Mommy tell you not to tell me?"

Aaliyah dipped her nugget into the sweet and sour sauce and bit again. "Because she was saying . . . she was crying because she couldn't fix something. And I told her God could fix it, and she said she didn't think God could fix it. Then I said she should tell you because you said nothing was too hard for God."

"Wow, you told Mommy all of that?"

"Yes," Aaliyah said in her almost-too-grown-up-for-her-age voice. "I tried to help her, but I don't think I did a good job. So I told her to do what you always tell me to do when I'm sad."

Marcus was fascinated as he listened to his little girl. He smiled. "And what's that?"

"You know, Daddy. We get down on our knees and we pray. You said that's the answer to whatever ails us. When we're sad, we should pray. When we're happy, we should pray. When we don't know what to do, we should pray. You said prayer was the an-swer to whatever is wrong." Aaliyah looked serious and she stared directly at her father. "Mommy was sad. Mommy was crying. I told her to talk to you if she didn't think God could fix it. She didn't want to tell you, so all I knew to do was pray."

"You know, you are wise beyond your years," Marcus said.

"Mommy says I'm just like you!"

The phone rang. Marcus got up. He looked at the Caller ID. It was Melissa. He answered it.

"Hey," he said.

"Hey, yourself. What are you doing?"

"Sitting here eating and talking with Aaliyah," Marcus said as he looked over at his daughter.

"I was just thinking about you. I miss you and I just wanted to hear your voice," Melissa said. "I got your message that you were going to get Aaliyah. Sorry I was out of pocket when you called."

"Well, I was thinking about you, too. Why don't you come over tonight? Aaliyah and I are just going to play a few games. Just like Jell-O, you know: there's always room for more," Marcus said, reciting an old television commercial.

"That's tempting, but I don't want to crash your and Aaliyah's night together."

"You wouldn't be crashing our night. It would be fun. Now, you know how much Aaliyah likes having you around. In fact, I'm starting to get a little jealous the way you two leave me out of the loop when you're together."

"And that's exactly the reason why I'm not coming over tonight. You and Aaliyah have fun."

"I didn't mean it that way. You were supposed to take that as a good thing," Marcus said.

"Oh, I took it as a compliment. I just know how important it is for little girls to have time with their fathers. Well, I would know personally had my father spent a little more time with me before he died." Melissa made a popping sound with her mouth. "Maybe that explains why some women grow up chasing after the wrong kinds of men. I don't think your daughter will have that problem when she grows up."

"I'm not sure what factors go into how children turn out. My mother raised all of us the exact same way and look what happened with my baby brother. He's upset with me now because he feels I should shell out more money for a lawyer to get him out of prison. I helped my mother pay off the bill she incurred when he was on trial. But he thinks I should pay some high-powered lawyer he's found to get him out. So who can say what causes children to do what they do or turn out like they do," Marcus said.

"You're right. Nae-nae's mother was real strict and very religious. They practically lived at church. You would think that Nae-nae would be in church big time now."

"She doesn't go to church?"

"She goes, but it's more out of tradition. Nae-nae became quite cynical about the church. She's put off by all the money talk from the pulpit when she's struggling to pay her light bill and keep food on the table. She gets even madder when she's being told that she's struggling because she's not putting even more money in church."

"So she doesn't go to the same church as you?" Marcus asked. "Pastor Landris's church seems different from most churches I've attended. I love going there."

"No, I haven't been able to get her to visit us. She says all these churches are pretty much the same. That's the downside when preachers and churches disappoint. It can be hard to get back those who have just given up on them completely. Nae-nae still goes to church, her home church, whenever she has to take her mother. And Nae-nae's mother is not ever going to leave that church. Not until she takes her leave for heaven. That's just how some people are when it comes to churches. It doesn't matter whether or not their needs are being met. Many stay out of tradition."

Marcus rubbed his goatee. "Well, I think if we could get her to give Followers of Jesus Faith Worship Center a chance, we might be able to get her back."

Melissa laughed. "Did I miss something? What's all this *we* thing? I don't recall you walking to the front of our church to become a member yet."

"I'm thinking seriously about it. I really love Pastor Landris's teaching. And he and I have talked. He's positively an impressive man and a man of God. Not perfect, so don't get me wrong. There are a few things I don't totally see eye to eye with him on. But ninety-nine percent, he's right on it." Marcus looked over at Aaliyah. She was almost finished eating. "You know, you might as well put on your shoes and come on over."

"And how do you know I don't have my shoes on?" Melissa asked.

It was Marcus's turn to laugh. "I think I know you pretty well now after four months. So put your shoes on and come over. Aaliyah would love to see you."

"I'm finished!" Aaliyah said, holding up her empty plate. She got up from the table and walked toward Marcus. "Can we play the memory card game first?"

"I hear Aaliyah. You go on and spend time with her. You and I will talk later," Melissa said.

"Does that mean you're coming over?" Marcus asked.

"Bye." Melissa softly sang the word.

"Are you coming over?" Marcus pressed again.

Melissa giggled. "Bye-e-e."

Melissa thought about going to his house. She really did enjoy spending time with both of them. But she also didn't want to be so selfish that she felt things had to revolve around her. So she decided to stay home, at least for tonight.

Maybe tomorrow. But tonight—tonight she would leave father and daughter to have their time together.

Chapter 37

Late Saturday afternoon, Tiffany Connors called and asked me if I could watch her three children for her. I hated saying no, even though I had vowed I would work on that a little more. It wasn't as if Tiffany asked me to keep her children often or asked me so she could hang out in the streets. Darius hardly ever took her anywhere, but tonight he was taking her out to dinner.

"It's the weekend before Valentine's Day, which I'm sure you already know is Tuesday," Tiffany said. "Darius wants to take me out tonight instead of Tuesday since it would be easier to get a sitter on the weekend than during the week. The teenager who was coming over just called and said something came up and she can't do it tonight. I've called the one other teen I trust and have used before, but she already has plans. Melissa, I know this is short notice, and if you can't keep them, it will be okay."

"No, it's not a problem. I can do that for you. What time do you want me to come over?" I said.

"If you'd prefer, I can bring them to your house. I'm already asking a lot. It's not like you don't have your own life and probably your own plans," Tiffany said.

Tiffany really was a sweet person. She always seemed to put others first. I couldn't understand why, with her good looks and smarts, she hadn't figured out what a jerk Darius was and dumped him. She had to know he was cheating on her. That's most likely why he was insisting on taking her out tonight instead of on Valentine's Day. I guarantee you if I call on Tuesday around eight or nine at night and ask her where he is, he'll not be home. Now if I can see this, surely Tiffany has to be able to.

Sometimes I just want to shake her and say, "Wake up! How does a beautiful, intelligent, kind woman like you continue to take junk like this off somebody like him? You either need to put your foot down or tell him to get to stepping."

Then I look back over my own life and the lives of so many others, and see I have no room to judge. Why did I let Cass and all the others treat me like dirt the way I had? If I'm so bad, why didn't I put my own foot down? Why do I let people, not just men, still run over me now and not stand up for myself? It's funny how we can easily defend other people's honor, but somehow we fail to see what's happening with ourselves. I can see where I've made a vast improvement over the past guys I've chosen to give pieces of my life to. But then again, I wasn't even trying to talk to Marcus. He didn't seem my type.

I was wrong. Maybe that's the lesson I need to see and take away from all of this. I think I know what's best for me, but what I tend to go for eventually treats me like I'm nothing and a nobody. When God is in the mix . . . when I yield to *His* voice and *His* leading, I end up with the most remarkable man I could ever have asked for. Granted, it's only been four months. Still, I can't help but think of the scriptures that emphasize how in all our ways we should acknowledge God and lean not to our own understanding, to let God direct our path. I now truly understand why.

"Tiffany," I said, "I'll come over there. It makes no sense for you to have to get all three of them ready and drag them to my house when it's easier for me to come to you. Besides, they'll feel more comfortable in their own environment."

"Are you sure?"

"Absolutely."

"And I'm not interfering with any plans you may have had?" Tiffany asked.

I thought about Marcus and how he was spending time with Aaliyah. I had indicated I might come over tonight, but this was all working out just fine. I would call Marcus and let him know what I was doing.

So I went over to Tiffany's a little before six o'clock. Darius wasn't home when I got there, although I was a little early. I played with the children while Tiffany finished getting ready. He had told her to dress for a night out on the town. Suggested she wear a dress he'd uncharacteristically surprised her with. She had definitely dressed up, and then some.

"Are you sure I look all right in this?" Tiffany asked me as she twirled around in the A-line, beaded, knee-length purple dress for me to get a good look from all angles. "This isn't something I would *ever* have bought myself. But Darius said I was worth this splurge even though I was pregnant when he gave it to me back in May."

"Well, you look stunning," I said, and I meant that.

"For real? I still have a little baby fat." She smoothed down her abdominal area.

"I wish I had your body. If I did, I wouldn't be asking anybody *anything*," I said about her size-eight body.

"Oh, Melissa. You look great with the body you have. I wish I had curves the way you do," Tiffany said.

Tiffany and Darius's five-year-old daughter Jada walked up to Tiffany. "Wow, you look pretty, Mommy."

"Oh, thank you, baby." Tiffany bent down and gave her daughter a big hug and a kiss on the top of her head.

"Yeah, you look pretty, Mommy," Dana, her three-year-old daughter, said as she waited for a hug and a kiss from her mother. Tiffany was more than happy to oblige.

It was past time for Darius to be home. Tiffany checked her watch. I checked mine. It was now seven o'clock. Tiffany paced the floor, picking up a few toys that were scattered around the room. I worked to keep the children occupied so they wouldn't bother her. At twenty minutes past seven, she called Darius again on his cell phone.

Darius came through the door just as she was hanging up.

"I'm so sorry I'm late. I had to run by the office to get something I left there yesterday." He kissed Tiffany. "There were folks working overtime on a project due Monday, asking me to help with this and that. I had to let them know I wasn't getting paid overtime like they were. But you know how hard it is for me to turn away anyone who needs my help. On top of that, I couldn't find what I went to get. Then I remembered it was in the jacket I had on Thursday." Darius started laughing. "Wouldn't you just know? What I was looking for was here at the house the whole time. So I wasted all that time gone for nothing."

"Oh, it's fine," Tiffany said. "You're here now."

I looked at Tiffany like she had lost her ever-loving mind. I couldn't believe she was actually buying his story.

"So Darius, what did you go to get?" I asked.

"Hi, Melissa," he said, trying not to show just how much he really didn't like me. He wasn't doing a great job of it.

"Hi, Darius. So," I said, refusing to let him change the subject, which I knew he was planning to do, "what did you go back to your job to get?"

Tiffany stood there and waited for his answer. Darius looked at her like he couldn't believe she wasn't putting a stop to my question.

He did all sorts of things. Pressed his lips together, puckered them out, scratched his head, then laughed. "It's a surprise for my wife."

"Oh, so does that mean you're going to go get it and give it to her so I can see what it is?" I said. "You know how nosy I am." I exaggerated a grin.

"Yeah, I'm sure you'd like to see what it is, but like I said, it's a surprise for my wife." He turned to Tiffany. "Give me a few minutes, and we'll be on our way. Okay?"

Tiffany smiled and nodded slightly as he left and trotted up the stairs.

"Melissa," Tiffany said, "I appreciate what you're trying to do. Darius and I are like most married couples. We have our share of problems for sure. I'm not as naïve or clueless as you might think. I know you care about me, but let me handle this. Okay?"

I nodded. "Sure. I didn't mean to cause any problems or overstep my bounds." I picked up Dana. Little D. was asleep in his bassinet. "I sure don't mean to get in your business."

Darius returned holding a small box in his hand. "I was going to give this to you tonight," Darius said. "But since I get the impression I'm under suspicion about having a gift for you, I decided to give it to you now." He handed a small velvet box to Tiffany.

Tiffany opened it. "Oh, Darius. It's beautiful," she said, taking the ring out of the box.

"Let me put it on," Darius said. He took the ring and placed it on the finger next to her ring finger. "I know how much women like jewelry. You can't go wrong with a ring. That's what I always say." He held her hand up and looked at it. "Do you really like it?"

"Oh, yes!" Tiffany kissed him. "Look," Tiffany said, showing me the ring.

"That's beautiful," I said, and it was.

"It's one carat," Darius said. "Nothing but the best for my baby."

"Well, I suppose you two had better get going," I said.

"Yeah, we do need to get going," Darius said to Tiffany before cutting his eyes over at me and smirking just a little.

Tiffany hugged me. "If you need me, call. I'll have my cell phone on," she said.

"No, she won't," Darius said. "This is our night out. Melissa can handle anything that might come up. Can't you, Melissa?"

"Darius is right. Turn your cell phone off and have a great time. We're going to be fine here." I looked at the three-year-old I held. "Aren't we, Dana?"

Dana nodded.

I looked down at Jada. "Aren't we, Jada?"

"Right," Jada said with a quick nod.

"So you two just go and have a great time. And take your time coming home. We're going to have lots of fun," I said.

Tiffany kissed the kids once more and she and Darius left.

Chapter 38

And sent his servant at supper time to say to them that were bidden, Come; for all things are now ready.

—Luke 14:17

Marcus took Aaliyah home earlier than he normally did on regular visits. Sasha had called Saturday night and asked him to. But in truth, he was a bit concerned about what was going on with her anyway.

Sasha appeared to be much better Sunday afternoon than when he picked Aaliyah up on Friday. She'd even cooked dinner, including many of his favorite dishes.

"Now, I just know you're going to stay and eat with us," Sasha said, the dining room table set for three when he and Aaliyah arrived.

Marcus hadn't planned on staying. In fact, when he had talked to Melissa the previous night, he told her he was going to take her out to dinner after he learned Sasha wanted him to bring Aaliyah home by two o'clock instead of his normal six o'clock. His plan was to take Aaliyah home right after church, then go by and pick up Melissa.

He and Aaliyah had gone to his church this Sunday. Despite the worship service starting at eleven o'clock (most churches had long ago begun having morning services at either ten thirty or ten forty-five), they didn't get out of church until around one thirty. Marcus still attended his own church even though he had visited and liked Melissa's church, Followers of

Jesus Faith Worship Center. Aaliyah preferred going to Followers of Jesus, but Marcus was both a member and a minister at Divine Conquerors Church. And every since Reverend Walker had learned Marcus had visited Pastor Landris's church more than a few times, he'd assigned him more duties on Sundays at his own church.

Melissa had been fine about going out to eat. She usually ate breakfast on Sundays and didn't care to eat dinner until two or three o'clock anyway.

Melissa had grown up in a community where at one point they still had the pastor, his wife, and children (if he had any) over for dinner after church. The church members took turns each Sunday hosting the First Family. Their pastor and wife usually ate dinner at their house three times a year because there were some families who either couldn't afford to or just didn't want to have the pastor and his wife over.

Melissa liked having their pastor for dinner because that's when her family really went all out, cooking all kinds of food. It was a true spread, which was why their pastor, despite forever saying he was going to, could never successfully go on a diet or lose weight.

When people cook that much food to make you feel welcomed and loved, you didn't dare hurt their feelings by not at least tasting everything set before you, did you? And Melissa's mother generally cooked three different kinds of cake and some kind of pie with vanilla ice cream on the side. That's probably another reason why Melissa was the size she'd become. Her mother could straight up throw down in the kitchen!

"Sister Anderson," Reverend Mackey used to say, "now you *know* you went and put your foot in these collards greens." Putting your foot in something when referring to cooking meant it was awesome, the best ever tasted.

"And the potato salad and the macaroni and cheese and these black-eyed peas," his wife would add to that putting-your-foot-in list. "You know, you really should think about opening up a restaurant."

"Sister Mackey, now don't you be starting nothing," Reverend Mackey would say to his wife as he piled more of everything onto his plate. "If she did have a restaurant, she would be rich. 'Cause I would be there practically every single day and get a carry-out on Saturday for my Sundays," Reverend Mackey said.

So Melissa had grown up accustomed to her family eating no earlier than two, two thirty on Sundays even when the pastor and his wife didn't eat with them. It just didn't feel right to her to eat before two. Not on Sundays. Marcus coming after two was perfect.

Marcus wasn't expecting Sasha to have cooked. And he certainly hadn't expected her to want him to stay for dinner.

Marcus scanned the laid-out dinner table. "This all looks great. But I can't stay today," he said.

"Oh, Marcus, please. Aaliyah wants you to stay, don't you, honey?" Sasha looked at Aaliyah.

Aaliyah jumped up and down, her two long pigtails jumping with her. "Yes, Daddy. Please stay. Please, please, please." She put her hands together in a prayer-like fashion and begged as she pulled on his arm.

Sasha walked over to Marcus and started mocking her daughter. "Please," Sasha said, grabbing his other arm. "Please." She smiled warmly. "It would mean the world to Aaliyah, you know it would."

"But I've already made plans," Marcus said.

"Then call her and tell her you'll be a little late," Sasha said. "Dinner's all done and the table is all set. How long would it take for you to sit and eat? Just tell her you'll be a little later getting there."

Marcus looked at Sasha. He started to respond to that *her* reference. He didn't like the way she had said it. After debating a few seconds with himself, he decided to just let it go.

"Sasha, I appreciate you for asking but—"

"Aaliyah, get your daddy to stay and eat with us. He might be able to say no to me, but he can't say no to you," Sasha said.

"Look at that sad face." Sasha looked over at Aaliyah who, right on cue, changed her face to look sad. "Are you going to break her little heart like that?"

Marcus couldn't help but laugh. Sasha was pulling out all the stops today. She had cooked, which was something she hardly ever did much of when they were married. She had cooked almost all of his favorite foods. She had the table set so it wasn't like he couldn't sit down right then, eat, and still take Melissa out. And now she was conspiring with his daughter to tug on his heart.

Sasha could tell she was getting to him. "When is the last time we all sat down and ate dinner together as a family?"

"A family?" Marcus said before he could stop the words from coming out of his mouth.

"Yes, Marc. In spite of everything that has happened, we're still a family. Aaliyah will forever connect me and you together. Now you two go and wash up. We'll sit down and eat. And"— she smiled—"we'll have a fun time just like we used to long ago. Today, ironically, the pastor's sermon was the parable about the person who prepared all of this food and invited his friends over for supper. When they didn't show up, he had them to go out into the streets, the highways and byways, and get people— the poor, the maimed, the cripple, the blind, and eventually, whoever would—to come and eat what had been prepared," Sasha said.

"So are you saying you invited some friends over to eat today and they didn't show up? And now you're getting anyone who is willing to come in and partake of the feast that was prepared for another?" Marcus asked jokingly.

Sasha smiled. "If I say yes, will you feel sorry for me and decide to stay?"

Marcus looked at her. "I suppose I would," he said.

"Well, the truth is, you're that friend I have invited to a feast prepared especially for you. If you don't partake, then I guess I'll have to go out on the streets and find someone to eat it. Please don't make me have to do that after spending so much time doing this for you and Aaliyah."

Sasha lowered her head, looked up and wiped her eyes as though there were tears. "Marcus, I just wanted to do something to thank you—that's all." She shrugged. "I know you have more important things to do, but I wanted to do something for you and Aaliyah. I'm always asking something *of* you. Today I wanted to do something *for* you."

Marcus looked at Sasha, then at Aaliyah. Sasha had gone to a lot of trouble to fix all of this. And if she went to church today, that meant she was either cooking last night or early this morning. "Come on, Aaliyah," Marcus said. "Let's go wash up."

Sasha began to smile. "Thank you," she said. After Marcus and Aaliyah left the room, she looked toward heaven. "Thank you," she said as she smiled. "Thank you."

Chapter 39

Give us this day our daily bread.
—Matthew 6:11

On Sunday, Marcus called and said he would be a little late coming over. That was great. In fact, I told him not to worry about coming until the evening.

Tiffany and Darius had stayed out on Saturday until almost three A.M. I was asleep on their couch when they came home. I was going to leave, but Tiffany insisted I stay where I was and go home in the morning. I could tell Darius had been drinking because he couldn't walk straight or without assistance. Honestly, I didn't feel like getting up and leaving, especially after I looked at my watch and saw how late it was. If I fully woke up, which is what I would have to do to drive home, I wouldn't have been able to go back to sleep that easily. So I told them good night, adjusted the blanket I had covering me, then went right on back to sleep.

When I woke up again, it was close to nine o'clock. Tiffany was not only up but cooking breakfast. It had been the smell of bacon and coffee that had awakened me. For a split second, I thought I was back home with my mother. That's the way Sunday mornings began in our house. My mother would get up and start cooking. She would put on a pot of coffee, especially when my daddy was still alive. After he died in that car accident, she would still fix a pot of coffee even though she was the only one to drink it until my grandmother came to live with us.

Grandmother was cool. Mama wouldn't let me or Diddy-bo drink coffee, and we asked her enough times.

"Coffee will make you black," Mama would say.

I thought she was serious. When Grandmother came to live with us, she saw me looking as she drank her coffee. "You want some?" Grandmother asked.

I shook my head. "Mama says we can't have any."

"Why not?"

I repeated my mother's words. "She says coffee will make me black."

Grandmother started laughing. "Is she still telling that?" Grandmother laughed even more. "That's what I used to tell her when she'd beg for my coffee." Grandmother went and got a cup and filled a fourth of that cup with coffee, then an equal amount of milk. She added three teaspoons of sugar and stirred before setting it before me. "I'll let you in on a little secret. Only black coffee makes you black. Brown coffee will keep you brown. Go on, drink up."

When I got older, I figured out that both my mother and my grandmother hadn't told the truth about coffee. I still make my coffee brown, but that's because I can't stand to drink coffee black, although the older I get, the less milk I use. And that's how I started drinking coffee. I don't make it much when I'm at home. During the week, I drink a cup each morning at work.

So smelling coffee brewing at Tiffany's house caused me to become a bit nostalgic. I got up and walked into the kitchen. Tiffany had the little ones in there with her. As she cooked, the girls sat patiently at the table. The baby was in his swing.

"Well, good morning," I said.

"Good morning," Tiffany said.

I went over and kissed the top of Jada's and Dana's heads. "You girls sure are good and quiet." I went over to touch Little D.'s hand as he played with things on the swing.

"You and Darius were still asleep. I didn't want the children to wake either of you." Tiffany set plates down before the girls. "Breakfast is ready if you'd like to eat something now. I have coffee ready as well."

"It all smells so good! I had to check my bearings at first just to make sure I wasn't a little girl at home with my mother," I said, picking one of the plates up off the counter as I fixed myself breakfast. "Look at this. Homemade biscuits?" I took two.

Tiffany nodded about the biscuits as she placed food on another plate. When she finished, I thought she was going to sit down and eat. Instead, she placed the plate along with juice and coffee on a tray. "I'm taking this up to Darius. I'll be right back."

"Sure," I said as I bowed my head and said grace. The biscuits were hot and flaky, just the way my mother used to make them from scratch.

I knew I had to hurry if I planned on getting to church on time. That's one thing about our church, we started on time. I hear that's due to Pastor Landris. One of the original members was noted for saying that since the beginning, if no one was there when the service was supposed to begin, Pastor Landris would start it with just him and his wife. Now everybody runs to get to church on time because we don't want to miss a thing.

When Tiffany came back downstairs, she had the baby's clothes in her hands. I finished eating while she got Little D. ready for church.

"Are you not going to eat anything?" I asked.

"Don't have time," Tiffany said. "I want to get to church on time, or at least as close to on time as I can. I've already combed the girls' hair, so I'm almost there."

"Is Darius going to church?" I don't know why I keep doing that: getting into her business. Old habits are hard to break. When I saw the look on her face, I really wished I could take back my question.

"He's tired," she said.

I was smart enough this time to keep my mouth closed, except to open it for the bacon I was finishing up.

"Do you want me to help you get the girls ready?" It was the least I could do, considering how much Tiffany had to do by herself.

"Thanks, but you need to get home so you can get ready for church." She walked over to me, reached into her housecoat pocket, and handed me an envelope. "This is for keeping the children for us last night. I *really*, really appreciate it." There was a glistening in her eyes.

I shook my head. "You don't owe me one thing," I said. "I had so much fun with them. You keep that."

"I can't do that. I've always been one to pay my way. If it hadn't been for you, I wouldn't have had anyone to keep the children last night. You don't know how much you mean to me. I would never take advantage of your generosity. Never."

"I appreciate you as well," I said, standing and giving her a hug. "You're one of the few people I know for certain has a good and kind heart. I'm just glad I was available to help out. But you don't owe me anything. Really. And I mean that."

She held out the envelope to me. "If you won't let me pay you, then I'll feel bad about ever asking you again. So if you won't take it as payment, will you at least accept this as a blessing from me? Allow me to sow a seed in your life, so that I can be blessed. Don't block my blessings by not allowing me to give you this. Can you do that for me?"

When she put it that way, how could I not accept it? I know what it's like to want to give to someone who doesn't want to take it for whatever reason. Those are usually the people who are always giving to others and don't know how to receive. But people who give *must* learn how to receive. I took the envelope, not because I wanted to be paid for what I had done, but because I really didn't want to block her blessings. I also didn't want her to have a reason not to reach out to me if and when she ever needed me again.

"I pray a tenfold return to you," I said, holding the envelope up in the air before I hugged her. "Be blessed."

When I got home, I had to hustle to get ready to get to church on time. Marcus and I had planned to go out to dinner later. But honestly, I was tired and wanted to take a nap. Who would think that taking care of three children could wear a person out? So when Marcus called and asked if we could go to dinner later than we'd originally planned, I cut him off from explaining why, and I suggested we cancel dinner altogether and him just come over later that night.

This way I was able to eat a sandwich and take a long nap. Everything worked out perfectly.

Chapter 40

Do not err, my beloved brethren.
—James 1:16

Marcus, Sasha, and Aaliyah had a great dinner. After they finished, Aaliyah wanted to play a game of Go Fish, so both mother and father obliged. Sasha seemed more relaxed and played more than Marcus had ever seen her do. Whatever had happened had been recent, and was truly affecting her in what appeared today to be a positive way.

Marcus looked at his watch. It was almost five o'clock. He jumped up. "Oh my, look at the time. I have got to get out of here," he said.

Sasha smiled and stood up. "Well, thank you for spending time with us today. I really enjoyed it."

"Yeah. Me, too." He turned in the direction of Aaliyah. "Come on, Princess, and give Daddy a hug and a kiss good-bye," he said.

Aaliyah moped over toward him. "I don't want you to go, Daddy. Can't you stay a little while longer? Please."

"No, I have to go. We'll spend time with each other again soon," Marcus said.

"But not with Mommy there. Not like we did today. I liked playing with both of you. It was fun."

"We'll do this again," Sasha said. "I promise. I rather enjoyed myself today as well." Although Sasha was originally speaking to Aaliyah, she ended her last sentence looking softly at Marcus as she hunched her shoulders.

It was different having Sasha being nice to him. Marcus was used to her attacking or criticizing him but not being so agreeable and almost adoring again. She was being almost the way she had been when he tutored her in high school. The way she was when he first realized she was actually interested in dating him. When she had thrown out hints but he hadn't picked up on them. The first time they went on a date was when she asked him out. He couldn't help but wonder what was going on with Sasha now or what she was truly up to.

Marcus had gone home before going to see Melissa. When he arrived at Melissa's around six, she answered the door dressed in a purple satin lounging dress.

"I was a lot more tired than I knew," she said as they sat down on the couch together. "Would you believe I'm just now getting up? Those children must have really worn me out," Melissa said. "My hat goes off to Tiffany. I don't know how she does it all. So, how was your day? How did everything go with Aaliyah?"

"It was a good day," Marcus said. "And as always, Aaliyah and I had a great time." Marcus was debating whether or not he should tell her about Sasha and the dinner she'd prepared. It wasn't as if it were that big a deal. But he didn't want to start the habit of keeping or hiding anything from Melissa. Not since he was looking to ask her to marry him soon.

He knew what half-truths and keeping things from the other person could do to a relationship. He had been the one on the receiving end of Sasha's untruths, half-truths, secrets, and attempts at constant manipulation. He had told Sasha how he felt about all of those things, although it didn't make her stop doing them. So he knew he didn't want to have even the *appearance* of doing anything like that with Melissa.

Melissa was wonderful. She was open and honest. Marcus didn't have to search deep to find her heart because she put it out there for all to see. That, in Marcus's opinion, although liberating could be dangerous. He knew from personal experience that people weren't always so careful when handling some-one else's heart.

After Melissa got past the divorce drawback, she and Marcus had talked openly and honestly about what each of them was looking for in a marriage. Marcus told her he wasn't looking for a trial-and-error relationship.

"Trial and error?" Melissa had asked.

"Yes. You know, let's try it and see if it works out. If it works for me at the time or works out, then I'll stick around. If it doesn't, then I'm out of here. I'll try you because I really don't have that much to lose since it's pretty easy to walk away. If you're not the right one, I'll admit my error and keep trying. No fault, no foul; trial and error."

"May I ask you a question?" Melissa asked.

"Go ahead."

"Do you wish things had worked out for you and Sasha?" When Melissa noted his hesitation in answering her, she added, "Honestly."

"Honestly, I would have preferred that she and I had worked things out," he said with a serious look on his face. "I'm going to tell you this: I hate that my family was torn apart. I loved Sasha. And I didn't want Aaliyah to have to grow up shuttling back and forth from one house to the other. I didn't and still don't want Aaliyah in the middle of whatever Sasha and I may be working out at the time."

Melissa's expression became even more serious. "If Sasha agreed to take you back right now, would you be interested?"

Marcus leaned his head back, rubbed his face with both his hands, then turned back to Melissa. "That's kind of a hard question," he said.

"Not really. Not if you answer it truthfully."

"But you're asking a hypothetical. None of us knows what we would really do in any given situation. I mean, how many times has someone ever said, If someone had done something like that to me, then I would have done such-and-such? Then when it happens to them, they react totally differently than they thought they would."

Melissa's expression remained the same. "If you had a chance to get back with your ex-wife right now, would you go for it? If Sasha were to come to you and tell you she was wrong about whatever happened between you two, or even if she didn't say she was wrong—if she came to you and asked that the two of you work out your differences, put aside your own selfish desires, get back together, and honestly work at your marriage, would you consider it?"

"Wow, you ask some hard questions," Marcus said. "But can I say that *that* is something that's not ever going to happen."

"You never know," Melissa said. "Women do things in the heat of the moment. They get bad advice from their family and friends. They find out things aren't so good over on the other side. That the grass, as well as its upkeep, costs a lot more on that side than anyone ever imagined just by looking over there. Then they realize what they had and see how foolish they had been to ever let it get away. A strong woman, a strong man will admit she or he was wrong. And—"

"But," Marcus said, interrupting her, "but—"

"But nothing. I'm not trying to put you on the spot, Marcus. I'm not trying to trick you or make you confess something just to make me feel better." Melissa took his hand. "You know, in spite of my zealous effort in the beginning not to, I've fallen deeply in love with you."

Marcus smiled. "And I with you."

Melissa blushed. "And that's why we need to talk about this now. I don't want to get deeper into this relationship with you just to have your ex-wife come back into the picture and we end up with a problem. I know you still have love for your ex-wife. That's just the type of person you are," Melissa said. "When a person really loves someone, they still have love for them unless that person does something horrible enough to turn that love into hate. I don't sense that has happened at all between the two of you."

"Of course I don't hate Sasha. She's the mother of my child," Marcus said. "We were married for five years. We were good friends before that. But Sasha and I are over. She's made that abundantly clear." He turned his body squarely toward Melissa. "When we talk about it like this, it sounds like I have a lot of baggage that you don't have. The question is: are you willing to be with me knowing I have all of this baggage?"

Melissa smiled. "Aaliyah is not baggage," she said.

"I don't mean Aaliyah is baggage. But she is my child, and I'm not ever going to abandon her."

"And I not only respect that, I admire it. That's what makes me love you so much. I've seen how you are with your mother. I see how you are with your daughter. I figure any man who knows how to treat his mother and knows how to take care of his child is a good man. That's the kind of man I would like to have in my life."

"And my ex-wife?" Marcus said. "How do you feel about her being in the mix?"

"Truthfully, whatever it is, it is what it is," Melissa said. "And trying to pretend or look at how things might be if they were not as they are is not going to make it so. I just need to know that if you're committed to me, you really are committed to *me*. The rest, you and I can work out together."

Melissa began to shake her head slowly. "But I can't have you doing things behind my back. I don't need a man trying to protect my feelings and keeping secrets in the guise of protecting me. If something is going on, then man up and tell me straight on. Anything else in my book is a cop-out and, frankly, dishonest."

Marcus had laughed at her after she'd said that a little more than a month ago. Now as he sat with Melissa, having had a wonderful time with Sasha and Aaliyah earlier this Sunday afternoon, he was trying to decide whether or not he should tell her about something as simple as their dinner. It really wasn't that big a deal. It had only been dinner, and Sasha had been rather pleasant for a change.

So why was it such a difficult thing for Marcus to bring up right now to Melissa?

Chapter 41

I could tell something was bothering Marcus. He seemed hesitant about sharing it with me. I wanted to make him feel comfortable, which is why I was chatting on and on about the previous night with Tiffany's children. I really wanted to tell him what I thought about Darius and that ring deal.

I think it was great he actually had bought Tiffany a gift. But there was something about that whole scene that didn't sit well with my spirit. I can't prove this and really don't have any basis to go on other than a feeling I have, but I wonder if it's possible he bought that ring for some other woman. And maybe she'd either given it back to him when they broke up or maybe he hadn't had a chance to give it to her yet. And *maybe* my asking to see the gift he claimed he had, essentially putting him on the spot, forced him to give it to Tiffany to prove something to both of us. Darius is a tricky little devil.

My mother tells me I need to stay out of other folks' business. I honestly try, but it's hard when I see other people being done wrong. I want to defend them even if it can be fairly said that I don't tend to rise to that level when it comes to defending myself. I don't think Tiffany appreciated my doing what I did, even though she knows something's not right. For whatever reason, she's willing to turn her head the other way rather than to confront certain things when it comes to Darius. I've seen him around other women, and I'm sure something is going on with him. I hear he has put the moves on quite a few women right in our church. I wouldn't put it past him to have hooked up with one or two of them. Again, it's not my business, and I need to focus on what's going on with me.

Marcus has something on his mind. Something happened, and I get the feeling he's hedging about sharing it with me. If this were happening to someone else, I would have jumped to challenge him to come clean. When it's me, I'm sitting here muzzling my mouth, waiting for him to decide what he wants to do. If that was ever going to change, I had to make a start.

"Tell me what's on your mind, Marcus," I said.

He smiled, then sighed. "Sasha fixed dinner for me and Aaliyah," he said.

I scrunched my face. "Well, that was nice," I said. *That was it?*

"Yes, it was nice. But she specifically fixed dinner."

"Yeah, I get that. You took Aaliyah home and your ex fixed you dinner."

He shook his head. "I'm not doing this right. She didn't just fix me dinner because I happened to be there. She planned it."

"So, she was trying to be nice. I think that's great," I said. The last thing I wanted him to think was that I was overly jealous. I've learned that being too possessive of anyone or anything can be dangerous for both parties. Been on both sides of that fence.

"Maybe I'm making too much about this. But then again, you would have to know Sasha to fully appreciate the significance. First off, Sasha is not a cook. She never liked to cook when we were married. And to cook a full-course meal like she did, that's something I can't say she's ever done. Not on that level, anyway."

"Well, I bet you she just wanted to thank you for being the great person that you are. You take such good care of Aaliyah. And you did just buy that piano recently. Most women have to fight to get child support. She asks you to buy a piano for your daughter and you buy it without batting an eye." I moved the remote control off the couch and placed it on the table so I could draw my legs up under me.

"That's what she said. She wanted to thank me." Marcus turned more toward me now that I was more relaxed.

"That's been about a month now. Has the piano arrived yet?"

"I think she said it would take four to six weeks to get here, so no, it hasn't."

I smiled. "I always wanted to take piano lessons, but I never got the chance."

"So what's stopping you now?"

I laughed. "I think at twenty-eight, almost twenty-nine, it's a little too late to start learning now."

"Nonsense," Marcus said. "As long as there is breath in your body, it's never too late to do a thing. I think you should find a teacher and get started."

"Oh, and are you going to buy me a piano, too, so I can practice?" I said. I was clearly teasing.

"You know, I just may buy one for my house. That way both you and Aaliyah will have it at your convenience."

I stopped when he said that. I wasn't sure what he intended to imply by that statement. Was he saying he would have the piano there so I would have more of an excuse to come to his house? Or was he saying something to indicate *his* house would someday soon be *our* house? I hated it when other women let their thoughts run wild like this when it came to what a guy said, trying to figure out what he really meant. Now here I was letting my imagination get the best of me.

I had decided I was not going to sit with my thoughts. Marcus and I were committed to keeping ourselves until we married, whether it was to each other or someone else. I must admit, he seemed to be handling this keeping himself much better than I was. I suppose it's because he's a preacher and preachers preach, or at least they are *supposed* to preach, against fornication, which Marcus has said he has no intention of committing. And after Cass, before I started dating Marcus, I had already vowed to become a revirgin.

"A revirgin?" Karen, my other friend who has tried several

times to do right, said as she laughed at me. "What in the world is a revirgin?"

"It means a virgin again. It means I'm not going to have sex until my wedding night."

She continued to laugh. "Well, good luck with that one." Later, after she knew Marcus and I were a couple, she asked how my revirginity was going. "And you made this commitment right before you started dating Marcus? Maybe he'll help you keep it, but I'm not so sure even he is for real. Folks talk the talk, but we all know people believe what's done behind closed doors is nobody's business unless and until you get caught."

Just when I was about to ask Marcus what he meant by his comment about buying a piano for his house, my telephone rang. I started not to answer it, but thought I at least should check the Caller ID.

"Hello, Angel." I said as soon as I saw who was on the other end.

"Hi, Melissa. I just needed to talk to someone. Brent is out of town assisting Pastor Landris who was to preach at four o'clock this afternoon. Johnnie Mae went with Pastor Landris. Are you busy? Do you have time to talk?"

I looked at Marcus, who was always such a good sport whenever I got a call I needed to take. He had been especially supportive since my event planning business had picked up. Angela's wedding was one of the reasons for that increased traffic. I could sense from the tone of Angela's voice, the slight shake as her words escaped her mouth, that something wasn't *terribly* wrong, but it wasn't quite right either.

And yes, I was nosy to some extent—a character flaw I confess to and absolutely do need to work on curbing—but it was more my concern now for one who had become a friend that caused me to reply, "No, I'm not busy. I have time to talk."

Marcus looked at me in a different way than in the past when I took a call. I couldn't help but wonder what was so different this time. We had been talking about his ex-wife and her fixing him dinner. I didn't have a problem with it. He had just seemed to open the door for us to talk about marriage, but it wasn't like he had asked me or anything—although he did tell me he had something special planned for Valentine's Day, which was only two days away. Maybe he was going to ask me to marry him. But if that were the case, I doubt he would ruin that moment by discussing marriage tonight. Besides, I was only going to be a minute, fifteen minutes tops, to find out what was troubling Angela. He and I had the rest of the night to talk.

He then shocked me when he stood up, kissed me on the cheek, then mouthed the word, "Good night," after which he walked over to the door and left before I could stop him.

"Melissa, are you still there?" I heard Angela's voice break through.

"Yes, I'm here," I said, shaking the thoughts loose from inside my head about Marcus and what was really going on. I focused on Angela. "So what's wrong?"

Angela brought me up to speed on a few developments regarding Arletha. Brent had an investigator check her out and he hadn't found anything. It was as if she had fallen out of the sky. She had just turned sixty-two on January 28. She had lived in Birmingham for forty-six years. There was no record of where she had lived for the sixteen years before that. No record of her ever marrying anyone..

"So is that what's bothering you?"

"No," Angela said. "My great-grandmother recorded her daughter Arletha's birthday as January 28, 1944—the exact same date as Arletha Brown. Brent and I had a huge disagreement on this, our first major one since we got married, really, about whether or not I should use that information to see if it would get Arletha Brown to confess the truth."

"What did Brent say?"

"He thinks I should let it rest. That even if my suspicions are correct, I couldn't force her to admit anything, so what difference does it make." Angela sighed deeply. "I keep telling everybody that I'm not trying to make Arletha Brown admit anything. I just want to get to the truth." She started to cry.

"I thought you had decided you would let it go," I said, recalling our last conversation. In all the time I had known Angela, she had seemed pretty grounded. But since she'd learned of Arletha's existence, she had become more emotional. Then I remembered that she was pregnant, and pregnant women have hormonal shifts, especially those first and last months.

"I had, and that's why Brent is more upset with himself than he is with me. He feels if he had not had someone dig deeper, I wouldn't be back on this. I'm trying so hard to let go, to put it out of my mind. But what if my feelings are correct? So I'm sitting here alone, without Brent home to calm or talk me down. Melissa, I'm going over to visit Arletha."

"You're *what?*"

"Right now, before Brent gets home tonight, I'm going over to see her."

"So you called me to talk you out of this ridiculous idea?" I asked, trying to figure out what my role was supposed to be in this.

"No, I called to ask you to come with me. If you will." I don't know if she could feel the hesitation or just figured it out because I hadn't given voice to my thoughts, but then she added, "Please, Melissa. I haven't shared what's going on with me with anyone here in Birmingham except for you and Johnnie Mae. You've been to Arletha's house. You know her. I don't want to go by myself, but for some reason that I can't quite explain, I feel in my spirit that I need to go over there tonight."

I knew I could effectively argue why this was a bad idea. But I also knew from experience that when a person feels something strongly in their spirit, they need to acknowledge it and act accordingly. Angela didn't need to go to Arletha's place alone. And I had a feeling in *my* spirit that if I told her I couldn't or wouldn't go, she was going to go anyway.

"Sure. I'll go with you," I said.

She let out a sigh. "Thank you. I'll be there to pick you up in about fifteen minutes," Angela said.

"I'll be ready," I said as I looked first at the lounger I was wearing that I needed to change out of, then at the clock that told me I didn't have much time to waste.

After I hung up, I called Marcus. The way he left didn't feel right to me either. I wanted to be sure he was all right . . . that *we* were all right. He said everything was fine. He just didn't want to crowd me or make me feel rushed.

As I hurried to change into my favorite pink jogging suit with the hoodie, the one Marcus bought me for Christmas, I replayed in my head our conversation about Sasha. I was trying to figure out what I might have missed.

I really didn't see anything, unless he was having second thoughts about his ex-wife being an ex, and he had needed someone to talk that out with. Unless when he needed to talk, I had chosen someone else over him and hurt his feelings.

I was looking out of my apartment window when I saw Angela pull up. I went out and got into her car. First I would take care of this. Then I would do a better job of finding out what was truthfully going on with Marcus.

Chapter 42

A friend loveth at all times, and a brother is born for adversity.

—Proverbs 17:17

Angela pulled up in Arletha's driveway. We sat there for at least five minutes. I wasn't going to say anything to push her one way or the other. Frankly, I thought going there was not a great idea. But I also realized this was something Angela felt she had to do.

Angela touched her purse a few times, then said, "Well, let's get this over with."

We walked to the front door and knocked on the door. After a minute with no answer, Angela knocked several times in succession.

I was actually relieved there was no answer. "Looks like she's either not here or asleep," I said.

Angela started to walk away. She stopped and tried to peek in a window on the porch.

"There's a light on in the back," Angela said, then she trotted off the porch and, to my surprise, headed toward the back of the house. I followed her, not because I really wanted to, but because I didn't think going around to the back of someone's house alone, at night, was either a smart or a safe thing to do. I took out my cell phone and held it ready in my hand.

Angela walked up onto the back deck. She started trying to look through the patio door. Vertical blinds obstructed a clear view, but Angela was determined to angle her body just right to see something.

Out of nowhere, Angela started trying to open the glass patio door, to no avail. "I see her," she said. "She's lying on the floor in the kitchen."

Not being able to budge the patio door, Angela then headed toward the front of the house. The whole time I was thinking that we couldn't just break into this woman's house like this, even if something had happened to her. I started dialing 911 as I trotted to keep up with Angela, thinking that, being pregnant, she didn't need to be running around like that.

I was talking to the dispatch operator when Angela reached the front door again. She was trying to open it as though she thought it might possibly have been left unlocked. The police and the ambulance arrived almost at the same time. They gained entry into the house quickly. Angela and I followed them, although we stayed out of their way.

A paramedic put Arletha on the stretcher.

"Is she alive?" Angela asked. "Is she going to be all right?"

"Are you a relative?" one of the paramedics asked.

"Yes," Angela said. "I'm her granddaughter."

"Well, you can follow us over to the hospital. For now, she's still breathing. You need to bring her information with you."

Angela asked which hospital they were taking her to. After they told her, she looked at me. Without even having to ask, I just said, "We're there."

Angela grabbed my arm as they made their way out. She pulled me off to the side, out of earshot. "We don't have her information," Angela whispered. "We need to find her purse, see if her insurance card is in there, and then take it to the hospital."

The more I thought about this, the more I could see this was not going at all according to plan. What disturbed me even more was the answer Angela had given when she was asked if she was a relative.

"Why did you say you were her granddaughter?"

"Relax. I had to make sure they'd let us follow them to the hospital."

Angela told the police we would lock up on our way out. When they left, we began to search the rooms looking for her purse. As tempting as I'm sure it was for Angela, she didn't take the opportunity to look through Arletha's things.

"Found it," Angela said. She opened it up and looked through her wallet. "I don't see a health insurance card in here." Angela found Arletha's driver's license, which gave her address and date of birth, but no social security number, which might have helped them with an insurance number. "She's only sixty-two, not old enough for Medicare yet."

"Where do you think she would have put an insurance card if not in her purse?"

"That's if she has one," Angela said. "There are a lot of people who don't have health insurance at all. They just hope they don't get sick or ever have to go to the hospital."

We continued to look in various bedroom drawers. "Well, if they find out she doesn't have health insurance they're going to transfer her to Cooper Green."

"Thank God for Cooper Green. I'm just thankful people have somewhere to go at times like these. It's sad how people right here in America are having to live without access to medical care. It's sad and it's really a shame."

I found something with Arletha's social security number on it. We decided to take that with her purse containing her driver's license.

"Let's check the bathroom," Angela said.

"For what?"

"To see if she takes any type of medication. The hospital will need to know if she is allergic to anything or is taking any prescription drugs."

I thought about it a second. "Maybe you should level with the hospital and tell them you're really just a friend and you don't know anything about her."

"Yeah, I was just thinking that."

I don't know if I just hadn't noticed it before or whether she had just started, but Angela was trembling. I gave her a hug. "Let's go. Give me your keys, and I'll drive us to the hospital."

She nodded and handed me her keys. We locked Arletha's house using the keys for the dead bolt we found in her purse. Fortunately, when they broke in, the dead bolt wasn't on, so the doorjamb wasn't damaged. This all seemed like it had taken a long time, but in truth, only fifteen minutes had passed since the ambulance had taken her away. It always amazes me how truly relative time is. The way it seems to speed up and go quickly for some things, while with other things, it feels like an ant trying to crawl through molasses.

We arrived at the hospital fifteen minutes later. They gave Angela a hard time because she didn't have much of the information they needed. I called Marcus and told him what was going on.

Marcus asked, "Is Brent there?"

"No, he went to a church where Pastor Landris was to speak this afternoon in Montgomery. He should be home soon, though."

"Well, I'll call him on his cell phone and let him know what's going on. How's Angel?" Marcus asked, calling Angela by the name everybody else except me seemed to call her. I had tried calling her Angel. But when you first meet someone and they tell you one name and you get used to, it's hard to switch. Angela had said either name I chose to use suited her. So I stuck with Angela. Especially since she was getting married when I met her and everything that was done in the course of her wedding used her legal name.

"Thanks, Marcus."

"I'll come over to the hospital after I finish," Marcus said.

"You don't have to."

"I know. But you never know. I might end up being some help. If not, I just want to make sure the two of you are okay."

I looked at Angela, who did seem to be a lot more upset than I was. She liked Marcus. If Brent couldn't be here with her, Marcus might help keep her mind off all the things I'm sure were going through her head.

I walked back over to Angela. "Marcus is calling Brent to let him know what's going on, and then he's coming over."

"He didn't have to do that," Angela said.

"You know Marcus," I said.

She smiled. "Yeah. Marcus is one of a kind for sure. I hope things work out for the two of you. He deserves to have a good woman in his life."

"Well, we'll see where things go." I took a deep long breath.

Fifteen minutes later, a nurse came into the waiting room "Mrs. Underwood?" she said, looking out among the sea of people sitting there.

"Yes," Angela said, standing up and walking toward her.

"Dr. Madison wants to talk with you."

Just then Marcus came up. He hugged Angela.

"You want us to go with you?" I asked.

She shook her head. "I'll be all right. After all, she's not really my grandmother, right? She's just a woman I met, what, once? A woman who came to my wedding and didn't even think enough to speak to me? You and I just happened to be at her house and found her lying unconscious on the floor. That's all."

Marcus grabbed Angela's hand and then mine. "Let's say a word of prayer right now," he said.

As he prayed, I felt a calm wash over me. Angela then followed the nurse to find out what was going on as Marcus and I continued to hold hands and wait together.

Chapter 43

For I know the thoughts that I think toward you, saith the Lord, thoughts of peace, and not of evil, to give you an expected end.

—Jeremiah 29:11

Brent called Marcus back as soon as he got his message. Pastor Landris brought him to the hospital, which really worked out well. This way Brent could drive Angela's car home and Marcus could take me home. Angela definitely was in no shape to drive. Pastor Landris was there for about ten minutes. He prayed with us before he left to go home. It was a little after ten o'clock—a bit late now, especially to be at a hospital.

Angela had learned from the doctor that an aneurysm had burst in Arletha's brain.

"They're not sure she's going to pull through," Angela said. "But the doctor said if we hadn't found her when we did, and if they hadn't gotten her to the hospital as quickly as they did, she'd be dead now."

"What were you doing over there?" Brent asked.

"It was God. God led her to go over there at that time," I said, once again sticking my nose where it didn't belong. But I knew where Brent was likely going with this.

I was telling the truth. God had led her. Angela believed in her spirit that she was supposed to go over there on this night at that time. Had she not yielded to the voice of the Lord, Arletha would most likely be dead. At least now, she had somewhat of a fighting chance. And it didn't matter whether she was really Angela's grandmother or not. She was a human being who was in need of help. Somehow in God's wisdom, He was able to move Angela on this night to go over there. No one knows the plans of God, but I was seeing more and more that if we don't just talk to God, but also listen, He truly will direct our path. He will order our steps.

Marcus put his arm around my shoulder and gave me a squeeze. It's as though he knew what I was thinking. Ironically, I didn't realize until he did that just how much I needed a hug at that precise moment.

"I'm glad you followed what your spirit was telling you to do. Whatever your initial reasons may have been, God used it," Brent said to Angela. "Do you want any coffee or anything?" he asked, still looking at his wife.

Angela shook her head. "I'm trying to cut back on caffeine, remember?"

"Oh, why is that?" Marcus asked.

Angela looked at Brent. "You haven't told him yet?" Angela said.

"We hadn't seen each other or talked in a while," Brent said.

I looked at Brent, not believing he was just now about to tell Marcus, one of his closest friends, if not his best friend, that he was going to be a father.

"So what's going on?" Marcus asked, looking at Brent." Haven't told me what?"

I tried to act like I didn't know since I hadn't told him either. Then again, I was asked not to so Brent would have the pleasure.

"We're going to have a baby," Brent said. "July . . ." he looked at Angela for help with the exact due date.

"July ninth," Angela said, smiling and rubbing her abdomen.

"I thought there was something different about you," Marcus said to Angela. "Oh, man, that is so great." He addressed his last comment to Brent as he gave him one of their manly hugs.

"Thank you, guys, for staying here with me. I know Arletha is no kin to any of us. But she doesn't have anyone, that we know of," Angela said.

"Do you really believe that or are you just saying that to throw me off the trail?" Brent asked Angela in a serious tone.

"Believe what?" Angela said

"That this woman is no kin to you?"

Angela lowered her head, then looked back up. "I'm pretty sure she's not my grandmother."

"How is it you're so certain all of a sudden?" Brent asked.

"I just know. It's time I faced reality. No matter how much I wish a thing to be true, it's not going to make it so. That woman in there fighting for her life needs our prayers. That's all I'm going to concentrate on now."

"Did they find her insurance information?" I asked.

"It doesn't look like she has any health insurance," Angela said.

"That's not good," Marcus said, shaking his head.

"I know," Angela said. "They asked who would be responsible for the bill if they kept her here, not that they could transfer her out at this point."

Brent looked at Angela. "And what did you tell them?"

Angela didn't answer him.

"Please tell me you didn't say you. Please tell me you didn't," Brent said.

"Brent, the woman needs care. They brought her in here to get help. What was I supposed to do?"

"You do what everybody else does. You stay out of it if it doesn't concern you directly. Especially something like this," Brent said.

"The worst-case scenario would have been to take her to another hospital. Do you have any idea how much it costs per day just to stay at a hospital?" Marcus said. "This woman from our church was in the hospital a few months ago. She was there for four days. Her bill was over ten thousand dollars. And that didn't include the doctor's bill."

"What was I supposed to do?" Angela repeated. "If they had tried to transfer her, she would have died. She wasn't in any shape to be moved just because she doesn't have insurance. Are we not our brothers' keepers? Are we not our sisters' keepers?"

"Yeah, but you could have just let her be responsible for her own bill," Brent said. "Look, baby. I'm not trying to sound harsh or insensitive or anything. But if you signed to be responsible for her bill, that means they are going to be looking for you to pay it if she doesn't. Sure, we have a little money, but we don't have money like that."

"Oh, I get it. We go to church. We talk about love. We talk about caring for the poor. We talk about whatsoever we do unto the least of these who can't do for themselves that we do it to Christ. We talk about missionary work in other countries. But when we have an opportunity to practice what we preach, practice what we're sitting in church week after week supposedly hearing and learning every single Sunday and Wednesday right here in our communities, we don't translate that into doing." Angela stood and walked away from Brent.

"I'm sorry," she said. "I feel I am supposed to do more than just talk about what a great Christian I am. I don't expect to have to pay this bill completely by myself." She turned to her husband. "I would never do anything like that to us. But I couldn't just turn my back on this woman. I'll do what I can, put together a fund-raiser. And no, I didn't do it thinking she's my grandmother and that I needed to be sure she was okay for that reason."

"Are you sure?" Brent asked, gently grasping Angela by her shoulders. "Are you sure you're not thinking this is your grandmother and maybe prolonging her life will help you get to the truth? Are you sure you aren't doing this thinking she will feel she owes you if she pulls through? Thinking that this will cause her to level with you?"

Angela leaned her head back and looked up toward the ceiling. She looked back at Brent. "This is neither the time nor the place for us to be having this discussion. I'm sure neither Melissa nor Marcus wants to hear us hash this out."

"Angel, baby. I know you're a caring woman. That's what I love so much about you. That's why I love you so much."

"So what do you want me to do, Brent?" She looked at her

husband. "What do you want me to do now? Do you want me to go in there and tell them I've changed my mind?"

"I don't know what I want you to do now," Brent said. "I'll tell you what. Why don't we just go home, and we can sort through all of this there."

"Fine," Angela said as she headed toward the exit.

It was at that moment that I realized how uncomfortable it made me to hear married people argue. I hated hearing my mother and father when they argued. There was always that scary thought in the back of my mind that they would divorce, and I would end up like so many of the other children in our neighborhood who didn't have a father around. Diddy-bo and I were always the envy of our community. We were one of the few families who had a mother *and* a father in the house, living together as husband and wife. Yes, there were plenty of men and women who lived with each other. For whatever reason, those people may have been together for years but they never married. But our family and about three others in the community were like an endangered species.

Then my daddy died suddenly in that car accident, and we became like the other children who didn't have a father in the house. Still, I had my memories. And the only bad memories I really had that I managed to bury were my parents' arguments. I hated when they fussed with each other.

I felt this way hearing Angela and Brent. I knew they loved each other. But most couples who marry loved each other at one time before something happened. The next thing you know, they don't love each other enough to stay together and make it work.

When I finally marry, I want things to be different. I always dream of things being different for me and my husband. But as I watched these two who I know love each other dearly, I realized that in real life there would be problems and disagreements in a marriage. But we have to learn how to work through them, not cut and run at the first sign of trouble.

Marcus took me home. It was eleven thirty. After he turned

off the ignition, and we sat there for a few minutes, I touched his hand.

"You and I need to talk," I said.

"I was just thinking the same thing," he said.

We went inside, knowing we needed to lay some things on the table.

Chapter 44

They search out iniquities; they accomplish a dili-
gent search: both the inward thought of every one
of them, and the heart, is deep.

—Psalm 64:6

Marcus knew he needed to have a heart-to-heart talk with Melissa. He had danced around this thing with Sasha. Yes, he had fallen in love with Melissa. His plans were to ask her to marry him on Valentine's Day because he knew how close they had gotten. Sure, they could date for a year, then get engaged for a year before getting married. But given the way he felt about her, that wasn't going to work for him. He also knew he shouldn't move too fast and end up making a mistake he would later regret.

"May I go first?" Melissa asked. She cleared her throat. "You were trying to tell me something about Sasha earlier today. I wasn't hearing what you were really trying to say. Would you please just tell me without me having to guess? What's going on with you and Sasha?"

He nodded. "I was struggling with something you and I have discussed in the past."

"What's that?"

"You asked me that if Sasha wanted to get back together, would that be something I would consider."

"Yeah. And you usually avoid the question by saying that nothing like that is ever going to ever happen."

"Right. Because that's what I've always believed. But today, this weekend really, I feel something is going on with her. She was acting so different," Marcus said.

"How?"

"Okay. Friday when I picked up Aaliyah, Sasha actually had everything ready when I arrived. Also, she was more subdued. Then later Aaliyah told me Sasha had been crying and had told her not to tell me." He chuckled a little. "Now, don't get me wrong. Crying, for Sasha, is a sport that she knows how to play very well. But usually when she cries, she makes an effort not to waste it."

"Do you think she did that with Aaliyah to up her game? Maybe she actually told Aaliyah to tell you, but to tell you she said not to tell you."

Marcus smiled for a second, then he shook his head. "No. She genuinely didn't want Aaliyah to tell me. Whatever it is, she told Aaliyah she didn't think even God could fix it."

"Do you think she's sick or something? That's how people act when they've gotten a bad report from the doctor. They don't like to tell people at first, and they internalize it."

He shrugged. "I don't know. But when I went over there earlier this afternoon, she seemed fine. She was happy, laughing, playing with me and Aaliyah. She had cooked this feast like I've never seen from her. That took quite a lot of time and effort. Then she told me she'd cooked all of that, many of the foods being my favorite dishes, because she wanted to thank me."

"See, that sounds like a person who may have been told some bad news. About five years ago, one of my friends found out she had cancer and she acted almost the same way. First she cried. Then she resigned herself to what was going on. She made up with her ex-husband because they had two little children and she wanted to make sure he got them and took care of them if she didn't make it," Melissa said. "She pulled through fine. And because of that tragedy, they got back together, and now their marriage is stronger than ever."

"So you think Sasha may be sick and just doesn't want to tell me?"

"That's a possibility," Melissa said. She didn't like the feel of any of this conversation. Especially after she remembered her friend and how things had turned out with her and her ex-husband, now devoted husband again. "So what do you want to do?"

"What do you mean?"

"I mean, are you planning to ask her and get to the bottom of what's going on?"

Marcus shook his head. "I can't just ask her something like that. What if that's not it? What if something else is going on?"

"Then just ask her what's going on straight out."

"Today," Marcus said, "she was a different woman."

"Okay. Let me ask you something, and will you promise you'll answer me no matter what?" Melissa said.

"If I can."

"If Sasha wants to get back with you now, are you open to that? And please don't skirt the question by saying she doesn't. I'm not asking you about her. I'm asking you about you. I need to know where *you* are. I need to know where your heart is."

Marcus stood up, walked around the room as he scratched his head, then sat back down next to Melissa. "I love you, Melissa. You have changed my life. You brought me back my laughter, my joy. I'm so glad I found you. I thank God for you. You give me a reason to look forward to the next day and then the next. Whatever Sasha and I had, it's over. I don't want to be her enemy, so if we can be cordial to one another, all the better."

"So your answer is no?"

"My answer is no. No, I wouldn't want to get back with her. That chapter in our lives is over, done. She has moved on, and so have I."

Melissa nodded.

He stood and pulled her up. "You are who I'm focused on right now."

Melissa smiled. She knew that's what he *thought*. She only wished she could be sure he truly believed it. She laid her head on his shoulder and allowed him to hold her.

Chapter 45

*Teaching us that, denying ungodliness and worldly
lusts, we should live soberly, righteously, and godly,
in the present world.*

—Titus 2:11

Sasha had to do something quick. She had made Marcus dinner hoping to see how he was really feeling toward her. Right now, she needed money to pay her bills. Her mother was having a fit about her own bills and the money she had lost that was to have paid them. Sasha knew Marcus would eventually get over the piano deal and the money she'd lost for it. Even if he got mad, he would still get over it. Marcus always got over the things she did. And she'd done some pretty horrid things in the past.

Sasha knew Marcus loved her—always had and always would. He hadn't wanted the divorce. He had done everything in his power to keep them together as a family. She was the one who had pushed it forward. She was the one who had done whatever she could to hurt him. She had lied to everybody, making him out to be the bad guy, an abuser. In the beginning, she had insinuated it, then later, she accused him outright of physically abusing her when he hadn't. All he'd ever done was love her and try to make her happy.

When Marcus didn't bow to Sasha's and her mother's whims and demands, mother and daughter teamed up with an unspoken vow to make his life miserable.

"He loves that child," Sasha's mother had said. "You want to hurt him the way he has hurt you? Then take that child away from him. That will bring him to his knees. Either he'll get in line with the program, or he'll find himself on the outside looking in."

The only thing was, Sasha had gotten her divorce, just as she'd wanted. And she had enjoyed a few months with the "guy friend" she'd continued talking with during her marriage. Of course, he dumped her as soon as he saw how much trouble she really was. Then she met another guy at a club. He seemed really into her. He would take her here and there, but he wasn't all that crazy about children. So every chance he could, he got Sasha to send her daughter off to someone else's place when he was around. Sasha spun so many tales of emergencies, she could have starred in her own television drama.

Her mother caught on to what she was doing rather quickly. But of course, her mother was the master of deception herself. She stopped keeping Aaliyah altogether. They both could visit her, but she wasn't keeping anybody. Sasha's cousin would keep Aaliyah, but she wasn't quite stable and everybody in the family knew it. Whenever Marcus found out his daughter had been left at Thelma's house, he would have a fit.

"If you ever need someone to keep our daughter, call me, okay? I don't want her staying with any- and everybody," Marcus said. "All right, Sasha?"

So when Sasha was asked to go out of town with this guy or that, and she didn't have anyone to keep Aaliyah for a few days, she'd call Marcus. Other times, when she didn't want to merely ask him, she would create phony emergencies. And when Marcus questioned her about these supposed emergencies, she did what she always did with him: she wouldn't answer the question and would quickly turn it back on him.

There was one thing Sasha noted about all the guys she had been with since she divorced. They would start out wooing her, using their money at first, then her own, to pay for their outings, to "Can I hold a few Andrew Jacksons until I get paid?" (Five Andrews were the equivalent of one Benjamin.) Then somehow, these wonderful men would tell her she was too high maintenance, and they were out of there like a streak of lightning. On to their next conquest.

In truth, they were looking for an excuse to walk away. But Marcus never did. It was finally starting to register with Sasha what a great man and husband she had had in Marcus. He loved her and she now knew that. He had always helped her with Aaliyah without complaint. He had paid all the bills. And even at the rare times when she worked during their marriage, she was able to use her money for whatever she wanted. Had she still been married to Marcus, she would have been able to help her mother out more after her father died.

But Sasha had totally miscalculated. She saw the fun of being single but not the responsibility. Aaliyah adored her father. It had been a mistake for Sasha ever to have pushed Marcus out of her life the way she had. She now understood that. The question she faced was: what at this point could she do to fix things between them?

She had cooked dinner for him hoping for an opening to let him know what she was thinking and feeling. Yes, on Friday she had been upset about the money and all that what had just happened had represented. But after Aaliyah went over to her father's house, Sasha had time to think, time to reflect, and time to earnestly pray about her life.

Yes, she admitted she had sinned and fallen short. The relationship she had claimed was just a friendship with her guy friend had been more than that. And when her own mother realized that, she had encouraged her, running interference to assist her in her deceit. Especially when her mother got upset with Marcus and wanted to show him who was really in charge. Sasha knew that was the real motive behind her mother's rallied support of her. And as much as Sasha hated to admit it, she had craved *something* from her mother other than the hurt she had felt over the years. When her mother got behind her and encouraged her to leave Marcus, she was just glad her mother seemed to be paying her any attention. So she took it and ran with it.

Yes, she had lied about the real deal surrounding her and Marcus. She had purposely and deliberately led everybody to believe that behind that thoughtful and caring exterior resided a man horrible enough to be an abuser. She didn't have to prove that. All she had to do was lead people to believe it was so. She did think, because of Marcus's generous nature, that if they divorced, he would give her whatever amount of money she asked for just because he loved her and his daughter so. Sasha truly believed she could have the best of both worlds if she and Marcus divorced: Marcus's undying attention and access to his money, coupled with the freedom to date and to do as she pleased.

Yes, she loved her daughter the same way she was certain her own mother loved her. What she hadn't realized, until this weekend, was how much she was treating Aaliyah the way her mother had treated her. While in prayer on Friday night, Sasha saw how her father had adored her, always doing whatever he could for her. How he had loved her unconditionally, just like Marcus loved his child. Sasha now saw how jealous her mother had been because of the love her father had for her. She didn't blame her mother completely. She now realized it was a spirit, that this was spiritual warfare. Seeing how she was repeating that same pattern, she understood how easily something like that can creep up and take over without your ever really noticing it. Like boiling a frog in hot water—gradually, and over time.

Why had she wanted so much to be free of Marcus? Marcus, whose only offense it seemed was to love her and love his child with all of his heart. Isn't that what most women desire in a man? That's why she went from one man to the next after she and Marcus separated and then divorced. Like an idiot, she was searching for what she already had.

God showed her all of this as she was first bowed before Him in prayer, then completely facedown on the floor. She had cried out to God and He had shown her the errors in judgment she'd made by not consulting Him. She confessed her sins and asked God to forgive her. She then reminded God of His Word as Marcus had often said we need to do. "Not because God doesn't remember," Marcus had said in a sermon, "but to let God know that you know what His Word says. That's what God is looking for from us. That and faith."

God, You said that if we will confess our sins and ask forgiveness, you will forgive us and cleanse us from all our unrighteousness. I'm asking you to forgive me right now. Lord, I was wrong. I should have acknowledged You in all of my ways. But instead, I went about trying to establish my own way. Please forgive me.

That Sunday, she had gone to church, something she had slacked off on quite a bit over the past two years, mostly because there was always some guy who wanted to stay out late from a Saturday night date well into early Sunday morning. At other times, she just wanted to stay in bed and catch up on her rest from having been out so much.

It had seemed fun at first, the guys. But then she realized none of them really cared about her. She had heard it and said it herself before: they were only after what they could get from her. They didn't really care about her, and they certainly didn't respect her. But when you get caught up in their web, you don't see these things as objectively. She thought she was enjoying herself and her life. But pausing at this point and evaluating things, she saw clearly that she was far from having fun *or* being happy. And when it came to Marcus, she at least needed to make amends. That's why on Saturday night, she called and asked him to bring Aaliyah home earlier on Sunday than he normally would. The very least she could do was surprise him by making them all a nice dinner.

Sunday, she had gone to a new church that people at her office were constantly talking about. They would bring tapes of the pastor's sermons and pass them around. Sasha had not been interested in hearing him, hearing about him, or hearing about his church. But after she prayed Saturday night, she listened to one of the tapes a coworker had given her. It was on "Strongholds" and how they can keep you from attaining all God has for you. That message ministered deeply to her. Like most everybody, she had her own stronghold. So she got directions to the church off the Internet, and on Sunday morning, she got up and made her way to the early-morning service at Followers of Jesus Faith Worship Center.

Pastor George Landris was preaching on, of all things, "Generational Curses." How a thing may have begun with our great-great-great-grandparents before making its way down through the generations to find us. And we're left not even realizing why we do what we do.

"Yes, it may have originated with your grandmother. Yes, your mother may have done the exact same thing," Pastor Landris said. "Yes, you may be doing it right now. And if you have children, you may very well be passing it on to them. At some point, we must realize that it is a curse, and curses can be broken. But we must first acknowledge there's a problem. Too many people want to act like they don't see there's something wrong in their lives. Church, it's time-out for playing church." He bobbed his head up and down. "I said it's time-out for playing church."

Sasha found herself engrossed in his every word. He was speaking to her in plain English. This man was speaking to her where she lived. He was indeed a different kind of a preacher than what she had grown to think was the true standard of what a preacher was. He spoke in today's terms, talked about the things people are dealing with in real life. He spoke so that his words would be heard and observed without distraction.

"Amen," she said softly. *Yes, too many people are merely playing church.*

"People of God, the Bible gives us plenty of instances where folks were cursed because of things they either did or didn't do. Yes, you may be under a curse right now. And yes, maybe it wasn't anything you yourself chose, it was just passed down from one generation to the next. When I was growing up, before welfare reform kicked in, you would find where the great-grandmother might have been an unwed mother at fifteen. She would sign up to get a welfare check. She may or may not have ever gotten married, although I believe lots of these women wanted to marry the men they ended up living with. But the way the government worked the welfare system, if you married, they would cut your check off. It didn't matter if you were struggling and needed a helping hand. If you married or had a man helping you out in any form, and they found out, your check would be cut."

Pastor Landris rubbed his chin. "Can't you just see Satan's hand in all of this? If you needed help, you could get help as long as you didn't marry. I won't go into the history behind keeping the men out of the picture in order to get that welfare check, but suffice it to say that the system was structured to keep the men out of the home and out of children's lives. All of this: from the mother being unwed and having children, to finding ways to keep the men out of their children's lives, to keeping people from ever marrying, became generational curses. And after that generation, the next generation would come along doing exactly what they saw. If you don't know any differently, how can you do any differently? So that young girl who became a mother at fifteen now has a daughter who comes along and does the exact same thing at fifteen, and the cycle continues."

Pastor Landris shook his head. "But let's not get caught up in the old welfare system of things. Some of our rich and well-off brothers and sisters have their own generational curses. Their family may have lied and cheated to get their wealth; now the next generation lies and cheats to keep the wealth. People divorcing, changing spouses like they change their winter clothes for spring, spring for summer, summer for fall. You all know what I'm talking about. Some people say getting rid of the old model for the new."

People laughed as they nodded.

"So let's not start pointing fingers at just the have-nots, trying to say they are under a generational curse," Pastor Landris said. "Let me assure you, those who *have* have their own problems, too. And you can believe that. Just like God is not a respecter of persons. Well, problems and generational curses are not a respecter of persons—they are an equal-opportunity employer. It rains on the just and the unjust. But children of God, it's high time to lay these generational curses down. Jesus is the answer to breaking these curses. Jesus has redeemed us. We who have received Him are no longer cursed. We are blessed."

He pounded the lectern. "Did you hear what I just said? I said we are blessed! And I don't care what anyone tries to tell you. I don't care how many letters he or she has after his or her name. I don't care how many degrees they may have. I don't care how many fancy cars they own. I don't even care if they have their own jet or not. I don't care what anyone tries to tell you, from this day forward, nobody, nobody, nobody can curse what God has blessed! Nobody can curse what God has blessed!"

The congregation erupted into shouts and praise.

"When God blesses you, no devil in hell can prevail against you," Pastor Landris said. "Jesus said, 'Upon this rock I will build my church, and the gates of hell shall not prevail against it.' You are the church. Not some building. You are the church. Oh, the devil might get in your head and whisper things to try and get you to use your tongue to curse yourself. But once you take hold of this revelation, the revelation that if God be for you then *who* can be against you? Once you get this, no one, no one, no one can snatch you from the blessings God has for you. Blessings delayed are not blessings denied. That's why I keep telling you to put a watch over your mouth. Watch the words you allow to come out of your mouth because your words spoken over your life have power. Life and death are in the power of the tongue."

Pastor Landris paced a few times as he wound down. "Generational curses, generational curses, generational curses. It's time-out for generational curses! However your mother was, whatever your daddy did or didn't do, you are the redeemed! You have been bought with a price, you have been emancipated. You have been set free! Let the redeemed of the Lord say so. Let the redeemed of the Lord say so! Recognize what you're doing to keep these generational curses going, and then repent."

He began to nod vigorously. "Yes, that's what I said. Repent. And repent means to turn around, to head in a different direction. Repent and stop this nonsense! God has better for you. I say God has better for you. But you have to choose the better. Why do you want to wallow in the way things have been instead of walk in what God has prepared for you? You need to head in a different direction. If you don't, you're going to miss out on God's blessings. And you'll have nobody to blame but yourself. You can't blame Mama, you can't blame Daddy, you can't blame sister, brother, spouse, cousin, or your friend. You can't even blame the devil. If your life is not working to the fullness of God's blessing, look in the mirror and have a nice little chat with that person who's looking back at you."

Pastor Landris walked down the stairs from where he was speaking. "If you've messed up, repent and go in a different direction. I know some of you think what you've done is so bad that not even God can forgive you. God not only *can* but He *will* forgive you. I know some of you think God can't fix whatever you've messed up, but we serve an awesome and an incredible God. Jesus, the name above all names. Don't sell God short. Don't underestimate our God. God is able to do exceedingly, abundantly, above all that you can ever ask or think. But you have to get things right with God. And if you have wronged anyone, go and make it right with that person. Don't let Satan keep you in that ball of confusion. God's grace is sufficient. It's time to break your curse. It's time to break free of generational curses. Your children and your children's children deserve better. *You* deserve better! Step out on God's Word and watch God as He takes you to higher heights."

Sasha was certain God was speaking to her. She had been married to a good man. Now she needed to make things right. She knew Marcus was involved with another woman now. She wasn't sure how serious they had really become, but she knew how devoted to God Marcus was. He knew the scriptures. She was ready to admit she had been wrong to push for that divorce. She had been wrong to listen to others when she should have been praying and listening to God. She wanted a better life for herself and her daughter. Marcus had loved her without condition before. He had wanted to reconcile and work through their differences, whatever those differences were, whatever they needed to do to fix them. Marcus had wanted to save their marriage and he had told her so unashamedly.

"Whatever we need to do to be a family," he had said, "I'll do that. I'll do it."

She had spurned him, laughed in his face, made fun of him, and enjoyed seeing him almost beg her to give them a chance.

Now she needed to know, did they still have a chance? Did Marcus still want his family back? God hated divorce. She now wanted to make things right.

Chapter 46

And as ye would that men should do to you, do ye also to them likewise.

—Luke 6:31

Angela had gone by the hospital to see Arletha every day for the past four days. Arletha had not regained consciousness in all of that time. Angela didn't stay long. It wasn't as if she had anything she could say to her as she lay there. She had mostly gone because she realized Arletha really didn't have anyone who cared.

The day after Arletha's surgery, Angela and Brent had gone to Arletha's house to look through her things. They had wanted to find someone to call to let know what was going on. They found no address book, no names or phone numbers written anywhere. Not inside the phone book, not on slips of paper, nothing. Arletha didn't have an answering machine, so they couldn't replay messages to find a lead on anyone who might have called her in the past. Arletha didn't appear to have a soul in the world who cared whether she lived or died. At least, there was no evidence of such a person.

Going through a stack of things on a bottom shelf in a curio cabinet, Brent found a book that looked like a church directory. It was a year old. He flipped through it and saw that Arletha had been an usher there. He showed the directory to Angela.

"Let's call the church," she said. Using her cell phone, she called the church's office, telling the person who answered her name and why she was calling. The woman told her she did know Arletha Brown, but that as far as they knew, she had left their church after years of being a faithful member. She didn't know what church Arletha was attending now. When Angela asked her at least to let the pastor know what was going on, she was shocked by the woman's response.

"I'll tell him. But quite frankly, she hasn't been here in a while. As far as we're concerned, she's no longer a member. I'm sure he won't bother to call you back about it."

Angela couldn't believe how cold that had sounded. Her heart went out to Arletha. What must it feel like to live a life where no one cares about you? What must it feel like not to have anyone when you need people praying and caring the most? Yes, it's likely that the life Arletha lived had caused this. But as Christians, weren't we called to love those who don't necessarily love us back? Aren't we to reach out and show God's love to others, people in this world, in order to win them to Christ? *If we only do good to those who return it to us, what is the reward for that?* Angela thought.

Yes, Arletha could have been nicer to her. And did Angela believe it was possible that Arletha Brown could be her long-lost grandmother? Yes, she believed it was possible, even though she had told Brent differently. She wasn't concentrating on that now. This was a human being who might not have treated people right, but that was no excuse for them to return the favor.

Angela heard the words her great-grandmother often spoke. "We must learn to love even the unlovable, reach the unreachable. Words come a dime a dozen. But a person's action, now *that* shows what they're really saying. Baby, always be true to who God has called you to be."

So Angela went to visit Arletha, hearing the words of Jesus each time she stepped into her room. "When I was sick, you visited me." She didn't consider what she was doing for Arletha as much as she considered it was being done unto the Lord. She resigned herself that if she was going to do a thing, she would do it as Colossians 3:23 instructed: "And whatsoever ye do, do it heartily, as to the Lord, and not unto men," realizing that verse twenty-four held a promise. "Knowing that of the Lord ye shall receive the reward of the inheritance: for ye serve the Lord Christ."

On the fifth day, Arletha opened her eyes. Angela alerted a nurse. A doctor came in and checked her. There appeared to be no brain damage. The following day, Arletha was moved out of ICU to a regular room. Three days later, Arletha was well enough to speak at length.

"Why are you here?" Arletha asked as soon as Angela sat down next to her bed.

"Just checking on you," Angela said.

"Why?"

"Because I want to be sure you're okay."

"I told you I'm not who you think I am," Arletha said, pushing her body back into her stacked pillows.

"I know."

She looked into Angela's eyes. "So why come here? I wake up, and you're here."

Angela smiled. "Whether you are who I thought and wished you would be or not, you still need someone to care. You still need someone to check on you."

Arletha turned away. "How did you know I was here?"

"I was the one who found you. Well, actually it was me and my friend Melissa. We were the ones who called for help."

Arletha turned back toward her. "Don't get me wrong. I thank you. Lord knows, I thank you. But what were you doing at my house in the first place?"

"I came to see you. It was the strangest thing. You were so strong on my mind and my heart. I believe it was God making sure you were all right."

Without any warning, Arletha began to cry. Angela stood up.

"Are you all right?" Angela asked. "Do I need to get the nurse for you?"

Arletha shook her head. "No, I'm fine." She smiled and touched Angela's hand. "Sit, sit," she said slowly. "I'm okay."

Angela sat back down.

"That night, I wasn't feeling well. My head felt differently than it had ever felt before in my life. I went to the kitchen to get some water. I felt something strange taking place." Arletha slowly shook her head as she spoke. "I didn't have time to pray a long prayer. All my religiosity, my grandstand stance went right out the door. All I could say was, 'Lord, save me,' because at that moment, I knew something awful was happening. And it occurred to me that I wasn't sure if I died right then that I would go to Heaven."

Angela stood up and handed Arletha the tissue box and a cup of water.

Arletha dabbed her eyes, took a sip of water, and continued. "I realized I had been trying to live so righteous, thinking that my works alone were enough to save me. At that precise moment, I knew I had come up short. That if I died right then and I had to be judged on my works instead of on what Jesus had done on the cross, I would not make it into Heaven. In those few precious seconds, I confessed Jesus as Lord, acknowledged that I believed Jesus had died on the cross and that God had raised Him from the dead, and I asked Jesus to come into my heart. Just as I finished, I heard a pop in the back of my head, and all I could say was, 'Lord, save me.' That's the last thing I remember until I opened my eyes in a strange place and saw someone looking down at me."

"That was me," Angela said. "I've come by every day since you were admitted to check on you. I was happy when you opened your eyes. I went and got the nurse."

"So you're the person who was here every day? One of the nurses said she thought my granddaughter had been here. I told her she was mistaken since I don't have a granddaughter. She kept insisting that I did, as though my mind wasn't fully functioning."

"Please forgive me for that. I said I was a relative so the hospital would keep me informed about your condition. I also signed for your medical care because we couldn't find anything stating you had insurance. I was afraid they might try and move you."

"You did all of that for me?" Arletha asked, wiping her eyes.

"Yes." Angela leaned forward. "And it's not because I believe you're my grandmother. You needed help, and I just wanted to help you."

"Well," she said, struggling to swallow, "I do have health insurance."

Angela smiled with a sign of relief. "That's good. Oh, and I have your purse. It's locked inside my car trunk. I took it from your house the night you were brought here."

Arletha shrugged as she shook her head. "My card's not in my purse," she said.

"Yeah, I know. I looked."

Arletha motioned for more water. Angela got up and poured her some. "I suppose since you have my purse and the keys to my house, you've been snooping around my place trying to find out whether I told you the truth or not," Arletha said. She tried putting the cup on the tray after she sipped a few more times, but her hand shook.

Angela took the cup and set it down. "No, I haven't been snooping around for anything like that. But I did go back to your house to see if there was anyone we could call and let know you were in the hospital," Angela said.

"I don't have anybody."

"Yeah, I kind of figured that out."

Arletha looked away. "Sad, huh?"

"What?"

"That I've lived all of these years and have no one who cares what happens to me one way or the other." Arletha turned back toward Angela. "I want to thank you for stopping by that night. If it weren't for you, I"—she placed her hand to her mouth—"I wouldn't have this chance to right some wrongs I've made in my life."

"Arletha, we're all only human. We've all made mistakes. Sometimes we get it right. Sometimes we miss it altogether. We just need to ask God to forgive us and work at doing better the next time. That's what my pastor, Pastor Landris, teaches us."

Arletha nodded. She pointed to Angela's abdomen. "Are you expecting?"

Angela looked down at her abdomen and beamed as she touched it. "Yes."

"Why did you come to my house to see me that night?"

Angela reached into her purse. "Honestly, I wanted to bring this little journal my great-grandmother had written. Great-granny was the best. I would love for you to read some of what she wrote." She held up the journal. "My great-granny was so wise, so funny, and so on point about life. People didn't always appreciate her words of wisdom. Sometimes, her tongue could cut sharp. For some reason, I guess I was hoping maybe you would appreciate them. Also, I heard you came to my wedding. You signed my guest book. I know what you said about us not being related, but I would still like for us to possibly be friends. That's if you don't mind," Angela said.

Angela didn't bring up that the birth date written inside that journal matched what she had discovered, first from Brent and later from Arletha's own driver's license.

"Of course. I'd like to be friends. You may have saved my life. It's because of your being obedient to our loving and merciful God and His leading you to my house that I have been granted a second chance at life. Another opportunity to get it right. But I'm not sure you were correct in thinking I would want to read your great-grandmother's personal thoughts."

"Well, I'll leave the journal here in case you get bored and just want something to do." Angela laid it down on the bedside table. "Great-granny had this secret family recipe for German chocolate cake people used to go nuts over. She wouldn't tell anyone her secret." Angela started for the door. "She put her recipe in that notebook." Angela turned back to Arletha when she reached the door. "If it's all right with you, I'd still like to come by and visit while you're here. We're still family, related by the blood of Jesus."

Arletha nodded. "I'd like that just fine."

Angela smiled. "I'll see you tomorrow then." Angela opened the door.

Just as Angela was about to walk out, Arletha said, "Double the vanilla extract and make sure the icing is cool before you add the chopped pecans." Arletha was attempting to reach the journal. She was still weak and straining to get to it.

Angela quickly walked back over to Arletha's bedside and handed the journal to her. "What did you just say?" Angela asked as she gazed at Arletha.

"Double the vanilla extract to two teaspoons and make sure the icing is cool before you add the cup of chopped pecans," Arletha repeated as she ran her hand over the front of the journal.

Angela sat down slowly beside her. "How would you happen to know that?" Tears rolled down her face.

"That's how my mother made her German chocolate cake," Arletha said as she began to cry as well. She rubbed her hand over the cover of the journal, then hugged it.

Angela placed her hand over her mouth to hold in any sound that might try to escape on its own. With her other hand, she touched Arletha's hand, which lay on the bed.

Arletha grabbed Angela's hand and squeezed it. "Please forgive me," she said.

Angela stood up as she nodded.

"I've asked God to forgive me. The night I collapsed, I asked Jesus to come into my life and save me. God has given me a second chance. My life needs to count for something now. You've shown me the love of God. You've treated me better than I have you. I've lived a life not so pleasing or a testament to God's love. I need to do better. I want to do better. Whatever time I have left on this earth, I want God to get the glory. Not I, but the Christ who lives in me."

"But why? Why didn't you tell me the truth from the beginning?"

"I wanted the Arletha that everybody knew from my past to be gone. I worked all of my life to make it as though that old creature that had disappointed and hurt so many no longer existed. Because of the way I lived my life as a teenager, my mother told me once that she was sorry I had ever been born. She then said if I couldn't abide by her rules, to leave her house. I saw to it that her desires were done. I left and made it as though I had never been born."

Angela shook her head in disagreement. "That's not the person I knew. She was loving and patient and kind. But Great-granny did write in that journal that she was sorry for a lot of things she'd said and done. Many things she wished she could take back or redo completely. As I said, we're all human and we all make mistakes. She was human."

"I know. If only I could go back and redo parts of my life, I would. I was too busy trying to be someone that I wasn't. After my mother told me I could either abide by her rules or leave, I left. At sixteen, I ran away with a thirty-year-old man who claimed he loved me and wanted to take care of me. I left my newborn in my mother's care. The man I left with lived in a town in Alabama called the Colony. He claimed he was only in Asheville to work on a special project. Leaving with him was a huge mistake. I learned all too soon he didn't care anything about me. He used me, turned me into a full-fledged teenage prostitute. I became even more of a disgrace to all my mother had raised me to be and all God had created me to be. I figured out too late that I'd thrown my life away following behind him. But there I was stuck, with no way home.

"I was a disgrace. I wanted the Arletha Black everyone knew to die. After that man put me out when I bucked him, I met a missionary at a revival. She was on her way to Birmingham. I came up here with her, and there began my journey of becoming a true Christian—a new creature who wanted nothing more than to live for God. That old Arletha was now dead. Arletha Black had officially become Arletha Brown. I became the person I thought God desired me to be. But in the process, I suppose I became an overly religious, judgmental person. Someone who thought I was better than everyone else because I was trying to live such a perfect life. I was on my way to Heaven anyhow.

Then, after all those years, you come along. My never-truly-forgotten daughter, Rebecca's daughter—Angel," Arletha said.

She squeezed Angela's hand again. "You showed up, and despite my nastiness to you, your cousin, and your friend, you still reached out to me. You even invited me to your wedding. Oh, I can't tell you how much that meant to me. And I was so proud watching you. I was accustomed to people talking about me behind my back, making fun of me and my religion. But you had reached out to me. Now don't get me wrong. I was fine with the persecution because I felt I was being persecuted for the sake of Christ. And persecution for Christians, in my book, was always a good thing. That meant I was on the right track. The Bible tells us men will hate us and come against us. So I was proud I was disliked." Arletha slowly shook her head.

"But you, you showed me what a true Christian is—one who can look past the hurt and work to heal it. You signed for me to get care just because you thought it was the right thing to do. No one has ever done anything like that for me. I was a faithful member of a church for over forty years. I left about a year ago in search of a new church home. I didn't find one, and my membership is still with the same church. Do you know how many people at my church would have done what you did for me?"

Angela thought about it. She knew that when she called to let them know Arletha was in the hospital, no one seemed to care. She had yet to hear back from the pastor, and Angela had called again just to be certain her message had been delivered.

"Yes, he got the message. In fact, we announced it at Wednesday night services," Angela was told by the person who answered the phone.

As far as Angela knew, no one had come by as yet. Angela shook her head in answer to Arletha's question about how many people would have done what she did.

"Not many, if any," Arletha said. She chuckled a little. "You know, for years I thought I was saved. As a child, I had gone forward and shaken the preacher's hand. I'd been baptized. But on that night when I knew something wasn't right, I realized that what I thought was saved was not. I had given the preacher my hand, but I hadn't given Jesus my heart. I had tradition, but I didn't have Christ. I had to make it right with the Lord. The scriptures state that if any man be in Christ he is a new creature. Today, I realize fully what that means. The old Arletha has truly passed away now, not because I left everything and everyone I knew and took on a different identity. I am a new creature because of who I am in Christ."

"Thank you," Angela said as she wiped away her tears. "Thank you for the gift you have just given to me.

"May I ask something of you at this time?"

"Of course. Whatever you need." Angela continued to wipe her tears.

"Can you and I be friends?"

"What do you mean?"

"I know you were searching for your grandmother. Honestly, at this point in my life, I'm still not the one you seek. I don't have many friends, as we've pretty much established. I would love it if you and I could do as you suggested earlier and become friends first. We can get to know each other better and allow things to develop from there."

Angela cried even more. She wiped her eyes with her tissue. "Yes, of course." She nodded. "Of course. Whatever you feel comfortable with." Angela leaned over and she and Arletha held each other as if they never wanted to let go.

When Angela did let go, she said, "As Great-granny would say were she here: Welcome home. Welcome home. Now come on in, and stay a spell."

Arletha closed her eyes. "Thank you, baby. Thank you. And thank you, Jesus."

Chapter 47

Not that we are sufficient of ourselves to think any thing as of ourselves; but our sufficiency is of God.
—2 Corinthians 3:5

Sasha packed a suitcase and Aaliyah's weekend bag. On Monday, after she left work, she picked up Aaliyah and drove to Marcus's house. Marcus opened the door.

"Hi, Daddy!" Aaliyah said.

"Well, hello there," Marcus said, looking from Aaliyah to Sasha. Aaliyah ran into his arms and he picked her up. "To what do I owe this pleasure?" He smiled at Aaliyah, then turned his gaze to Sasha.

Sasha smiled as she walked past him without giving him an answer. He closed the door and followed her.

"Is something going on?" Marcus asked.

"Nope," Sasha said, as she took off her coat, placed it on a chair, then headed straight for the kitchen.

Marcus set Aaliyah down and helped her get out of her coat. He picked Aaliyah up again and carried her into the kitchen.

Sasha was at the sink running water. "I should have brought some of the leftovers from yesterday. We had so much food, there's plenty still in the refrigerator. Maybe I'll run and get it later and we can have that tomorrow. I'll just make something quick for us to eat now."

Marcus sat Aaliyah in a chair. "You don't have to cook tonight. Yesterday was more than enough."

"We have to eat," she said. "I'm not planning on fixing much. Besides, from the look of your refrigerator, and pantry, you don't have a lot to work with. Maybe I'll go buy some groceries later tonight, too."

"Why would you do that?" Marcus asked.

She took out the skillet and placed it on the stove. "I'm going to cook that steak you have in the refrigerator, maybe with some mashed potatoes. Do you have any of the instant kind? I hate peeling potatoes." She found a box of instant potatoes in the cabinet next to the stove. "Here it is."

"I was planning on using that steak tomorrow," Marcus said, thinking of the special night he had planned for Melissa for Valentine's Day.

"I'll buy you another package," Sasha said, running the water over the steak, then patting it dry with a paper towel. "I saw Paula Deen—or was it Rachael Ray?" Sasha said as she stopped to think. "Whichever one it was, she made this great dish using steak. Although I think the cut she used was a lot thinner than this thick piece you have. Why would you buy such a thick steak, anyway? I'll need to slice it if I want to make what I saw her do on TV."

"Honey, why don't you go in the den and watch television while Mommy and I talk," Marcus said to Aaliyah.

Aaliyah got up and began to walk like a zombie. "All right," Aaliyah said, giggling as she went.

After Aaliyah left the room, Marcus walked over to Sasha just as she turned on one of the eyes of the stove under the pot of water mixed with milk for the mashed potatoes.

"Sasha, what are you doing?"

"I told you, I'm making dinner for us."

"But why are you making dinner for us tonight?"

She stopped and smiled. "Do me a favor." She pulled her keys out of her pocket. "Go out to my car and get my suitcase and Aaliyah's weekend bag and bring them in."

"What suitcase?"

"Mine and also Aaliyah's weekend bag."

"And why are your and Aaliyah's bags in your car?"

She smiled and opened her eyes wider. "We're moving in with you," she said, laying the keys on the counter when he didn't take them immediately. She started pounding the steak with a mallet to tenderize it.

Marcus walked over and grabbed her wrist in midair before she could pound again. "Hold on, hold on. Put this down and come over here and talk to me," he said.

She put down the steel mallet, went to the sink, rinsed off her hands, and dried them on a paper towel as she walked over and sat down.

"Talk to me," Marcus said.

"There's nothing much to say. Aaliyah and I are moving in with you."

"Okay, that's where I'm missing something. Aaliyah moving in I might understand. You, on the other hand, are . . . how do I say this without it coming out the wrong way? You are no longer my wife. You have no right or good reason to move in."

She grabbed his hand. "I was going to talk to you about this later, but if you prefer, we can talk about it now. Marcus, I was wrong."

"You were wrong? About what?"

"About everything. Everything that had to do with us. Everything except marrying you to begin with."

"Sasha—"

"Let me finish. Look, Marcus. You are a wonderful man, a fantastic father, a great provider, a learned minister of the gospel, an incredible businessman. And Marcus, you were the best husband any woman could ever ask for." She caressed his hand. "I should never have left you. I shouldn't have pushed so hard for that divorce. I should have worked harder to make our marriage work, as hard as you worked."

"Well, things are as they are. You've told me repeatedly that I need to accept that fact. I've accepted it. Now, as you've also said, we both need to just move on."

"But I don't want to accept it. I was wrong, Marcus. I was wrong. You deserved better. I was immature and spoiled. I listened to all the wrong people when I should have listened to what God was saying and to my heart." She moved in closer. "Well, I'm listening to God now. We've got to make right what I worked so hard to make wrong."

Marcus stood up and took a few steps away as he rubbed his head. "Sasha, I'm with someone else now."

Sasha stood up. "But you already have a family. You have me and Aaliyah. And I'm willing to work at us being the family you always dreamed of. Think of the testament this will be to other Christians if you and I can show how God can restore and re-pair even a marriage that once ended in divorce. You're a preacher. It's like you said to me when I was pushing so hard to get this divorce: It doesn't look great when a Christian's mar-riage ends in divorce. It looks even worse when it's a preacher. You were right."

She grabbed his hand again. "I was the one who wanted the divorce. And now I am the one who is admitting she was wrong and letting you know I want us to be a family again. Aaliyah de-serves that much from both of us. We have to do this, not just for us, but for our daughter."

Aaliyah's name caused him to gaze into Sasha's eyes. "Aaliyah has accepted that you and I are no longer together like that."

"No, she hasn't. She's coping. I know that, and so do you. She hates having to leave my house to come to yours and to have to leave yours to come back to mine. What kind of life is that for a child? I was selfish and ended up causing you and Aaliyah to pay for my being so consumed with myself and what I thought the world had to offer me. What I wanted or *thought* I wanted. Well, I'm coming to you right now, first to say I was wrong, and second to ask for your forgiveness."

He gently grabbed her by the shoulders. "Sasha, I forgave you a long time ago."

"Then tell me what I need to do to make things right with us. What do I need to do to fix this? You know how hard this is for me. I'm not good at admitting my mistakes, and I sure don't like doing it and having to beg along with it. But if I have to beg, then I'm putting aside my pride. You know the Bible says that pride goes before destruction." She grabbed him by his tie and pulled him down toward her, kissing him lightly on his lips.

Marcus stepped back from her.

"Marcus, please. Just go to my car and get our bags. Let's you and I talk about this. Let's just see how things go if we give this relationship another try."

"You can't stay here with me like that," Marcus said.

"Why not?"

"We're not husband and wife anymore."

"But we *were*. And in God's sight, we're still husband and wife."

"No, in God's sight we are *not*. We legally married in the state of Alabama. God recognized that. We legally divorced, dissolved that marriage in the state of Alabama. And God recognizes that. Which means we are no longer married in the sight of God."

"But the Bible says what God has joined together, let not man put asunder. Sure, we legally divorced. But God put us together and no paper can put that asunder," Sasha said.

"That scripture you're quoting does say that. But think about it, Sasha. It's a statement of fact, not a mandate. It lets us know that whatever God puts together nothing or no one can ever break up. If God had put you and me together, there is nothing or no one that would have been able to come against us and break us up. But something did break us up."

"Yes. My foolishness," Sasha said. "But isn't this just showing you that God wants you and me to be together? Think about it, Marcus. Do you think if this was just me that I would be here literally begging you to take me back?"

He laughed a little. "Not the Sasha I know."

She smiled. "You didn't have to agree with me so quickly." She stepped up to him once more. "Marcus, you were good for me. You brought out the best in me."

"And the worst," Marcus added. "Some of the things you've said and done over the course of our marriage and our divorce were *definitely* not the best in you."

"But look where I am now. Here I am with my bags packed,

asking—no, begging—you to give us another try. You and I don't need to date. In fact, we could go find a justice of the peace or one of your preacher friends tomorrow and get re-married. I was the problem. I've confessed my sins. If God can forgive me and treat me as though it never happened, then how can you who call yourself a preacher and a follower of God not follow His lead? We need to think about Aaliyah for a change instead of our own desire."

"I always put Aaliyah's needs first. Always."

"I know, Marcus. I wasn't implying that you don't. What I'm saying is: our baby needs us to grow up and act like adults. You were being the adult. I was being childish. I went out there to see what the world has to offer. Frankly, I don't like it. I like being in a world with you in it. I'm ready to settle down now and be a real wife and mother."

"But I'm in love with someone else."

Sasha laughed that off before taking her hands and pressing them to her face. "You're not in love with anyone else. You thought we were through. You were trying to move on, the way I told you that you needed to do. But we can work this out be-cause I'm a different person today than I was even just yester-day. God is working on me, Marcus. And with you there, I know I'm going to be all that God has called me to be. Please, hear my heart. Listen to my heart."

"Aren't you listening to me? I'm in love with Melissa. In fact, I was planning to ask her to marry me tomorrow."

Sasha burst into a laugh as she shook her head. "But you're not going to do that now."

"Yes, I am."

She shook her head even more. "Nope. Because you know you would be wrong to walk away from us." She went over to the stove and turned it off. "You preach forgiveness. You preach on the God of a second chance. You preach on doing the right thing even when the right thing is hard. The right thing is for you and me to make that vow we took in front of all those peo-ple work. For better, for worse; for richer, for poorer. We have just gone through the 'for worse' part.

"You preach about doing the right thing. You preach about family and the importance of families staying together. You preached to *me* against us getting a divorce, especially when you saw I was not planning on changing my mind. And you've preached about rebuilding that which has been torn down. Our relationship was torn down. But we can rebuild it stronger and better that it ever was. I'm asking you, Marcus, to give us a chance. I'm asking you to simply start practicing what you preach. Right now. Right here with me and your daughter. Let's begin again. Practice what you preach."

The doorbell rang. Marcus looked at Sasha. It rang again. He went to answer it.

"Marcus, how are you?" Melissa said as she hurried inside. "I know we're seeing each other tomorrow, and I can see you have company so I won't be but a few minutes. But I have some great news about a wedding I just got a call to do. It's huge! Huge! I didn't want to tell you about it over the phone so I came right over. I'm sorry. I didn't even think you might be busy."

Sasha walked in, drying her hand with a towel. Melissa stopped when she saw the tall, perfect size six, *Vogue* model designer-wearing, stunning beauty of a woman enter Marcus's foyer.

"Oh, I'm sorry," Melissa said. "I see I really am interrupting something." She threw a questioning look toward Marcus.

Marcus turned to look at Sasha standing behind him, then back at Melissa.

"You must be Melissa," Sasha said as she walked up and graciously shook Melissa's hand.

Melissa forced a smile. "Yes, I am." She looked again at Marcus.

Sasha realized Marcus wasn't planning on introducing them, so she said, "I'm Sasha Peeples."

"Oh, Sasha. It's so nice to meet you," Melissa said.

"You, too. Well, I'm going to get back in here and finish making supper. It's good to finally put a face with a name," Sasha said to Melissa. To Marcus, she said, "Supper should be ready in no more than fifteen minutes." She bowed at her waist slightly, then left.

Melissa tilted her head and mouthed her words to Marcus in case Sasha was still in hearing distance, "What's that all about?"

Marcus grabbed her by the elbow and led her into the living room out of earshot of Sasha. "I don't know what's going on. Out of the blue, she just showed up."

"So what does she want?"

Marcus knew he needed to come totally clean with Melissa. "She wants us to get back together. She wants to become a family again."

Melissa laughed. "Well, I suppose that answers my question about what she wants. So what did you say about that?"

"I told her the truth. That I loved someone else," Marcus said. "That I love you."

Melissa shook her head. "This is not good. This is not good at all."

"I know, but I'm taking care of it."

"So why is she here cooking supper?"

Marcus began rubbing his forehead. "She wants to move in with me. Tonight."

Melissa took a few steps back. "Oh. Well, now. She must feel pretty sure about you and her then if she just shows up and thinks it's that easy to get you back. Look, Marcus. I've never been one to fight over a man. So if you want to try and make things work with Sasha, you won't get any drama out of me. My goodness, she's gorgeous! Absolutely stunning! Why would you want to be with someone like me when you can have a supermodel like her?" Melissa started to walk away. She stopped and turned back to him. "I'm going to make this real easy for all of us. I'm going to go get in my car, go home, then go on with my life just the way I was doing before you entered my world."

Marcus ran and grabbed Melissa and pulled her close to him. "I love you."

"Yes, I believe that you do. But Marcus, this is no longer a rhetorical question. You have a determined woman in your kitchen cooking as though she lives here. And according to you, she wants to get back with you. The two of you have a wonderful daughter together. You and Sasha have a history. What do you and I have? A great time dancing at a wedding reception and four good months of knowing each other, three good months of actual dating? I can't compete with what you and Sasha have. I can't! So I'm going to get out while the getting is good."

"Melissa, please don't do this." Marcus held both her hands.

Sasha walked into the room. "Oh, I'm sorry. I thought you had left already," she said to Melissa. She turned her attention to Marcus. "I was coming to let you know the food is finally ready. Melissa, we have plenty. You're welcome to stay and eat if you like."

"That's quite all right. I was just about to leave," Melissa said.

Marcus wouldn't let go of her hands. "No. You're *not* leaving."

Melissa looked up at Marcus. "Yes, I *am*. So let go of me." She tried to pull her hands out of his. He held on tight. "Let go," she said.

"No. You're not leaving." Marcus knelt down on one knee as he held her left hand tight. "Melissa Anderson, I love you. I want to spend the rest of my life with you. I was going to do this tomorrow but—Melissa Anderson, will you marry me?"

Melissa put her right hand over her mouth. "What?"

He grinned. "I love you. I want to spend my life with you. Will you marry me?"

"Are you for real, Marcus? Do you really mean it?"

He stood up. "Stand right here. I'll show you just how much I mean it." He hurried out of the room. When he came back, he knelt down on one knee once again and opened a ring box. He took the ring out of the box and slipped the two-carat marquis-cut diamond ring onto her ring finger. "Melissa Anderson, will you be my wife?"

"For real, Marcus? For real?" Melissa said.

Marcus put his glasses on. "Will you marry me now?" he said. She giggled.

He pulled his glasses off. "How about now? Will you marry me now?"

"Yes!" she said as she pulled at him to stand up. "You're so silly. Yes, I'll marry you!" He stood up, leaned down, and kissed her.

The front door closed and made a noise when it did. Both Marcus and Melissa turned toward its direction.

"Sasha," Melissa said, almost whispering her name. "We forgot all about Sasha."

Marcus went and looked out the window. Sasha was helping Aaliyah into the backseat of the car. She fastened Aaliyah in her booster seat, closed the door, got in her seat, and quickly backed her car out of the driveway. "She's gone," he said as he watched her drive away.

"I'm sorry," Melissa said. "I'm so sorry." She wrapped her arm around his.

"Sorry for what?"

"We could have done this a better way. I'm sure Sasha is hurt by this. If I hadn't acted the way I did, you could have handled things in a different way with her," Melissa said.

"Melissa, I love you. I want the world to know that I love you. Sasha needed to know. Listen, I don't intend to allow anything or anyone get in the way of how I intend to treat you as my bride or protect you as my wife. I don't ever want you to doubt my love for you. I don't ever want you to wonder where you fit in my life." He smiled. "So, is your answer still yes to being my wife?"

"Yes," she said. "Yes, yes, yes!"

Marcus laughed, then picked her up off the floor as he hugged her and began to twirl her beautiful self around. "God is good," Marcus said.

"All the time," Melissa said as she gazed into his eyes and smiled. "And all the time . . ."

"God is good!" Marcus said.

PRACTICING WHAT YOU PREACH

Vanessa Davis Griggs

The following questions are intended
to enhance your group's discussion
of this book.

Discussion Questions

1. Melissa Anderson admitted to having problems saying no. What are your thoughts when it comes to things like that?

2. Do you believe Nae-nae was a true friend? Why or why not?

3. What were your views when it came to Marcus Peeples? Did those views change?

4. Discuss Melissa and Marcus's first date as well as the Bible study lesson they attended.

5. What were your thoughts regarding Melissa's reason for not dating Marcus?

6. Gayle Cane's visit with her cousin Angela Gabriel brought with it quite a few revelations of secrets. Talk about those and what happened subsequently.

7. What were your thoughts about Sasha Peeples?

8. Discuss Marcus and Sasha's relationship, both their younger and later years.

9. What did you think of Marcus's interaction with his daughter Aaliyah?

10. What are your views when it comes to the social issues touched upon in this novel?

11. Discuss Angela's meeting with Arletha Brown and the things that transpired later.

12. Do you believe Sasha was right to treat Marcus the way she did? Why or why not?

13. Discuss the teachings that address divorce. What were your views before? Did your views change? If so, why?

14. Marcus spoke about the spirit of Jezebel. Discuss your thoughts regarding Jezebel.

15. Marcus gave money to Sasha to purchase a piano. How did you feel about what happened, and her subsequent actions?

16. What are your feelings when it comes to child support payments? Do you believe if one doesn't pay that he or she shouldn't be able to see their child until that debt is paid?

17. What were your thoughts when it came to Tiffany and Darius Connors? Do you believe Melissa overstepped boundaries? Why or why not? What would you have done?

18. Discuss Arletha and her final revelation.

19. At the end, do you believe Marcus made the right decision? Why or why not?